The Figurehead

Bill Kirton

Long-listed for the International Rubery Award, 2012.

ISBN: 1479143421
ISBN-13: 978-1479143429

DEDICATION

For Gill, Ginge, Ron, Les and Bob
And especially dedicated to the memory of my brother-in-law, brother and
real friend, Pete Perring

ACKNOWLEDGMENTS

Even more than usual, I'm indebted to many for their help and suggestions. My friend, Mike Lloyd-Wiggins, told me that I should write about a figurehead carver.

Sculptor Chris Bailey is as good a teacher as he is an artist.

David Atherton and Simon Spalding opened up various contacts and indicated useful directions to follow.

However obscure the questions I asked them, John Edwards, the Keeper of Science and Maritime History and Ann Scott, the Librarian at the wonderful Aberdeen Maritime Museum, always found the answers and gave up their time to guide me.

My wife, Carolyn, read the first draft and suggested many very helpful changes and additions.

Among the many books I have consulted and which have provided me with lots of my material are:

Archibald Simpson by Cuthbert Graham

Tools of the Maritime Trades by John E Horsley

Sail's Last Century Editor Robert Gardiner

Older Ship Figureheads and Sterns by L G Carr Lawton

Ships' figureheads by Peter Norton

British Figurehead and Ship Carvers by P. N. Thomas

The Whale Hunters by Robert Smith

Footdee by Diane Morgan

The East Neuk Chronicles by William Skene

Scotland's North Sea Gateway by John R Turner

A Thousand Years Of Aberdeen by Alexander Keith

Emigration from North East Scotland (2 vols) by Marjory Harper

The Great Days of Sail by Andrew Shewan.

The Diced Cap by Hamish Irvine

Food in England by Dorothy Hartley

Many of the background characters in this story are real people who did exist in the Aberdeen of 1840 but, although my principal characters bear very well-known Aberdonian names, they are all fictional and not intended to represent any actual persons, living or dead.

DEDICATION

For Gill, Ginge, Ron, Les and Bob
And especially dedicated to the memory of my brother-in-law, brother and
real friend, Pete Perring

ACKNOWLEDGMENTS

Even more than usual, I'm indebted to many for their help and suggestions.
My friend, Mike Lloyd-Wiggins, told me that I should write about a
figurehead carver.
Sculptor Chris Bailey is as good a teacher as he is an artist.
David Atherton and Simon Spalding opened up various contacts and
indicated useful directions to follow.
However obscure the questions I asked them, John Edwards, the Keeper of
Science and Maritime History and Ann Scott, the Librarian at the
wonderful Aberdeen Maritime Museum, always found the answers and
gave up their time to guide me.
My wife, Carolyn, read the first draft and suggested many very helpful
changes and additions.

Among the many books I have consulted and which have provided me with
lots of my material are:
Archibald Simpson by Cuthbert Graham
Tools of the Maritime Trades by John E Horsley
Sail's Last Century Editor Robert Gardiner
Older Ship Figureheads and Sterns by L G Carr Lawton
Ships' figureheads by Peter Norton
British Figurehead and Ship Carvers by P. N. Thomas
The Whale Hunters by Robert Smith
Footdee by Diane Morgan
The East Neuk Chronicles by William Skene
Scotland's North Sea Gateway by John R Turner
A Thousand Years Of Aberdeen by Alexander Keith
Emigration from North East Scotland (2 vols) by Marjory Harper
The Great Days of Sail by Andrew Shewan.
The Diced Cap by Hamish Irvine
Food in England by Dorothy Hartley

Many of the background characters in this story are real people who did
exist in the Aberdeen of 1840 but, although my principal characters bear
very well-known Aberdonian names, they are all fictional and not intended
to represent any actual persons, living or dead.

What others said about *The Figurehead*:

"…an exciting, page-turning murder mystery … interesting, thoughtful and thoroughly absorbing"—Mary O Farrington

"…a splendid romance of … exquisite tenderness, *The Figurehead* satisfies on every level, giving the reader authenticity, characters to care about, a mystery, and a romance."
—Diane Nelson

"…a real page turner"—L.P.Taylor

"…*The Figurehead* deserves a 5-star rating because it's artfully written and leaves the reader wanting more."—Jean Henry Mead

"…a hugely satisfying read, by a writer whose love and knowledge of the sea in all its phases shines through on every page."—Myra Duffy

"Bill Kirton weaves a fine net of words that will keep you trapped from the beginning to the end."—P.D.Allen

"*The Figurehead* is a surprising, satisfying book and a memorable read for anyone with an interest in ships and the sea of course, but also for anyone who might want to see how it's done, the right way."—Richard Sutton

CHAPTER ONE

Bessie Rennie was on her usual Sunday morning beach trawl. It was the one day of the week when she could comb the sands in peace. Most of the other residents of Aberdeen were either tucked up in their granite villas, curled in blankets and sacks in the poorer areas of town, or lying about the alleys and closes around the Mercat Cross, sleeping off the mayhem of a normal Saturday night. The prostitutes in Mason's Court were having a well-earned rest and none of the Castle Street traders would be setting up their stalls on the Sabbath. The yards hung motionless on the masts of the ships in the harbor, some of them with sails still bent on them and gathered up into tight bunches. The decks were empty and the quays deserted, echoing back the clicks and rustles of the rigging in the quiet air. Any citizens who were up and about would be getting ready for church. Bessie was safe to forage.

She was looking for whatever she could get but hoping, as usual, that one of the frequent wrecks along the north east coast would send her a body or two, their pockets still holding purses, watches or anything that might persuade a pawnbroker to part with a couple of shillings. So far, she'd been wasting her time. With a half-moon still bright in the sky, she'd started near the river Don and worked her way south toward the Dee, collecting just three bottles which might fetch some pennies in Ma Cameron's public house and a waistcoat which was so far gone that not even she would think of wearing it. Her habitual muttering to herself was becoming progressively more blasphemous as she castigated the citizens of Aberdeen for being so sparing with corpses on their beach.

She'd almost reached the pier at the end of the harbor when she saw the sort of bundle she'd been hoping for. It was high on the beach near the wall which ran along the north east edge of the village of Footdee,

1

protecting it from the sea, the sands and the big easterlies that snarled in from Scandinavia. She peered hard as she climbed through the soft sand toward the dark shape, fearing that it might be just another tangle of tarred ropes or seaweed that the tide had flung ashore. But her breath came faster and a smile cracked her leathery features as she saw that the long dark cylinder stretching out from the side of the bundle had a hand on the end of it, and that the twisted material at its seaward end was indeed a pair of trousers which clearly still had legs in them.

As she came closer, her smile developed into a little cackle of secret delight that her patience had been rewarded. It was a man. But he was dressed not in the rags of a sailor or the tatters of a wrecked mariner who'd been floating a long while in hard seas, but in a pair of woolen broadfall trousers with a cravat at his throat and a full jacket. Over this was a heavy overcoat and, hanging loosely around his neck, a light-colored scarf. From Bessie's perspective, more items of clothing meant more pockets. Then, as she stopped beside the body and bent to begin her search, her excitement was stilled as quickly as it had been generated. This man came from no shipwreck. His hair, still wet, was plastered across most of his face but she recognized him at once. It was Jimmie Crombie, the shipwright from Waterloo Quay. His sodden clothes were not the ones he would wear to work but the sort of thing he'd put on for a night out.

Bessie could guess what had brought him here. It was a familiar story. Too much Saturday drink, a staggering walk home along Regent and Waterloo Quays and, in the darkness before the moon had appeared, a stumble over the edge into the harbor. The river would then quickly grab him and drag him along the channel beside the north pier, slamming him against the rocks that regularly claimed ships trying to make their way in or out of the harbor mouth, and then twirling him round the corner onto the beach. It had happened to so many over the months and years that, at last, there was talk of erecting pillars and chains to guard the quay's edge. They would be too late for Jimmie, though. His jacket and shirt had been torn open on the top left hand side of his chest and Bessie saw the scrapings and batterings he'd suffered as the river had bounced him along its rocky banks and down into its depths. The flesh of his face, shoulder and chest was raw, shining silver and black in the growing light, the skin peeling back from it here and there and the cuts and grazes stretching down out of sight inside his shirt.

For Bessie, it was a dilemma. If he'd fallen in after a night's drinking, the odds were that he'd still be carrying some money. But this was not just some strange soul who'd tumbled from the deck of a passing barque; it was one of her own. And everyone knew she never missed a Sunday morning on the beach so she would have to tell someone that she'd found him. She stood looking at the watch chain that stretched across his belly and wondered what to do.

****

John Grant had slept badly. He'd walked the full length of the beach the previous night to tire himself, slept for a couple of hours then, suddenly, woke with his thoughts galloping. It happened now and again, usually when he'd been reminded in some way of his girlfriend, Marie McLeish. Just two months before they were due to be married, she'd been assaulted and left to die slowly and painfully behind the sheds on the fish quay. The killer had never been found and, from time to time, John felt a hunger that he'd never be able to satisfy.

Few of the people he knew were aware of his occasional insomnias. He was too curious about everything to let them get in the way. As a young boy in Glasgow, he'd watched the ships being towed out into the Clyde. As the flood caught them, they'd set their sails and point their bows toward the ocean. John longed to join one of them, to satisfy his curiosity about the bigger brotherhood whose experiences stretched further than Scotland and England to the African ports, the Colony of Newfoundland, Cape Horn, and the South and China Seas. But his mother, who'd lost a father and three brothers at sea, knew only too well the truths of shipboard life and she managed to keep diverting him from his impulses until he'd accepted that, while she lived, he would never be able to sail away with a clear conscience.

In fact, it was his conscience that had driven him into his trade. One night, with three of his friends in Glasgow, he'd stolen a bottle of whisky from a sailor who'd fallen asleep on the quayside. None of the four boys was past thirteen years old and they'd drunk the liquor quickly and climbed aboard a brig looking for mischief. When John woke the next day, his head and body hurting badly from the whisky, he'd gone back to the quay and been amazed by how much damage they'd done. The ship's owners had offered a reward for the capture of those responsible but the fear of discovery was nothing compared to the shame of having hacked huge splinters from the sweeping bow of such a pretty vessel and thrown a tangle of cut halyards and sheets over every fitting on its deck.

They'd never been caught, but the experience had burned into John's brain and its guilt had never entirely left him so, when the time came to begin a trade, he chose one that would counterbalance his vandalism. He was a figurehead and ship carver, a calling that let him sail the world by proxy. His own knowledge of Australia, Canada, and the West Indies was still only second hand, but many of the figures he'd shaped had driven through the winds to ride all the world's waters.

He'd started his apprenticeship in Glasgow and worked in yards from Southampton and Bristol to Hull and Sunderland before finally settling in Aberdeen. The city's growing need for coasters as well as for bigger ships for the Chinese, North American, and South Seas trades kept him in full employment. The shipwrights and owners who called for him knew that they'd have to pay a little extra but that they'd get a degree of artistry worthy of the finest vessel. Too many figureheads were crude, stereotypical carvings of improbable figures, busts with featureless cylindrical necks, women with breasts like half melons thrown high on their chests and wild, staring eyes set wide and angled outwards like those of horses. A figurehead held the spirit of a ship and too many fine vessels had suffered the humiliation of carrying ugly symbols which said more of their makers' inadequacies than of the ships' own capabilities.

John was sitting in the small kitchen of his house in North Square in Footdee, the kettle beginning to hiss over the fire and two thick bannocks cooling on the table beside him. As he reached for the kettle, the Sunday stillness outside was split by a noise between a shout and a scream. He set the kettle aside, opened his door and went out into the square. Other doors began to open and gray faces blinked round them to see what was going on. From the north side of the square, Bessie Rennie appeared, still wailing and calling, flapping her arms and rolling along in a parody of running.

John went to meet her as others came out into the street.

"What's up, Bessie?" he said, as the two of them met and she put her hand on his arm to steady herself.

She pointed back the way she'd come.

"Down there. On the beach."

"What is it."

"Jimmie Crombie. He's dead."

As she said the words, she crossed herself, which surprised John because, in all the years he'd known her, he'd never seen her do it before.

"All right, lass," he said. "Come on. Show me."

For a big man, the voice was soft. Although he'd been living in the northeast for almost ten years, before his arrival he'd moved wherever his work took him. The effect of this had been to leave no particular accent in his tones. The lilt and rhythms of his speech were Scottish but whether they had been learned in the east or the west, the Highlands or the Borders, it was impossible to say.

Bessie had come to find John because, for anyone around the harbor with a puzzle to solve or a trick to understand, he was the first port of call. He was fascinated by the unexplained things that were thrown up by life

along the quays and on the ships leaning at their moorings. He'd often helped the watch to tease out the mysteries of robberies and corpses. People with troubles preferred to visit him rather than endure the scorn and lack of interest of advocates and police. He wasn't always sympathetic, but he did listen and, if his interest was caught, he had a way of looking at things which sometimes found truths that others had missed. He had little doubt himself that the urge that drove him in these activities was linked with the fact that no one had solved the mystery of the violence that had been done to Marie.

Bessie was breathing hard but still tried to explain her find on the beach as they turned out of the square toward the brae leading down onto the sand.

"God rest his poor soul," she panted. "Such a fine man. Such a good neighbor."

John wondered where both her religious fervor and her high opinion of Jimmie had come from. Usually, her mutterings were provoked by hellish rather than heavenly associations as she cursed traders for cheating her, wee boys for taunting her and anyone in earshot for being part of the conspiracy that kept her poor. As for Jimmie Crombie, he was a good enough shipwright, but never eager to pay his bills. John had done one or two jobs for him and had had to resort to threats to get the few pounds he was owed on each occasion. Jimmie withheld wages from his apprentices without reason, treated his wife, Jessie, like a washerwoman and was expert at slowing down work on a ship he was building until the owner could be persuaded to part with extra funds to hurry things along. There would be no more such transactions now.

Bessie stopped some paces away from the body and left John to walk up beside it. He looked down at the twisted shape, its arm flung out to the side, its face half turned into the sand and the ragged chest now showing its blacks, reds and pinks to the early sun. John felt no pity or revulsion. He'd seen bodies washed ashore in much worse condition than this. Besides, the memories of Marie's twisted body hunched behind the shed where she'd died, her eyes dull and staring, the dried blood caking over her pretty face and the marks of the knife on her neck were stronger than the immediacy of this still death on a quiet beach.

As he looked at Jimmie and the sand around him, he saw at once that this was not a simple matter. Jimmie probably had been drinking and there were plenty of examples of people falling into the harbor, but if they didn't manage to get ashore, the waters of the Dee wouldn't cradle them gently round this corner onto the beach; they would sweep them far and fast out into the German Ocean. They might well come back on another tide but that would be long after their disappearance and they'd be dumped up toward or beyond the Don, or on the rocks further south. The likelihood of them fetching up just outside the north pier was remote.

He touched the lapel of Jimmie's overcoat. It was still wet but John knew, for an absolute certainty, that it was not from the sea. The wall protecting Footdee was only some ten yards away. John had walked that way last night before going to bed and, although he could easily have missed it, being absorbed in his own thinking, he was fairly sure that there'd been nothing there. He looked at the sea spilling along the beach. It was nearing high water. That meant that there'd been no tide in the night that could have brought Jimmie up the sand. And, even if there had been, they were neap tides, which had a rise of only eight feet at the mouth of the Dee. Jimmie's body was well above the high water mark. Whatever had brought him here, it wasn't the sea.

The sand between Jimmie and the brae was well trampled and told him nothing. He bent closer to the body and looked hard at the marks on the face, neck and chest. They certainly could have been caused by rocks as the corpse was dragged over them, but they could equally well have happened onshore. John had seen enough accidents in the shipyards and the whaling boil houses to know that human flesh is a fragile substance when it comes into contact with some of the more solid and lethal things amongst which it passes.

Then he saw the marks that finally convinced him that he was right. In the top center of the chest, just in the soft depression at the base of the throat, was a puncture mark about three quarters of an inch across. It was perfectly square. As he looked hard at it, he saw another, partly hidden by the other grazes and cuts on the left hand side of the chest. The flesh over it had been severely torn but, deeper than the rags of skin, there was the same unmistakable square hole. Jimmie had been stabbed.

For once, John's mind held no trace of Marie. He'd forgotten Bessie, too, and was unaware of the neighbors who had followed them down from North Square and were gathering around the body, shaking their heads and speaking in low whispers as if there were something sacred in the scene. John lifted the end of the pale scarf to look at more of the lacerations on Jimmie's neck. There, too, he saw the evidence that this had been no accident. A clear, continuous raw mark ran across Jimmie's throat. It was high on his neck under his chin and led upwards behind his ears. John bent even closer. The central part of the mark was deep and dark. Toward the edges it grew paler and John could see that it was made of lots of individual cuts, the sort that might be made by sharp fibers being pulled into the skin.

It was not something that any of the Footdee people could deal with. John had little faith in the police force and even less in those in charge of them but this was their business. He stored the information away for consideration later, stood up and said, "Send somebody to tell the watch. They'll have to come and fetch him."

The others looked at one another. None of them had much more confidence than John in the force and Bessie, whose duty it really was since she'd found the corpse, always went out of her way to avoid contact with them in any form. John didn't wait to see how they resolved the matter. With a last look at the remains of Jimmie Crombie, he turned and walked back to his kettle and the waiting bannocks.

As he sat outside his house eating his breakfast, the ghost of Marie McLeish was kept at bay by the mystery of Jimmie's last hours.

CHAPTER TWO

Dinner at William Anderson's house on Regent Quay was a grand affair. Despite the fact that only Anderson, his wife and their daughter were at table, the rump of beef that was carried in was big enough to feed a dozen. The cook had stuffed it with sweet herbs, beef suet and anchovies and, after a long slow roasting, had made up a sauce of claret and Elder vinegar, thickened it with egg yolks, dropped in butter, onions, oysters and mushrooms and sent it all up to the dining room with steaming dishes of potatoes, carrots and leeks.

Anderson set about the carving as his wife, Elizabeth, checked the vegetables and passed him their plates one by one. She'd long since accepted the restrictions of her role as accessory to one of Aberdeen's richest merchants, knowing that, as long as she supervised the cooks and servants efficiently, she would live an easy life, with all the leisure time she needed to reflect on the frustration of being female.

It was a frustration shared but tolerated with less equanimity by her daughter, Helen. Unusually, Helen was an only child. Despite all the efforts of Aberdeen's best doctors, two other little Andersons had died in infancy and a subsequent miscarriage had damaged Elizabeth so severely that she lost the ability to conceive. At first, William had regretted the lack of a male heir but the incessant calls of business soon distracted him and commerce took the place of procreation.

When they were served, Anderson and his wife bowed their heads as he said grace. Helen sat, her knife and fork already in her hands, waiting for them to finish. It earned her the usual look from her father but he'd given up trying to impose his will on her on the day that she proved, philosophically and at great length, that religion was invented by a few medieval families to keep funds flowing upward toward them and their

9

peers. Seeing nothing wrong with such an arrangement but unable to counter her arguments, Anderson had sent her to her room, where, throughout their meal, she'd sung very loudly with her door wide open. The matter had never been raised again.

As they ate, Helen talked of how the building of Marischal College was progressing. She'd been walking there with friends that morning and was impressed at how high they'd made the central tower and how the granite arms of the extensions on either side of it reached out toward Broad Street. Granite, which had, in the words of one of Anderson's commercial acquaintances, "brought gold to Aberdeen", was one of the few local commodities in which he had only a limited financial interest. One or two of his ships took cargoes of it to London, where it was used to pave roads and face bridges, but his profits from the carriage were paltry beside those of the producers. Their quarries were working incessantly not only to export the material but also to supply the town's own needs. Aberdeen was growing fast. It was a wealthy city with an established, progressive reputation. The new streets, crescents and buildings with their huge classical facades and pillars were the outward signs of the confidence its wealthier citizens felt in their future.

"A waste of time and money," said Anderson. "I see neither sense nor advantage in maintaining two separate universities in a city like ours. We're a fraction the size of London, Glasgow, or Edinburgh, and they don't indulge in such foolishness. Too, many professors, that's the root of the problem."

"I thought you admired learning," said Helen. "You're always telling me how important it is."

"Yes, it is," he said. "But it has its place. It shouldn't be allowed to spread like some uncontrolled pestilence. Giving these academics more lecterns to preach from, more pulpits from which to spread the contagion of their theories. We'll be the laughing stock of Scotland, you'll see."

"We already are," said Helen. "I heard a man in the mail coach office saying that horses die younger in Aberdeen because our coaches carry twice the passengers of those in other cities."

Her mother tutted. "I wish you wouldn't go to these places," she said. "I'm sure there are no other girls of your age in them."

"Nonsense, mother," said Helen. "Sarah and Bella are always there. There's a boy who brings the packages in on Wednesdays and Fridays who…"

"Enough," said Anderson. "Your mother's right. You have no idea of the dangers…"

It was Helen's turn to interrupt. She didn't want another lecture on the way she lived.

"They found a body on the beach this morning," she said, her tone light and her knife cutting into the beef on her plate.

The change of subject took her parents by surprise. They stopped eating, looked at her, then at one another before her mother said, "How on earth do you know about such things?"

"Oh, mother. Everyone's talking about it."

She stopped, allowed a little pause to develop, then added, "It was one of your men, father."

Anderson looked at her. She said nothing, wanting his curiosity to grow.

"My men?" he said at last. "What do you mean?"

"One of the men building your new boat."

Again she stopped short. Her father was silent, looking at her as if he suspected some trick on her part. It was her mother's curiosity that broke the silence.

"Well, who was it?"

"Mr. Crombie, the shipwright. He is working for you, isn't he, father?"

Anderson was about to put a forkful of potato into his mouth but stopped as he heard the name and put the fork back on his plate.

"Are you certain?" he asked.

"That's what they're saying," she said. "A woman found him on the beach. Half of his throat had been cut away, they say."

"Helen!" said her mother.

"I'm just repeating what I heard," said Helen, pleased to have had an effect.

Anderson laid his napkin on the table beside his plate and stood up. He walked over to the window. He was a handsome man, already in his late fifties, tall and without too much of a belly. His face was pale and framed by neatly cut hair that was nearer white than gray. It wasn't just his money that earned him respect in town; he had bearing, presence and there was an undeniable power about him. It was evident now as he looked out at the masts along the quay. The two women waited.

"Wonderful news. And now where am I going to get another shipwright?" he said at last.

"There are ships on all the stocks in all the yards. I'll have to bring one over from the Clyde or up from Newcastle."

"Not a very Christian reaction to a fellow creature's demise," said Helen, her voice low but loud enough for him to hear if he chose to.

"Mr. Crombie was not a very Christian person," he said, turning back to face her. "He was a drunkard, a thief and... well, lots more besides. If I could have replaced him, I would have done so at the very beginning of the contract."

"And what of his wife and family?" said Helen. "I suppose he has one."

"I have no idea," said Anderson. "He was an employee, not an acquaintance."

"And now he's dead," insisted Helen, more to provoke him than out of any real feeling for Crombie.

"People are dying every day," said Anderson. He knew his daughter's ways and was usually ready to counter her high flying ideas. "The old woman they found on The Links last Tuesday. Died of cold. The watchman in Correction Wynd. Apoplectic fit. Fever, cholera, accidents. Of course people are dying. But this one was supposed to be building my boat. Forgive me if my Christian reactions are somewhat restrained."

He'd crossed to the door as he was speaking and, on his last words, he opened it, left the room and shut it behind him. They listened to his footsteps until they heard him close another door, that of his study.

"Why do you always provoke him?" said Elizabeth, standing and preparing to call a servant to clear the table.

Helen reached across and put a hand on her arm, pulling her back down into her chair.

"I haven't finished eating yet. And this really is delicious."

Her mother watched her put a small piece of beef into her mouth. She loved her daughter and knew that the fire and drive in her were those of her father and, that, in a way, he'd encouraged her independence. Having resigned himself to the fact that his only heir was a woman, he'd allowed Helen a much broader education than was considered proper for a female. Everyone said how lovely Helen was and Elizabeth knew it was true. The glow of her skin and the sparkle in her eyes reminded Elizabeth of how she herself had looked when she was just in her twenties. But in Helen, it was a more forceful beauty, refusing to lie passively on her features, like some painter's confection. The passions which drove her added a dynamic quality to her appeal. Hers was a beauty which did not simply sit waiting to be appreciated and feathered with compliments; it burned into the air around her. She looked up, caught her mother's gaze and let a smile creep onto her lips.

"It's fun when I manage to surprise him, isn't it?" she said.

****

At Rose and Joe Drummond's house, the food was less extravagant and very few words were exchanged as it was eaten. Rose worked with her

12

sister, Jessie, at the fish market, loading and carrying baskets from the boats up to the stalls in Castle Street. Her husband, Joe, was the skipper of a small trawler. He spent most of his shore time at home, tending a little plot of ground outside their rented house. He was a big man with a thick, black beard and a face beaten almost as dark by wind and weather. There was little love between the two of them anymore and, usually, he and Rose kept out of one another's way. When the catch had been particularly good or he'd come into some sort of windfall, he'd duly hand her some of the coins, but then go and celebrate his fortune in the traditional way; by drinking himself unconscious.

That's how he'd spent the previous evening. Like most of the fishermen in Torry, he sometimes earned extra money by acting as a pilot to guide the bigger ships into the channels. They'd let the pilotage fees build up and share-outs were always on Saturday nights. This week, the purses had been full and Joe's head and stomach were still feeling the effects of how he'd spent his bonus.

When he'd scraped the last of the grease from his plate, he pushed it away from him, belched, and began to fill his pipe. Rose stood up, gathered the dishes together and took them to the sink in the corner.

"I'm away to Jessie's," she said. "Are you comin'?"

Joe belched again and shook his head, concentrating on getting his pipe to draw.

"You've no respect," she said. "You're just a pig."

Like "rabbit," "bunny" and others, "pig" was one of the words no trawler man liked to hear. Joe stared at her and spat on the floor, touching the wood of the table to deflect the bad luck the word could bring. He reached into his waistcoat pocket and felt the small round object inside it. He took it out, keeping his fingers closed round it and stroking it with his thumb.

Rose looked over his shoulder but his hand closed quickly.

"What're you playin' with now?" she said.

"None o' your business," Joe muttered, pushing his hand back into his pocket.

Rose grabbed her shawl from the hook beside the door and hitched it around her shoulders.

"Why d'you no' come?" she said, trying to soften her voice. "Jessie's had a terrible shock."

"I'm just no' comin'," snapped Joe.

Rose felt her anger rise in her throat.

"You spend your time drinkin' with the man but you canna find time to comfort his widow," she said. "You're a disgrace."

Joe looked away, deliberately scraping the chair round to turn his back to her. It was true that he'd been drinking with Jimmie Crombie the previous evening, but he didn't like being made to remember it.

"And there's nothin' you want to say to her?" Rose asked, her hand already on the door latch.

Joe didn't move. The smoke from his pipe curled back over his shoulder toward her.

"Pig," she said again, and quickly opened the door and ran out as he kicked his chair back and spun to come at her. She knew he'd remember and that the fists would still have to be faced later, but she didn't want to parade fresh cuts and bruises in front of Jessie. Not tonight.

CHAPTER THREE

The end of Waterloo Quay nearer to Footdee was just a wilderness of stone yards, stacked logs of wood and a few workshops. Jessie Crombie lived in a little house in York Place, the street running away from the harbor at the eastern end of the quay. In the late afternoon, John Grant had decided to go along and see how she was coping. The murmurs of conversation from inside as he knocked on the door told him that other people had had the same idea. He went in and found Jessie with Rose, Tom Leach, the ropemaker, his wife Mary and their son Wee Tam, Willie and Freda Marshall from Pilot Square in Footdee and three other women from Torry, the village on the other side of the Dee, who worked with Jessie at the market.

The air in the cramped room was warm and thick with the smoke from Tom and Willie's pipes and the two oil lamps on the mantelpiece. A strong smell of fish hung around Jessie and her workmates. For anyone who lived near fishermen and their families, it was such a familiar smell that it was hardly ever noticed, but in a small space such as this, it seemed to thicken and, as John said "Aye, Jessie" and bent to kiss her on the cheek, it was sickly in his throat.

All the questions he'd been going to ask her, about how she was coping, but also about Jimmie, were left unasked. The gathering of friends had already said everything that needed saying and, despite the tragedy that had brought them there, the main feeling in the room was one of strength and comfort. These people had come along because they cared.

The men, though, were fidgeting. Tom and Wee Tam had already been there for the best part of an hour and Willie had arrived not long after them. Their contributions had mainly been to give Jessie a quick hug, then stand nodding their heads as the women spoke of the disgraceful lack of

15

warnings and protective structures at the water's edge and the problems of drink. Mary Leach was a member of a Temperance Society but was sensitive enough not to use Jimmie's death to preach her gospel. The time for that would come in the weeks that followed.

John noticed that no one, including Jessie, tried to say anything very nice about Jimmie. There were none of the usual maudlin wailings about how good the dead man had been, how popular at work and how well he looked after his family. No one in the room was under any illusion; Jimmie had had more enemies than friends. As a husband, all that could be said was that he paid the bills—mostly late, but he did pay them. He was good at his job but loath to admit that co-operation with his fellow artisans—shipwrights, ropemakers and sailmakers—was worth the effort. He put the timbers together and the other craftsmen had to work to his schedules. The people gathered in the little house were there not out of respect for Jimmie but out of love for Jessie.

John wanted to ask her about the ideas he'd had as he'd thought about the stabbing and about why anyone might want to do such a terrible thing. But, so far, no one else had mentioned the square wounds or the weal around the neck. He doubted very much whether the police would bother to look closely at the corpse. There were so few of them and their reactions to events they met with in the course of their everyday work tended to be totally predictable. Davie Donne, the day patrolman for the harbor area, was fixed in his ways. When women came bruised and bleeding to him complaining of being assaulted, he listened patiently enough, then sent them home to the husbands who were probably responsible for the attack. When shopkeepers dragged thieving boys to him or citizens frog-marched pickpockets into the watch house, he always took the word of the accuser and the unfortunate captive was routinely condemned. And the Circuit Court judges on their rounds invariably upheld the police's rulings. On their last visit, a woman who had stolen a man's pocket handkerchief was transported for seven years, exactly the same sentence as that pronounced on a man who had drawn a knife and cut deep wounds into three separate individuals after a squabble in the London Tavern. Crime was a cut and dried affair. There were honest citizens and rogues. Jimmie would be seen as just another drowned drunk, and any of the town's worthies who heard of the matter would secretly feel that he'd got exactly what he deserved.

But John had had most of the day to reflect on what he'd seen on the beach. He had worked out two different versions of what could have happened. The first was that there'd been a fight and that, as well as punching and tearing at Jimmie's head and chest, his opponent had stabbed him. The second version was more sinister but it was one which John found more convincing because of other details he'd noticed. Somebody had killed Jimmie in cold blood by pushing the sharp point twice into his chest. Then whoever it was had beaten and torn the flesh around the wounds in order to hide them.

It was the mark looping around his neck and his soaking hair and clothes that made John prefer the second version. Neither had anything to do with a fight. He couldn't guess at the significance of the strangulation mark but the wet clothes were easier to understand. Whoever was responsible for the stabbing must have deliberately soaked him with water to make it look as if he'd drowned. And then they'd dragged or carried him to the beach, dropped him by the Footdee wall, and covered their tracks back up to the brae. This was no tavern brawl. It was all too deliberate. The killer had gone to a lot of trouble.

A knock on the door stilled the murmuring in the house. It was short, timid, not the sort with which they were all familiar. John, who was nearest to the entrance, looked at Jessie, who nodded to him. He lifted the latch, swung back the door and was as surprised as everyone else in the room by what he saw. Framed against the darkness outside was Helen Anderson. Most of them knew her, having seen her around the shipyards when her father's boats were being built or launched, or when she and her mother had to stand with him at civic events. She was wearing a dark dress, with a short jacket over it, buttoned to her neck. She looked at the group inside and her hesitation suggested that she hadn't expected to see so many people. She'd come to see Jimmie's wife but had no idea which one of these women it was. John sensed her confusion briefly, but it was overwhelmed by his own. What was Anderson's daughter doing here alone this late in the day? It must be connected with Jimmie's death. Anything else would be too much of a coincidence.

"Good evening, Miss Anderson," he said. "Have you missed your way?"

He knew she hadn't but someone had to say something. Helen looked at him and gave a small shake of her head.

"I heard the dreadful news about Mr. Crombie. I came to... to offer Mrs. Crombie my sympathy and that of my family."

Jessie stood up.

"Come in, please," she said, looking around but knowing that there was no chair on which Helen could sit without ruining her dress. Helen stepped inside and went directly to her.

"I will not stay, Mrs. Crombie," she said, her expression betraying nothing of the nausea she felt as the smell of the interior caught her. "I am glad to see that you have your friends around you. I merely wished to tell you how very sorry we were to hear about your husband. He was working so hard on my father's... Well, I simply wished to say that if there is anything we can do..."

She left the offer hanging in the air. Such a large audience made her acutely aware that she was intruding. She'd wanted to offer specific financial help, pretending that it came from her father as a token of his thanks for the work Jimmie had done on his ship, but the mood was wrong. To stand in her finery amidst their sorrow and drabness and talk of money would be unfeeling and insulting.

Jessie was as embarrassed as she was.

"You're very kind," she said. "I'm pleased my Jimmie was to your likin'. But I don't need nothin', thanks."

Helen smiled.

"Well, if you do, just..."

She gave a little nod, not knowing how on earth the woman would contact her or ask for anything. The visit, made for the best of reasons, had proved to be of no value whatsoever. It had added discomfort and confusion to the woman's grief and offered her nothing.

"Please, forgive me for intruding," she said, before turning and forcing herself to walk very slowly back out into the evening. John shut the door behind her.

Jessie sat down in her chair again and Helen would have been pleased to know that, rather than embarrassment, her visit had brought a change of emphasis and a flash of novelty which warmed Jessie and lifted her out of the orthodoxy of dutiful mourning.

Only Willie Marshall seemed unimpressed.

"What was all that about?" he said.

Outside, Helen walked quickly away through the darkness. She knew the danger of being in such a place at night but her mind was too full of the Crombie interior to dwell on her fears. She knew she was insulated from the real lives of the people she saw working on the ships and quays, and ignorant of the passions and preoccupations that filled their days. She was far too sensible to believe that these dark houses were filled with the noble savages which peopled the cheaper novels she read, but she also doubted that they sheltered the villains and cripples that filled the London of Mr. Dickens. She wished that she could meet and talk with them, disguised as one of their kind, to save them having to filter their responses through the acknowledgement that she was William Anderson's daughter. Even in their own homes, the deference that she hated so much was obvious. Her cheeks burned at the thought and she scolded herself for having acted so inappropriately. Her intention had been positive, strong, and yet all she'd managed were some feeble muttered condolences and she no doubt left Mrs. Crombie and her friends bewildered as to why she'd bothered to come at all. Her pace quickened and she resolved even more fiercely to do something definite to help Mrs. Crombie as soon as she could.

****

John's present contract was for a barque being built by the Duthie brothers. The figurehead itself was ready and John had done most of the work on the stern ornament and name boards. Before etching the finer details of the scrollwork on the trailboards, the timber facings needed to be blocked out. It was a job that could be handled by his apprentice, Jamie Forsyth. John took him through the schedule, demonstrating angles and curves and marking corners and edges which needed to be shaved away. Jamie listened, nodded, asked some questions and was pleased when John eventually clapped him on the back and went out of the workshop, stopping only briefly at the door to say, "Any mistakes and you lose a week's wages and your left eye".

Even though he was used to it, the stench of the harbor at low water caught his nostrils. It was like a huge cesspool. In fact, on the rare occasions that the authorities had arranged to clear out the upper harbor, the work had produced tons of manure, which they'd advertised for sale in the Aberdeen Journal. When the summer came, it would get even worse and there'd be the usual public meetings and promises to do something about it, promises which would only be kept if they didn't interfere with profits.

For all the smell, though, the harbor was the place John always wanted to be. The masts and spars swayed lazily across one another against the sky, the ropes and rigging slapped their gentle rhythms and hummed quietly in the wind. The hulls rolled slowly in the water or sat still on the mud, resting before their next battle with sea and ocean. At the Waterloo Quay basin, barges were being loaded with lime, bones and dung to be taken up the canal to the fields around Inverurie. The grain they'd brought down with them had already been loaded onto carts and hauled away to storage. The long waterfront and the little streets that led down to it were noisy and full of bustling people, all seeming to move with a definite purpose.

John exchanged greetings with lots of them as he walked along, eventually turning north, away from the harbor, to cut across York Street toward The Links and the beach. Tom and Wee Tam Leach had a small ropeworks beside the much larger building of Catto, Thomson and Co. Much of the work they did was sub-contracted to them by the big firm and, like John, they were rarely idle.

John pushed through the big door and saw Tom half way down the rope walk, a streak of hemp around his waist with its ends sticking out the back like the bristles of a big, well used shaving brush. The other end of the hemp was looped over one of the eyes of a big spinning wheel which was being turned by Wee Tam. Wee Tam had to spend anything up to ten hours at the wheel every working day so it was just as well that he was over six feet tall and as solid as granite.

John had known Tom ever since he first came to Aberdeen. The ropemaker had got him his first job by recommending him to a shipwright who needed some trailboards in a hurry. Without particularly seeking one another's company, they found themselves spending time together wandering along The Links, drinking in the Pilot's Tavern on Waterloo Quay or just sitting outside John's house. Tom shared John's curiosity about things and was always wanting to hear more of what John had done over in the west and down in England. Since Tom had never taken the trouble to learn to read, John was also his primary source of stories and news from the papers. He admired and envied the carver's learning and John was happy to share it with him.

But it was a horse that gave their friendship its present strength and depth. One day, Tom had stepped out of John's workshop straight into its path. It had been frightened by a pile of timber which had crashed from a pallet just beside it and bolted down the quay, its cart jumping and rattling behind it. Tom had leapt back, fallen, stretched out his right hand to save himself and dislocated the middle two fingers. John came out and found him lying in the road, gray with pain and drifting in and out of consciousness. Without hesitation, he grabbed each of the fingers in turn and heaved them back into place. Tom screamed once but the pain immediately began to subside and he could soon start flexing his hand again. It was all done so quickly that there was no lasting damage to the tendons or joints and he was back at work just a couple of hours later. That evening, fingers and senses all dulled by whisky, he'd insisted that, without John's help, he would have lost the dexterity his job demanded and so was convinced that he owed him his livelihood.

Neither of the rope makers had seen John and he watched as Tom walked backward toward him, letting out more hemp for spinning on the way. As he came nearer the door, John moved across to the rope walk and came up beside him.

"Aye, big man," said Tom.

John nodded at him and waved to Wee Tam. He walked slowly alongside Tom as he continued to spin his rope.

"What're you doin' here?" asked Tom.

John shrugged his shoulders.

"Jimmie," he said.

Tom nodded.

"How was Jessie when you left her last night?" asked John.

Tom looked at him and stopped for a moment before starting to move backwards again.

"Ach, as good as she could be, I suppose. Her man's away, but she's better off without him."

"I can't get the two of them out of my head," said John.

"How?"

"Never thought he'd be that daft."

"The drink makes us all daft," said Tom, smiling. "You should know that."

John ignored the gibe.

"Did you see him Saturday night, then?" he said.

"Me? No, don't think so. I was in the Union and the Royal. He never came in there."

Nowadays, John rarely spent much time in the taverns or public houses. Tom was right. Drink loosened his tongue and his past carried too many regrets at observations he'd made and things he'd done that owed more to whisky than to wisdom.

"Where did Jimmie usually drink, then?" he asked.

Tom's spinning rhythm didn't vary as he brushed a hand across his nose and sniffed.

"Cruickshank's in Schoolhill. Sometimes the Risin' Sun in Huxter Row. Mostly Cruickshank's though. What difference does it make? Doesna matter where he got the stuff. It killed him anyway."

"Maybe."

Tom looked up from the rope again.

"Aye, aye," he said. "You're sniffin' around again, are ye?"

"Maybe," said John again.

"What d'ye mean, maybe? If it wasna the drink, what was it?"

"Did you not think...? Where Bessie found him... It was a bit far up the beach?"

"Aye. I see what you're sayin'. I didna see for myself but I heard."

"Aye."

Tom stopped and gave a single sharp whistle. Wee Tam stopped turning the wheel.

"What're you thinkin' then, John?"

"Well, that far up, well beyond the tide... How did he get there?"

Tom looked at him and nodded.

"I wondered myself. Are you thinkin' it's maybe no' a drownin'?"

"Well," said John, "if it wasn't the sea..."

He left the unsaid suspicion hanging.

"He could've crawled," said Tom. "He was drunk, fell in. That would've sobered him up fast enough. He managed to swim ashore, crawl up the beach but... well, he'd've been freezin' by then. Cold just got to him."

But for the mark on his throat and the two square holes in Jimmie's chest, it was a fair enough guess. The waving strands of hemp at Tom's back caught John's eye. He reached over and felt it, letting it run through his fingers. Its fibers were thin and sharp. He twisted them around his fist and saw how they formed a tight rope in the center with looser individual threads at its edges. Tom watched, bemused. John caught his expression and smiled.

"There were other things," he said.

"What things?"

"A mark round his neck for a start. And two holes in his chest." He flicked at the hemp. "I reckon somebody wrapped a piece of this around his throat."

Tom's face showed that John's words had had their effect.

"What, hemp? Raw?"

"Aye. I saw the marks. If it'd been spun it'd show the lay of the rope. There'd have been tar, too. No, I reckon somebody just grabbed some and turned it round to make a thong."

Tom thought for a while, nodding slowly.

"And the holes. Did nobody else see them?"

"Don't know."

Tom continued his nodding.

"Well, well. So somebody'd finally had enough."

"What d'you mean?"

"Aw, come on, John. You knew Jimmie as well as I did. He was never short of money. And usually it was somebody else's. He must've met up with somebody he was owin' something. Maybe they'd had a drink or two, tried to get what they was owed and..."

He made a throat slitting noise and gesture. John noted that he didn't seem particularly disturbed by the scenario he'd described.

"Was he owing you?" he asked.

"Aye. As usual. Why? You askin' if I killed him?"

John laughed.

"No, no. I can't see you going to all the trouble of dragging him down the beach, soaking him with water and all the rest of it."

"Why not?"

"You're too bloody lazy."

It was Tom's turn to laugh.

"Still, I won't see my money now though, will I? Canna ask Jessie for it." He paused to think, then went on. "It's Willie Johnston who'll be the real loser."

"How?"

"Jimmie bought two loads o' timber from him last month. I say 'bought' but he never paid for it. Willie'd kill Jimmie if he wasna already dead."

John managed to smile but inwardly he was struck by the words. If he was looking for someone who might have killed Jimmie, he'd find plenty of people who hated him enough to do so if they could get away with it. The problem was that most of them hated him because he owed them money and killing him would guarantee that they never got it.

Tom gave another whistle, the wheel started turning and he moved backwards again.

"Have you told the watch about the mark and the holes?" he asked.

John shook his head. A huge smile spread across Tom's tanned face.

"That'd be somethin', if we caught him, wouldn't it?" he said.

"Aye, it would, too. If there was time."

"We can make time," said Tom. "Have you told anybody else?"

John shook his head.

"Right, best to keep it just the two of us. You and me, eh?"

"If you like," said John, amused by the older man's enthusiasm. He knew that it came from boredom rather than any real interest in justice. Tom's life took him from home to the rope walk and back, with a diversion to the taverns at weekends. It was like everyone else's but he was constantly speaking of signing on for one of the ships leaving the harbor and he'd often given John glimpses of his minor dissatisfactions. Whenever John came across one of his mysteries, Tom was always wanting to be part of it. It was a little road that led him away from middle age for a while.

John stayed on the rope walk until Tom had finished the length he was spinning and started to coil it. Wee Tam walked down to join them and they talked of Jessie. She was still a young woman. Everybody had always said she was too good and too pretty to belong to Jimmie. None of the dislike that attached to him tainted her and she didn't deserve to suffer just because she'd been unlucky in the man who'd chosen to marry her.

"I just hope she's got enough to keep her going," said John.

"Don't worry about Jessie," said Tom. "She's got friends in all the right places."

"What d'you mean?"

"You know what I mean. That Anderson wifey. What was she doin' there last night?"

It was a question that John had asked himself, too. As his mind had turned on the troubling little details of Jimmie's body, the image of Helen Anderson framed in Jessie's doorway had occasionally flashed up at him and added fresh confusion. The worlds of people like the Andersons and the Crombies didn't overlap very much, certainly not to the extent of either making social calls on the other, however extreme the circumstances. It was tempting to think that Jimmie's involvements were wider than any of them knew. If so, John's chances of satisfying his curiosity were even more remote.

"I wouldn't call her a wifey," he said.

Tom laughed.

"They've all got the same thing under their skirts, John," he said.

To his surprise, John felt a little heat come into his cheek. Tom's reduction of Helen Anderson to the level of the whores in Mason's Court or the fishwives who carried the creels from the fishing boats up to the market was disturbing. It might well be true but it was a truth he preferred not to think of.

"She didn't need to come. It was a... Christian thing to do," said John, knowing the words were not expressing what he really meant to say.

"If that's what Christianity brings to your door, I think I might start prayin' again," said Wee Tam.

John shook his head.

"You'll go to hell. Both of you," he said.

"See you there," said Tom.

John left them as they started walking back toward the wheel to hook up another streak of hemp. Outside, he stopped, leaned against Tom's little handcart and looked out across The Links. The sun was bright and the wind made the narrow band of grasses between him and the beach wave and flow. Far out to sea, he saw the white smudges of four sets of sails. Nearer the shore, three other ships lay at anchor, waiting for the tide which would take them up the Dee and into the harbor. Briefly, he remembered the walks he'd taken with Marie along the water's edge, the plans they'd made, the dream of one day sailing out of the harbor together to find a new freedom and new riches in America or Canada. Marie's face came back to him, her pale golden hair, her big brown eyes with their strange feline tilt, the laugh that made it impossible to be angry with her.

Tom's whistle and the sound of the turning wheel from inside the rope works cut through his rememberings. Marie's was just one more brutal death, something that happened too frequently in towns all over Scotland. John forced his thoughts away from her darkness and back to the conversation he'd just had. Tom's eagerness to look for Jimmie's killer had been genuine and they'd more or less agreed to do some investigating. As he pushed himself upright and started back to his workshop, he began reflecting on where to begin looking and realized that he had no idea.

CHAPTER FOUR

Molly Cameron had been with the Andersons for four years, starting as a junior housemaid but with ambitions to become if not a housekeeper, then certainly a cook in one of the grander houses in Perthshire or maybe somewhere in the west of Scotland. The work was hard and long but she enjoyed the privileges of living and eating in a fine interior. Her own room was clean and simple but carried little indicators of the elegance she would like to spread further into her life. In the corner was a cane bedroom chair, beside it a painted pine chest of drawers and, dominating the room, a cast-iron bedstead. The little patches of flowers embroidered on its quilt and the prints on each of the walls were bright splashes against the room's dark wallpaper and polished floor. On a small table beside the bed was her Bible, the page from which she had last been reading marked with a light blue silk tassel which she had made herself from an offcut from one of her mistress's dresses.

In the middle of the morning, Molly had come to check a list of special chores that the housekeeper had given her for the coming week. She heard a knock on the door and was surprised that anyone else was up near the servants' rooms at such a time. It was Helen. She was carrying a small bundle, wrapped in paper.

"I heard you coming up here," she said with a smile. "I've been meaning to give you this."

She gave the package to Molly, who bobbed a quick curtsey and stood back, inviting her into the room. Although she felt slightly embarrassed at being visited by her mistress, it had happened on many previous occasions, usually when Helen had some little present for her. Helen came in and stood at the door as Molly unwrapped the package. It contained a pelerine, a little cape. It was made of sheer white cotton and had a pattern of intertwined flowers embroidered around its edges.

"I haven't worn it for a very long time. I thought that you might like it."

Molly held it up and admired the stitching.

"Oh, I do, Miss. Thank you very much. You're very kind."

"I know you're busy, Molly," said Helen. "You always are. But I wondered if I might ask you a favor while I'm here."

Molly folded the pelerine and laid it across the cane chair.

"Of course, miss."

Helen patted the bed.

"May I sit here?" she asked.

"Of course, miss," said Molly again.

Helen did so. There was a rustle of quilt and a single squeak from the bedsprings.

"And will you sit beside me for a moment?"

Molly was used to Helen's unique ways with her and the other servants but this was a new departure. She hesitated a moment, then took a step to the side of the bed and perched uncomfortably on the edge, leaving a more than respectable distance between herself and her mistress. The springs squeaked again.

"I've asked you many things over the years, haven't I?" said Helen, eager to get to the point.

"Yes, miss."

"Some of them more than a little strange."

She waited, encouraging a little smile from Molly.

"It's because, for all my schools and tutors and books, there are still so many parts of life about which I know nothing. You have many things you can teach me, Molly."

Secretly, Molly agreed with her but she wasn't prepared to say so.

"So I'd like you to tell me how you feel about me coming into your room, sitting on your bed and asking you questions."

The words threw Molly into complete confusion. She had no idea what to say.

"I don't want you to think about it. Just tell me how it makes you feel. Embarrassed? Angry? Something else?"

Desperately, Molly searched for words, any words that might unblock her mind.

"Not angry, miss."

"Embarrassed, then?"

"A little. Not really, though."

Helen gave a long sigh.

"I'm sorry, Molly. It isn't fair. How can you know what I'm looking for? You see, what I really want is your advice."

"Advice, miss?"

"Yes."

Helen moved along the bed toward her, making the springs creak louder and longer than before. She leaned forward, her initial embarrassment at invading Molly's space eased aside by her eagerness to know her opinion.

"You've heard of poor Mr. Crombie's death."

"Yes, miss."

"Do you know his wife?"

"No, miss."

"A pity. I'm very anxious to meet her. Losing her husband must be very distressing for her. You see, Mr. Crombie was working for my father. I feel we should try to help her."

"I'm sorry, miss. I don't know her at all."

Helen smiled again, reached out and put her hand on Molly's arm. It was an unconscious gesture, one which, in Helen's mind, drew them closer together, but in Molly's set up a small tension. Helen must have seen something in her face. With a single squeeze, she withdrew the hand again.

"I am so clumsy," she said. "I know I should just be able to go to Mrs. Crombie and say, 'I want to help you. What can I do?' But I have no idea how she might respond to such an approach. What do you think, Molly?"

"I don't know, miss. It is the Christian thing to do."

"Yes. But I don't just mean Christian charity. I want to talk to her, discover how she feels, give her something other than money. Do you suppose she would think I was merely interfering? Intruding into her grief?"

As it had in the past, her openness conveyed itself to Molly and she began to feel that the distance which normally separated them had been set aside.

"I mean, I burst into your room, sit on your bed and here I am talking to you like a sister. There are those who would find it offensive that I feel free to do such things."

Molly thought for a moment.

"I know what you mean, miss," she said at last, "but I take no offence. None of us do. We know you. It is—strange, as you said, and at first, it feels wrong for you to be so—friendly with us. But I've never felt there was any harm in your actions. Anyway, you have the right to do whatever you wish."

"No, I don't. I don't have the right. This is your room. I'm forcing myself upon you, taking up your time. I only have the right to do that if you don't mind."

"Well, I don't."

"But, think, Molly, if you wished to do the same thing—ask my advice, I mean—would you feel able to come to me as I have to you?"

The answer was obvious. Molly dropped her eyes and shook her head.

"No, you see? It's so difficult. That's why I wonder how Mrs. Crombie might feel. You see, I have no idea what she may think of me. She may see only the daughter of William Anderson. It brings me many privileges but it is also a barrier between others and myself."

Molly knew exactly what she meant. Mr. Anderson would never be this familiar. He had always been fair with her, but her friends often said it was a shame that she had to work for such a man. Helen was a model mistress; her father kept his distances and, so the gossip went, had his secrets.

An awkward little silence grew between them. Helen seemed to be waiting for her to say something.

"May I speak honestly, miss?" Molly asked.

"That is why I came to you."

"I think you should have no fear that your father's name will be an obstacle."

"Why?"

Molly looked shyly at her, feeling the fragility of her position in such a conversation.

"Because Mrs. Crombie is a woman. Your father is a very important man in Aberdeen, but women have different beliefs."

She stopped.

"Beliefs?" said Helen, a little frown on her brow.

"About—trade, business. I don't know Mrs. Crombie but I would be surprised if she did not welcome you into her home. The way you talk with her will depend on you, not on your father. I can't say how she'll feel if you approach her. You can only find out by going to her."

Helen smiled at her.

"Do you think she might be as understanding as you are, Molly?"

The smile invited a complicity which Molly was at last ready to give.

"You've had four years to train me, miss."

The answer, accompanied with a shy little smile, still seemed equivocal. Helen, though, found it reassuring. Molly was saying that strangers might respond less readily to Helen's boldness in setting aside the normal social constraints, but the freedom with which she expressed her opinion and the fact that she was even prepared to risk a tiny joke confirmed that simple, honest contacts were always possible. There was surely every chance that Jessie Crombie, free from the need to be respectful that necessarily cramped Molly's attitudes, might not be overawed by the visit of an Anderson. And it would perhaps give Helen the chance to satisfy her curiosity about the death of her husband.

****

John remembered Tom's remark about Willie Johnston and decided to look in on him on his way back to the harbor. Willie had made a success of his business by setting up a permanent sawpit, working regular hours and spending what he earned on improving the place. He hadn't yet made enough to install one of the new steam engines and still relied on horses to drive the long blades up and down through the timber.

There was a smell of resin and freshly cut wood which overlaid the stench of the nearby harbor as Willie and his apprentices used their axes to block out the masts and spars of the barque on which Jimmie had been working. Willie was too busy to stop but, as they spoke, was surprisingly forgiving about Jimmie Crombie. As Tom had said, he was angry at what Jimmie had cost him, but he also seemed anxious to spread some of the blame.

"It was Mr. Anderson who was askin' for it," he said. "Jimmie said he was pushin' him to get the boat finished. You don't argue with Anderson, do you?"

"Did Anderson talk to you, then?"

Willie's expression was scornful.

"No. He doesna come near us. It was just Jimmie. 'Mr. Anderson this' and 'Mr. Anderson that.'"

"D'you think he was spinning a yarn?"

"You could never tell with Jimmie. He'd do anythin' for money."

He suddenly dropped the axe against the spar and stood up. John waited, wondering why he'd stopped.

"He wasna brought up by the tide though, was he?" said Willie, his voice quieter.

"No," said John, taken by surprise at the turn of the conversation.

"Somebody got their money off of him. He was robbed."

"Robbed?"

"Aye. I checked his pockets. Nothin'. No' even a penny piece. No watch. Nothin'."

"I didn't know you'd seen him."

"Aye. I came when they were gettin' ready to take him away."

"Did you see anything else?"

Willie wiped his forehead with a red handkerchief.

"You mean the..."

He stopped and pointed twice at his own chest with a stabbing motion. John nodded.

"Aye, I saw. Somebody's done for him. He drank himself stupid and they must've caught him on the way home. And, you know, I don't care."

"But that's murder, Willie."

"Aye. And good luck to them."

He grabbed the axe and began hacking at the spar again, the strain evident as he continued to speak.

"Anyway, I'll maybe get paid yet. There was a shipwright came in earlier. From Dundee. Said he was lookin' for Anderson. Wantin' to take over Jimmie's job. I'm no' for jumpin' into a dead man's shoes but if he pays his way..."

"Aye," said John. "There's no other shipwrights free that I know of. Maybe you'll be getting your money after all."

"Aye," said Willie. "And maybe Anderson'll kick his arse back to Dundee."

CHAPTER FIVE

Across the road from the Town House beside the Mercat Cross was a raised pavement, known as the Plainstones. It was one of the places where gentlemen gathered to walk and discuss their business. Its proximity to the harbor meant that many of these discussions involved ships, cargoes, and everything connected with them. The ships' captains and others who actually made their living on board the vessels were easy to distinguish. Their walks replicated those they took on board as they criss-crossed their quarter deck. While the landsmen wandered the length of the Plainstones, paused now and then, set off at different angles, the seamen stalked back and forth, covering the same few yards over and over again, each turning at exactly the same time as the others as if some signal had been given.

William Anderson was having to fall in with this rhythm as he spoke with Egil Thorsen, the captain of one of his vessels on the Atlantic routes. It had brought timber from Canada in December and was nearly ready to make the return voyage. For this trip, the holds, which had held the trunks of North American pines and oaks, had been cleaned and fitted out with rudimentary tables and bunks ready for the emigrants who were looking for a new life away from Scotland. Twice a year, two of Anderson's vessels made this return voyage, importing timber and exporting people.

In spite of the din of traders at the top of Marischal Street and the crowds in Castle Street, Anderson kept his voice low.

"The trouble with the crew you spoke of, is it dealt with?"

Thorsen nodded.

"I set two of the starboard watch ashore in Quebec. We'll see no more of them," he said in an accent which carried only the slightest evidence of his Norwegian origins. "The men I took on as replacements just wanted to work their passage. I'll find others."

"And the cook?"

"He was drunk, too often. I gave him the choice when we docked in Liverpool. Paid him off and he disappeared."

"Do you know of another one? One we can trust?"

"I think so. The extra shilling helps."

Anderson paid his crews slightly more than the going rate. It meant that he was never short of personnel when a sudden opportunity presented itself. He could get a ship loaded and out to sea faster than any of his competitors. And if rules had sometimes to be twisted in order to produce more revenue, silence bought at a shilling a month was cheap enough.

"I think we should raise the cook's wage to three pounds," said Anderson. "That might help us to find the right man."

Thorsen nodded slowly, seeing at once the wisdom of buying the trust of a figure who in Anderson's way of arranging things, could add significantly to their income.

"Good," said Anderson. "That's what we'll do."

From the Castle Street stalls came the smells of mutton pies, fish and baking. Groups of boys ran amongst the women with their baskets and tried to trick the milk maids into leaving their pitches on the corner of Justice Street so that they could help themselves to a few ladles of the creamy yellow contents of their pails. The beggars that the city's leaders found so unsightly were either sitting at the sides of the street or dragging their way through the crowds, limping extravagantly, hands outstretched as they whined their troubles right and left. None of them dared venture onto the Plainstones. Insinuating themselves into the world of business would be the fastest way of booking a place on the horse-drawn green caravan known to everyone as the Rose Street omnibus. It had no windows, just a door at the back, and it carried prisoners to the city's two jails.

"There was another matter I wanted to sound you about," said Anderson as they turned to retrace their steps once more. "These voyages to Canada and America, they're relatively short, and, whatever we do, news does get back. It would be unfortunate if any unfavorable reports from our passengers began to appear here. It could be very... damaging."

Thorsen knew that this was true. There was so much interest in emigration that journals were being published which gave advice to anyone thinking of taking advantage of the offers of land and life in the colonies. Many of the articles in them spoke enthusiastically of the pleasures of the climate, the country and the opportunities that previous emigrants had found. Others, though, carried warnings of misleading contracts, inaccessible tracts of land and malpractice on the part of ship owners and their captains. Potential emigrants, already anxious at the thought of uprooting their families, would always ask questions about the ship on which they were due to embark. The slightest suspicion could turn them away.

"Of course," Anderson continued, "that's an issue that's far less pressing if the destination is Sydney or the islands of New Zealand. What do you think?"

Thorsen had only twice made trips into the southern ocean and each had been undemanding. But others had spoken of its mountainous seas, its storms and its fog-shrouded icebergs and he knew that it could be fearsome. He thought for a while before replying.

"It's a dangerous passage but I suppose it could not be worse than chasing the whales."

He'd spent six years sailing back and forth to the North West Atlantic, sometimes bringing back a ship groaning with whales and seals, but just as often limping into harbor months later than planned, most of the surviving crew members broken by disease, their gums peeling from their teeth with scurvy, their hands useless because their fingers had been eaten away by the frost. There was no glory in the trade, little room for seamanship when the ice closed in.

"If I got the right vessel," said Anderson, ignoring the reservation carried in Thorsen's words, "would you take it to New Zealand for me?"

"I'll answer you when I see her," replied Thorsen.

As they turned again at the eastern end of their walk, they were stopped by a call from an individual who had stepped onto the Plainstones and was hurrying toward them. He was slightly built, with thick brown hair and a full beard. There was no doubting his trade. The rule dangling from his overalls was the universal badge of the shipwright. It gave them a strange precedence over other craftsmen such as carpenters or sailmakers, allowing them to jump the queue at the barber shop or get the best seats on coaches. He introduced himself as Alexander Glover, a shipwright from Dundee. As he apologized for the manner of his approach and began to explain the reason for it, however, Anderson's interest grew. He'd already been enquiring about shipwrights but, as he feared, they were all busy with other commissions. He listened, asked Glover the names of owners for whom he'd worked and who might supply appropriate references and was soon content to have apparently found an answer to the problem caused by Jimmie's death.

"I arrived this past weekend," Glover was saying. "I was hoping to speak to Mr. Crombie about a joint enterprise. It's a terrible tragedy. I only met him a few times but we spoke about the sort of work he's been doing. He seemed a worthy shipwright."

His words were clipped, unnatural, as if he were trying very hard to use the right ones but wasn't certain of success.

"What do you know of my ship?" asked Anderson.

Glover pulled at his beard and nodded.

"A fine vessel. Sound, strong. She'll serve you well."

"But when?" asked Anderson.

Glover's hand moved under his chin to scratch the hairs on his neck.

"She could be launched in five, six weeks," he said.

Anderson was surprised.

"Five or six? Crombie told me there was another two months' work at least."

Glover smiled and raised an eyebrow.

"Mr. Anderson," he said, "if you put the plans and papers into my keeping this week, she'll be felted and coppered, fitted out and ready for the water by the beginning of June."

It was a tempting prospect but Anderson's conviction that villains were far more numerous than honest citizens checked his impulse to sign Glover on at once.

"You will understand if I first make some enquiries of your previous employers," he said.

"Naturally," said Glover. "But I should tell you that I have nothing else to hold me here in Aberdeen and I have a yard waiting for me in Dundee. I hope that your enquiries will not take too long."

"I shall make it my business to settle the matter at once."

They talked a little more of the ship and the various tasks and fittings that still needed to be arranged, then they shook hands and arranged for Glover to call at Anderson's house at the end of the week.

"What did you think?" Anderson asked Thorsen as the shipwright walked away from them.

"I didn't," said Thorsen.

****

After her chat with Molly, Helen saw no point in agonizing over whether or not to go to see Jessie Crombie. It was a practical not a theoretical issue and the only way of resolving it was to make the visit and find out how she was received. There was no point in discussing it with Bella or any of the other friends with whom she usually spent her time; they would be incapable of understanding her desire to make contact with a fishwife. For Helen, however, it was an exciting antidote to the predictability of their habitual social exchanges, which bored her and which she frequently tried to avoid. Her mind was made up.

She changed into the plainest of her dresses, chose a simple, unadorned bonnet, and slipped out of the house on Regent Quay, telling her mother that she was simply going on an errand and would be back almost at once. It was a short enough walk along Waterloo Quay to York Place and, with the working day already well advanced, few people took much notice of her as she hurried through the crowds. When she tapped on Jessie's door, she still had no idea what to say or how to explain her visit. In fact, she wasn't even sure herself why she was so anxious to make it. The initial impulse had been one of sympathy and, while that was still important, there was another, more confused motive.

The scene she'd witnessed on her visit the previous evening had stirred a curiosity in her. The interior had been dark, the smell of it nauseating, but the group that the opening of the door had revealed was like those depicted in the paintings she'd seen in Edinburgh and London. Drawn together to support the widow, the little huddle of people had a unity, a strength of comradeship that she saw nowhere in her own world. Helen wondered why that should be, why individuals deprived of the privileges that were so natural to her should be capable of generating such a positive force. She envied their seemingly easy harmony. And, of course, they'd been brought together by a mystery toward which Helen was drawn in a way that her mother would have described as unhealthy.

When the door opened, both women felt a rush of surprise; Jessie at the identity of her visitor and Helen at the discovery that the dark widow she'd expected was, in fact, a fresh, pretty young woman with little sign of grief in anything about her.

"I'm sorry. You must think me something of a nuisance, Mrs. Crombie," said Helen, speaking quickly to prevent her surprise showing. "But my visit yesterday evening was so brief and so... inadequate, that I felt I must come and explain myself to you properly."

"There was no need," said Jessie, with a little stammer and a sudden flush in her cheeks.

"I'm glad you think so, but I am less forgiving of my conduct than you are."

The two women stood looking at one another, each with a half-smile on her lips. Despite the distant harbor noises, the silence in York Place seemed total. To break it, Jessie said, "Well," then looked up and down the street, stepped back and gestured for Helen to come in.

The smell was still there but, without the warmth of the people to stir it, it was less insistent. Jessie dusted a chair and invited her guest to sit. When she did so, Jessie sat opposite her, her hands folded in her lap and her glance flicking round the room to check for anything she might prefer Helen not to see. It was clear that the silence would soon climb between them once more but Helen had no wish to repeat the embarrassment of her first visit.

"Two visits in as many days may strike you as rather surprising and certainly excessive," she said. "But I simply wanted to tell you that my offer of help was sincere and that we do appreciate the work your husband was doing for us."

"That's very kind," replied Jessie.

"That's why I came this morning. I really would like to do something to help in some way."

Jessie's head was shaking before she'd finished speaking.

"I don't need nothin'," she said. "My husband made sure that we had enough money. I don't want for nothin'. But thank you for your kindness."

Her refusal was respectful but firm. Helen was pleased to sense that the presence of an Anderson in her house seemed not to impress her unduly.

"I know it must be difficult for you at the moment," she said. "Yesterday evening, I was very aware that I did not belong here with you and your friends. I was intruding on your grief and I'm sorry to have been so thoughtless."

Jessie surprised her by smiling.

"No, no. I was happy to see you. It took my mind off all the gloom."

"I'm glad."

"Aye," said Jessie, warming to the memory. "It was a shock to hear about Jimmie, but that's all. It soon went away. Look at me. Do I look as if I'm mournin'?"

Helen was surprised to find that Jessie had taken the initiative.

"Well... no," she said, a smile of her own flashing to match Jessie's.

"There then. Ach, it was tears and worryin' last night when they was all here. Couldna be anything else when your man's killed. You wonder what'll happen. Your life's changed so sudden, like. But it wasna really grief or mournin'. I had to pretend a bit. That's how it was... different when you came."

"Different?"

"Unexpected. It helped us all to think o' somethin' else. We could stop tryin' to think o' the right things to say."

Helen was amazed at the ease with which Jessie was confessing such secrets. There seemed to be no guilt attaching to her failure to honor her dead husband and, despite the fact that she was a stranger to her, Jessie was speaking with an openness that Helen always craved with her own acquaintances but rarely achieved. She'd also noticed that Jessie had said that her husband had not just died, but been killed.

"Your bravery is astonishing," she said.

"Bravery?"

"Well, whatever you say about not grieving, you've still been left alone, with no one to provide for you. It will not be easy."

Jessie studied her for a moment, the smile away from her lips, a serious expression on her face.

"Have you a man, Miss Anderson?"

Helen laughed, delighted as much with Jessie's willingness to be direct with her as with the prospect of herself having "a man".

"No, Mrs. Crombie. Not even a boy."

It brought the smile back to Jessie's face.

"It's no' always better to have one. My sister's married to a fisherman. They don't have many rows. D'you know why?"

Helen shook her head.

"'cause he's usually at sea."

She laughed, got up and, without asking Helen if she wanted any, put out two cups and saucers. She took the pot from the range on which it was gently simmering and poured tea for the two of them. It was so natural, so normal. Neither of them felt the need to follow the polite protocols that usually governed contacts between people of such different estates. For Jessie, it had quickly been obvious that she didn't need to. Helen was just grateful that she hadn't had to work to break through them.

She was less grateful for the tea. It was strong, brackish and had obviously been brewing for a long time. With Jimmie keeping a tight hold of the family purse, Jessie couldn't afford to buy fresh leaves so, like most of her neighbors, she had to buy them second hand. They'd already been used by wealthier folks and, to get any strength out of them, they had to stand for a long time. As Helen sipped at it, she did everything she could to suppress the shudder she felt, but it was hard. To her dismay, Jessie noticed her reaction.

"You'd maybe like me to make a fresh pot," she said.

Helen shook her head at once.

"Certainly not. It's... it's just that I'm not used to it being strong. It'll be good for me. It may educate my palate."

"Aye, or destroy it completely."

Helen gave Jessie a smile wide enough to prevent her insisting.

"But tell me," she went on, "why do you have such a low opinion of marriage?"

"Ah," said Jessie, the sound suggesting that her reasons would take a very long time to relate. With little prompting from Helen, she began to list all the drawbacks of having a husband, staying mostly with generalizations and not referring specifically to her own. It seemed to Helen that, some of the time, her remarks were meant to apply to all men, not just married ones. Jessie's opinions spilled happily out, expressing on the one hand a confidence in her own strength as a woman but on the other the vulnerability of her sex to the brutish whims of men. She had obviously had many unpleasant experiences in her relationships but she still believed that, however strong and theoretically superior men were, women would always survive and overcome their baseness, even though it took a long and painful time. At one point, she asked whether marriages "in society", as she put it, were any better than those she was describing. Helen had to think for a moment before answering that it was difficult to say because no one ever admitted to anything. She added that, like the pairings being described by Jessie, those "in society" made very infrequent use of the word "love".

It wasn't until they'd finished their tea that Helen took the subject back to Jimmie. At first, she spoke again of his work on her father's ship.

"Aye," said Jessie, "he was good enough at his work. But now he's gone, I can tell you he was makin' your father pay plenty for what he was gettin'."

"What do you mean?"

"Jimmie never asked for four shillin's when he could get six. He always found ways of addin' a wee extra here and there. You winna be losin' by hirin' another shipwright."

"He must have been a clever man," said Helen, "to get more from my father than he was owed. My father plays the commerce game as well as any and better than most."

Jessie was content to raise her eyebrows to confirm that Jimmie was indeed that skilful.

"You said he was killed," Helen said suddenly. "Why?"

"Why was he killed?"

"No, why did you say that?"

The serious expression came back to Jessie's face. She was thinking hard about her reply. Helen waited.

"Because it would make more sense if he was," said Jessie at last, her words slow and her tone quiet.

"Why?"

Jessie gave a little shake of the head.

"Jimmie wouldna fall in the water, however drunk he was. I knew him. He's come home when he was so drunk he couldna even see, and he never went near the edge."

"But that's not the same as saying that someone killed him."

Jessie looked at her.

"If he didna fall, he was pushed. That's all it could've been."

"Who would want to push him?"

To Helen's surprise, Jessie laughed out loud.

"You didna ken him, did you?" she said.

"No."

"No, because if you did, you'd have been in the queue, too."

Helen was intrigued. Jessie was joking about it but was her husband really so universally disliked?

"Have you told the watch about this?" she asked.

Jessie shook her head.

"I've told nobody. 'cept you." She stopped, suddenly aware of what she was saying. "Why did I do that? Why did I tell you?"

"Because I asked you," said Helen. "Because I'm curious, inquisitive. I push my unwelcome nose into other people's business. Are you going to tell the watch?"

"They wouldna arrest you for that."

"No, not about my nosiness, about your husband being killed," said Helen with a laugh.

Quickly, Jessie shook her head. "I just want it all to go away. I want to forget it." She got up and started to clear away the cups. It was obviously a signal to Helen, who stood up at once to help her.

"No, no," said Jessie. "I'll do it. It's just two cups."

"I must go," said Helen. "I've already held you up for too long."

Jessie turned and smiled at her.

"It was nice. Nicer than I'd've thought," she said.

"Am I supposed to be bad company, then?"

Jessie laughed.

"I dinna ken. I hope so, though."

Helen laughed with her.

"Are you sure there's nothing I can do? No way I can..."

Jessie shook her head again.

"Thank you for comin'," she said. "It brightened up this wee place."

Helen went to the door and opened it.

"I'll maybe think of something I can do," she said.

"Don't try," said Jessie. "You've already helped me."

As she saw Helen out, she looked up and down the street again before stepping outside. The two of them said goodbye and shook hands, the only formality in all their contact, and Helen turned to make her way home. The meeting had been a joy for her. Her apprehension about intruding on Jessie's privacy had not only been unfounded, the two of them had talked like friends and equals. It was a completely unfamiliar experience for her. And, on top of everything else, Jessie had deepened the mystery. Jimmie Crombie had been cheating her father. And someone had pushed him into the water. Whatever Jessie thought about her visit, Helen knew that she would want to repeat it in the very near future.

CHAPTER SIX

Joe Drummond was hurrying to catch the tide. His crew had just let go the fore and aft mooring ropes and he was shouting at them to free off the halyards ready for hauling. There was no need to. The men went through the rituals of setting sail automatically and they wondered why he suddenly felt the need to treat them as if they were boys on their first trip.

"Didna get it from Rosie last night," said one of them.

"Aye, that'd be it," said another.

In fact, since Sunday's silent meal, Joe had seen only glimpses of Rose and she'd managed to stay out of his way long enough to escape his anger at her using the curly-tail word. He'd cut his own chunks of bread and cheese, wrapped them in a cloth and stowed them in his tiny charthouse beside the small keg of ale he kept for his private use.

The tide had just turned and the combination of its ebb and the flow of the river Dee carried the boat quickly out into open water. With more shouts and growling coming at them, the crew broke out the mainsail and felt the boat surge immediately as it cracked full in the wind. Only when the sails were trimmed and the men were sitting sorting out the nets ready for shooting when they reached the fishing grounds did Joe feel the tension ease from him. It was a feeling he got every time he sailed but, after Saturday night's troubles and Jimmie's dying, he needed it more than ever.

He'd wanted to speak to someone, tell them what had happened, but his only friendships depended on a ready flow of beer and whisky and there was no sense to be had in them. There was a time that he might have been able to talk to Rose but, in his eyes, she'd become an anchor that forever held him in a dismal silence, pulling him back from the prizes and pleasures of the bigger world. Maybe the time had come to sign up for a trip across the Atlantic. That would get him away from the dangers and miseries that stalked the streets of Aberdeen nowadays. There were a couple of new ships on the stocks. The owners would soon be looking for men to crew them. Some of the things Jimmie had said on Saturday about Anderson and the ship he was building for him made Joe think that he would probably find it easy to get a berth on her. Glad to be away from the troubles onshore, he looked up at the sails, turned the bow a whisper to port to catch more wind, and wished he was on the deck of a brig headed for the West Indies.

****

It was lunchtime and John and Jamie sat in the workshop, a big loaf of bread and a lump of cheese on the bench between them. Jamie had a jug of ale. John preferred the city's natural water, which was filtered and pumped up from the Dee to the Waterhouse in Union Place. Around their feet were the chips and shavings of the wood Jamie had gouged and chiseled away during the morning. He'd made a very good job of the scrollwork, not only roughing out the general shapes but actually beginning the finer cuts which etched swirls into the design and sent them curling up the trail boards toward where the figurehead would sit astride the main stem piece. John ran his left hand over the work and nodded his appreciation.

"You'll be ready to set up on your own before long," he said. "This is good work."

John was acknowledged by most to be one of the finest carvers in Scotland and Jamie knew that praise from him was the most precious testimonial he could get.

"I won't be stayin' here, though," he said. "No' if Jenny has any say in it."

"How's that?"

Jamie reached into the pocket of his overalls and brought out a cutting from the Aberdeen Journal. He passed it to John, who scanned quickly through it. It said that the Eastern Coast of Central America Commercial and Agricultural Company would, for twenty pounds, convey a man and his wife to a settlement on the river Polochic, feed them on board ship throughout the six to eight week passage and give them forty acres of freehold land on arrival.

"So you'll be a farmer?" said John.

Jamie nodded his head, though without much conviction.

"There's other jobs," he said. "As soon as folk get there, they get work straight away. Good wages, too. And the Journal says that there'll still be plenty even if ten times more go over there."

John remembered that he'd felt the same excitement when he and Marie had toyed with the idea of emigrating. The stories told of a huge country where there was space for everyone and where owning land wasn't just the privilege of a few but an automatic right for every family. For those driven from the Highlands or put out of work by the new machines or simply too poor to make any sort of start in Scotland, it seemed an opportunity devised by God himself.

"Well, there's no shortage of timber there, that's true," said John, handing the cutting back. "You'll be able to make yourself a fine cabin. Maybe make some carvings in its beams. Set up as a house carver."

Jamie smiled and reached out to flick a curl of shaving away from the scrollwork.

"Got to get the twenty pounds first," he said.

For what it was buying it wasn't a great sum but for an apprentice with a girl friend who worked as a chamber maid, it might as well have been two hundred.

"Have you been saving?" asked John.

Jamie nodded.

"Over a year. We've got six pounds twelve shillin's."

On the sort of wages he and Jenny earned, it was a significant amount and it proved that they were serious about their plans.

"Two more years then," said John.

Jamie's young face was set grimly as he replied, "Aye."

In his eagerness to see the new world and set up home with Jenny, two years probably sounded like a lifetime.

"You'll maybe change your mind meantime," said John.

"I don't think so, John," said Jamie. "What am I goin' to be here?"

"One of the best carvers in town."

Jamie smiled.

"Aye, and I'm proud to hear you say it, but can you ever see me walkin' the Plainstones, settin' up in a villa in Ferry Hill, ridin' up to Deeside to shoot the deer?"

John was surprised at the words.

"Is that what you want?"

Jamie laughed.

"I don't know. But I see others doin' it and I know I canna. And that doesna feel right."

It was a feeling John himself had had many times. The gap between those who seemed to have everything and those who had precious little was evident throughout the city. There were enlightened attitudes toward the poor and the sick but the feeling was still that there was a natural order which separated society into layers that were a necessary part of its processes.

"You're serious then, are you? Talked about it?"

"Aye. No question. It was just dreamin' at first but when you see the folk that've gone already... It's no' just dreams, John. Jenny's wantin' away from bobbin' and curtseyin' all the time."

"How about you?"

"Oh you know fine I'm glad to be workin' with you, but I've got itchy feet. I want to see things."

John smiled. Once again, he remembered the frustrations that had hedged around the plans he and Marie had made, qualifying them, forcing them to think small thoughts when they wanted to shake the world.

"Aye, well," he said, "if you're wanting help finding the twenty pounds, you just have to say. I'll lend you what I can."

Jamie looked down at the bench, then away at the far wall of the workshop. When he looked back at John again, tears were beginning to shine in his eyes.

"Would you do that, John?"

John saw that he'd had to swallow before risking his voice.

"I don't care how much it costs. Just as long as I get rid of you," he said.

Jamie smiled and rubbed his eyes with the back of his hand.

"It's just..." He stopped, sniffed and continued in a rush. "It's just that Jenny's pa says he can let us have some and my ma's the same and I've got a few things I could sell if we're leavin' and... well, I worked it out. We just need seven pounds to take us past the twenty."

It was a lot of money but Jamie had always worked well and responded honestly to the challenges he'd been set. He was worth more than John was allowed to pay him and, since the only reason that John had money saved was to be ready for the unexpected, the opportunity was clear.

"Seven pounds," said John. "A fortune. I'll want interest. I think maybe a thousand per cent might cover it."

"Only a thousand?" said Jamie.

"Well, I'll expect to have unlimited access to your wife if I'm ever in your part of the world."

Jamie shook his head.

"No, it's too much."

"All right," said John. "Just a loan. We'll talk about the interest later. You pay me back when you can."

He held out his hand. Jamie took it then suddenly jumped up, reached across and hugged him.

"God, John. I don't know how I... But I'll pay you back. With interest, too. You won't be..."

He gave a final squeeze and disentangled himself.

"The first wages I get," he said, "before I spend anythin' over there, I'll send them back to you."

"You haven't even booked your ticket yet," said John. "I think you'd better speak with Jenny about it." He stood up and banged the flat of his hand against the trail boards. "Anyway, you're not going anywhere until these are finished."

The tears had gone from Jamie's eyes and a wide smile lit his face.

"God blessed me when he sent me to you John," he said.

"Aye, and the devil will start munching on your arse if you don't get back to work," said John. "D'you think you can finish the trail boards yourself?"

The question surprised Jamie. Usually, John did the detailed work himself. Entrusting it to Jamie was a further sign of the change that had taken place. He knew that it was John's way of setting him free, telling him that he had what was needed to succeed on the other side of the ocean. He resisted the temptation to hug John again and, instead, picked up a small straight gouge and started studying the timber on the workbench.

His pleasure made John feel good. He knew that, when the news got out that he needed a new apprentice, there would be lots of boys to choose from, but Jamie had been a fast learner and he worked well. He put a hand on the lad's shoulder, gave it a squeeze and left him once more to work unsupervised.

He walked out once again into the bright April afternoon and strolled slowly back toward Footdee. He had no clear purpose in mind and, as he walked, he thought of Jamie and Jenny and the excitement of the two of them setting out on their adventure. There would be the weeks of boredom and sickness in the hold of some barque as she punched her way across the Atlantic against the prevailing winds, but then, with luck, they'd find that the land they'd bought was cleared, with roads leading them easily to it and friends and neighbors who'd made the same choices and knew what they needed to get them started.

To his surprise, the thoughts of Marie that came to him held less bitterness than usual. As he tried to recapture the sound of her laughing and the glow of her golden hair, another image came unbidden to replace her. It was one that had flicked in and out of his mind many times already; the pale, simple silhouette of Helen Anderson, elegant against the darkness outside Jessie Crombie's doorway. He remembered the smell of her as she'd passed him, the flash of her eyes in the lamplight, the low, respectful music of her voice as she'd spoken to Jessie.

He shook his head to rid himself of such fancies. Women only complicated things. He'd be better worrying away at the death of Jimmie Crombie. He saw that he was near York Place and decided to call again on Jessie. He knew that she would not yet have gone back to her work and he'd still not had the chance to ask her the things he'd wanted to the day they'd found Jimmie's body.

He was just a few paces from her door when it opened and Wee Tam came out. Each of the men was as surprised as the other.

"Aye John," said Wee Tam, before calling back through the door, "And Pa says there's no hurry."

"Leave it open," said John. "I was coming to see Jessie myself."

Wee Tam nodded and called again.

"Another visitor, Jessie. You're a popular girl today."

Jessie appeared at the door. She looked pink and flushed and a total stranger to grief. John was pleased to see it.

"Jamie given you the sack, has he?" asked Wee Tam.

"No," said John. "I'm a man of leisure, like yourself."

The big man laughed.

"I just brought a few things across from Pa. It's break time anyway. I'd best be gettin' back, though. Take care, now Jessie."

"Aye Tam. Thanks."

As Wee Tam walked away, Jessie went back inside, holding the door for John to follow her.

"Cup of tea?" she asked. "It's fresh made."

"No thanks," said John.

"I'm drinkin' it day and night, with all the folks that keeps comin' to see me."

"Oh sorry. Did you want me to... ?"

"Sit down," said Jessie. "It wasna a complaint. I'm havin' a better time now than I've had for ages."

"Aye," said John. "You're looking well."

"I am well."

And it was true. There was a shine in her eyes and a lift to her lips that made her look as young as she really was. The days with Jimmie, his moods, his brutality and his demands had clamped her into an oppression that had threatened to smother her in middle age before she'd even taken hold of her youth. What John could see in her was her release from a sentence. Jimmie's wife had vanished; Jessie had taken her place.

"I was wondering if there was anything you're needing," said John.

"You too?" said Jessie with a laugh.

"What d'you mean?"

Jessie shook her head.

"Nothin'. Anyway, folks is showerin' me with stuff. You wouldna believe it."

The light from the window silvered the edges of her dark hair and dropped soft shadows into her cheeks and eyes. The blouse she was wearing was loose and two folds curved down from its neck to the points of her breasts, where they divided into several smaller folds which disappeared into the waist of her skirt. She tugged at the material of one of her sleeves.

"Did he owe you anythin'?" she asked suddenly.

"Jimmie? No," said John. "No, I'm not here collecting debts."

Jessie smiled again.

"None of them says they are but I know that that's what some of them wants. He was a terrible man for not payin', wasn't he?"

John shrugged. Another silence fell between them.

"Well," Jessie went on. "Somebody got paid all right."

"How d'you mean?"

"They got his watch from him."

"His watch?"

"Aye. It wasna in his pocket. Somebody's took it. In fact, his pockets was empty. Everythin' gone. Mind you, he could've spent it all, knowing him."

John didn't say that Willie Johnston had already told him the same thing. He was just grateful that he could steer their talk toward the questions he wanted to ask.

"You think he was robbed then?" he asked.

Jessie shrugged.

"Maybe," she said. "There was certainly nothin' left on him."

She scratched at her cheek and was thoughtful for a moment.

"They even took his black pebble," she said.

John had no idea what she was talking about. Jessie saw the frown on his face.

"Maybe that's why he drowned," she added. "He picked it up on the beach, years ago. Shiny wee pebble. Black as pitch, with a kind of white marbly streak in it. Fixed an eye on the end of it and wore it round his neck. It was his lucky stone."

She gave a short laugh at the irony of what she was saying.

"So they left nothing," said John.

She looked up at him and gave a small shake of her head.

"It doesna matter," she said. "Anyway, he was gettin' worse. Lately... I dinna ken if it was the work or what else, but he was always arguin' with folk, complainin'."

She stopped short of revealing just how he'd used her to unload his angers at home.

"What about?" asked John.

Jessie was still picking at her sleeve.

"I didna listen much. It was always the same story. And he was drinkin' more than he used to."

"D'you know where he was drinking Saturday night?"

Jessie looked away for a moment, then shook her head.

"He was meetin' somebody. Said he had some business. On a Saturday night. I didna believe him. I didna care neither."

"So he didn't mention any names?"

"Only Mr. Anderson."

"What about him?"

"Nothin' special. He was always speakin' about him."

"But what sort of things did he say?"

"Jimmie was robbin' him. Kept gettin' extra money for timber, wages for workers who werena there, that kind of thing. It was the only thing that made him laugh. He said he coulda had the job finished weeks ago."

This surprised John. Jimmie's ways with money were well known but he was no match for people like Anderson. The sort of fraud Jessie was describing could never pay in the long run. Her voice cut across his thoughts.

"Ken this, John, you're as bad as Davie Donne."

"How?" asked John.

"He's been here askin' all the same questions."

John felt a little shiver of interest at the fact that the police had begun an investigation. It obviously showed on his face.

"Aye, now that's started you thinkin', eh?" said Jessie, with a smile.

"What do you mean?"

"Oh, you ken fine," she said, with a wee tap on his arm. "If Davie's lookin' for somethin', you'll want to find it first."

John smiled back at her. She was right. As well as looking after law and order, Davie and the five other policemen who formed the Day Patrol were responsible for hygiene, sanitation and keeping the streets clean, but what drove Davie was crime. It was even part of the way he worked. He supplemented his weekly wage of ten shillings and sixpence by accepting free drinks from publicans and, when his arrests fell below his expectations, used alcohol to bribe people — guilty and innocent—to confess. His opinion of his investigative ability was unaccountably high and John frequently took a childish pleasure in solving some puzzle which had kept Davie occupied for days or more.

"Anyway," said Jessie, "whether Jimmie fell in or somebody pushed him, I don't care. I may be a wicked woman to say it but it suits me fine."

The dust sparkled in the light's rays and there was silence in the little house. The quays and workshops were not so far away but their clattering was muted by the walls and the other houses, and very few horses ever came along York Place. Only the handcarts rattling by with their cargo boxes or coils of rope gave occasional reminders that they were at the edge of a tangle of noise and bustle. John took a cup of tea after all and the two of them spoke of other things, the changes in the city and the harbor, the glories of the royal wedding and the celebrations it had unleashed up and down the country, the strangeness of having a queen instead of a king and the difference that would make to women.

"None," was John's opinion.

"Aye, it will," said Jessie. "Her Majesty's at the top of the heap. You men winna be able to pretend we canna think for ourselves."

"Women? Thinking?" said John. "Whatever next?"

Jessie smiled and he stood up. To his surprise, Jessie got up too, then reached up and pulled his head down to kiss him on the mouth. It was a quick kiss of friendship but it was the first time she'd ever done such a thing.

"I wish there was more like you," she said.

"Aye, a fine place the world'd be then," said John.

"It's true," insisted Jessie, still holding him and looking straight into his eyes. "You shouldna be on your own. You could be doing some lassie a great big favor."

He laughed.

"No, Jessie. Not with all my dark secrets. You wouldn't believe what I get up to in that wee house of mine."

"Maybe I'll come along and you can show me."

The twinkle in her eyes allowed him to bend to her, kiss her on the mouth in his turn—the same, quick peck of a friend—then wag his finger at her.

"You're an evil woman," he said. "But I'm glad to see you're well."

She smiled and let go of his arm.

"Aye. I'm fine, John."

"Remember, you'll tell me if you need anything."

She nodded and opened the door for him. The brightness flooded in and, once again, the memory of the woman who had come across that threshold on Sunday evening flashed in his mind. As he walked back toward the harbor, basking in the early spring warmth, the thoughts of Jimmie and his murder mingled with the brush of Jessie's kiss and the lingering image of Helen Anderson.

CHAPTER SEVEN

In the drawing room of the house on Regent Quay, Elizabeth Anderson was at work crocheting a shawl—a present for the new baby of one of her nieces. She would have preferred to be making it for a grandchild but she kept the idea to herself because, when she'd brought the topic up on previous occasions, her daughter had been quick to let her know that she didn't consider herself to be a "baby manufactory".

Helen was at the window, looking out at the sunshine and the activity along the quays. For her, being forced to stay indoors, reading, making music or filling the hours with needlework, was a constant frustration. She watched the women carrying their baskets, helping to push handcarts, scurrying on errands and, although she had no wish to exchange her soft linens and luxuries for the hardships with which they lived, she envied them their freedoms and involvements. Her conversation with Jessie had reawakened in her hungers that she'd suppressed for too long.

"How many ships has father got?" she asked suddenly.

Her mother stopped, considered and replied, "I have no idea. Why do you ask?"

"Because it's important to us. It's why we have this house, these clothes. It's the reason we can spend all day doing absolutely nothing. I find it natural to take an interest in the thing that shapes our lives so directly."

"Well, I'm sure I don't know, my dear."

Helen turned with her back to the window and looked at her. "And do you know what these ships carry? Where they go? Do you know anything about any of the people who work on them?"

Elizabeth thought again, and her face became serious. "I did when I was younger. But then, it was mostly whaling and they were across the

Atlantic, near Canada and Greenland. And the stories I heard were distressing. I was glad not to have to listen to them." She picked up the shawl and began pushing her hook through it again. "It's a very long time since your father and I spoke of such things."

Helen turned to look outside again. Her father never acknowledged the appetite she had for tales of the world his trading laid open. Each time she walked along the quays, she saw the black faces among the ships' crews, the Orientals with their fascinating eyes, she heard the twanging accents of the Americans and Canadians, the conversations in the strange musics of Swedish and Norwegian. The bales and goods which came ashore in the tenders brought with them materials, textures and spices which fed her imaginings of islands and people living dream-lives on them. The goods that had come from them confirmed their reality but, for her, they were as insubstantial as the perfumes which hung around the emptying holds of the ships. Names like Newfoundland, the Tasman Sea, and Pennsylvania charmed and frustrated her. She wanted to see the places, watch and listen to the people there. She wanted to understand the links and bridges that connected them with her father and therefore with herself. As her father's ships were winched out of harbor and towed clear of its mouth to set their sails into the breathing wind, she wanted to be on them, spreading away from her tiny, narrow world.

"I think we should be told more about the things father does. These men and their secrets... They stifle me."

"You're far too curious, my dear. It's always leading you into trouble."

With a quick, loud sigh, Helen moved across and sat beside her mother. She put her hand out and stopped the moving crochet hook.

"I need to be curious, mother. I need to know about father's business. Who will look after it when he's older?"

Her mother frowned. "I'm sure I don't know. And I don't think he would be pleased to hear you speaking of this."

Helen lifted her mother's hand away from the shawl and held it in her own. "No, he would not. Because he knows that I have ideas of my own, which might not sit easily with his."

Her mother was shaking her head. "Keep your ideas to yourself. They will only cause more trouble."

Helen smiled and looked into her face. "Do you really have no curiosity at all about the places he sends his men? The Americas? The South Seas?"

Elizabeth smiled back, eased her hand away and said, "None," before pushing her hook into the shawl again. "In any case, I shall soon be going there," she added, without raising her eyes from her work.

Helen looked at her. "What do you mean?" she said.

Elizabeth teased her curiosity out a little further by remaining silent, seemingly intent on the hook with its wool.

"Mother," insisted Helen.

Elizabeth stopped and looked up.

"The new barque, the one that's being built, he's chosen a name for it at last."

"And?"

"It's to be called the Elizabeth Anderson." She obviously felt a little pride at the news but it was nothing beside the delight it gave to Helen. She threw her arms around her mother's shoulders and hugged her hard.

"That's wonderful," she said. "I shall even kiss father to thank him myself."

Elizabeth laughed.

"He'll think you're plotting something if you do," she said.

As Helen asked her for more details about when the decision had been made, what her father had actually said, where the boat would be trading and all the other trivia that came with her excitement, she saw the ship with her mother's name on its bow slipping through green and blue waters, lying alongside quays thousands of miles from Scotland as the scents and dusts of exotic places blew from the land onto its decks and spars. And she imagined shining, dark-skinned people looking at the name and wondering what this Elizabeth Anderson was like, how important she was and why her name sat beside others like Nelson, Conqueror, the British Queen and the Earl of Fife.

"When is she to be launched?" she asked.

"I don't know. Not for a long time. She isn't even finished yet. And with the death of that unfortunate man, your father thinks there may be even more delays."

Helen remembered the interior of Jessie's house. The memory contrasted strongly with the visions of her mother's ship riding grandly in foreign ports. She was silent for a moment, then said, "I went to visit his wife."

Elizabeth was used to being shocked by her daughter but she was never prepared for it. She opened her mouth to remonstrate with her but Helen placed a finger against her lips.

"I know what you're going to say. Ladies don't do such things. Well, I think you're wrong. They do. They do if they care about people. She's lost a husband, one who's been working to build a ship for us. I wanted to tell her that we knew about it, that we were sorry. I wanted to show her that her husband meant more to us than... than the timber he was using. And I was right. The ship he's been building isn't just any ship, it's the Elizabeth Anderson."

****

The people on the fish quays were surprised to see Jessie back at work so soon. Mourning usually dragged on for several days. Some made it stretch for weeks. But, as they carried their baskets up the hill, Jessie told the other women that she'd had enough of sitting in her house and putting up with people who all had the lowest possible opinion of Jimmie and yet, for the most part, spoke of his passing in solemn, mournful tones.

"In God's name," she told Rose, "it's me that's the widow, but it's like I was havin' to cheer them up."

Rose smiled. "They meant well," she said.

"Aye, I ken. But they was sayin' things I didna understand. And I don't think they even believed them theirselves. Wantin' me to be greetin' an wailin'. They knew what he was like." She paused, shook her head, then went on again. "Ach, they was kind enough, but I'll tell you, by yesterday evenin', I'd had enough. I was ready to be back."

Rose heaved her own basket higher on her shoulders. The fish inside it slithered about, making its weight shift and forcing her to pause for balance.

"To this?" she said. "You're mad, Jessie."

Jessie laughed and they walked on again in silence, their arms held high to steady the baskets, whose bottom edges dug into their shoulders. They both knew that it was right for Jessie to be back in the world. She probably didn't need to work as much. In fact, she'd never really needed to work at all after her marriage and Jimmie had even suggested once or twice that a shipwright's wife should be occupying herself with something more refined than hoisting baskets of fish onto her hips and shoulders. She'd ignored him though, partly to keep a small independence but mainly because of the pleasure she got from working with her friends. If she'd stopped, she'd have vanished into her little rooms in York Place.

Today, the comforts that Jimmie's money had brought her might be fewer, but they were still there. The house was hers and it would only need a couple of days work a week to keep it and feed herself. Rose had asked about money and Jessie had told her that, in fact, Jimmie had been earning more than usual lately. On three occasions in the past two weeks, he'd emptied his pockets onto the table and Jessie had been stunned at the amounts he was carrying. When she asked where it had come from he'd told her to mind her own business but he'd hinted that there was more to

come. She suspected it had something to do with Mr. Anderson and his
ship but she didn't know for sure.

"How's Joe?" she asked, as they turned right off Regent Quay.

Rose was silent for a moment, then just shook her head.

"Trouble?" asked Jessie.

"To be honest, I dinna ken," said Rose.

"How?"

Rose sighed deeply.

"I don't see him all that much, to tell you the truth. We never say
nothin' to each other. He's out every night he can." She paused, stopped
walking for a moment, and said, "And I don't care either."

"There's many would say the same about their men," said Jessie, who
knew something of the troubles her sister had had.

The two of them started walking again.

"Aye, but just sittin' there, sayin' nothin'. I mean, you want to talk,
don't you? You want somethin' to bring the world into your house. With
Joe, there's nothin'. I dinna ken where he goes, what he does, nothin'."

"Don't worry," said Jessie, trying to get the smile back onto Rose's
lips, "that's easy. He's either on the boat or in the alehouse. There's no'
many secrets with Joe."

The smile flickered only briefly.

"I'm no' so sure, Jessie. He's been in a black mood these couple of
days. He's changin'."

"Is he out today?"

"Aye. He sailed yesterday. And I bet he's still feelin' sorry for
hisself."

"How?"

"His head'll still be sore from Saturday night. And he'll be
rememberin' all the money he spent."

"And they wonder why I'm not cryin' myself to sleep for losin'
Jimmie," said Jessie, nudging her elbow into Rose's side.

Rose looked at her but couldn't manage a smile.

"Are you sure you're better off without him?" she asked.

"What do you think?" said Jessie.

"I hope so," said Rose, taking one hand from her basket and reaching
over to squeeze Jessie's arm. "I really do, Jessie darlin'."

Jessie smiled and they fell silent, saving their breath as they climbed
Marischal Street. It was very steep and, when they eventually turned right
at the top into Castle Street, they immediately felt the muscles in their
calves ease. Their stride lengthened and they were soon dumping the
contents of their baskets into the trays of one of the fishmongers. The white
and silver streams gushed across the top of those already lying there and

added to the pungency of the air. The two sisters turned, heaved their empty baskets onto their hips, Rose to the left, Jessie to the right, and set off back down toward the boats.

"That Helen Anderson came back, you know," said Jessie.

"What d'you mean?"

"To my place. Came to see me. Wantin' to help."

"What, again?"

"Aye. She meant it, too. She's a fine lassie. No airs and graces."

"Aye, maybe."

"She is, I'm tellin' you. We had a nice talk. Very friendly, she was."

"Wake up, Jessie."

"What?"

"Helen Anderson? A friend of yours?"

"Rather her than some of Jimmie's pals."

"How?"

Jessie smiled again.

"Oh, I could tell you things," she said.

"What things?"

"I had some offers."

"Offers?"

"Aye."

"What offers?"

"To warm my bed for me."

Rose stopped, her eyes wide and her mouth open.

"In the name o'..."

Jessie laughed out loud.

"Aye," she said. "I winna say who but they werena the ones I'd pick myself."

"What did they say?"

"Och, it's more what they did. The kiss on my cheek that found its way round the front onto my mouth, the hand round my back squeezin', then slippin' round the front. And telling me what a fine woman I was."

"What did you say? What did you do?"

"Said it was no use to me now that poor Jimmie was gone. One of the cheeky buggers said he'd be glad to take his place. I told him the only man I was thinkin' of was Jesus."

The two of them laughed again but, a few paces further on, Rose reached her right hand across and brushed Jessie's hair back from her neck. She let her arm stay around Jessie's shoulders as they walked on.

"You winna be carin' about getting' a new man, then," she said.

Jessie smiled and put her left arm around Rose's waist.

"I winna be goin' short," she said. "But I'm no' in a hurry to get shackled up to another one. I canna tell you the peace since Jimmie's been away. I just want a wee bit of time to myself before I start humpin' and heavin' about in the sheets again."

Rose pushed her away.

"You're disgustin', Jessie," she said with a grin.

"Oh," said Jessie. "Do you no' hump and heave then? I thought it was only educated women who lay there and let their men get on with it."

People turned to look at them as they both screeched with laughter again and there were some who thought that Jessie's manner was unworthy of a grieving widow.

****

When Anderson came home that evening, the warmth of his daughter's greeting took him by surprise. Her embrace and kiss made him blush with the unexpected pleasure but also, as Elizabeth had foretold, wonder what was behind it all. She had already told the maid to bring the glass of whisky he always drank when he arrived home and, as he settled back to drink it, she sat on the arm of his chair and said, "Well, well."

He stopped in mid sip and looked up at her.

"What?" he said warily.

"Will you soon be reading Lord Byron? Or Percy Shelley perhaps?"

"Helen, I have had a busy day. What are you planning?"

"Nothing at all. I'm simply overwhelmed with the pleasure of discovering that my busy father has time to be a romantic."

Anderson looked at his wife for help. She raised her eyebrows and smiled. He looked back at Helen, who reached down and took the glass from his hand. She raised it to him and said, "To the poet of Regent Quay," before sipping a little of the liquid and immediately coughing as it burned her throat and quickly handing the glass back to him.

"Has she gone completely mad?" he asked his wife.

"Yes," said Elizabeth.

"I'm sorry, father," said Helen, dabbing her lips with her handkerchief. "It's just that mother told me that you'd decided to give your new ship her name. I think that's wonderful."

"It's as pretty a name as any of the others in the harbor. Prettier than most," said Anderson, with a quick, fond look at his wife. "But I'm afraid it may be some time before it's ready. The loss of a shipwright is a major blow."

"Are there no others?" asked Helen.

"There is one. He came to see me today. I must find out more about him, though, before I trust him with the job."

"Yes. Especially as this is to be the finest ship in Aberdeen harbor," said Helen.

"That, I'm afraid, is not possible."

"How can you say such a thing?"

Anderson sipped at his whisky and swirled it round in his glass.

"Last year, the Halls built a new type of ship. Her bow shears down to the water in a way that no others do. She's called the Scottish Maid and everyone is talking about her."

"Well, I'm more interested in the Scottish maid known as Elizabeth Anderson," said Helen. "When will you know if the new man is honest?"

"I shall ask some people. It will not be long. It cannot be long. There's work already waiting for the vessel," said Anderson. "And, my dear," he added, addressing his wife, "we must arrange some sittings."

"Sittings?" she said.

"For the figurehead. If the ship is to be named Elizabeth Anderson, then the figurehead must look like you."

"Nonsense," said Elizabeth, a blush coming to her neck and cheeks at the thought.

"Not at all," said Anderson. "It's become common practice."

"Of course it has, mother," said Helen, delighted at this extra piece of excitement which was about to ripple even more glamour into her mother's life. "I've heard them talking about their figureheads. They are the eyes and the spirit of the ship. You have no choice."

Elizabeth was unconvinced but recognized that, with both of them decided, her protests would be swept aside.

"Who will be making the figure?" asked Helen.

"I'd like to use the new man the Halls have brought up from London. He did a lot of work for the Navy and has a good reputation but I think he has enough to do for them at present. It'll have to be one of the others. That new shipwright thinks we have one of the best already here. I'm inclined to agree."

"Who is it?"

"John Grant. I shall speak with him tomorrow."

CHAPTER EIGHT

John was surprised at how his mood had kept on shifting since Bessie's discovery of Jimmie's body. The questions that needed answering and the thought of Jamie's imminent plans for a life across the ocean forced the wider world into his musings. And now, on Donald Simpson's bench, he'd seen something else which had set more thoughts rattling around and added another edge to the mystery of Jimmie's death.

Donald was a sailmaker. His loft was in York Street and he'd called John in as he was walking by. In the normal course of events, John would have declined the invitation. Donald liked to gossip and a visit to his loft was rarely brief. But John was in no hurry to be back at his own workshop, where he'd just sit watching Jamie and maybe sharpening gouges and chisels to occupy his hands as his thoughts wandered elsewhere.

Donald was going bald and his head always shone with Atkinson's Bears Grease, for which he paid two shillings and sixpence a bottle. It was supposed to promote hair growth but, after months of applications, it had only succeeded in adding a slightly rancid tinge to the smells of the materials in his loft. He was launched on a long anecdote about a piece he'd read in the Aberdeen Journal. Some poor, unsuspecting dog had nosed its way into the shop of an apothecary at the bottom of Union Street. The apothecary was furious, grabbed the dog and poured turpentine into its eyes, ears and nostrils. The idea was to teach the dog not to come back. It cost the apothecary a three guinea fine, which he chose to pay rather than spend sixty days in jail.

As Donald moved on to tales of the abominations carters visited on their horses, John's eyes wandered around the loft. A shape big enough to be a mainsail was chalked out on the floor. The sail prickers driven in at each corner held tight lengths of twine which had been snapped round more prickers and awls banged in at intervals along them to give them the required curve. When he'd seen John outside, Donald was in the process of running the first bolt of canvas across the pattern ready for cutting. But it was when John's eye moved to the bench that his attention was suddenly caught.

It was about eight feet long with stretching hooks set into it. Hanging on the seat was a bag full of grommets, brass eyelets, eyelet punches and cases of needles. At one end of the bench itself was a series of holes which held prickers, awls and fids. Fids were wooden or bone spikes, which sailmakers used to open the cloth when they were reaming out grommets, sewing or splicing. To avoid tearing the cloth, the fids had to be needle sharp and they could be as much as ten inches long. The holes they sat in kept their points clear of the floor and, as he looked at them, John wondered why he hadn't realized before that the square profile of their long tapered points matched the wounds in Jimmie's chest. Three of the holes were empty.

"Seen Jessie Crombie lately?" asked Donald, pausing in his narratives.

"Aye. She's doing fine," said John, his mind still on the square fids.

"Aye, poor lassie," said Donald. "The drink's done her a favor all right."

At first, John didn't understand the reference but quickly realized that Donald was taking the conventional view of the cause of Jimmie's death.

"More than it has for the rest of us," Donald went on.

"Owed you too, did he?" said John.

Donald waved a hand to indicate the area all around them.

"You try to find somebody here he doesna owe something," he said.

"It's funny that nobody knows where he did his drinking on Saturday," said John.

"What d'you mean? I saw him myself," said Donald. "No' long after seven o'clock."

"Where?"

"Huh! Pensioners' Court, and he was already half seas gone."

Along with Sinclair's Close, Pensioners' Court was one of the most disreputable alleys in town. The only people who went there were drunks, prostitutes and people like Bessie Rennie, looking for the chance to empty the pockets of the folks lying about the pavements, too drunk to know they were being robbed. It was a strange street, strung between extremes. In its shadows, flesh was cut and mauled, diseases were transmitted, bastards were conceived and death was a frequent visitor. The picture that Donald now began to paint was typical not just of Friday and Saturday nights, but of every night of every week; it was only the presence of Jimmie there that made this occasion significant.

Donald had seen him staggering along with Joe Drummond and another man he didn't recognize, a little man with a big beard. They had their arms round each other's shoulders and were singing a song about:
"Legs o' lassies, lang and white,
Spread out wide in the pale moonlight."

As the three of them stepped or stumbled over the bodies that lay on the pavements and in the gutters, many different pairs of eyes followed them. Their clothes showed that they were men who could afford to buy things and the state they were in suggested that tonight they'd been spending and that their pockets might not yet be empty. The spying eyes belonged to both men and women, the latter confident that, by lifting their skirts or loosening the drawstrings on their coarse linen blouses, they could show the men pleasures worth sixpence or more. The watching men had higher ambitions. The younger ones among them would use speed of hand and foot to whirl past the three drunks, dip quickly into their pockets and be gone with what they found there before the spinning men knew which way they were facing. The best hope of Jimmie and the others was that the women or the boys would get to them first because the older watchers would use neither pleasure nor bewilderment to achieve their aims. Their methods were more direct. They would take whatever came to hand, stones from the street, glasses or metal jugs, thongs or spare ends of rope, to beat and throttle them senseless. That way, they would have the time and liberty to help themselves to everything from money to watches to pieces of clothing.

Donald was there to look for a neighbor who, unaccountably, took enormous pleasure in having sex with vile women against the slippery walls of the alcoves and alleyways off the main court. The neighbor's wife, ever afraid that his obsession would deprive her of her home, often asked Donald to find him and bring him back. Tonight, there was no sign of him and, even when Donald noticed Jimmie and the others, he hurried on, away from all the troubles waiting in the shadows. He saw them stop beside a young girl in a doorway. Jimmie pushed the other two aside and stumbled forward, his hands reaching for the girl's chest. She stood her ground and he fell against her, his right arm dropping down to grab at her skirts and start pulling them up to her waist. The small man with the beard just watched as Joe joined the couple and started his own fumbling between the girl's legs. Jimmie pushed him away and he and Joe started shoving at one another, each trying to hang on to the wee girl who stood between them. Sickened, Donald turned the corner and hurried to the next dank haunt in which his neighbor might be taking his pleasure.

"It's a terrible place to do your drinking," said Donald. "And I could never see myself fornicating there neither, however bonnie the lassie was."

As he spoke, he wiped his hand across the top of his head, then on his trousers, where a dark stain indicated a long build-up of Atkinson's Bears Grease. John shuddered inwardly at the thought of Donald fornicating. Any whore who took him on would certainly be earning her money.

"It was funny seeing Jimmie there, though," Donald continued, "'cause we'd just been speaking about him."

"We?"

"Tom and Wee Tam Leach and Willie Johnston was here in the loft. We was all owed stuff for Mr. Anderson's boat. They came round to talk about going to see him about Jimmie. See whether we couldna get him to pay us straight. Or maybe we could sort Jimmie out so's he'd settle up."

"Sort him out?"

"Aye. Threaten him, like."

"What did you decide?"

Donald laughed again.

"None of us was willing to do it. You don't want to get on the wrong side of Anderson, do you? He could cost you a lot more than Jimmie. It just needs him and his pals to decide to start buying steamers and that's us scratching around for work."

John thought that the likelihood of Aberdeen's merchants all moving from sail to steam was slim. It was seven years since the first steamship, the Royal William, had crossed the Atlantic under its own power, but coal had to be bought and the wind was free, and boilers and engines took up space that could be carrying cargoes.

"Not much chance of that," said John.

Donald shook his head.

"I wouldna be so sure. Yon steamers that go to Dundee and London every week; they're always full."

John wandered over to the bench and picked up one of the fids.

"Aye, but the Halls' and the Duthies' order books are full of wooden boats. It's the Clyde that's making the iron ones. Don't worry, there'll still be plenty of storms to blow out seams for you. You'll not be short of work."

As he spoke, John pushed the point of the fid gently against his palm and realized how easy it would be to penetrate the flesh and draw blood with it. It would need neither strength nor speed. But why would anyone use such a thing? Almost everywhere you looked around the harbor, there were marlin spikes, cargo hooks, knives of all sorts within reach. Why use something which left such a distinctive hole? Nobody carried fids around with them. He turned the fid in his fingers again, then held it up for Donald to see.

"Couple of your fids're missing," he said.

Donald looked around the loft, as if he expected to see the missing items somewhere.

"Aye, I noticed. I'll be needing them soon, too. For this main."

He scratched his slippery head.

"They'll be under some of Billy's stuff there," he said, pointing to a corner which was piled high with rigging. He shared his loft with Billy Murray, a rigger.

"Where is Billy?" asked John.

By way of answer, Donald simply held his hands up in front of him, their backs toward John. John nodded his understanding. Splicing rigging was notorious for the damage it did to hands. Billy had been at it for years and, although he'd formed calluses as thick as horses' hooves, they still lifted off each day and the fibers tore at his fingers and palms. All around the harbor, riggers would arrive for work in the mornings with their hands tightly bandaged to stem the previous day's bleeding. Predictably, by the end of the day, the bandages were loose, red and sticky with blood once more. It made John even more grateful that his trade was in timber. It had its own dangers but little of the day to day lacerations of sail making and rigging.

He put the fid back in its hole and noticed the brown stains on and under the bench. Some of them still had a dark reddish tint.

"He's been bleeding on your bench, too, I see," he said.

Donald came across to look and rubbed at the stains on the top.

"Och, that coulda been me," he said. "It's probably Billy, though. Amazin' how much blood we've got in us. I'm surprised he's got any left."

With a laugh, John said that it was time he was back at his workshop and set off along York Street once more. As he walked beside the lines of ships lying alongside the quays, he wondered idly whether Donald's missing fids were connected with the holes in Jimmie's chest. And, if they were, where were they now?

CHAPTER NINE

Although fashion and propriety dictated that young women should employ middle aged companions and guides, Helen had always refused to conform. Having to be imprisoned in layers of petticoats and a heavy cotton corset, with its whalebone forcing her bust high and cinching her waist, was bad enough in itself, without the added indignity of a jailer. The only older woman who ever acted as her companion was her mother and they'd taken advantage of the fine weather to take the air away from the town's noise and smells. Their carriage had taken them up Union Street, turning left at the top onto the main South Road, then left again through Justice Mills toward the Hard Gate. There, they'd told the coachman to stop and been helped down, choosing to walk the path through the fields toward Ferry Hill. From there, the intention was to go on down to the river and meet up with the carriage once more on the other South Road.

Part of the attraction of this particular walk was the view it gave of the recently completed Bon Accord Terrace, a grand curve of granite houses on top of the hill to their left as they strolled along the path through the grasses.

"That's where we should live," said Helen.

Elizabeth looked up at the sparkles in the stone and nodded her head in agreement.

"They are lovely. But your father needs to be near the harbor."

"Well, he shall stay there and buy one of those for the two of us."

Elizabeth smiled. Helen picked a long feathery grass stalk and flicked it across her cheek as they continued on up the hill. At the top, they stopped and looked down at the river sweeping in a long curve toward the harbor and sea. Further downstream, on its left bank, were the tradesmen's storage sheds, houses and main workshops. Beside them, the tangle of masts looked like a small, bare forest. On the other side, fishing boats were pulled up onto the mud and the houses of Torry climbed up toward Girdleness lighthouse. Elizabeth had lived here all her life and seen the rapid changes the century had brought, but this view of the city let her blot out the miseries of some of its citizens and the industrial processes that were taking place further up river. Watching the Dee slip out through the channel from this distance was a peaceful, comforting experience, a reassurance that none of the changes were fundamental.

At last, they began to walk down toward the river. The sound of the harbor's business came to them as a light babble, not much louder than the wind in the grasses. Helen's thoughts went back to the death of Jessie's husband and the business dealings he'd had with her father.

"Father really is a very rich man, isn't he?" she said.

"Yes, fortunately for us," said her mother.

"Then why do you think he still works so hard?"

She saw a smile play across her mother's lips.

"It's his way of entertaining himself," she said.

"Entertaining himself?" said Helen.

"Yes. It's as if he's playing a game. He needs to keep his wits sharp. Every day is a contest. It's the way he's always lived."

"It's not a game, though, is it?" said Helen, after some reflection. "Some men are broken by it. Their families suffer."

Elizabeth made no reply.

"Do you never think of those who are less successful than father?" Helen insisted.

Elizabeth's face was serious.

"I should not be able to do anything about it, so I put it from my mind," she said. "And, before you chide me for that, you should remember that I have seen far more of it than you. And," she went on, as Helen made to interrupt her, "the suffering is not confined to those who don't succeed."

"What do you mean?"

"It's better that you don't know."

Helen took her mother's arm and stopped her.

"You cannot do such a thing," she said.

"What?"

"You know very well. You stir my curiosity by hinting at some secrets, then you simply hold your tongue. It's a very wicked and unforgivable way to behave."

Elizabeth put her arm through her daughter's and they began walking again.

"Well?" insisted Helen, refusing to be silenced.

Elizabeth sighed and tapped her fingers on Helen's arm.

"I've always thought that your father is driven by other motives, motives I know nothing of."

She spoke slowly, thinking about her words before uttering them. Helen waited, giving her the time to shape her thoughts.

"He never speaks to me of his commerce, and I never ask him about it. From the time we met, it was a separate pursuit, conducted by someone other than the man I was to marry. A darker man."

She fell silent again. Helen forced herself to say nothing.

"His own father was still alive then, of course. You never knew him. He was strong, quiet. I was rather afraid of him."

"Afraid?"

"I don't know why. He was kind to me, welcomed me into his home. But he belonged in the world of business. Your father learned everything from him and I'm sure that some of it went rather further than he liked."

"In what way?"

Elizabeth shook her head slowly.

"I've never sought to understand but, for example, his Union Street enterprise was... shall we say doubtful. Although even I could see the skill of it."

"Tell me," said Helen, excited by a subject of conversation they'd never shared before.

"Oh, everyone was talking about it," said Elizabeth, her own eyes shining with the memory. "A grand, central road that would bring glory to the city, the spirit of the new century, it was to be a marvel. But your grandfather saw only that it would need to bridge the Denburn, and so he bought land on both sides of the river just where they would need to build the supports for the arch."

"How astute," said Helen.

Elizabeth looked at her.

"You are indeed you father's daughter," she said. "Yes, it was clever."

"And he sold them back to the town."

"Yes. They cost him very little. They were good for nothing at the time. But he made the city and its people, and even the government, pay dearly for them when the time came. Indeed, they say that it cost more to buy them than to clear the slum dwellings at the top of Shiprow."

"And you say that father didn't approve?"

"No, no. It was not that. He saw the envy of the other merchants, the respect even, but he also saw how many enemies your grandfather made among the city's councilors. He saw the bitterness which started there. He thought that it was that which led to your grandfather's death."

"How?"

Elizabeth shook her head again.

"I don't know. We've only spoken of it rarely, but it seems that it was a cruel death. William was only twenty-six when it happened. I think... no, I know it changed him. He worked even harder. It was many months before I saw the gentler person again. Indeed, I'm sure that it was your arrival that brought him back."

Helen was about to ask yet another question when her mother squeezed her arm and said, "There. That's all I want to say of this. It's bringing a darkness into the morning. It's a chapter that's closed."

Helen's frustration was hot, but the clouds in her mother's face stopped the questions that were spilling into her mind. She would find some other way of opening up this mystery. She leaned across and kissed her mother on the cheek.

"You're right," she said. "Father's world is even less pleasant than I'd imagined."

"Yes. I think it is," said Elizabeth.

She fell silent again, seeming to reflect on the darkness of their conversation. At last, she stopped walking and it was Helen's turn to have to stop with her.

"I have an idea," she said. "But I want you to listen to all of it before you say anything. Promise me?"

"Of course."

They began walking on again, their pace slower than before.

"This figurehead that your father wants to have made for the new boat. I don't think it's such a good idea."

"But mother. There's always..." Helen began, before a look from Elizabeth reminded her of her promise.

"Sorry," she said.

"I know the ship must have one and I know it's to be named after me, but no sailor wants his ship adorned by the likeness of an old lady."

"I must break my promise," said Helen. "You are not an old lady."

Elizabeth smiled.

"I'm not a young lady, though."

She raised her finger to her lips as Helen was about to say more.

"In any case, I find the prospect of sitting while this carver stares at me and decides how to give his timber the forms of my nose and ears most unattractive. And that is where my idea came from. I think you should take my place."

Helen raised her hand, seeking permission to speak. Elizabeth nodded.

"But the ship is the Elizabeth Anderson, not the Helen Anderson."

"I know," said Elizabeth, "but you know that everyone says how much you resemble me. I can see it myself. At your age, I had the same eyes, the same hair, even the same sulk when I didn't get my way."

Helen forced her lips into an extravagant, deliberate pout.

"Just so," said Elizabeth. "Anyway, with you sitting for the figurehead, the sailors will get the young beauty they prefer and the Elizabeth Anderson that sails into foreign ports will be the beautiful one I used to be rather than the old witch I've become."

"But, old witch," said Helen, "what if I dislike the idea of being stared at by the carver as much as you do?"

"You will obey me because I am your mother."

They both laughed out loud at this extraordinary assertion.

"And what does father have to say about your idea?"

"He knows nothing of it. He's not my keeper," said Elizabeth, the twinkle in her eye proving indeed that she had once been just like her daughter was now.

"Do you not intend to tell him then?"

"Perhaps. Perhaps not. We shall see how discreet the carver can be."

****

Anderson's office was a long way from the tranquility of the fields through which his wife and daughter had been strolling. Outside its windows flowed a perpetual stream of carts, carriages and people. The shouts of street traders floated from one direction while from the other came the bangings and callings of the shipyards. The room was a sober, somber place, its dark walls brightened only by paintings of some of his ships and shipwrights' plans of others. He sat at his desk, his cravat pinned high on his linen pullover shirt to cover his throat, his double breasted jacket with its shawl collar tight around him. The warmth of the sun outside had not penetrated the building's granite walls.

Anderson, as usual, gave little attention to his surroundings or matters meteorological. On the desk before him were books of accounts relating to Thorsen's last three voyages. Thorsen himself had kept them, scrolling the ledger entries in immaculate copperplate and accounting for every cut of pork and beef, every pound of butter and cask of ale. Supplies for the ship's carpenter and sailmaker were detailed in other books but it was the food that preoccupied Anderson this morning. He was expecting a visit from Thorsen and the new cook he'd found for the coming trip to Canada and he needed to be clear on the economics of victualing.

When they arrived, his first thought was that the cook was a poor advertisement for his profession. He was a thin, sallow man with lank, dirty hair pulled back into a thin pigtail. His sunken cheeks and hollow chest gave him an undernourished look. Thorsen introduced him as Peter Perring, a Cornishman who'd been a cook in the navy before transferring to merchant ships on the transatlantic routes. As Anderson began asking his questions, Perring weighed his replies carefully. He hoped that Thorsen hadn't been able to access his service record. He'd taken a lot of trouble to make it disappear from the various registers. He'd never been a model of good conduct but his last trip had moved him into a category that owners preferred to avoid. On the passage home, he'd been treated appallingly by the first mate, a big Swede who'd lost half an arm once when a capstan spun more quickly than he'd anticipated. The Swede treated his crews so badly that many of them suspected that his real aim was to bully them into indiscretions which would result in more limbs being lost. Theirs, not his.

One night, with the ship being bowled along on a good, warm trade wind, he began to complain of abdominal pains. By the morning, he was delirious, screaming in agony and cursing both watches. When he eventually died, late in the afternoon, his bunk was awash with blood and vomit and the crew knew that his last hours had been more hellish than they could imagine.

Everyone suspected that he'd been poisoned and the captain's enquiry found that he had indeed been served with fish they'd caught when they were in the doldrums not long before. Perring, as cook, was the prime suspect, but no one could prove his guilt and, with so many of the crew having equally strong motives, he couldn't safely be prosecuted. He was paid off at the end of the voyage and word spread of the incident. Part of the reason that he'd come so far north was that, in ports from Bristol to Liverpool and across to Hull, poisons of all sorts were being referred to as "Perring's herrings'.

Soon after arriving in Aberdeen, he'd heard of Anderson's reputation and knew the advantages that came to those he favored. As the man talked now, he listened, gave every impression that he was reflecting with great care on what was being said, and replied with the respect that rose naturally in him whenever money was involved. He needed to be sharp; Anderson kept shifting direction, testing him. At one point, he turned one of the ledgers in front of him and pushed it toward Perring.

"What's your opinion of that?" he asked.

Perring looked. It was a typical victualing account with a list of the sort of things he'd load for an ocean passage—beef, pork, hulled barley, cheese, dried cod, biscuits, butter, oatmeal, bread, ale—and the cost of each item. The difference was that another list of figures, its ink fresher than the rest, had been added in the right-hand margin to amend the original costing. In each case, the amount was lower, sometimes by shillings and pence, often by pounds. Perring had no idea what he was supposed to make of it.

"You're familiar with such documents, I take it?" said Anderson.

"Yes, sir."

"Well?"

"The second set of figures," said Perring, fumbling for the right response, "I don't understand them. What are they?"

"They're the reason I can pay my crews better wages than others," said Anderson. "Every vessel that's victualed brings good business to the butchers and grocers who supply her. And when you have as many ships as I, you can make people rich."

"I'd heard that, sir."

"Aye, well it's true. But I'm not a charity, Mr. Perring, and if I'm making someone wealthy, I expect to be shown some gratitude."

He drew the ledger back and looked at it.

"This second column is what I'm suggesting we should offer to pay for these victuals. We will dictate to our suppliers what we're willing to pay, and if they fail to agree, there are always others who may be more persuadable."

"That seems a reasonable attitude," said Perring.

"It's one you'll have to encourage if we sign you on," said Anderson. "Your wages will depend on it."

He closed the book and changed tack again.

"When they brought in roller reefing for topsails, what difference d'you think that made?" he asked.

Perring was getting used to the switches.

"Not my part of ship, sir," he said. "I'm sure they..."

"Not so," said Anderson. "If you can roll the reefs in and out, you need fewer hands to man the yards. And fewer hands means fewer victuals, reduced costs and a bigger share of premiums at the end of the voyage. So it's very much your part of ship, sir."

Perring nodded and even managed a smile. Anderson tapped the book in front of him.

"You'll notice there's no fruit on this list," he said.

"Yes, I did," said Perring, grateful to be back on familiar ground.

"Should there be?"

Perring trod carefully.

"Well, sir. They do say that it's what stops the scurvy but there's plenty that's gone without it for months and never seen no ill effects."

Anderson tutted.

"That may well be, sir," he said. "But it's not our way. We don't risk that on our ships, do we, Captain Thorsen."

Perring turned to look at Thorsen, who gave the smallest shake of his head.

"The authorities care little if the paupers we ship over there for them are landed alive or dead, but that's not the way I work."

Perring listened. Concern for passengers was a new, unexpected element in the equation.

"No, no. If you become Captain Thorsen's cook, he and I will both expect you to ship plenty of apples and other healthy stores. Our passengers are promised as much in their contracts."

"Very fine sentiments, sir," said Perring, although his little eyes betrayed what he really thought of such generosity.

"Very profitable, too," said Anderson, "if you have a cook who knows how to handle things."

Once again, Perring was surprised. His inclination was to wait again but he was afraid that Anderson would begin to think him witless.

"Sir, I've been a cook for many years," he said, "and I knows my trade. But there's things you'm tellin me that I've never thought of before. And I'm always ready to learn. Just tell me what it is I've got to handle."

Anderson leaned forward across the desk and looked straight into his eyes. Perring forced himself not to look away.

"Good food is a rarity at sea, right?" said Anderson and, without waiting for an answer, continued, "So luxuries are prized. And the scarcer they are, the higher their value. We provide fruit and other good things as part of our service, but it's not in my nature to run a charity and the contracts state that such provisions are only possible while supplies last. Now if, in mid-Atlantic or down past the Bay of Biscay on the way to New Zealand, you were to become concerned about the sufficiency of your supplies and feel the need to begin a system of rationing, there are those passengers who would pay handsomely to keep on receiving a varied, healthy diet."

As he spoke, he was pleased to see a smile spreading across Perring's face. He sat back again.

"So, you understand that you'll not only be expected to cook but also to contribute in other ways to the success of the whole enterprise?"

"I do, sir, and I can see that it's a blessed opportunity for the right man."

"And you think you may be the man?"

"I knows I am," said Perring, confident now that he could fit easily into Anderson's ways of working and that it would line his pockets more quickly than they'd ever been lined before. In addition to that, the mention of a destination as distant as New Zealand, a place where "Perring's herrings" might not yet have surfaced, was an added incentive to show Anderson that he was indeed the man for the job.

"Very well," said Anderson. "If Captain Thorsen thinks you will make a useful member of his crew, I shall be happy to engage you. We will talk of wages later as well as any premiums there might be if you manage your stores with care."

There was no question of a handshake to seal the bargain; the social distance between them was too great for that. As Perring was gushing his thanks, Thorsen stood up and, with a tap on his shoulder, indicated that they should leave. Anderson went to the door with them.

"I hope you're applying your thoughts to the New Zealand venture," he said to Thorsen.

"Aye," said the captain. "With the right ship."

****

Joe had stayed out for longer than usual but his catch was still only average. The weather had been fair enough and the sea kind, but he didn't manage to find the shoals he was looking for. He'd been lying off the beach for the past two hours, waiting for the tide to turn and take him back up to his berth, less anxious than usual to get back ashore, even though the inns were open. His crew, though, was more than ready. The bawling and shouting he'd started before they'd even left had gone on through the trip and, as they searched in vain for the fish, his temper had got worse. They looked with grateful eyes as they came abreast of the point where Joe would swing the bow to starboard and nose in alongside the quay.

The maneuver was an automatic one, calling for no special seamanship or even much attention and, as he spun the wheel over, Joe was looking along the quayside, scanning the faces. There were the usual huddles of women with their baskets. He saw Rose in one group but gave no wave to her. She stood still, her eyes fixed on the boat, and showed no sign of recognition or welcome. Two men came forward to catch the lines the crew was preparing to heave ashore. And, as the boat slid round into its berth, Joe saw the face he'd been half-expecting. Standing back from the crowd, leaning against a post, was John Grant.

CHAPTER TEN

Anderson had business down at the harbor but, before leaving, he called in one of his clerks to prepare a letter to the Union Whale Fishing Company. With interest in whaling shifting to Dundee and Peterhead, their boil houses at Footdee no longer sent the smell of blood and blubber up the river and into town on the easterly winds. They were advertised for let in the Journal but Anderson had it in mind to offer to buy them outright. He had no immediate need for them but the harbor was growing and space and buildings were getting more valuable all the time. If he found no use for them himself, he was sure that someone would.

When the letter was finished, he signed and sealed it and sent the clerk to deliver it by hand. He himself set out for the shipyard where the barque he was already calling the Elizabeth Anderson was sitting high on the stocks. He'd arranged to meet Glover there to find out exactly how the shipwright would deliver his promise to finish the work in a time so much shorter than Crombie's estimate.

He could see the top of his ship's hull over the wall of the small yard that Crombie had hired to build her but only felt the full impact of the rake of her bow and the sweep of her sides and quarters when he turned through the gate. She'd been framed up in green oak and left to season on the stocks before Crombie had braced the deck beams between her frames and bent the planks into place to form the hull. The timber shone softly in the sun, the blending of its grain broken only where the edges of the planking butted together into long parallel lines.

Glover had been halfway up the scaffolding on her starboard side talking to some men when he saw Anderson arrive. He hurried down and came across to greet him.

"A fine ship," he said. "Mr. Crombie's done you proud so far."

Anderson simply nodded. He was disinclined to dwell with small talk, however, and began walking along the side of the ship, forcing Glover to follow him.

"You said she could be ready by June," he said.

"That's right," said Glover. "The bulkheads are already set. We could lay the decks and put in all the fittings in a couple of weeks. Caulking, felting, coppering—they can be getting on with that at the same time."

They walked on, Anderson asking questions about specific aspects of the ship, Glover always ready with the answers. After a while, Anderson stopped walking and turned to look at Glover.

"You seem to know a lot about my ship," he said.

Glover paused before replying.

"I've made it my business to."

"Why?"

"Have you spoken to any of the owners I've worked for?"

"Not yet."

"Well, even so, you'll know from their names that I prefer to associate myself with success."

Anderson made a sound like a snort.

"Oh, please, Mr. Glover. I thought you were more subtle. Flattery is dull."

"I mean no flattery, sir," said Glover. "I'm simply pointing out a fact. Long ago, I saw that doing a good job wins nothing unless people know about it, see it. For me, that means building ships which are always in and out of port. It matters little if I build the most beautiful ship that ever floated if she's stuck on a cheap coastal run, looking for business in little harbors scattered around the land's edge. That's why success attracts me so."

It was an attitude that Anderson understood but he showed nothing of his reaction.

"So you're pursuing me."

Glover smiled and scratched at his beard.

"I'm pursuing success, sir. I've been here a short while. I heard about Mr. Crombie's ways and I knew they'd work against him in the long run. I met him once or twice and we talked of your ship. That's why, when I heard the sad news, I decided to be bold with you and offer to finish the job."

Within himself, Anderson was already decided. With no other shipwrights available he had little choice.

"By June," he said at last.

Glover nodded.

"And what will it cost me?"

78

Glover took a piece of paper out of his pocket. It was a tidy, itemized list of fittings, timber requirements, wage estimates. The most interesting point was the last one which gave June the fifth as the completion date. Glover's proposal was that, if he finished the job before then, he would be paid a premium for each day gained and that, if the job was delayed, an equivalent daily amount would be subtracted from the final cost. For Anderson, used to the mumblings and evasions of Jimmie Crombie, its clarity and commercial precision were admirable. He read the whole list once more, lingering over some items, making a mental note to renegotiate others and, at last, held it for Glover to take back. Glover shook his head.

"I have a copy, sir. If you approve, that may serve as the basis for our contract."

Anderson folded the paper and pushed it inside his jacket.

"I leave contracts to my lawyers," he said.

"Of course," said Glover. "But will you be content to use these figures?"

Anderson looked carefully at him before reaching into his pocket and taking from it a key and a single sheet of paper.

"The job is yours," he said.

He handed the key and the piece of paper to Glover and pointed to a small wooden building beside the wall of the yard.

"This is the key to the cupboards in Crombie's office there and this authorizes you to have access to his records, his papers and the plans of the ship. I shall have our agreement drawn up today."

The two men shook hands and Anderson started striding away. After half a dozen paces, he stopped and turned.

"You may wait until it's signed or you may prefer to start at once, to keep time on your side," he called back. "And, by the way, the ship is to be called the Elizabeth Anderson."

He turned away, then back again as he seemed to have another thought.

"And the completion date will be June the third."

****

John waited for Joe to come ashore and sign off for the boxes that had been unloaded from his boat.

"Come on, big man," he said, as Joe hoisted his bag on his shoulder, "I'll buy you a drink."

Joe said nothing. Before he'd sailed, he'd heard that John had seen Jimmie on the beach and he knew that he wouldn't be able to resist asking questions about it. John was clever; he could see things that others didn't notice. But a drink was a drink and Joe's private keg had soon been emptied while he was fishing.

As they made their way to the Pilots' Tavern on Waterloo Quay, John asked about the trip and the catch. Joe complained that there'd been no fish about but secretly knew that the problem lay elsewhere. The shoals had been there but he'd been unable to find them. He was maybe losing his touch.

When they were sitting with two big jugs of ale in front of them, Joe's already half empty from the first long draught he'd taken from it, John wasted no time.

"You'll have been surprised to see me on the quay there," he said.

Joe just shook his head.

"No?" said John. "How?"

Joe looked him straight in the eye.

"You'll be wantin' to talk about Jimmie," he said.

"Aye, but why with you?"

"That's for you to tell me."

"All right. What did you do on Saturday night?"

"I was out for a drink."

"Who with?"

"On my own."

John took a swig of beer and waited. Joe was scratching patterns on the wooden table and looking around at the other men in the smokey fug.

"You met Jimmie, didn't you?" said John.

Joe looked down at his fingers and, after a pause, gave a small nod.

"What happened, Joe?"

Joe looked quickly up at him.

"Nothin'. We had a few drinks."

"We? Who else was there?"

Joe waved a dismissive hand.

"Plenty. We went around a bit."

"Yes. How about when you went to Pensioners' Court? Who was there then?"

Joe screwed his eyes up as he tried to remember.

"Just me and Jimmie... and this other one. Don't know who he was. Jimmie said he was doin' business with him, but he was too far into his drink to make any sense. We was all the same. No point askin' me about it."

"Where'd you go after you left there?"

Once again, Joe held his silence. John was getting impatient.

"Did you go with the lassie?"

"What lassie?"

John suddenly leaned forward and grabbed Joe's arm hard.

"Joe, you're wasting my time. You don't want to talk to me and I'm not interested in just passing the time of day, so let's say what we have to say, eh? I'm just curious. I need to know things. If you don't tell me, I hear Davie Donne's looking out for folk who might know something. You could tell him."

Joe looked quickly at him, pulled his arm away and raised his fist. In a fight, there'd be little to choose between the two, but Joe just wanted the questions to be over. The set of John's face told him that he'd be better saying what he had to say as quickly as possible. If necessary, the fight could come later. He banged his fist down onto the table.

"Aye, all right. I went with the lassie."

"Where?"

"Edge of The Links. It didna take long."

"Did the others go with you?"

Joe shook his head.

"Where did they go, then?"

"The new boat," said Joe, after a pause.

"Why?"

"No idea. They was talkin' about a box."

"What box?"

"A box. I don't know. Jimmie said it was worth a heap of money."

"And you weren't interested?"

"I was interested, but I was busy."

"Aye, with the lassie. I thought Jimmie wanted her, too. I heard you were fighting over her."

To his surprise, Joe laughed.

"You don't fight over women like that," he said.

"I heard she wasn't a woman. She was a girl."

"She knew what she was doin'."

"So you took her."

"Aye. Jimmie went off for another woman."

"I thought he went to his boat."

"Aye, that, too," said Joe.

"What time did you leave him?"

"I didna even ken what day it was, never mind what time. It was late."

"And, after you'd had the lassie, where did you go?"

Joe hesitated, looked around the bar then drained the last of his ale.

"Home," he said at last.

"So you didn't see Jimmie after you'd left him in Pensioners' Court."

Joe banged his empty jug on the table, then lifted it high to get the attention of the landlord.

"No," he said. "And I'm sick of your bloody questions. Who d'you think you are?"

"Somebody who spits on liars," said John. "I care that Jessie's had her man taken away."

"Nothin' to do with me."

"You sure?"

Joe banged his jug on the table again and reached over to grab John's shirt with his free hand and pull him forward. John clamped his fingers around Joe's wrist and twisted. Joe's flesh burned but he tightened his grip.

"Nobody killed Jimmie," he said, his lips inches away from John's face, the flecks of spittle spraying against John's cheeks. "He died. It was maybe the drink, but it was natural."

The words took John by surprise. For a moment, he held Joe's gaze, looking for the truth in his eyes, but seeing only his fear and anger. He gave a quick, hard turn of his wrist, broke Joe's grip on his shirt and pushed him back into his seat. At nearby tables, others looked across but without much interest. The landlord began filling two more jugs with ale.

John was angry with himself. He'd let his temper loose again and found it hard to concentrate on the questions he still needed to ask. All he wanted to do now was drag Joe outside and bang his head against a wall. Joe, too, was ready to unload some of his frustrations. He rubbed at his sore wrist. The conversation was over. John leaned forward and forced himself to speak quietly.

"First you say Jimmie went off to his boat, then he's off to see a woman. And he wasn't killed, you say. It's all lies. You'd better find another story."

Joe just stared at him.

"You're going to have to tell somebody the truth," John went on. "Me, or Davie Donne. I don't care. So think about it."

The landlord arrived with the two full jugs. John shook his head.

"Not for me," he said. "But he'll drink both of them."

The landlord looked at Joe, who nodded and reached into his pocket. John stood up to go as Joe pulled out a handful of coins. Among them was a shiny black pebble.

CHAPTER ELEVEN

John wondered about the black pebble all the way back to his workshop. He had no doubt that it was the one Jessie had described—Jimmie's lucky stone. She'd said it had been taken along with his money and watch. He'd wanted to go back and ask Joe about it, but Joe would simply deny everything and John's temper was still too hot. He needed to work off the anger before he could think clearly again.

Jamie was waiting for him and, together, they manhandled a block of English oak into the middle of the workshop. It was heavy, strong grained, very dense wood and would be hard for him to work but he preferred it because of its durability. There were many tales of oak figureheads which had outlasted the ships for which they'd been carved. As he strained with the weight, Jamie was full of talk of emigration.

"You see, New Zealand's no good," he said. "Sixteen pounds each is what they'd charge us for that and that's just the passage. And you never hear what's goin' on there, do you? You've no idea what you're sailin' to, what land costs, what sort of livin' a man can get. We talked about it but no' seriously. No' with so much waitin' for us in America."

The words rushed out. Now that the move was a reality, his enthusiasm was hard to check.

"And Canada, well, Canada's all right but it's cold. Colder than here."

"And from what you hear," said John, glad to shift his attention away from his subsiding anger, "with the number of folk who've gone there from Aberdeen, it'd be just like staying here. Hardly worth the trip."

"Aye. There's no doubt about it. America's the best country for the poor man."

They slid the block a few more feet and rocked it into the position John had indicated with chalk marks on the floor. As Jamie went to fetch some wedges to jam it into place, John walked round it, his hand running over its surface, his fingers picking at stray splinters and teasing into the raised grain. It was a familiar therapy.

"One way we won't be goin', though," said Jamie, as he brought the wedges across and started to bang them under the base of the block. "On Mr. Anderson's boats."

"How's that?" asked John.

Jamie shook his head.

"There's stories. Things are goin' on. Nobody knows for sure but folk say you shouldna trust him."

"What's he offering?"

"Well, there's his ships, but Davie Reid was telling me about how he's an agent now, too."

"What sort of agent?"

"Land agent. There's blocks of it inland, bought up by some Marine and Fire Insurance Company—Wisconsin or Winscontin or somethin'. He's workin' as their agent over here. Sellin' berths on his boats and pieces of land for when you get there. No thanks. No' if he's involved in it."

"You're a hard man, Jamie," said John.

"Aye, with a man like him about the place, you need to be."

"He's bringing lots of work to Aberdeen."

"So's he can fill his pockets even fuller."

John was surprised at the vehemence of Jamie's dislike of Anderson. He'd heard some of the stories and knew that many of them were born of old-fashioned envy at the man's success. He took no prisoners, drove hard bargains but was no worse than many who did their trading around the water's edge. In his own dealings with the man, John had been impressed with his directness and had more than once detected a stubbornness that was born of something other than commercial advantage. He knew that Anderson was no ordinary trader and John's scorn was not for the man but for the structure in which he operated. It was not the hypocrisy and lies on which it thrived that disgusted him but the fundamental assumption that everything was reducible to a patchwork of profits and losses. According to its vision of things, life was sustained not by blood and air but by money.

"I tell you, John," said Jamie, "the sooner I get to where I don't need to have dealin's with the likes of Anderson, the better I'll feel."

John laughed.

"You do a lot of business with him then, do you?"

Jamie laughed too.

"No. Thank God," he said.

It was as well that they fell silent then to concentrate on setting the final wedges. Not many minutes later, there was a knock at the door and a call from outside. As the two of them straightened up to see who it was, they were surprised in different ways by the person who walked in. It was William Anderson.

****

The smell of drink was strong as Joe banged the front door open and stumbled in. Rose jumped at the sudden noise, then turned back to the range to start scrubbing at its black bars once more. With so little fish being landed, she had fewer creels than usual to carry up to the stalls and had come home to do some cleaning.

Joe kicked his boots off and left them on the floor just inside the door. He pulled some coins from his trouser pocket, selected a few, threw them onto the table and put the rest back in his pocket. His fingers touched the pebble there and he stroked its shiny surface before bringing his empty hand out again. Rose looked across at the coins.

"Not much," she said. "Bad trip?"

Joe half fell into a chair and grunted.

"Nothin' out there," he said. "Wastin' my time. Time to sign on one of the big ones."

Rose said nothing. It was a familiar refrain. Unless he'd come back with his decks groaning with the catch, he was always threatening to join the crew of a ship bound for the Americas. Every time, she wished he'd get on with it.

"Could've, too, if your brother-in-law wasna such a thief," he added, the words tumbling into one another.

This was new.

"What d'you mean?" asked Rose, stopping her scrubbing and turning at the waist to look at him.

"He could've had that ship finished weeks ago. I could've been away. But he was wantin' more and more money. Bleedin' Anderson dry."

He shook his head and muttered a few things she couldn't hear.

"Is that what you've been talkin' to John Grant about?" she asked.

He looked at her, a frown on his face.

"I saw you with him on the quay," she said.

"He'd do better to mind his own business," said Joe.

"Aye," said Rose. "What did he want?"

"Nothin'. More about Jimmie."

"About Saturday night?"

"Aye."

"What did you say?"

"Just told him what happened."

"What was that?"

"Jesus, woman, you're as bad as he is. I told him I left Jimmie and the other one and came home."

"You must've gone out again, then. You werena here when I got back."

Joe stood up quickly. His chair tipped over with a bang.

"No. I winna be here much longer, neither," he shouted.

"Good," said Rose, standing up ready to dodge an attack.

Joe stumbled against the table and almost fell.

"Where's my tea?" he said.

"In the pan," said Rose. "And you can get it yourself. I'm away out to see Jessie."

"Aye, and you can tell her from me she's better off without her man. She doesna ken just how bad he was."

Rose was shrugging on her shawl at the door.

"I think she does," she said.

****

Jessie had come home from work, scrubbed herself and prepared the potatoes for the stovies she'd be making for her supper. She was determined to resist the temptation not to bother with cooking just for herself and was looking forward to eating her meal in her own time and without the need to act as Jimmie's servant. When she answered a knock at the door and saw that, once again, it was Helen Anderson, she didn't bother hiding her surprise. She simply opened the door wider and waved her in.

"Maybe I should give you a key," she said with a smile. "You'll have a cup of tea?"

As she said it, Jessie remembered Helen's reaction to her last cup.

"Or maybe, you winna," she added.

When Helen hesitated, Jessie said, "It's all right. I'll make a fresh pot."

Helen smiled and nodded. She was carrying a small package. She put it on the table and began to unwrap the paper.

"I hope you're not offended but I brought this shortbread for us to have. Our cook makes it and I've never tasted better. It's almost pure butter."

Jessie laughed and set the kettle to boil.

"I don't understand how folks like you can stand up."

"What?"

"By rights, you should be a great dumplin' of a woman instead o' the slender wee thing that you are. If I had all the nice things to eat you do, and somebody preparin' it for me, I'd just be sittin' like a big sow fillin' myself up."

Helen could only manage a small smile. Her sanitized reality was still a long way from that of Jessie. Jessie noticed.

"You don't really know much about me, do you?" she said.

"No," said Helen. "And everywhere I turn, I fall into more examples of my ignorance. I'm sorry."

"Don't be silly. How could you know? What d'you think I know about you? Nothin'."

Once again, they'd moved quickly into an easy familiarity. The tea was fresh and, though still too strong for Helen, much better than the stewed variety she'd had last time. As they drank it and crumbled and melted the delicious shortbread on their tongues, they talked of the differences between them, each trying to correct the misapprehensions of the other and painting opposite but equally fascinating worlds.

At one point, Jessie gestured to indicate the room they were in.

"But this is luxury for most," she said. "Jimmie was a shipwright, remember. We've got lots of space here. You should see where my sister Rose lives. Her place is no' so bad. They've even got a wee bitty of garden. But some of the families around her; eight, ten, twelve of them, all in the one room."

"Yes. I've heard," said Helen.

Each time she was reminded of the injustice of things, her reaction was always anger. She knew better than to think that everyone could be equal, but she saw no need for the vast difference in degree there was between herself and the people crammed into dark, tiny rooms or deprived of accommodation altogether. She'd read essays about it, tried with little success to understand the social theories of Rousseau and been frustrated by every effort she'd made to discuss the subject with Sarah, Bella and her other friends. It was part of her deeper curiosity about life, one which she could not satisfy in the drawing rooms she visited with her mother.

Jessie was sitting in a rocking chair and the slight creak of its runners brought a soothing rhythm into the silence which settled between them.

"I've been thinking lots about what you were saying yesterday," said Helen at last. "Some of it troubles me."

Jessie looked at her, waiting for her to go on and Helen, almost as if she was thinking aloud, prodded away at the things that had kept coming into her mind. Her surprise that someone should cheat her father was still strong and she remembered the uncompromising way in which he'd dealt with others who'd tried to do the same thing. She could not conceive that someone might dislike Jimmie enough to actually kill him. In spite of the daily experience of thefts, assaults and cruelties reported in the papers and relayed in hushed but fascinated tones over tea and coffee, she preferred to believe that murder required a grander motive.

The more she thought this, the more she was concerned that Jimmie's punishment might be connected with her father, especially after her mother's revelations about the murkiness of some of his family's dealings. For a long time, Jessie's husband's primary occupation had been the building of his new boat. All his recent activities would somehow relate to that and, if the reason for his death was hidden within them, it was necessarily linked with her father. Not that he himself could possibly be involved, of course, but she knew that there were others who were paid to protect his interests and his reputation and who were no doubt capable of pursuing their own extreme forms of justice. Helen was still perhaps a little naïve about the lifestyles of Jessie and Rose but she'd met and listened to too many of her father's business acquaintances to be in any doubt about their capacity for crime when money was the motivation.

Jessie listened with interest but Helen's deepening concern seemed only to amuse her.

"You take things too seriously," she said. "My Jimmie wasna worth that much trouble. The extra money he was makin' was pennies really. I don't think anybody'd risk killin' him for pennies."

"But what else? What other reasons could..."

Jessie held up a hand to stop her.

"I think you're better no' askin' things like that. My Jimmie was guilty of things you wouldna dream of. People didna think I knew. They kept quiet about them. But I did. You canna be married to somebody and not know things like that."

"Are they things you can tell me about?"

Jessie thought, then shook her head.

"No. Better not to. But you can stop blamin' your father. Jimmie had as many women for enemies as he had men."

"But no woman could push a man into the river."

"Why not?"

"He would resist, struggle."

"Maybe you couldna do it," said Jessie, with a smile, "but for women who spend all day carryin' creels up and down Marischal Street, upendin' a staggerin' drunk's as easy as spittin'."

Helen didn't spit but she took the point. Talking with Jessie really was revealing how imperfect her understanding was.

"Do you really think it was a woman who killed him then?" she asked.

Jessie shook her head.

"I dinna ken. Maybe it was two women, or three. Or maybe it really was Mr. Anderson."

"You're teasing me, Mrs. Crombie."

"Can you no' call me Jessie?"

"Of course. And you'll call me Helen."

Again Jessie shook her head, not to refuse the suggestion but in wonder at Helen's relaxed manner.

"What you need is a man," she said.

Helen felt a flush come to her cheeks.

"Don't say that. That's what my mother always says. Anyway, you said yesterday that having a man wasn't necessarily to be desired."

"Did I?"

"Yes. And why do I need a man if you don't?"

"Ah, but I've got one," said Jessie, wagging her finger at Helen.

"Already?" said Helen, before realizing that it implied some impropriety on Jessie's part and adding, "Oh, I'm sorry."

Jessie just laughed.

"There are some things that men are good for," she said and the look on her face left no doubt about what she meant.

Helen suddenly felt another great chasm open between Jessie and herself. Jessie had had a husband; she was now claiming to have perhaps a lover. And how many other men had she known in her years as a girl living by the docks? She was a mature, experienced woman. Helen herself knew nothing of physical relationships with men.

"I've shocked you, haven't I?" said Jessie, amused by Helen's sudden confusion.

"I have lots to learn," said Helen.

"Don't worry. I'll teach you. They're only men."

"Jessie," said Helen, recovering herself and pretending to be outraged.

"Helen," said Jessie, and the two of them gave in to their laughter.

In the street outside, Rose had just lifted her hand to knock at Jessie's door when she heard them. She recognized Jessie's voice but not the stranger's. She wanted to talk to her sister but her mood was a long way from their merriment. As the giggling bubbled on inside, she let her hand drop, pulled her shawl around her shoulders and started back toward her own house.

CHAPTER TWELVE

Anderson's arrival in John's workshop left John in some confusion at first. He'd featured heavily in a conversation John had had the previous evening. He'd finished his meal and was washing up his single pot and plate when Tom had arrived and suggested they go for a drink. John was surprised but it was obvious that Tom's eagerness to delve into Jimmie's death had brought a little excitement into his life. John suggested that a walk along the beach might be a better idea than a crowded tavern since there, they'd have no eavesdroppers.

It was another still, shining evening as they walked down the brae onto the sand. John's stride was slow, Tom, the smaller man, had to shuffle quick, short steps to stay beside him. There were couples and little groups of threes and fours dotted here and there but, with the beach stretching away in a huge curve to the dunes of Balmedie and beyond to Peterhead, the main impression was of space and quiet. Out on the sea, the big sky was still a pale blue and, over to their left, peach colored strands of cloud were draped behind the steeples of the city's skyline. John liked these spring evenings. They were made for loving and couples and silly, small conversations about subjects that were trivial but totally absorbing for the people having them.

Tom apparently failed to feel their magic. Even before they reached the spot where Bessie had found the body, he was talking blood and murder.

"So they strangled him, stabbed him, cut him up, soaked him with water and dumped him on the beach. No' takin' no chances, was they?"

John sighed and forced his mind to focus on Jimmie.

"I don't think they strangled him. I think it was a hanging."

Tom turned his head to look at John and wait for an explanation. John raised his hand and held it against his own throat, high under his chin.

"You see, the mark was up here. And then, round by his ears, it went up sharply toward the back. It didn't go right round. It disappeared into his hair. So I don't think they just tied it round his neck and choked him. I think it was pulling upwards."

Tom whistled.

"I see what you mean."

"And the holes, they were square," John went on. "Like they were made with fids."

Tom thought about the new information.

"So it was somebody from around the harbor," he said at last.

"Why?"

"Hemp. Fids. No' the sort of things you find anywhere else."

John nodded.

"Maybe," he said. "But who'd want to do it? And what for? I mean, I know he was owing money everywhere but it's not going to be one of his creditors, is it? That way, they'd never get paid."

"Could've just lost their temper. Had enough. Wantin' to teach him a lesson."

It was possible. John just gave a nod and, for a while, they were quiet, each trying to isolate individuals amongst the crowds of people with reason to dislike Jimmie. Their thoughts took separate directions. While Tom tried to picture the struggle and actions of the Saturday night or Sunday morning, John had a wider perspective. There was certainly no shortage of thieves in the Saturday night shadows and that was possibly the most likely if rather obvious explanation, but it was too mundane and it failed to acknowledge the complexities. The combination of hanging and stabbing, the subterfuge of the soaking to suggest a drowning, all demanded a much more fanciful resolution. And he still hadn't worked out where Joe fit into it all.

Just past the bathing station, Tom stopped to catch his breath and, paradoxically, light up his pipe. John watched as the tobacco glowed more strongly with each puff.

"Donald Simpson saw him, you know," he said. "Saturday night. With Joe Drummond and somebody with a beard."

Tom looked through the smoke at him, still puffing.

"Have you talked to Joe?"

"Aye." He says he left him in Pensioners' Court."

"That's where the killer will have seen him, then."

"Maybe," said John.

Knowing the nature of the place, it was a conclusion that most people would have reached. Tom thumbed down his tobacco, inspected it and put the pipe back in his mouth.

"Canna think that Joe would do somethin' like that," he said.

John considered the remark as he looked out at a sail coming in from the east. He'd have said the same thing before he'd had that drink with Joe, but he'd seen the pebble, and Joe's insistence that Jimmie's death was natural seemed strange. He was probably ashamed of the episode with the lassie, too. He'd admitted in the end that she was barely more than a child, but most of his answers about Jimmie had either been hesitant or they'd come out so fast that they sounded like protests.

The two men walked on again, this time at a much slower pace.

"I can't imagine anybody doing it," said John at last. "Killing somebody, I mean. Taking the life out of them with them right there, in front of you. I'd have 'guilty' burning on my face forever after."

Tom sucked at his pipe and nodded his agreement.

"I haven't seen that on anybody's face yet, have you?" John went on.

"No. Why? Are you thinkin' it's somebody we know?"

John didn't answer him directly, his thoughts still on the enormity of witnessing a person cross the threshold into death because of something you'd done to them. He allowed a little list of possibilities to form in his mind.

"Maybe it gets easy after you've done it," he said at last. "Especially when everybody says he deserved it. Maybe Willie Johnston or one of the other creditors reckoned he was the reason they were in trouble."

"Willie Johnston? Never."

John shrugged.

"How about Jessie, then?" he said. "All the beatings he's given her. Maybe he went home drunk and gave her one too many."

"Aye, so she hangs him, stabs him and carries him down the beach," said Tom, the words dragging, slow with irony.

"Maybe she wasn't on her own. Maybe there's somebody comes round to comfort her when he's out drinking."

The thought swung Tom away from irony. This was something that hadn't occurred to him.

"So it wasna Jessie who did it," he said. "It was her man. Jimmie comes home, finds him there and there's a fight."

His tone made it sound as if he even took some pleasure at the prospect.

"And how about the fellow from Dundee, the one who was asking Willie Johnston about Jimmie's work," said John. "Maybe he got rid of

Jimmie just to get his job. Or maybe it wasn't personal. Maybe it was nothing to do with Jimmie."

"Nothin' to do with Jimmie?"

"No. Maybe somebody just didn't want the boat to be finished. Somebody who doesn't like Anderson."

Tom let out a snort of laughter, which developed into a rich, productive cough as he inadvertently gulped down a mouthful of pipe smoke.

"That's just about everybody on the quays, then," he said when he'd recovered.

"Aye, he doesn't seem to bother with making friends, does he?"

"Never has," said Tom. "Started when his pa died, they say."

"What d'you mean?"

"Folk say he was a lively lad. Always in trouble, specially with the women."

"Anderson? Never."

"That's what they say. Then he gets married, his pa dies and, all of a sudden, he's got his finger in every pie round the harbor."

"He's a merchant. His family had property, ships. It's natural," said John.

"Aye, but there's other merchants, other owners, and you never hear nothin' about them. No' as much, anyway."

He stopped and tapped some of the ash out of his pipe against the sole of his shoe.

"It wouldna surprise me if he's got somethin' to do with Jimmie's killin', you know."

"Yes," said John, "I can see him down on the beach strangling Jimmie then brushing the sand and blood off his frock coat and getting back into his carriage."

The irony was delivered with a lighter touch than Tom had used but still provoked a reaction.

"You think he wouldna do it? Ask Billy Walker's folks."

John knew the name and the story. Billy Walker was the captain of the Lady of Dee, a whaler of Anderson's which had been caught in Baffin Bay and the Davis Strait in the great freeze of 1835-36 along with several other British ships. When the spring came and the Lady of Dee limped back home with more than half her crew dead and most of the rest cured forever of the desire to go to sea, Anderson had given Walker just three weeks to recover, then sent him up to Stromness to take on a new crew and get them ready for the trip back to Greenland. There were always plenty of men in Orkney ready to sign on and Walker was back in Aberdeen with a full complement by the end of March. But the iron grip of the North Atlantic winter he'd just endured still held his mind. He'd told his friends tales of cannibalism, disease and on board conditions beyond endurance. The sick and the healthy lay close together for warmth, the smell of gangrene drifting over them, their bodies wrapped in blankets crawling with lice. They tried leaving their bedding pegged out on the ice during the short hours of daylight to get rid of the infestation but it had no effect. And, as all these nightmares were stampeding through Billy Walker's mind, Anderson was forcing him to concentrate on victualing up and pressing for an early departure date.

The tension between them ended on the night of April 23rd. Billy climbed to the fore topgallant yard and threw himself down to the deck, breaking his back and splitting his skull on the edge of the fo'c's'le hatch. It shook Anderson very badly. No one saw him on the quays for weeks but then he was back again and, by the end of May, he'd found another skipper and the Lady of Dee was on her way to Greenland.

"Billy was sick," said John, lamely.

"Aye, and he wasna given no chance to get better, was he?" said Tom.

"So it's suicide, then?" said John. "Jimmie stabbed himself, hanged himself, soaked himself with water, lay down and died. All because Mr. Anderson was nagging at him to get the boat finished."

"Aye, that'll be it," said Tom.

"Oh aye, and he robbed himself while he was at it," said John.

"How?"

"Jessie told me. There was nothing in his pockets, his watch was taken and some stone he used to wear around his neck. That was gone, too."

"Ah, his black pebble," said Tom, with a grin.

"You knew he had it?"

"Aye. He was as bad as the rest of them. I saw it one night in Ma Cameron's. Wee Tam and me was there and this Polish sailor threw a glass at the bar. Broke a mirror on the wall. Jimmie pulls at this piece of string round his neck, takes out this stone and starts rubbin' away at it. 'What you doin'?' I says. He just shook his head, dead serious. 'Bad luck,' he says. And he tells us it's his lucky stone, his black pebble. Mind you, he wasna the only one. There's fishermen pullin' all sorts of stuff out of their pouches and belts and rubbin' away like they was possessed."

They turned to make their way back toward Footdee. Knowing how difficult it was for Tom to keep secrets, John decided not to mention the fact that Joe had Jimmie's stone now. He wondered, too, whether he should add Anderson to the list of suspects he'd started to make. The Billy Walker episode seemed to suggest that there was little compassion in him and that, if a person stood in his way, he would somehow have him removed. But would he really take the risk of actually killing someone, or having him killed? Jimmie might have been costing him money but being found guilty of murder would cost him everything.

"Anyway, why would he want to kill Jimmie?" asked John, breaking what had been a long silence.

"Who?"

"Anderson."

"Who said he did?"

"You did."

"Did I?"

"Yes. Just now."

"No, no. It's Jessie's man that did it."

"Oh? And who's he?"

"That's what we're going to have to find out."

The enthusiasm was back in Tom's voice. John smiled to himself and accepted that their collaboration was unlikely to produce any agreement about any aspect of the incident except that Jimmie was definitely dead.

****

Davie Donne was never enthusiastic but he had his reasons for giving Jimmie's killing a little more attention than usual. Investigation was never a strong part of his working methods; he preferred to make his decisions quickly and move on. He knew all about Jimmie's enemies and their reasons for getting rid of him, but they'd been around for a long time and they'd done nothing before. No, the only thing that had changed in Jimmie's circumstances recently was the fact that he'd been trying his tricks on William Anderson. And Davie knew that Anderson wasn't a man to have as an enemy.

And that was all he needed by way of proof. He was certain that Anderson had paid some of the villains who frequented Castle Street to rid him of Jimmie. The problem now was not how to find the evidence needed to take action against him but how to shift the blame onto someone else. If he could do that and make sure that Anderson knew he was protecting him, life would become so much easier. He might at last be lifted out of patrolling the degradation of the streets around the harbor and made Superintendent of the Night Watch. With an annual salary of seventy five pounds, it paid twenty pounds more than the Day Watch and there were fewer dignitaries around to oversee his conduct. Even better, he would be removed from the proximity of the vile women of the streets, with their indecent and blasphemous language and their fetid attentions. However many times they were moved on, they always returned, their mouths fouler than before and their obscenities more grotesque. Prison meant nothing to them. Indeed, in winter they welcomed its shelter and relative warmth.

Davie's size and appearance, as well as his profession, always made him the butt of their coarseness. No one had ever seen him chasing a felon; his bulk did not allow it, even when the thief was an older woman. In any case, he'd always preferred the company of men. The streets offered him nothing to appease his appetites. So, having made up his mind that Anderson was the guilty man, he'd begun to consider which people he could accuse in his place. They were nearly all women and the first name on his list was Jessie.

CHAPTER THIRTEEN

As he walked into the workshop, Anderson knew that it was unnecessary to introduce himself but he did so anyway, adding straight away that, if John was interested, he had come with a commission. Gratefully, Jamie excused himself, saying that there was stock to be shifted in the loft over the workshop.

"It's a normal sort of figurehead. How long will it take?" asked Anderson.

Slowly, John arranged some spare wedges on the bench beside him.

"That would depend on size, the pattern you wanted, what you mean by 'normal'," he said. "Is it the ship Jimmie Crombie was working on?"

"Yes. It's being finished by another shipwright. Mr. Glover, from Dundee."

John nodded. Willie Johnston might be paid after all.

"Sad news. About Jimmie," he said.

"Indeed," replied Anderson. "No one is spared grief for long. But I'm here on business, Mr. Grant, and if..."

"Not a very lucky ship, is she?" said John. "I mean, with Jimmie being killed."

"We make or own luck," replied Anderson.

John noticed the lack of reaction to the word "killed". Was it already common knowledge then? Was the watch investigating?

"I don't think that's of any importance," Anderson continued.

"It is for your crews," said John.

Anderson tapped his cane against his palm.

"Yes, I know. Superstition is as natural as breathing for them."

"Then it's something we should take notice of."

Anderson looked at him, a slight frown on his face, as if he were assessing John, looking for what was behind his words.

"Mr. Grant," he said, "I think I might find it difficult to accommodate some of their fancies in any of my commercial calculations. What allowance do you think I should make, for example, for skippers who don't dare to count their crew before a voyage for fear that not all of them will come home, or who refuse to sail if they have to turn back for something on their way down to the harbor? I've lost count of the taboos they've quoted to me, the words which must never be uttered: rabbit, pig, devil and more. Woman, even. They're a strange breed, and they make accounting difficult."

"They look for help where they can find it. The sea isn't very forgiving."

Anderson looked at the open door and nodded.

"Nor is the city," he said. "But there's little time there for such dallying. Now, are you available for this commission or not?"

"I am," said John.

With a gesture of his arm, he invited Anderson to follow him across to a table at a window in the corner. It was the one on which he made his drawings and did his accounts. It was clean and had three chairs set around it. John waited for Anderson to sit, then pulled a sheaf of designs and some clean sheets of paper from a shelf, took a crayon from a box and sat opposite him.

"These are some of the classic designs," he said, beginning to spread the papers on the table. "Apollo, Minerva, Neptune. Or there are animals, horses, lions."

Anderson glanced quickly at them, then sat back.

"I hear that you can create passable likenesses," he said.

"I've done so in the past, yes."

"Then you can put those away. The ship is to be named after my wife. I would like the figurehead to resemble her."

John nodded slowly, bringing the memory of Anderson's wife into his mind. He'd seen her with him often and called up a picture of a handsome enough lady, always buttoned up to the neck and usually wearing a bonnet. In fact, she was barely distinguishable from the rest of the merchants' wives who were paraded on civic occasions and would be easy enough to copy into timber.

"Would Mrs. Anderson be prepared to sit for some drawings?" he asked.

"Of course. Now, how long will you need? The ship itself is to be ready by June the third. I hope that the figure may be completed and fitted by then."

John thought for a moment but knew that there was no problem. Fixing a date always helped to concentrate his mind and, once the shapes began to emerge, he was always eager to help them out of the wood.

"With Mrs. Anderson's co-operation, it will be ready before time," he said.

"Good," said Anderson. "Now, the necessary evil of cost. I've had such work done before, of course, and I've made enquiries round and about. It seems that I can get the figure I seek for no more than six pounds. What do you think?"

For the type of work they were discussing, John had been estimating that he would charge six pounds, twelve shillings. In terms of size and complexity, it was an undemanding enough commission and fell easily within the middle range of his normal rates. But Anderson's presumption in quoting a figure before any real discussion made him revise it.

"Seven pounds, twelve shillings," he said. Apart from anything else, the extra would help to buy Jamie's ticket.

The figure took Anderson by surprise.

"Well, well," he said, "that's more than I'd anticipated. How do you justify the extra charge?"

"It isn't extra," said John. "That is what the work is worth."

"And if I offered seven pounds, ten shillings?"

"I would refuse it. The cost is seven pounds, twelve shillings."

"I see."

There was silence, broken only by the noises Jamie was making as he moved things in the loft above them. John wanted the commission, wanted to get to know more about the links between Anderson and Jimmie and was attracted by the thought of working a figure from life again.

Anderson had never before had dealings with John but knew his reputation. He had come to him because he was probably the best, staying clear of the maneuverings that went on when contracts were being negotiated, seeming really to prefer the art of what he did to the commerce which commanded it. It was an attitude so foreign to Anderson that it held some fascination for him. Against all his own instincts, he resisted the temptation to haggle any further.

"Very well," he said. Seven pounds, twelve shillings it is. And I hope it will be money well spent."

John said nothing.

"Have you the materials?" Anderson went on.

John stood and took him back to the middle of the workshop and the block of oak he'd just placed there. He looked at it and ran his hand over its surfaces again.

"This is English oak," he said. "It will last longer than you, me and perhaps even your ship. I have some yellow pine, which is easier to work, but it hasn't the same strength. If you wish, this is the piece I'll use."

Anderson nodded. To him, it was a large trunk of grayish wood which would cost him seven pounds, twelve shillings.

"When will you start?" he asked.

"I'll need to get the rake of the bow, take some measurements," said John.

"Mr. Glover's there now. He has the plans and Mr. Crombie's papers. Tell him your needs and that you have my permission to go where you wish and see what you like. Now, about my wife's likeness." He looked around the workshop. "Your premises are well kept but I'm not certain they're fit for ladies to spend any time here."

John agreed with him.

"I shall need to make some drawings to begin with, and perhaps more later, once the work is well advanced, but they can be made wherever you choose."

"At my home, then," said Anderson immediately. "When can you begin?"

"As soon as you wish."

"Good," said Anderson. "Tomorrow. I shall tell my wife that you will be there at... shall we say... ten thirty in the morning?"

"Earlier, if you wish."

"No. I think ten thirty will be better. She will no doubt wish to spend some time preparing for you. You know the address?"

"Yes," said John.

Anderson nodded, shook John by the hand and went to the door.

"Ten thirty tomorrow morning then," he said. "Seven pounds, twelve shillings. And fitted before June the third."

"Yes, yes and yes," said John.

"I shall look forward to seeing the results of your art. Good day to you, John Grant."

"Good day, William Anderson."

Anderson smiled, gave a brief nod and left.

The whole encounter had had a curious undercurrent. John felt that Anderson had been testing him in some way, probing for something beyond his function as a carver. The money and the processes of doing the work had been secondary. John felt that there was more to know about him than his reputation suggested.

****

Bessie Rennie was in trouble again. It was a common enough occurrence but this time it was beginning to look more serious. During the winter, she'd managed very well on the bread and soup given out to the poor at the public kitchen, but May was coming and it would soon be closed. The winter had been particularly hard and, although it was being chased away now by an early spring, Bessie had suffered a lot and felt the need to cheer herself up. It had started as she'd walked past Mr. Coutt's lemonade factory and breathed in the sharp tang which had brought the saliva to her mouth. Lingering beside Old Murray's stand in Castle Street with its stacks of gingerbread snaps and Gibraltar Rock had made things worse and, when the two town drummers arrived on their rounds and started to read the latest news, the crowds that stopped to listen were too tempting.

She was not a particularly gifted pickpocket and preferred her victims to be either drunk or (better still) dead, but the woman standing beside John Black's stall trying to listen to the drummers and simultaneously control a small child looked an easy enough target. She wore a dark blue cotton day dress with a matching pelerine, and the ruffles on her white bonnet were large and extravagant enough to restrict her vision on both sides. In her hand was a small bag, the fastening of which had come undone as she tried to still the squirming child. Bessie saw an extra advantage in the fact that John Black had put away the pens and inkstands he used to write letters for his customers and gone to listen to the drummers himself. She could dip into the woman's bag, simply step back through the stall and disappear.

She moved slowly behind the woman and stopped, unnoticed by her or the child. The bag swung free, its black material bulging with the promise of money or trinkets. With a quick look each way to check that no one was watching her, Bessie reached forward and flicked open the top of the bag, slipping her fingers quickly inside it.

But she had never been lucky. As she felt the cold edges of some coins and reached deeper to take them, the child suddenly pulled again at the woman's hand, trying to get free. The woman bent to grab at the child, felt the pull on her bag, turned, saw what was happening and screamed. The child, frightened by the noise, joined in. The drummers paused, the crowd pressed around the woman and Bessie was grabbed by a young man in shirtsleeves and a butcher's apron.

He marched her, protesting, across the street to the High Tollbooth, the city's police headquarters, where the woman, deaf to Bessie's pleadings, made an official complaint and the child was given boiled sweets to suck while they wrote things on the necessary pieces of paper. Eventually, the young man, the woman and the child all went away, flushed with the success of their adventure, and Bessie was left with Davie

Donne and another watchman who were to take her to the Bridewell prison in Rose Street.

It was when she was emptying her belongings into a box for them to lock away that the trouble really started. The possessions she carried with her, bundled up in an old shawl which also served as her blanket at night, were mostly sorry things. There were beads and pieces of metal she'd picked up on the beach, stale lumps of bread and cake, rags of material and, incongruously, a pair of silk slippers that she'd found on the steps of Trinity Church and worn so often that they looked and smelled like two pieces of seaweed.

Davie was more interested in a bundle that, right at the start, she'd tried to push up inside her skirt. He had no intention of venturing anywhere near the horrors the skirt concealed, so he forced her to retrieve it and made her open it on the table before him. He gave a thick, phlegmy chuckle. His instincts were right. There were two necklaces, a snuff box, a small set of sailmakers' needles, awls and fids tied with twine and a watch and chain. On the back of the watch was an inscription: "Presented to James Crombie, 17th August 1831, on the launch of the Good Content".

CHAPTER FOURTEEN

John had slept badly again but, this time, there was no ghostly Marie beckoning him toward a horizon which refused to come closer. In her place came a succession of figureheads, men in military costumes, lions with curled claws outstretched, horses raising their hooves high before them, rearing out from the bows of indistinct ships. Now and then, in half-dreams, Anderson was in John's workshop, his features hardening to become timber and his posture angling into the thrust of a prow. And, in a few disturbing sequences, his face turned, softened and became, very briefly, that of his daughter.

The dream which eventually forced John to get up and start his day took this metamorphosis a stage further. He was standing in the bow of a barquentine looking across at a sister ship. At her stem was a finely carved bust of Anderson, his left arm across his chest, the right pointing forward. As the ship leapt into the waves, the spray glittered on him, making his cheeks and eyes shine and running glistening, foaming streams through the folds of his high-collared coat. Then came a succession of bigger waves with deeper troughs. The ships climbed and dropped, their bows digging harder into the faces of the oncoming seas, until the rush of water was so great that it broke over the bows themselves and the figure of Anderson dived down into the green wall. As the barquentine recovered and heaved herself back on an even keel, John was appalled to see that the carved figure of the merchant had disappeared. In its place was his daughter. Not the bust of his daughter but Helen herself, the sea pouring from her screaming mouth and plastering her hair against her seared and dripping skin. Her eyes were wide with terror, her arms imprisoned in the planking of the hull as the vessel lifted itself once more and tipped to spear her into the next fold of the ocean.

He set a pot of water onto the low black range to boil and chased the dream's residue from his mind. He knew that, whenever he was about to start a new commission, there was always an excitement inside him which tumbled his thoughts for a few days. Once he'd started shaping the wood, it would settle and he'd be back into his normal, gentle rhythms.

It was not yet eight o'clock when he set out for the yard where Anderson's boat sat on its stocks. Long before he got there, however, the ringing notes of maybe nine or ten caulking mallets told him that they were already at work. He saw them as soon as he turned through the gate, ranged along the side of the hull. There were nine of them, moving to and from four small heaps of oakum, pieces of blackened hemp which had been picked from old rope. They grabbed fistfuls of it, rolled it into long strands between their hand and their knee and pushed it into the seams between the planking. It was when their mallets hit hard against the caulking irons to press the oakum deeper that they made their music. Each shipwright tried to get his own, distinctive note by cutting a slot in the head of the mallet on each side of the haft hole. As a team of caulkers worked together, the sounds sang into one another, weaving a strange percussive music in the air.

John found Glover in the wooden hut that Jimmie had used as his office. He introduced himself and said that he had Anderson's permission to look over the vessel and take some measurements. Glover folded away the plans he was looking at and walked with John toward the scaffolding around the bow.

"She'll be a fine ship," said Glover. "Mr. Crombie knew his trade."

"Did you know him?" asked John.

Glover shook his head.

"Not really. Met him a couple of times. I'd heard about him though. Heard about his ways."

"Ways?"

Glover smiled and scratched at his beard.

"His business ways. Juggling with money."

"And news of that got as far as Dundee?"

Glover's smile became a laugh and he gestured at the town to his left and the country beyond it.

"You know what harbor folk are. I've no idea what's going on just a few streets away, but I can tell you plenty about characters in Leith, Great Yarmouth, even Stavanger."

John knew that this was true. In many ways, Boston and Quebec were closer to Aberdeen than Birmingham or London.

"You're moving up here from Dundee, are you?" he said.

"It's either that or getting work as a carpenter building houses. Aye, Aberdeen's the place to be. If you can unlock the door."

John had expected him to be wary, mistrustful even. After all, he'd stepped into the shoes of a local man, taken over a job in which most of the hard work had already been done. Instead, his tone was assured, confident.

"The door?" said John, although he knew very well what Glover meant.

"You're an incomer yourself. A stranger," said Glover. "You know how closed it is here. Advocates, university professors, doctors, country landowners, merchants—this town belongs to them. They keep their counsel. But they're canny, too. There's room for others, if they've got the enterprise. Do you not feel it yourself?"

John didn't answer. Despite the apparent enthusiasm in what he was saying, there was little passion in Glover's tone. His remarks were more like calculations. John felt that he was no pioneering spirit but rather a speculator balancing possibilities and looking for some personal gain.

They were walking beside the place where the caulkers were working. John waited until they'd passed them so that he wouldn't have to shout over the singing of their mallets.

"You think you'll make your way in Aberdeen, do you?" he asked.

Glover shrugged his shoulders and raised his eyebrows.

"It's in the lap of the gods and Mr. Anderson," he said.

"You know all about him too, I suppose."

"Enough," said Glover.

John waited for more but Glover was silent. They'd reached the foot of the scaffolding around the bow.

"You'll want to look around, take your measurements," said Glover. It wasn't a question. "I'll leave you to get on with it. I've got the plans and papers back in the office. Come along and look at them when you've finished if you like."

He turned and walked away, not waiting for a reply. John felt as if he'd been dismissed by an employer. Indeed, through most of their conversation, despite the fact that Glover had done nearly all of the talking, John had felt he was being assessed. Glover's eyes had been on him all the time, seeming to look for reactions, agreement, encouragement maybe. John suspected that, with that sort of single-mindedness, he probably would make his way in Aberdeen.

As he climbed up beside the bow, however, his thoughts turned away from Glover. He followed the sweep of the gripe up from the keel, the sweet, dark curve easing into his mind. Near the top, he reached out and trailed his fingers along the cheeks, cupping his palm over the point where they overlapped the apron and joined the main piece. Jimmie really had done a good job. The ship was almost ready to live.

John measured the stem piece at the top, examined the timber to look for the point at which he would cut into the grain to make the step for his figurehead, made the notes he needed, then clambered over the top rail to check the clearance under the bowsprit. The dirt and white splashes everywhere showed that this part of the ship had been finished long ago and that its only recent visitors had been seagulls. The fo'c's'le hatch was held open by a short length of timber. John pulled it free and lifted back the cover. The steps hadn't yet been fitted, so he lowered himself inside to see whether there were any interior fittings that might affect the way he mounted and secured his work. It was dark there and most of the examination had to be by touch and at first there were no surprises; planks curved sharply to the head, their smooth surfaces broken only by occasional ridges of oakum where the seams had been wider and the material had been forced in tightly to seal them. John's hands swept over them, testing the crevices well forward, looking for anything which didn't belong.

He found it low on the port side. He was lying on his stomach, with his left hand making a final sweep low down and well forward when he felt a square shape which shifted as he touched it. He thought it was a piece of loose timber that had fallen and been overlooked but, when he pulled at it, he realized that the shape was wrong. He slid it free, picked it up and took it to a spot directly underneath the open hatch.

It was a small ditty box, the sort used by sailors and fishermen to hold their personal belongings while they were at sea. Barely a foot long, eight inches wide and five deep, it had a hinged lid and two splashes of red paint on the back. Its edges and corners were rounded off, not by the person who'd made it, but by many years of handling. Screwed into it at the front, just below the catch, there was the usual brass plate, with the owner's name: J. CROMBIE.

****

Both Helen and her mother had woken early, excited for different reasons at the morning's appointment. Sitting for a bust was a distinct departure from the routine of their days. Elizabeth saw it as a source of interest but also of concern, especially as part of it involved deceiving her husband by substituting Helen for herself. Helen felt the excitement that anything new always brought to her. She'd spent longer than usual choosing her dress. In the end, she'd put on a pale yellow taffeta gown with a separate, short-sleeved day bodice whose neckline was so low that her mother insisted that she wear a fichu over it. She refused to put on a bonnet, however, saying that no self-respecting sailor wanted to be led over the oceans by a prim little churchgoer.

Fortunately, Anderson had had to leave before ten so they were free to discover whether the carver was prepared to agree to their deception. The minutes before his arrival were dragging, however, and although Elizabeth managed to occupy herself with her crochet work, Helen moved impatiently about the room, looking out of the window and talking all the time.

The person she was looking for appeared at twenty-six minutes past the hour. Out of respect for the ladies he was to visit, he'd gone straight home from the yard, stowed the ditty box in his bedroom, scrubbed himself thoroughly, and put on a blue cravat and a navy, single breasted jacket. His black leather boots were plain and had an elegance far greater than the pointed toes, high arches and elevated heels of the young men of Helen's normal acquaintance. And, as she already knew, he was a very handsome man, with thick black hair and dark eyes which made his face look paler than it really was. He walked with a long, slow stride, his shoulders dipping forward slightly with each step. She watched him cross the road, looking up at their windows, and resisted the urge to draw back into the room. He disappeared out of sight. She waited a while, then turned and moved slowly to her chair. She sat for a few moments, and then said, "I think Mr. Grant is here." Her voice was quiet, controlled. They heard the front door bell ring and, soon, a servant came in to announce John's arrival.

He was surprised to see Helen but disguised the fact, simply repeating for her the little bow he'd given to her mother. Elizabeth asked the servant to bring them tea and invited John to sit down, gesturing at a sofa with an extravagant scrolled back, cabriole legs and thick, buttoned crimson upholstery. The whole room had the same opulent feel about it. The wallpaper was a rich bottle green, and its dark tones carried down into the floral patterned Aubusson carpet. Under a large gilt mirror stood a marble-topped pier table. Opposite it, beside the fireplace, was an embroidered pole screen and, on the mantelpiece, two flowered Coalport porcelain vases. As well as the two chairs on which Helen and Elizabeth were sitting, there were three more small buttoned velvet and mahogany ones with loose cotton covers. It was an interior which cast Anderson in a better light, although John suspected that the elegance around him owed more to Mrs. Anderson.

A needlework sampler caught his eye. Its text was "Blessed are the meek" but what struck him was the fact that it was followed by an exclamation mark. It confirmed the overall impression that this was a room with conventional enough trappings but an edge of individuality.

"You're very punctual, Mr. Grant," said Elizabeth.

"It would do little for my reputation to be otherwise," he replied, aware of the formality of his tone but not yet feeling sufficiently at ease to be content with smiles and silence.

"What news have you of Mrs. Crombie?" asked Helen. "I hope she is beginning to recover from the shock of her husband's death."

"She's well, I think," replied John. "She has many friends to comfort her."

"Good. And what of Mr. Crombie?"

Elizabeth looked up sharply, wary at what scheming Helen might be unfolding.

"I don't understand your question, Miss Anderson," said John.

"There is talk that his death was not the accident it first appeared to be."

"Is there?" said John, wondering where she could have heard such a thing.

Helen looked hard at him. He really did seem to be ignorant of the things Jessie had told her and yet there was a reserve deep in his dark eyes that she could not decipher.

"I would have thought you would have heard some gossip."

"I have little time for it."

"I'm very glad to hear it," said Elizabeth, attempting to move away from such an unseemly topic.

"I think it's a pity," said Helen, pressing on and ignoring her mother's stare. "I think the unexplained death of a prominent local tradesman should be investigated. Do you not even have a little curiosity about it?"

John was caught. He had no wish to lie to her, but a drawing room such as this was hardly the setting for talk of stranglings and lacerations.

"If there is evidence of what you say, I would certainly be interested to hear it," he said.

"Ah, well that has yet to be uncovered," said Helen, her eyes bright with interest. "But it may well be something other than the obvious."

"I'm not sure that I quite understand you."

"A drunken fight," said Helen, as if it were self-evident.

"Helen," said Elizabeth sternly, before turning to John and saying, "Forgive my daughter, Mr. Grant. She sometimes has strange fancies."

"These are not fancies, mother. It's true that Mr. Crombie may have been the victim of thieves, but his death may also have been caused by a business acquaintance."

"Indeed?" said John.

"Yes. Or even some women," said Helen, deliberately giving the last suggestion a mysterious edge.

"Well, well," said John. "I shall listen very carefully to hear how this story develops."

"Was it not you who found the body?" asked Helen.

"That is enough," said Elizabeth. "This is a most unsuitable conversation for us to be having and I wish to hear no more of it."

In their separate ways, both John and Helen would have preferred to continue. He was intrigued to know how someone such as Helen could have learned that Jimmie had been killed. For her part, Helen was certain that he knew more about it than he had revealed. The choice, however, was not theirs; Elizabeth's tone had been unequivocal. The topic was closed.

At last, the servant reappeared carrying a Rockingham tea service on a papier-mâché mother of pearl tray and, with the tea ritual well under way and the initial exchanges freed by the small talk, Helen decided that they should waste no more time.

"We have a proposition to make," she said.

John looked at her, waiting to hear the next surprise that she had ready. Helen looked quickly at her mother, who was shaking her head, no longer sure that this was such a good idea, even though it was her own.

"I notice that you have been looking at Mama with great care as you've been speaking," Helen continued. "No doubt to become familiar with her features."

John looked at Elizabeth.

"Forgive me," he said. "I was not aware that I was being so indiscreet."

"Neither was I," said Elizabeth, with a frown toward Helen.

"Oh, it's not indiscretion if you're here to sketch a likeness," said Helen. "For goodness' sake, why are you both being so polite? It's natural that you should look at Mama. How could it be otherwise? But you are studying the wrong subject."

John looked from one to the other and opened his mouth to say something but had no idea what.

"You'll have to forgive my daughter, Mr. Grant," said Elizabeth after a quick scowl at Helen. "As you will already have discerned, for all her education, she seems to be lacking in many of the social graces."

"Well, graceful one, you tell him," said Helen.

Elizabeth sighed. Helen was right; the sooner they put the suggestion to him, the better. She set her tea cup in its saucer, laid it on the table beside her and folded her hands in her lap.

"Mr. Grant," she began. "I'm very flattered by my husband's decision to name his ship after me, but it's my opinion that its captain and crew would be better served by having a younger figure at its bow."

Once again, John didn't know what to say, but Elizabeth was not yet expecting an answer.

"I've seen the ships moored along the quays," she continued, "and they all carry powerful beasts, military figures, gods and goddesses. None of them are old women, are they?"

John thought for a moment before replying.

"I've seen many which are," he said at last.

Elizabeth looked at him, a smile on her lips. She was still a beautiful woman. Her hair had the shine of silver and the lines of her face were clear and carried none of the flabbiness that hung on the cheeks of many women of her age. She sat upright in her chair, her shoulders back and her gaze steady on him.

Helen was finding it difficult to remain seated. There were so many things she wished to ask, some of them secrets that she had not yet admitted to herself.

"Observation must be an important part of your work," she said. "I've heard that you have an interest in detection also."

John looked at her but said nothing. He wondered whether her changes of subject were deliberate attempts to unsettle him.

"Do you find any resemblance between Mama and myself?" Helen went on.

"That's enough, Helen," said Elizabeth, her tone sterner again and the smile gone from her face. "You are really treating Mr. Grant very unfairly."

"But..."

A glance and a gesture from Elizabeth were enough to stop Helen continuing.

"You must think that you have fallen amongst strange creatures," she said to John, "but the matter is really very simple. My daughter is right. People do say that we resemble one another and, despite your kind remarks, I would still prefer you to base your work on her features rather than my own. She is now what I once was."

John was silent, looking first at Elizabeth, then at Helen, studying their faces, looking for, and finding, the similarities Elizabeth spoke of. Helen watched his dark eyes flick quickly over her hair, face, neck and shoulders before lifting back to look directly into her own. She held his gaze. He was the first to look away.

"What of Mr. Anderson?" he asked.

"What of him?" said Helen.

"Have you spoken to him of your idea? It's he who has engaged me, after all."

Once again, Elizabeth had to hold up her hand to still Helen.

"We were hoping you might be prepared to agree without having to consult him," she said.

The morning was moving much too quickly for John. First, Jimmie's ditty box, now an invitation to join in a conspiracy.

"I'm not sure what to answer you," he said to Elizabeth. "I have agreed a contract and a price with your husband. I have to honor it."

"I understand," said Elizabeth, seeming to accept that John was not free to do what they were asking.

Helen looked at her with a frown.

"Are the likenesses you create always exact, then?" she asked.

"No," said John.

"So could you not make a figure that was both Mama and myself? Is that too great a challenge?"

John had made many, many figureheads in his time and his work was seen in ports all over the world, but the figures that he dreamed were elusive and he had never caught exactly the vision he was chasing each time.

"Every new piece is a challenge," he said. "I have to find what the wood holds. It's not simply the curve of a brow or the hollowness of a cheek."

"There you are, then," said Helen, sitting forward in her chair and letting some of her excitement into her voice. "That is what we're asking. Forget how Mama's lips are so tight when I embarrass her or make her angry, forget the way my hair flies loose when I become agitated, take the best from both of us and make a creature father will be proud of."

Her eyes had the brightness Elizabeth loved to see in them. John, too, felt their power but still wondered whether there was something else prompting her, some other need to provoke him, to compromise him. It was Elizabeth's voice which eventually forced an answer from him.

"My daughter's enthusiasm is very eloquent, Mr. Grant. She speaks for me also. Will you humor us and give my husband both his women in one?"

Two pairs of eyes were on him and the similarities between them were very clear. Their combined force was too great for John to resist. In a gesture he had known all along that he would make, he reached for his paper and crayons.

"I'd better get started," he said.

CHAPTER FIFTEEN

Thorsen pushed a list across the desk. "One mate, a bo's'n, a cook steward, and two watches of seven each," he said.

Anderson nodded. "Good. Fewer than last trip. Is it enough?"

Thorsen didn't bother to answer, the implication in his expression being that the question didn't need to be asked.

"And all the fitting out's finished?" said Anderson.

"We can sail in two weeks."

"Good."

Anderson took the list to a chest of drawers by his office window and put them into a box in the top drawer which was already half full of papers. These last few days before a ship sailed were always trying. There was little work for the crew to be doing before the trip began and yet they had to be paid a month in advance, a period known as dead horse time. With the money already in their pockets, there was little pressure on them to do anything to earn it and no amount of cajoling or threatening could increase their efforts. It was a system that was contrary to all of Anderson's instincts.

On top of that, he had to make sure that he met the requirements of the 1827 Passenger Act, which had tried, among other things, to ensure that passengers had enough space, adequate ventilation, and that single men and women were not berthed together. It was legislation that was hard to enforce but Anderson observed it strictly, preferring not to run the risk of a heavy fine and restriction of his trade.

He took a bundle tied in waxed paper from a shelf on the wall, went back to the desk and handed it to Thorsen.

"Testimonials," he said, pointing at it. "From some of, or previous passengers, addressed to the Journal, describing your excellence as a captain and the advantages of sailing with us."

Thorsen pushed the bundle into his bag without looking at it and said nothing. He had no need to ask where Anderson had acquired such treasures. The deliberate irony in his tone told him that they were fakes. It was normal business practice; no one told the truth about their enterprises. Every week the Journal carried letters praising all sorts of items with nothing to authenticate them. Last Thursday there had been a particularly effusive one about the efficacy of Dr. Parker's Gout and Rheumatism pills; its enthusiasm was such that Anderson had little doubt that it had been written by whomever was calling himself Dr. Parker.

"When you arrive," he said, "take them ashore to some place where you're not known. Get them stamped and sent back. Don't bring them back yourself. They're independent opinions."

They had no more business and Thorsen left Anderson to return to his correspondence on the acquisition of the boil houses at Footdee. The Union Whale Fishing Company had noted his interest but still preferred the option of retaining ownership and letting the premises. Anderson knew of no company with any interest in them and was content to wait.

****

Rose dropped her empty basket next to the fish boxes to be filled, stretched her arms and gave a long, wide yawn.

"You know, sometimes," she said to Jessie, who was scraping some scraps of fish from the bottom of her own basket, "I think I'd like to be workin' in a manufactory."

"Why?" asked Jessie.

"Oh, I'm no' sure, really, but I'd be inside, there'd be none of the stink of this stuff..."

"Aye, and they'd pay you pennies for workin' all God's hours."

"Well, I could be a parlor-maid then."

Jessie laughed.

"Who'd let you into their parlor?"

"Well... a laundry maid, maybe?"

"Further down."

"Scullery-maid?"

"That's more like it."

Rose smiled and pushed at Jessie's arm, then started back as two young boys came racing between them, jumping over their baskets and slithering among the fish scales on the cobbles. One half-fell but was on his feet again before the other could catch him and they ran on their screaming way.

"Strange that we've had no children of or own, isn't it?" said Rose.

"Count your blessin's," replied Jessie, pointing after the two boys. "Would you want to be havin' that day and night, year after year?"

There was a sadness in Rose's eyes.

"It'd be somebody to love," she said.

"Aye," said Jessie, reaching over and gently pushing her shoulder. "But think of what we have to do for it."

"What do you mean?"

"Well, how much pleasure have you ever had out of Joe?"

Rose simply shrugged.

"No," Jessie went on. "We lie there, or stand there—Jimmie always took it when he wanted it—and... well, there's just the filth and the smell... and it's all over."

To her surprise, she saw tears in Rose's eyes.

"Oh, now, come on, darlin'," she said, moving beside her and holding her close. "If you want bairns, there's still plenty o' time."

Rose shook herself and dabbed fiercely at her eyes.

"I wouldna want a child of Joe's," she said.

"Doesn't have to be," said Jessie, leaning to whisper in her ear. "Look at it. Men everywhere. One of them'll oblige you. You're a fine-lookin' woman."

"And you're disgustin'," replied Rose.

Their intimacy was broken by Jack Dorner, one the clerks of the trawler company they carried their loads for.

"Stopped for the day, have you?" he said, coming up beside them.

"We're waitin' for the baskets to..." Jessie started.

He shook his head and raised a hand to stop her.

"We need a horse fetched down from the stables. Off you go, Rose. Quick as you can."

He turned and went back toward the office.

"Maybe he'd be the one," said Jessie.

"What one?"

"You know," said Jessie and she thrust her hips back and forth.

Rose rubbed her hands on her rough apron to dry them.

"I'd rather have the horse," she said.

"That's just greedy," said Jessie.

Rose kissed her on the cheek and set off for Union Street.

****

117

As John spread his sketches of Elizabeth Anderson and her daughter on the table in his workshop, he was aware that the familiar excitement of starting a new piece of work had a different edge. He was about to create a likeness that would last for over a hundred years and more, but this time he had to combine two people in a single image. And one of them was already a part of his own dreaming.

He picked up the main sketch of her and looked at its lines. Her face was regular but he had noticed a difference between her eyes. The left carried more of her smile, the tiny creases on its lid curving up toward the eyebrow, which lifted slightly higher than the right one. They had none of the cat-like lift of Marie's but they looked straight out of the sketch with a surprising directness. He remembered their color, a blend of soft green and hazel, and knew that he would never find the paint to reproduce it. Her neck was long, pale and flawless, emerging from the fichu which perversely, though intended to cover the exposed top part of her breasts, called attention to them. Her auburn hair was parted in the middle, swept low across the sides of her cheeks and beneath her ears and held in a clasp at the back. On the left of her dress at the top was a diamond cluster starburst spray brooch, one of many inspired by the visit of Halley's Comet just five years earlier. John had sketched it both to add detail to the final piece and to mirror its effects in the scrollwork which would bind the figure into the lines of the ship's prow.

He held a sketch of her mother beside it to compare them. The resemblance was in the overall shape of the face, the slight tilt of the head toward the right and the character of the eyes. She, too, had a direct, amused look and had obviously been as great a beauty in her time. He took the two sketches across to the piece of English oak and walked round it, his eye carrying their lines into its grain, assessing angles, choosing the orientation and beginning to see the woman waiting inside the wood. He knew that he would bring her right hand across her breast and that it would hold not flowers but grasses and ribbons. He would use the tilt of the head to turn the face slightly to one side, knowing that this would capture the resemblance between the two women. At another level, he sensed that this was also a protective impulse, angling the pretty face so that it would not have to meet the wind and waves head on.

He called Jamie down from the loft and the two of them eased the block from its wedges and tilted it until it was lying on the floor with the surface which would be the front of the figurehead facing upwards. John fetched his crayons and, referring frequently to his sketches, drew an outline shape on the front and one of the sides. At this stage, there were no details, just the roundness of the head, the slopes of neck and shoulders and, in the profile sketch, the extra volume of wood which would be needed for the arm to be held across the breast. When he'd finished, he looked at the overall effect, accentuated one or two of the shapes then put the sketches back on his table.

Jamie had already taken out the saws and adzes they would use to rough out the primary shape before they lifted the block onto the wooden horses to begin to refine it.

"This might be your last bit of work with me," said John as he took one of the saws and chose where he would start. "So it'll be one for both of us to remember. It's an important one, too."

"Oh aye, of course. I ken. It's for Mr. Anderson."

"No," said John. "It's for Mrs. Anderson."

"And Miss Anderson, by the look of your drawings."

John pointed the saw at him.

"You keep your dirty wee mind to yourself, young man, or I'll detach you from Jenny's wedding present. Now, you start on that corner. Use the middle adze."

He started to cut out wedges of timber to create a very basic form as Jamie began whittling away at the top of the block. They stopped talking, each taking pleasure at the thought of what this shapeless lump of wood was about to become.

****

Anderson was just finishing his last boil house letter when one of his junior clerks brought the news that Glover had come to see him. No meeting had been arranged and Anderson's immediate instinct was to feel that Glover's time would be better spent getting on with the work. He told him so the moment he walked through the door.

"My absence makes no difference," Glover replied smoothly. "The teams are at work and this is my lunch time anyway. I thought I would take the opportunity to report on the program of work I've devised and its implementation."

"There is no need to report. My interest is in the finished item, not the processes that produce it."

"I appreciate that, Mr. Anderson, but I was confident that you would wish to be reassured that we will be meeting all the required regulations and respecting the necessary legislation."

He was using the same strangulated formalism that characterized so many of his business exchanges.

"I took it for granted that we would," said Anderson. "I cannot afford to transgress."

"Of course not," said Glover, his eyes unwavering as they held Anderson's gaze.

It was slightly unsettling because he'd suddenly dropped out of formality and given the words an inflection which suggested that Anderson's reply was ingenuous. Glover was no longer the supplicant eager to be employed; he had greater self-possession, a new boldness. Anderson sat back, resolved now to listen to the report and try to assess where the man had found this apparent confidence and why their relationship seemed to have altered.

As Glover listed the schedule of tasks and events, from the last of the caulking to the stepping of the masts, the hoisting of spars and the balancing of the standing rigging, Anderson kept his eyes on him and simply listened. Nothing he was saying was out of the ordinary. It was all standard procedure, a catalogue of the obvious, which merited no reporting or recording. So why was he here?

Glover spoke of his brief meeting with John but that, too, was information that Anderson didn't need. He waited, still offering no response, until Glover completed his report and put the list from which he had been reading on the desk. Instead of taking it or looking at it, Anderson stood and went to the window. Outside, the midday clatter was at its peak with workers and seamen coming past on their way to the pie stalls and taverns in and around Castle Street. People, handcarts and the occasional horse-drawn cart wove through the confusion, seeming to follow no rules as to the right of way and yet managing not to collide with one another or become compressed into a jam.

"What is the point of all this?" said Anderson at last, his back still turned toward Glover.

"Standard procedure for..."

Anderson was not interested in his reply. He hardly paused in what he was saying. "Because I wouldn't wish your business here to go the way it did in Dundee."

The silence in the office showed that the remark had had its effect. Anderson turned slowly to look at Glover.

"Did you think your deception would go unnoticed?" he said.

Still Glover said nothing, and Anderson was intrigued to note that, apart from his initial reaction, the information seemed not to have disturbed him unduly.

"Everyone knows how little work there is in Dundee. And yet you claim your skills were in demand, your order books were full."

To his surprise, Glover managed a smile.

"Yes," he said.

"And you were lying."

"Yes."

"Then you are more of a fool than you seem. I have many acquaintances with interests on the Tay. I spoke with them after you approached me. You have no full order books."

"No," said Glover, the smile still in place.

"Indeed you have no books at all, Mr. Glover. Your yard has been closed and its books sequestered. Am I not right?"

"Perfectly."

"And you are in debt."

Anderson's tone had been almost playful but there was a dangerous edge to it. Nonetheless, Glover was still smiling.

"I'm rather surprised to think that you should try to play me like a fish," said Anderson.

Glover waited for a few moments, then sat on the chair beside the desk.

"Have you never lied?" he said, his voice calm, steady.

Anderson, still standing, felt himself at a slight disadvantage. It was as if they were in Glover's office.

"I beg your pardon?"

"Never oversold cargoes? Never given less than you promised? Never seized an advantage which presented itself?"

It was Anderson's turn to smile. They were moving into insinuations and accusations. He knew he was a match for Glover, whatever the man had in mind.

"I think," he said, "that you do yourself a disservice by making such offensive suggestions."

"So you've never put profit before principles?" said Glover, shaking his head slowly, almost sadly.

Anderson waited.

"Mr. Anderson," said Glover, "I'm a good shipwright. It's no fault of mine that affairs have slowed in Dundee. I told you that I followed success. That's why I came here. That's why I lied to you to get your commission."

"And you believe that is the way to success?"

"It was for Mr. Crombie, wasn't it?"

Anderson looked at him again. This was more entertaining than he'd expected. Where was Glover leading them now?

"By all accounts," he went on, "he based all his commerce on untruths, deceptions, even extortion. Isn't that so?"

"So people said."

"Oh no. It was more than that. You were trapped by him yourself."

"Trapped?"

"I've seen his books. The sums he's asked of you over the past few weeks. Not all of them relate to actual work undertaken."

Anderson knew what he was talking about at once. He was confident, though, that his dealings with Crombie were secret.

"I paid what he asked," he said. "He was the shipwright. I was anxious for the job to be done."

"No, no. These items were separate. Oblique, one might say."

"If you have a point to make, do so," said Anderson.

The smile had gone from Glover's face but his confidence was intact.

"There are papers which Mr. Crombie kept very carefully, very well secured. I found them amongst his plans and accounts."

Anderson felt a little thrill of anxiety. This man played the game well. "What papers?"

Glover waved a hand to signify that he considered the matter trivial.

"Notes, jottings in Mr. Crombie's hand," he said. "References to letters and the like. They have no obvious connection with the Elizabeth Anderson and yet they're linked with payments he received from you."

Anderson could see that, despite the ignorance he was feigning, Glover was deliberately creating an effect; not just for the fun of it but to retain the contract and perhaps to gain some other imagined advantage. He toyed with the idea of dismissing him but that would not solve the problem of completing the Elizabeth Anderson. Instead, he forced himself to recover the composure which the mention of the papers had briefly undermined. He'd been giving Glover too much leeway. His own amusement had been suppressed.

"These... notes you've found. Am I to understand that they cause you to wish to cancel our arrangement?" he asked.

"Of course not."

"Or renegotiate its terms?"

When Glover hesitated and seemed to consider this option, Anderson continued, "Because they're not negotiable. Either the contract is completed on the terms we agreed or I award it to someone else."

Glover was silent for a moment before replying.

"In Aberdeen?"

"Or Dundee. There is no shortage there, as you know."

"No, no," said Glover, his smile reappearing. "If the papers prove to be of any significance, I shall of course tell you so. The fact that they seemed profitable for Mr. Crombie needn't alter the arrangements we've made. I shall keep them aside, in a safe place, and proceed with the work. There may, of course, be a need to insert a fresh clause into our contract."

The words carried a threat. Anderson chose not to give him the satisfaction of showing that it had registered with him.

"There'll be no 'fresh clauses'."

"I see," said Glover. "Well, I still consider my visit was worth making. We both know now exactly how matters stand."

Anderson looked sharply at him.

"With the construction of your ship," said Glover, innocence personified.

Anderson picked up the piece of paper which Glover had placed on his desk and handed it to him.

"Good day," he said.

Glover gave another of his self-satisfied smiles and went out. He felt that he had won a small victory, which he would extend on another occasion. Anderson, too, felt invigorated by the exchange. He loved the unexpected and always rose to its challenges. He was already considering how to ensure that Glover's creditors in Dundee got to know of his whereabouts. Once the Elizabeth Anderson was launched, of course.

CHAPTER SIXTEEN

After little more than an hour, John and Jamie stopped. The squareness of the block had gone but, apart from where Jamie's whittling had created rudimentary shoulders and a huge, bulbous head, it still showed nothing of what it was to become. Jamie went to pour a cup of tea, leaving John looking at the oak, letting his eye slip over its new contours, easing his fingers along the paler grain freshly exposed by their tools.

A shout made him turn. Tom was standing in the open doorway, dark against the bright afternoon. John waved him in. "Heard the tea pouring, did you?" he said.

"Too busy for that," said Tom, "but I'll take a cup if it's goin'."

John called to Jamie to bring an extra cup as Tom looked at the carved wood.

"Anderson's?"

"Yes. He wants it to look like his wife."

"It does already," said Tom.

John laughed.

"Why're you around here. No work?" he asked.

"Well, if you're supposed to be findin' out who killed Jimmie, I was just wonderin' if you'd heard the news."

"I've been busy. What news?"

"Davie Donne's put Bessie Rennie in the Bridewell."

"So? She spends more time in there than you do on your rope walk."

"Ah, but I was talkin' to Davie. This time, she had Jimmie's watch in her pouch."

He waited for John's reaction. It came as a slow smile.

"And," he went on, "what else d'you think she was carryin'?"

"A new will made out by Jimmie in her favor?"

125

"A bundle of fids," said Tom, with a triumphal finality that suggested that they'd found their murderer.

"But..."

"And there was blood on one of them. Dried up, of course, and she'd tried to wipe it off, but they found it there."

"So is Davie saying she killed him?"

Tom shook his head and frowned to show his disappointment. "No. She wasna brought in because o' Jimmie. It was for thievin'. Some wifey in Castle Street. Still, the watch, the fids... must be somethin' goin' on."

John nodded. It would be worth finding out a bit more about it if they could. "Can Davie get us in to see her?" he asked.

"He won't do nothin' fer nobody," said Tom. "But Charlie Dodds works there. He'll easy let us in."

There was no need to say any more. They called through to tell Jamie they were going and set off for the Bridewell, leaving him with three half pint mugs of hot tea.

They walked along Trinity Quay to the bottom of Market Street, turned right and were soon up on Union Street. It was like moving into a different world. They left behind the stench of the harbor and all the ropes and spars and timbers of their trades to walk past merchants dealing in quieter, more domestic commodities. Alexander Lumsden, a woolen draper; George Gauld, a grocer, tea and spirit dealer; Miss Black, who made straw hats and stays; and various bakers, cutlers, shoemakers, vintners, tea merchants and others. On the pavements, smartly dressed men and women wandered along in no great hurry, stepping back when carriages veered too close to them and stopping frequently to talk to other wanderers. Hats were raised, smiles exchanged. These were people with time to spare, living lives which spread an air of elegance and restraint over the city's turmoil.

John and Tom crossed the road just before they got to Crown Street. On the opposite corner, they met Rose leading a dray horse down Silver Street from Golden Square. She gave them a big smile. Spending time with the horses was the part of her job she liked best, taking them back and forth from the quayside stables with bigger loads of fish for the ice houses. Best of all was when she fetched a new animal like this one. It allowed her to stroll along, free of the smell and slither of fish, with no load on her back or hip and just the gentle clopping and blowing of the beast beside her.

"Aye, Rose. How's Jessie?" said Tom, as she hauled on the bridle and stopped the horse at the roadside. Automatically, John reached over and started to clap its neck and run his hands through its mane.

"Fine," said Rose. "Back at work and enjoyin' herself."

"No' missin' Jimmie then."

The smile died as she replied. "Who'd miss a waster like that?"

"Heard anythin' more about him?" asked Tom.

Rose looked at him, her brows furrowed. "What d'you mean?"

"I dinna ken. From the police, maybe. About how he died."

Rose's puzzlement increased. Her eyes were like her sister's. As they flicked from Tom to John they looked very dark in the afternoon sun.

"He drowned," she said, as if it was too obvious to bother mentioning.

"Aye, but..." Tom just shrugged.

"Och, yon Davie Donne's been makin' a nuisance of hisself as usual," said Rose. "Askin' daft questions. Tellin' her she doesna look all that upset and things."

"Well, he's got somethin' to ask questions about now," said Tom, enjoying his role as investigator. "Have you no' heard?"

"What?"

"Bessie Rennie. She's in the Bridewell. They found Jimmie's watch in her pouch. And she was carryin' some fids."

Rose's expression was one of utter bewilderment. "What's he babblin' about?" she said to John.

John shrugged, smiled and tapped his forefinger to his temple.

"Well, you say he drowned," Tom insisted, "but with all the cuts and bruises on him, it looked as if he might have been in some sort o' fight."

"With Bessie Rennie?" said Rose.

"Course not," said Tom. "Down round the harbor somewhere."

"Aye, well, there's plenty lookin' for that sort of thing Saturdays," said Rose. "Ask my Joe. Took his pilot's money with him and never come home till Sunday night."

"Sunday?" said John.

"Aye," said Rose. "Him and his crew got theirselves battered at the weekend. And there was two Norwegians and a Dutchman in."

Tom nodded. On top of everything else, with foreign sailors on shore leave, their pockets stuffed with back pay, the smallest spark was enough to ignite mayhem in the harbor's taverns.

"Foreign sailor," he said, turning to John. "I never thought of that."

John and Rose exchanged looks.

"What?" said John.

"Hemp, fids, drownin'. All things that sailors'd know about," said Tom, spreading his hands in a gesture that suggested the connection was obvious.

"Why d'you keep talkin' about fids?" asked Rose.

"He didna drown, Rose," said Tom before John could stop him, "Somebody stabbed him with a fid."

Rose was speechless, reduced to shaking her head in disbelief.

"We don't know that," said John. "Tom's just guessing. Getting excited."

"Have you told Jessie?" asked Rose, her voice small, hesitant.

"Nothing to tell yet," said John.

"What d'you mean, 'yet'?"

Tom answered before John could reassure her that there was nothing in what they were saying.

"John and me's askin' around, tryin' to find out what..."

John looked quickly at him and gave a little shake of the head.

"Don't listen to him, Rose," he said. "Your brain stops working when you get to his age."

The smile Rose gave in reply was weak. Tom's news had clearly upset her. "What have you found out?" she asked.

"Nothing," said John. "Jimmie was drunk, that's all."

"Aye," said Tom, at last realizing that he'd said too much. "Staggerin' around in Pensioners' Court. Probably had a fight and fell into the water."

Rose's eyes flashed. "Aye, I ken. Pensioners' Court. Just the place for him, with his whores and tinkers."

John noticed how Rose's fingers twisted the lead rein she was holding, pulling it hard into the folds of her hand. She clearly had little time for her brother-in-law's habits. The horse, which had been standing with the quiet patience of its kind, gave a sudden shake of its head, pulling away from the tightness of its bridle. John rubbed at its neck again.

"You say you've said nothin' to Jessie?" asked Rose.

John shook his head.

"I havena seen hide nor hair of her since Sunday," said Tom. "I was meanin' to find out if there was anythin' she was needin' but I thought she'd want to be left on her own for a while."

"Aye, she does," said Rose. "And I don't think you want to be tellin' her this sort of thing. She's well out of that marriage. She kens it, too. She wouldna want things stirrin' up."

"Nobody'll say anything to her," said John.

Rose nodded, looking straight into his face. "She's had enough," she said. "With Davie and his trouble-makin'. Don't give her no more pain."

"Is she working today?" asked John.

"Aye."

"Tell her I've got something for her. I'll bring it round tonight."

"I mean it, John," said Rose. "She's fine now. Don't say nothin' to bring it all back."

"I won't."

Rose held his gaze for a moment, then nodded and tugged at the bridle to get the horse moving. As she said her goodbyes, it was obvious that the meeting hadn't brought the pleasure her original smile had suggested it might. Tom and John turned to continue up Union Street.

"Shoulda' asked her about Joe," muttered Tom.

John shook his head. "No. He was there in Pensioners' Court with Jimmie. Better if she doesn't hear about that."

"Could've asked about Jessie's man, though."

"What man?"

"Her fancy man. I was supposed to be findin' out about him, remember? Rose would've known if she was seein' somebody."

John shook his head slowly. "You've said too much to her already," he said.

"How?"

"Worrying her. We won't get any answers by upsetting folk."

"Huh, we won't get no answers if we don't ask no questions," said Tom. "I'd like to know a bittie more about that new shipwright Glover. Seems he's been makin' some friends."

"Oh?"

"Aye. Willie Johnston, for a start."

"What d'you mean?"

"I saw him dinner time. Glover's been along to see him. Paid off some of what Jimmie owed him."

John whistled his surprise. Perhaps he'd need to reassess Glover.

"I wondered, though," said Tom. "That beard o' his."

"What about it?"

"Do you no' remember Donald Simpson tellin' you Jimmie was with Joe and another man with a beard. Coulda been him."

John nodded. There were plenty of bearded men around but it was a coincidence worth looking at.

"That's right," he said. "Jessie said Jimmie was doing some business on Saturday."

"There you are, then. Maybe I'll go and have a word with Donald. See whether it coulda been Glover he saw."

Mention of Donald reminded John of something which had stayed with him after his visit to the sail loft.

"Speaking of Donald," he said, "you remember I told you there was blood splashed around his place, from Billy Murray and himself?"

"Aye. That's nothin' new."

"No, but it made me start thinking about Jimmie." He paused and called back the image of the body on the beach. "He should've had blood all over him. From the fid holes. But he didn't. There were cuts and bruises, but not much blood."

"Maybe the water washed it away."

"Aye, maybe. But there wasn't even much staining on his clothes."

They'd arrived at the Bridewell's entrance.

"Well," said Tom. "You can ask Bessie about it."

The institution was only about thirty years old. Lots of municipal money had been spent to create an imposing, five storey building. The top floor was a hospital and, beyond its elegant gateway and porter's lodge, it had a garden and an area in which prisoners could exercise. Its intention was to remove petty felons from the sources of temptation and occupy them with useful work. But, despite the fact that it was heated by steam, it was still a place of incarceration and friendlessness. There were one hundred and nine cells, each one eight feet deep by seven feet wide and just over seven and a half feet high.

Moving through its big gate out of the sunlight, John and Tom felt the physical gloom matched the many miseries held within its walls. Once inside the building itself, they were in an alien world. Its dank silence held lots of little echoes and the scuffling of its restless inmates. Some of them banged and clanged things against the walls now and then but most of them knew that, once they were locked up, they'd left hope in the street outside. They lay in their cells, singing to themselves, coughing, wheezing and hungry for sleep. They worked until eight o'clock every night, starting at six in the morning in winter and five in summer. It was better than deportation but few recovered from it.

Charlie Dodds was on the day shift. He was one of Tom's drinking friends and asked no questions as he led them through the dark corridors and past the gray cell doors, which shone with substances John preferred not to ask about. The smells caught at their throats. With sewage in many of the streets and the fetid air that often hung over the mud in the harbor, they were used to the city's odors, but the closeness of the walls here and the dankness of the air gave the stench a sour, insistent edge. As they walked, John kept his breathing shallow to lessen its effects. At last, they stopped at the end of a row. Charlie unlocked the door, stood back for them to go in, then followed them and stood with his back to the corridor.

Bessie was squatting in a corner, looking as if she belonged in the dirt-smeared, squalid space. The light was dim and she squinted up at them, wondering what other torments they were bringing to her. When she saw that it was John and Tom, she brightened and felt an absurd hope. They couldn't possibly be there to accuse her.

"Bless you, Big John," she said, surprising him once again by crossing herself. "You've come to help me. Bless you, son."

Gently, John explained that by getting caught with her hand in the woman's bag, she'd made it difficult for anyone to do much in the way of help. All he could promise was that he'd speak on her behalf when the courts tried her and try to get them to be easy on her. They had to listen as she protested her innocence, said that the woman had made a mistake, pleaded hunger, illness and, in a final twist, even suggested that she was pushed against the woman by the real thief, although she had no idea who it was.

"Aye, aye," said John. "As I said, I'll do what I can. But that's not what we wanted to ask you about."

Immediately, she fell silent, unwilling to commit herself to anything until she knew the nature of the next accusation.

"You thinkin' o' becomin' a sailmaker?" asked Tom.

Still Bessie said nothing.

"Only I was wonderin' what you're doing with a bag full of fids."

Bessie's eyes looked away from them, searching the floor of the cell for an answer. The question had taken her by surprise.

"There's mad folk about these days," she said. "A girl needs to protect herself."

John looked at her. "Girl" was not a word he'd have used to describe her.

"You used one of them, too, didn't you?" he said.

"No."

The reply was too quick and her eyes continued to look anywhere but at their faces.

"They're going to ask you about it, Bessie," said John. "There was blood on one of the fids."

"It was old. I cut myself. Long time ago. Maybe it was from some meat. I use them sometimes to cut things."

"Bessie." John drew out the name, using the sound to tell her that they knew she was lying.

"It's... I..."

She gave up, at last looking up at him, her face pleading for help, showing the hopelessness of her state.

"What about Jimmie's watch?" asked Tom. "Where'd you get that?"

Bessie shook her head, started to deny any knowledge of it, then stopped and looked down again. By now, there were tears in her eyes. She rubbed at them with her sleeve. John took a step forward, turned and sat beside her, leaning back against the wall.

"Hellish place, this," he said.

Bessie said nothing.

"If they think you stole the watch, too, they'll keep you here a lot longer. Might even transport you."

This time she looked at him, her fear obvious.

"I don't know how you got the watch, Bessie. I don't know what you've been doing with that fid either. But I know you're not as evil as some in here, and I wouldn't want you staying here longer than you need to."

Bessie nodded. He could hear her half suppressed sobbing. He meant what he was saying to her. They'd come to get information but the sight of her hunched in the darkness dug at his pity.

"You could maybe say you found the watch. Didn't know it was Jimmie's. I could tell them that."

Bessie nodded her head toward where Charlie Dodds was standing, hearing everything they said.

"Ach, Charlie's all right," said John. "He knows who the real criminals are."

Charlie made a big show of pretending not to hear them.

"But they won't believe me, John. They never do."

"Aye they will, Just say you found it further along the beach."

Bessie thought about this, gradually controlling her snuffling and transferring more of the liquids running from her eyes and nose onto her greasy sleeve.

"Aye," she said at last. "Maybe they'll listen. I didna take the money, did I?"

"What money?"

"Jimmie's money."

John's silence told her that she'd surprised them, that they didn't know much at all. They were looking at her, waiting. It helped her to regain control of herself.

"I took the watch, right enough," she said, very quietly so that Charlie couldn't hear. John had to bend toward her to catch the words. It meant that he also caught more of her smell.

"But I left the money where it was."

"Bessie, what money?"

"In his coat pocket. Wee bag. Full of coins. Sovereigns, crowns, all gold and silver. I thought o' takin' it. Could've hid it. But it was too much. You don't find that much scrapin' along the beach. I'd have been caught. Folk woulda' known it wasna right."

John looked at Tom, who'd also squatted to hear her words. Neither of them knew how to react to the news. John tried to get it straight in his mind.

"You found a bag of money in his pocket?"

"Aye."

"And you put it back?"

Bessie nodded.

"You didn't keep any?"

She was silent.

"Bessie."

"Two half crowns," she said, her voice quieter. "There was so much, I didna think they'd be missed."

"Then what?"

"I came up to see you."

"So when we went back to Jimmie, the money was still in his pocket."

"Well, I didna take it."

And yet Jessie, and Willie Johnston too, had told John that Jimmie's pockets were empty. He remembered Joe and the black pebble.

"He used to wear a sort of stone around his neck on a cord. Did you see that?" he asked.

Bessie shook her head.

"I never saw his neck," said Bessie, quickly, the tears springing into her eyes again.

"All right, lass," said John. "Don't fret. We'll see what we can do."

Tom had a big grin on his face. The more complicated things got, the better he liked it. It wasn't a feeling which John shared. They'd come hoping to move nearer to a solution; instead, Bessie had added a new complication. What had happened to the money she'd left in his pocket?

CHAPTER SEVENTEEN

It was evening, and Helen was looking at her reflection in the long gilt mirror. She held her head at different angles, inspecting her neck, her cheeks, her eyes, licking the tip of her finger and running it over her lips, making them shine. She smoothed her bodice, adjusting its neckline where it swept down from her shoulders. The fichu had been discarded as soon as John had left that morning and she now let her fingers trail across the soft flesh at the top of her breasts. Her mother watched from her chair, her crochet work set aside on its arm.

"Stop admiring yourself for a moment," she said. "You've done little else since Mr. Grant left. It was bad enough that you were so forward with him."

"Forward?" said Helen.

"Yes. I cannot imagine why you should think of speaking of such things as the death of Mr. Crombie. You were shameless."

"If I was, I'm sorry, but I cannot still my curiosity, mother. Really, it is a mystery. He did not fall into the river, he was pushed."

"Who told you so?"

Helen waved a hand to suggest that that was unimportant.

"But no one is investigating it," she said. "It seems that the watch knows nothing of it."

"Then there is nothing to know."

"Yes there is. And I shall find out what it is."

"Helen," said Elizabeth, concern replacing her irritation. "I have no idea where these ideas come from but I forbid you to pursue this matter further."

"But mother..."

"Suppose for a moment that someone did push Mr. Crombie into the water. Such a person would be capable of doing the same thing to someone else. You must put aside any thoughts of speaking of this matter again."

"Mother..."

"Promise me."

Helen considered her reply. Her curiosity was too strong for her to be able to keep such a promise if she made it, and yet she wanted to reassure her mother.

"Mother, you were once twenty-three years old," she said.

Elizabeth waited, wondering what the relevance of the comment might be. Helen smiled.

"But it was hundreds of years ago and you have forgotten what it is like."

Elizabeth couldn't resist the smile on her lips and in her eyes. She brought her hands together, steepling her fingers in front of her chest.

"I think I must suggest to your father that you are in need of correction," she said.

"Then I shall leave home."

"Good."

The door opened and Anderson came in. He'd heard their voices as he climbed the stairs and they'd begun to draw from him some of the frustrations of his day and especially those generated by Glover's visit. He kissed his wife on the cheek, allowed his own to be pecked by Helen and eased himself gratefully into a chair. When the maid arrived with his glass of whisky, Helen went to take it from her and handed it to her father, seating herself in the chair beside his as she did so. He sipped, savored the warmth and the flavor then looked at her. Her eyes were fixed on his.

"Is there something you wish to tell me?" he asked, slightly disturbed by the intensity of her gaze.

She shook her head.

"No. It's just that Mama and I have had a very pleasant day and you've been working hard and it's nice that you can now relax. Tell us what you've been doing."

"No, no. It's all far too dull, and I'd rather not think about it. Tell me about your day. How did this morning's sitting go?"

He looked from one to the other of them and didn't notice the slight blush that colored Helen's neck and cheeks.

"Very well," said Elizabeth. "Mr. Grant is a very talented artist."

"What did he say about the figurehead?"

"Nothing at all. In fact, he said very little about anything, despite or daughter's constant chatter and incessant questions."

Anderson looked at Helen, a smile in his eyes.

"I suppose you now wish to be a figurehead carver."

Helen seemed to consider the question.

"Well," she said at last, adopting her serious voice, "I did discover that, for an average figurehead, I would need a block of American fir weighing some thirteen hundred pounds or more and that, at one shilling and eight pence per cubic foot, that would cost approximately three pounds."

Anderson laughed.

"Very reasonable."

"But, of course, my creative skills would multiply that fivefold."

"Fifteen pounds? No one will employ you at such rates."

"I know. And so, since mathematics is too taxing for a woman, I shall content myself with playing the piano after dinner, joining the Ladies Working Society and selling needlework."

It was the sort of remark she'd often made in anger so, to make sure he knew that this time she was joking, she ended the sentence with a huge, theatrical sigh.

"My sympathies are with the Ladies Working Society," said Elizabeth.

The three of them laughed and Helen, anxious not to return to talk of the sitting and its deception, wove more deliberate fantasies of the sort of employment opportunities available to her and to the other young ladies of Aberdeen. She painted pictures of women driving the mail coaches, their skirts flying as they drove their teams north from Edinburgh through the January blizzards. She saw them heaving at the wheel of a fishing smack half way to Scandinavia, running before a gale, with an all-female crew securing the gear on deck as the breaking seas washed around them. Then, with her parents' defenses lowered by her playfulness, she gradually shifted to scenes which she found far less fanciful, scenes where women bought and sold cargoes, organized crews and voyages, opened trading possibilities that had so far not occurred to the men who controlled the city's commerce. She was careful to keep the lightness in her tone and frequently had to bite back criticisms of her parents' maddeningly passive acceptance of traditional wisdoms. Indeed, her strategies were so effective that, when she took the chance to hint gently at the possibility that she might one day help her father in some of his work, he didn't dismiss the suggestion as being part of her usual frivolity. He obviously still found the notion to be faintly absurd but, for a change, he was prepared to talk about it.

"Of course, I know that there are limits," she said at one point, "but if I made sure that my horizons were very close to me, perhaps I could find some small successes. That would suffice."

Her father gave a small laugh.

"However limited your vision, you would always find something which obscured your ideals," he said.

"Even if I was buying just one spice from one trader in China and bringing it back to Aberdeen in a corner of one of your ships?"

As he answered, his eyes wandered to look through the window at the tops of some masts swaying as the tide lifted the vessels outside.

"I would not wish upon you any of the ills which that would involve," he said.

"I could bear them," she replied.

He shook his head and looked across at his wife.

"There are some..." he began, but then stopped as his wife returned his glance. "It's a cruel business," he went on. "It breaks the hardest of men and I would find it impossible to forgive myself if I exposed you to any of it."

"But if it were just a tiny corner of a ship, a single bale of material, a single barrel of spice."

"That would soon seem too small, even for you. It's so difficult to explain, but a step into commerce is the start of a journey which can be very frightening. Some think it's simply a matter of earning a living, making enough funds to buy a house, clothes for your back, food for your table. They know nothing of it. It's much more."

"Tell me," said Helen, eager to make the most of his unaccustomed expansiveness.

She was leaning toward him, her hands on the arm of his chair, her whole posture betraying the intensity of her interest. He looked at her face, her wide, bright eyes and knew that she had his own fierce energy in her and that, had she been a son, she would have fought the same battles as he had, with the same success. His wife, watching the two of them, felt the same conviction. Helen resembled her physically, but she was much more energetic, more self-sufficient. For many years now, Elizabeth had seen the evidence that Helen had indeed inherited much of her father's determination.

"In many ways, money is an evil invention," said Anderson. "Men pursue it not for what it can buy but simply for itself, simply to possess more and more of it."

"Is that what you do?" asked Helen, surprised at his words.

Anderson sipped his whisky slowly and considered her question. There was no smile in his face.

"I think perhaps I do at times. I used to think that it was simply a question of... well, power. And it is, of course. But it's also something else. A necessity maybe. And a destructive one, too."

He stopped, his thoughts far away.

"Helen," said Elizabeth, her voice very low. "Your father has been working very hard. I think we should speak of something else."

"Men want more and more," said Anderson, his thoughts still on some horizon inside him. "They already live pampered lives, they have more carriages than they can use, and they still struggle on. Why?"

"To be secure," said Helen.

"Yes, but there are merchants here who are more secure than the Bank of Scotland, yet they still haggle over pennies. No, it's... it's part of a process. One sets it in motion and it has to be maintained. And I'm part of it and successful and still I don't understand it."

He took another sip and looked from Helen to Elizabeth, expecting some sort of response. But the frankness of what he was saying left them stranded. Work and all its associations were usually left outside and yet here he was not just talking to them about it but also exposing the thoughts which lay behind it, the philosophy which his dealings concealed.

"Are you really so determined to try yourself in such a world?" he asked, taking Helen's hand in his own.

"Yes," she said.

He looked hard at her beautiful face and gave a little nod.

"It's a vile place," he said. "And I would do anything to protect you from it. But if you're determined, we shall see what you think of it when you've looked at it from the inside."

"What do you mean?" she asked, intrigued by his words.

"I shall make a bargain with you. A business arrangement."

"Very well."

"I'll open my study to you and you can look through the mountains of paper I need to negotiate. If that does not sicken you and if your curiosity still pricks you, we shall talk some more."

Helen's lips curled into a wide smile.

"But my hope," he went on, "is that you'll find it so tedious and so soul-less that you'll content yourself with the gentler things in life."

Elizabeth was shaking her head.

"You should not encourage her, William," she said, before wagging her finger at Helen and continuing, "And you would do better to leave the largest possible distance between yourself and the world of trade."

"But if I learn from what father says..." Helen began.

Anderson raised his hand and put a finger to her lips.

"Yes. Do," he said. "I learned my ways from your grandfather. He suffered far more than I ever have in commerce."

Once again, Elizabeth looked at him, her face serious, a little anxiety in her brow.

"His dealings were harsher," Anderson went on. "He taught me a lesson which you will no doubt deplore but which you would do well to consider. Value yourself above others. In business, you can rely on no one."

Helen raised her own hand and lifted his fingers away.

"That's a sad lesson, Papa."

"Sadder than you can imagine. From such a standpoint, the step to despising people is a very small one."

Elizabeth looked at the tableau of her husband and daughter, the two of them serious, somber, their mood deeper than a few moments ago when Helen was playing her games.

"Well, well," she said. "Your day must have contained some heavy news for you to come home so full of philosophy."

It had the desired effect. Anderson gave a small laugh.

"No, no," he said. "It's just that there are some things about business that cannot be explained."

"Never mind," said Helen. "That will all change when the Elizabeth Anderson is launched."

"Perhaps," said Anderson.

"Certainly," insisted Helen.

"Ah, if you but knew. This latest shipwright may still prove to be as troublesome as your late and unlamented Mr. Crombie. He is already finding ways to multiply expenses."

"Is that what Mr. Crombie did?" asked Helen, glad of the chance to speak of him while her father was in such an expansive mood.

"In many ways, yes."

"Did everyone know of it?"

Anderson looked at her.

"Everyone? How should everyone know of my dealings with him?"

"I just wondered whether other people found him... what did you call it?... troublesome."

"Oh, I'm sure of that," said Anderson. "Mr. Crombie was a very unpleasant, unpopular man."

"Because of money?"

Anderson drank the last of his whisky and stood to walk over to the window.

"You see? Here we are, back at the awful subject of squeezing money out of the air," he said. "It's far better for you to have nothing to do with the likes of Mr. Crombie. Forget your dreams of trade. You're a beautiful girl with a beautiful life."

He turned to look at her, his silhouette dark against the sky outside.

"And that brings me to the other side of our business arrangement," he said.

Helen was at once wary. She waited.

"You should marry."

Both Helen and Elizabeth were frozen by his words. It was a suggestion he had made before but Helen's progressively strengthening resistance to the idea had kept it at bay for a very long time. She felt an anger rise inside her but she held her tongue. There was no question of her agreeing, but she wanted the other part of the bargain and knew that, if she spoke her mind, it would be lost and the evening might well crumble into disputes and sulking. It was her father who broke the little silence that had fallen between them.

"Of all the choices I made, that was the best," he said, with a smile. "Your mother has helped me to keep this corner of the world apart from the troubles and trials of my work. Marriage is more of a blessing than even the church knows. Especially when you're fortunate enough to find someone as extraordinary as your mother."

Once again, he had rendered them speechless. Elizabeth wondered whether he had perhaps drunk something else before his whisky. It was a long time since she had heard him say such things. Helen was utterly bewildered. She found it hard to associate the opinions being expressed with her father. But his next words to her sent him spinning firmly back into his accustomed role.

"This may sound like idle talk, but I really do believe what I'm saying. I will do everything I can to protect my home and my family from the hurts that others can do. Nothing will turn me from such a goal. I'm sure that, with a family of your own to manage, you'll be just the same. So, let's banish all these thoughts of commerce. We must find you a husband."

CHAPTER EIGHTEEN

John had resisted the temptation to get back to his carving and, instead, went home to have some supper. It would have been easy for him to eat in one of the harbor's inns but he liked the relaxation of preparing and cooking meals, even though there was no one to share them. One of his neighbors had brought a thick chunk of cod back from the market for him. It was fresh and John was suddenly aware of his hunger as he washed it and began drying it with a cloth.

His mind wandered back over the day, finding that, despite the discovery of the ditty box and Bessie's revelations, it was not Jimmie Crombie who preoccupied him but Helen Anderson. As he'd been sketching her, she'd asked him so many questions, darted her thoughts in so many directions that the simple lines and curves on his paper were trying to catch not just a physical object but a presence which shifted like the air and moved in and out of colored shadows. At Jessie's it had been her beauty which had fascinated him; today, it was the mystery inside it which had drawn him deeper.

He dragged his thoughts back and realized that the fish was as dry as it was ever going to be. He dipped it into a mixture of flour, salt and pepper, patted the powder into both sides of it then dipped it in milk and back into the flour mixture again. He dropped it into a pan with some thinly sliced potatoes, where it spat and crackled.

After he'd eaten it and finished a wedge of cheese, he set off for Jessie's again. He heard the ships' bells sounding and guessed that it must be well after nine o'clock when he got there. The sky was full of a light like pale blue china and there were still men and horses at work along the quays. The ditty box was wrapped in a scrap of canvas under his left arm. He knew that it hadn't found its way into the bow of the ship by accident;

someone had put it there. Giving it to Jessie was a risky option because men often used their boxes to conceal things which they preferred their wives not to know about. It didn't matter to Jimmie now, of course, but Rose's warning had stayed with him and he wanted to do nothing which would cause Jessie any more grief.

As she opened the door and invited him in with a smile, he couldn't help noticing the smell of tobacco. It hung in the air, fresh and sweet, and had none of the stale smell of old smoke which had thickened and settled in furniture and hangings. The windows were too small to let in much of the late evening light and the room was lit by just one oil lamp, which made shadows jump in the far corners and threw a yellow tinge across the table and up into the ceiling.

She offered him a drink but he shook his head. He unwrapped the ditty box, put it on the table, sat down and told her how and where he'd found it. As she listened, her eyes stayed mainly on the box and the expression on her face was hard to read. When she did speak, her words surprised him.

"Do me a favor, John. Stop askin' about Jimmie."

He didn't know what to answer. She saw a frown come to his face as he looked away from her.

"Rose told me. About Bessie. All of it. I know fine somebody killed him. But I don't care. Davie Donne's been here pokin' about, askin' questions, stinkin' the place out with his bad breath. He won't let go of it, but I hope you'll let it lie."

"What sort of thing's he been saying?"

Jessie made the tossing away gesture with her hand.

"Ach, askin' how much Jimmie left me, where I was on Saturday. The fool thinks I had somethin' to do with it."

"Is that what he said?"

"No. He didna have to. I just knew. The man's a viper, John."

John nodded slowly.

"I'm not like him, Jessie, " he said. "I'm not asking things just from curiosity. I saw that it wasn't an accident..."

She reached over and laid her hand on his arm.

"I know that, Big John. But you know that Jimmie's no loss. I just want to forget all about him now. Get on with it. Make the most of it."

"Aye, lass, but it'll be a while yet before it's over. It's not just me that noticed. Willie Johnston saw the marks, and Tom Leach knows about them. There's probably others, too."

She gave him a small smile.

"Aye. You'd maybe be surprised if you knew," she said.

"I was. Earlier today. I was at Anderson's house, sketching his wife and daughter. She knew about it."

The smile vanished. Jessie was suddenly very quiet. Then, she broke the silence with a little laugh.

"She won't let things lie, that Helen."

"'Helen'? Is she a friend of yours then?"

The laugh subsided into a smile again.

"Aye. She came back, you know. Here. To see me. She's a kind-hearted lassie. It was me that told her about Jimmie. Dinna ken why."

The news surprised John. He didn't know how to respond. Jessie didn't give him time to.

"There must be others knows about it," she said, sitting back in her chair. "They'll all start askin' questions in the end. I suppose it's better if it's you. If you find out anythin', you'll maybe understand."

"What d'you mean, understand?"

She didn't look at him. Her eyes were on the pale square of window beside the front door. She was very still.

"Killin' somebody. It's no' always an evil thing. Folk do it for all sorts of reasons. If Jimmie was murdered, it wouldna surprise me. And maybe I wouldna want the murderer found out."

Although it was all very unexpected, John understood what she was saying. When she did eventually look across, the lamplight caught the tears in her eyes. It made him feel bad. Responsible.

"He's done me a favor, John," she said. "He's no' a murderer, he's a Good Samaritan."

She dabbed her eyes, shook her head and suddenly stood up.

"Well, maybe you don't want nothin', but I'm takin' a dram," she said, reaching up and taking a bottle from the top shelf of a dresser against the back wall.

"Well, well, just the one then," said John, glad of the chance to change the mood.

When she'd poured their drinks and they'd clinked glasses and sipped, she put down hers and pulled the ditty box toward her.

"I've seen this many times but never had the chance to look inside it," she said. "It must be worth somethin', though."

"Why's that?"

"The man Glover was here today askin' about it."

John looked quickly at her.

"What did he want?"

Jessie shrugged her ignorance.

"Said it had some things about the boat in it. Some plans or papers or somethin'. Jimmie'd told him it was here."

She was releasing the catch as she spoke. John was apprehensive that she might find something which would bring back her tears, but he was also curious about what might be in the box that made it worth hiding. The first thing she produced from it seemed to answer the question right away. It was a small leather bag. Its top was tied with a piece of hemp and the dull chinking from inside it suggested that it was some sort of purse. Jessie pulled at the hemp and poured the contents onto the table. They were both astonished by what they saw. There were coins, all gold and silver, which must have added up to fifteen pounds or more. Jessie stared at it, her head shaking slowly in disbelief.

"You're a rich woman," said John, to break the spell. "Will you marry me?"

It had the effect he'd wanted. She gave a big laugh.

"Yes, of course," she said. "You want to come up the stairs and have a wee practice first?"

"I would like to, but I've got a bad leg," he replied.

Her laugh subsided to a smile and, with the tears gone, the prettiness was back in her face.

"I knew this would be here," she said.

"How?"

"Saturday, when he came home. He took some out of it and put it in his pocket. I dinna ken how much."

John wondered whether to mention the fact that Bessie had found money on him and that it had vanished but decided to say nothing at present. There were already enough complications for Jessie to cope with.

"What a close bastard he was," she said. "Keepin' this away from me."

"Maybe that's what Glover was after."

"Aye, maybe. Or there's all this stuff," said Jessie, starting to take more things out of the box. There were scraps of paper, some letters and invoices, an old seaman's knife and a small bundle tied with twine. She started to look at them but, not being a particularly gifted reader, soon gave up and pushed them all back into the box. She picked up her glass and took a long swig of whisky. It bit at her throat and she had to wait a moment before speaking again.

"You can take it with you, John," she said. "There's maybe stuff there that Mr. Glover needs. I wouldna ken. And if there's anythin' else about me, I don't want to hear it. Do what you like with it. Burn it if it's no use to you."

She pushed the box to him, guiding it round the heap of money, which she began to pick up and put back into its pouch.

"I'll hang on to this, though, if you don't mind."

"You're marrying me, so I'll get it anyway," he said.

As she tied the hemp around the pouch, she smiled and said, "You're right, Big John. I am a rich woman now." She lifted the pouch. "No' just this neither. Folks is tryin' to give me money all the time. Willie Johnston was here today. Gave me nigh on seven pound. Said it was money he owed Jimmie."

John couldn't cope with this. Puzzles came tumbling in from all directions. Willie Johnston didn't owe Jimmie anything. In fact, it was the other way round; he'd complained about his debts. So why the reversal? It couldn't just be that he was being charitable. Not Willie.

"Willie owed Jimmie money?" he said.

Jessie nodded, all her original sadness gone.

"That's what he said."

"I don't understand any of this," said John.

"Don't try," said Jessie.

She drained her whisky and came round the table to stand in front of him. He got up and she put her arms round his waist. He was a good foot taller than she was and, as she looked up at him, the lamp lit the right hand side of her face, rounding her jaw line, throwing shadows into her eyes and glistening on her lower lip.

"Now then," she said, a smile playing through the words, "about us gettin' married. You sure you don't want to practice."

"It's this leg," he replied. "It's bad when I'm standing up, but even worse when I'm lying down."

She laughed, lifted herself onto her toes to kiss him and said, "We don't have to lie down."

For the rest of his visit, they managed to stay at the same level of lightness. Maybe it was the money which had done the trick, but John didn't care. He was happy enough to sit chatting with her, teasing and flirting. At one point, when her eyes were crinkled half shut in laughter, he had a sudden flash recollection of how Marie's eyes used to look even more cat-like than usual when she laughed. As ever, it sent ripples of regret through him but Jessie's mood didn't allow that to last. When he eventually left to go home, he apologized for the fact that his bad leg had prevented them practicing for marriage and adopted an extravagant, elaborate limp as he walked away. It brought more bubbles of laughter from her and the night felt warm and good.

He was tired but couldn't resist the pull of the box. Once inside his own house, he lit the lamp and started to sift through its contents. Most of the pieces of paper related to ships launched years before, some of which had since foundered while others were still trading up and down the coast. In each, there was some reference to the part Jimmie had played in their

147

construction. There were old invoices from as far back as 1819, all paid and all listing healthy sums handed over to "James Crombie, Shipwright". The letters were more interesting. Three were from a woman to whom Jimmie had obviously promised marriage and who scribbled her slow, careful love in phrases she must have taken from books. The romance had taken place eighteen years before and, whoever "Ruth" was, she had eventually said a bitter, tearful farewell on October 17th 1822, wondering "whether you ever felt for me the boundless sympathy my love sent out to you at every evening's dying".

But the items that were of real interest were in the small bundle. When he untied the twine, John saw right away that the pieces of paper it held were all more recent gatherings. There were cuttings from the Journal, mostly referring to the progress of Jimmie's present contract. Others featured Anderson and various business successes. There was even one from long ago which was a simple announcement of the death of Anderson's father. It gave no details, except to say that it followed hard on the heels of another misfortune, the loss of one of his vessels in the north Atlantic, which disappeared with all its crew and cargo.

The piece of paper which John found most intriguing, however, was an invoice from the editor of the Journal addressed to and apparently paid by Anderson. It purported to be for an advertisement in the issue of April 22nd but it was for a sum large enough to have bought several pages of space.

John set it aside and went to look in the basket sitting beside his hearth. He bought the Journal most Wednesdays and kept it to light the fire or to wrap bundles of kindling that he brought back from work. It had been too warm for fires recently and he knew he would find the copy he was looking for. He slid it from amongst the others, shook it free of dust and set it on the table. Carefully moving his eyes down the various columns on all the pages, he searched for whatever Anderson was paying for.

And found nothing. Dr. Allison was insisting that tooth extraction was a thing of the past thanks to just one application of his "unparalleled and specific cure for the toothache, rheumatism of the gums, etc." His "corn solvent" apparently worked equivalent wonders at the other end of the body. Others offered medicines, stallions to cover mares, passages on steamers, lessons in all sorts of disciplines, houses for let, but nothing that could remotely be connected with Anderson.

It was yet another puzzle but John's mind was now racing. It was past midnight but sleep felt far away. He boiled water to make a jug of coffee and sat with Jimmie's box and its papers on the table before him, forcing himself to concentrate on the meaning of the invoice and ponder why it was in Jimmie's possession. The money had certainly been paid, but not for anything in the paper. Perhaps there was a simple explanation but, if not, the document gave whoever owned it an interesting hold over Anderson. John couldn't guess at the dealings which the invoice concealed but the more he thought about it, the more certain he became that Jimmie had come by it illegally and had been using it. Jessie had said that she'd frequently seen him with sums of money which he'd claimed were connected with Anderson. Given Jimmie's character, John felt sure that he'd found out the secret of the contribution to the Journal and had used it to squeeze money out of the man. That was a dangerous game and Jimmie might have paid a high price for playing it.

CHAPTER NINETEEN

Helen had had a wakeful night. She had forced to the back of her mind her renewed anxieties that her father might be somehow entangled in Mr. Crombie's death. The fact that he had found him "troublesome" and that he knew that he was being cheated by him confirmed her earlier fears. The idea was too alarming to entertain, and yet it had made her mind work and kept sleep at bay. In the morning, after breakfast, she asked her father if she could walk with him to his office. It was an unusual request but one which pleased him. The previous evening had been exactly the antidote he needed and walking along the quays with his daughter on his arm would prolong it further.

Thanks to the continuing warm weather, the harbor smell was as strong as ever but, like everyone else, they accepted it as part of the landscape. The tide was rising again and, all along the quayside, hulls curved high above them and spars and yards dipped gently across one another, scratching familiar patterns against the pale morning sky. They threaded through the workers, many of whom raised their hats as they passed while crewmen on board their ships looked at Helen and thought thoughts that guaranteed their damnation.

"I need to ask you a question, Papa," she said as they passed the harbor office at the bottom of Marischal Street.

"Ah. I knew that walking with me was not just for the pleasure of my company."

She squeezed his arm. "Don't be silly. You know how I like seeing these poor creatures tremble before your power."

Anderson was never sure of how to distinguish truth from irony in her observations. He said nothing.

"What did you think when you heard of the death of Mr. Crombie?"

151

Anderson stopped and turned to look at her. "What an extraordinary question."

"And what is the answer?"

Anderson shook his head and continued walking. "I was angry."

"Because of the Elizabeth Anderson?"

"Yes."

"Were you surprised that he should have such an accident?"

Again, Anderson stopped. "Why on earth are you so interested in Crombie?"

"What if it wasn't an accident?" Helen went on, unwilling to stop now.

"But it was."

"But what if..."

He held up a hand to stop her and they began walking once more.

"Whether it was an accident or not, it's now of no consequence. The new man, Glover, is possibly as much of a scoundrel as Crombie was before him but the ship will be finished and he'll be back in Dundee, or in jail, before he can cause me any harm."

"But..."

"And that is all I wish to say about Messrs. Crombie and Glover."

Helen knew better than to insist.

"One other thing, then," she said after they had walked a good distance without speaking.

"About death and shipwrights?"

"No."

"Good."

"Last night, your talk of marriage. Did you mean it?"

"Helen, you're twenty-three years old."

"Never mind my age, Papa."

"But it matters. Unless you're intent on remaining a perpetual spinster of this parish."

"And what if I am?"

He stopped a third time, turning to look at her again. His mind had already begun to move toward the day's business and he preferred to keep family matters well removed from it.

"Helen," he said, "you're a beautiful young woman. Many of our friends remark on it and they all wonder why no man has yet asked for your hand. I know of your independence but I still find it very hard to believe that you don't wish even to look for a husband."

"Well, for the present, I don't."

He held her gaze for a moment then they turned and walked on.

On their right, a horse suddenly decided that it resented having to pull a loaded cart and neighed loudly, clattering its hooves on the cobbles and flinging its head up and down to pull clear of its bridle. Some shouting and hefty whipping from the man leading it, however, quickly convinced it that resistance brought only pain and, with just a couple of snorts and a final toss of the head, it accepted the inevitable and clopped passively on.

"If I did marry, would you let me choose the man?"

"Of course," said Anderson, adding quickly, "within reason."

They were silent for a while, then Helen broke the spell.

"If I really don't want to get married, will you make me?" she asked, staring ahead at the masts beside Trinity Quay.

Within himself, Anderson knew that such a course of action would be useless and would alienate her totally. It was certainly time for her to set up her own home but he knew he could never force her to do so. The pain his own father had caused him ensured that he would never knowingly cause his daughter any distress.

"Of course not. If you really are so set against it, I won't insist."

"But the other part of our bargain, the papers in your study, is that still open?"

Anderson smiled. "You know, my dear," he said. "You may already have what it takes to succeed."

"Why?"

"You've struck a bargain with William Anderson and succeeded in discarding your own responsibilities while retaining your advantage. There are few who could do the same."

"I'm my father's daughter," said Helen, giving him a peck on the cheek. "Can I start my education today?"

"Education?"

"My researches into the papers in your study."

"It would be better if I were there to guide you but I see no harm in you finding things for yourself. But don't make a mess. Put things back as you find them."

"Yes, sir," she said. "Now, tell me what you'll be doing today."

Although the day's projects were now at the front of his mind, he was reluctant to discuss them with her. She belonged to the refuge in which he escaped them, a world with different, sweeter limits. With her and Elizabeth he could play a gentler role and leave aside the compulsion for revenge.

He patted the hand which rested on his arm and said, "I shall be making money."

****

When Helen got home, she found so many drawers and cabinets and shelves in her father's study that she didn't know where to start. The temptation was to go straight to the papers relating to the Elizabeth Anderson to search out any clues there might be to his contacts with Mr. Crombie, but there was no easy way of identifying them. She decided instead to start at the beginning and, finding two cabinets with drawers labeled with years and months, she looked for the earliest days of her father's transactions.

His father had left him three fine properties and a substantial sum of money, and his own activities had begun in the 1820s when he'd bought shares in the Town and County Bank and the Aberdeen Banking Company. They'd cost him hundreds of pounds but the whole banking business had grown very quickly. As he'd worked to increase his inheritance, he'd also acquired more properties, ships and other assets. From her conversations with her friends and her parents, Helen knew that fashionable dwelling houses in Union Place now sold for six hundred fifty and the latest ships cost between fifteen hundred and two thousand pounds. When she added that to the fact that the original banking shares were now worth well over three thousand pounds each, she began to understand just how powerful a force William Anderson had become in the community, even more than his father before him.

But, as her father had hoped, after the initial excitement, she began to tire of these endlessly dry sheets of paper with columns of figures and details of ownership wrapped up in rebarbative legal terminology. She felt her father's guiding presence in them, knew that the buying and selling had been dictated by his acumen, but there was little to be seen of him as a person. The correspondence which accompanied the documents was as formal as they were and gave away nothing of the bitterness and struggles that her mother had spoken of when describing her grandfather's affairs. She needed to sense the people who lived in this commercial world.

She pushed back the drawer, closed the cabinet and went to sit at her father's desk. Papers were arranged in neat piles at each side of it and, at the back, rows of little shelves and pigeonholes carried more bundles, some flat, some rolled into tubes. She riffled through the piles without trying to read anything, not sure whether she should be touching things that her father was currently working on. Everywhere, she saw the long, strong strokes of his handwriting. There were few flourishes. He wrote with economy and directness. His instructions were sparing, almost abrupt, and gave the impression of a person who made decisions quickly and moved on.

Then, at the bottom of a pile, she saw a piece of paper which was different. It was filled with false starts, scribbles which had been crossed out, additions and amendments. She slid it toward her and began to read. But, at first, it was a puzzle. It spoke of the pleasant climate which the writer was experiencing, in a place called Illinois, and was lavish in its praise of the captain and crew of one of her father's ships. "Our voyage passed in dancing, playing and most remarkably good humor in every soul on board," it read. "Truly, there can have been no more contented collection of passengers ever on the High Seas. It gives me unbounded pleasure to bear witness to the delights and comforts assured by Captain Thorsen and his crew and to encourage those contemplating migration to these shores to dally no further but to fly at once to this most agreeable part of the Americas."

Helen had read such letters in the Journal but this was in her father's hand and, with all its corrections, clearly a first attempt. She sat back, her eyes still scanning the words, and she quickly guessed the purpose of the exercise. Rather than carry real news of conditions at sea and the delights of the destination, testimonials such as this served simply to bring commercial advantage to those responsible for the voyage. From all the papers she could have chosen, she'd selected one which gave proof of her father's dishonesty.

****

John sliced chunks from a smoked ham which he had in the larder, cooking potatoes, onions and a strong, dark cabbage to go with it. As usual, he only had water to wash it down with and was surprised and pleased when Tom arrived carrying a jug of ale for them to share.

"I stopped to get it on my way," he said. "I know you never have anythin' to drink here."

They took the jug and two big cups round to the beach and sat on the wall, the sun starting to set behind them and the sea in front of them as flat as a pond. The beach and the dunes, stretching away to their left, were completely deserted and the sounds of those still at work around the harbor came only infrequently as light, distant echoes.

"So what's this?" asked John, as Tom poured the black ale into his mug. "Good works to bring comfort to lonely bachelors?"

"I thought it was time we sorted everythin' out. I mean, Bessie and everythin'. What's goin' on, John?"

John nodded his agreement that it was time things were put in order. "Bessie's only part of it. Since then... well, let's start with her. She finds the body, steals the watch but leaves the money in his pocket. Well, she does take a couple of coins. Does that sound fair enough to you?"

Tom filled his own mug, put the jug on the wall and thought about it. "Aye," he said. "She'd take the watch. She couldna know his name was in it. And two half-crowns'd be a fortune for her."

John agreed. "And she wouldn't have known what to do with sovereigns and the like," he said. "Folk would've been suspicious."

"So where did the money go? Somebody else must've come along while Bessie was up fetchin' you."

John shook his head. "They'd need to be quick. We went right back down there. It must've been one of the others there."

"Who was that?"

"Nearly everybody in Footdee for a start."

Tom appeared to be ticking items off on a list in his head. "Right," he said. "So we need to talk to Bessie again. See what else she can tell us."

"Aye, but we'll need to offer her something, see if we can't help her out of there, or make sure she doesn't get too bad a punishment."

"Oh aye, and how're you goin' to manage that? You're a judge now, are you?"

John lifted his shoulders. "We'll have to give her a reason to tell us more. That's if there's any more for her to tell."

"Right then, that's the money dealt with," said Tom, becoming almost businesslike as he obviously returned to his mental list. "It's the killin' we should be lookin' at next."

"Go on," said John, smiling at his enthusiasm.

"Right. You say he was hanged, yes?"

John nodded.

"So that woulda been in one of the workshops maybe. His own yard. Somewhere there was ropes about the place. Or on board a ship. Plenty to choose from there. Buntlines, clewlines, downhauls, sheets, halyards, braces..."

John lifted a hand to stop the flow. "It wasn't a working rope, remember. There were no lay marks, no tar."

"Aye, I forgot." Tom's mind was working hard. "But anyway, I was thinkin' that whoever it was would need to be strong. That proves it."

"Maybe."

"No maybe about it. If it was just loopin' a clewline round him and haulin' on it, that'd be bad enough, but usin' just a stray piece of hemp... He'd have to sling it over a cross jack or a beam or somethin' and pull on it direct. No blocks. Nothin'. And Jimmie's no' gonna put his head in a noose to do somebody a favor, is he?"

"They could've knocked him out first. There's always handy pieces of timber lying around. And if it was on board, he'd have two hundred or more belaying pins to choose from."

"Ah, but he still has to haul him up, and with no blocks or nothin', he'd need to be the size of you to manage it. And then, when he's hung him good and proper, and he's dead, he has to carry him all the way to the beach. No, John, the man's got to be strong."

Despite the fact that they were talking about someone they'd known, Tom was actually enjoying his speculations. John, too, felt as if they were playing some sort of game. "Easy," he said. "They use a cart. Nobody would think twice about hearing one going along the quay, even at night."

"Maybe. They still have to lift him up on it, though."

"What if there was more than one person doing it?"

"Aye, I thought of that, too. But it wasna thieves, was it? I mean, why leave the money in his pocket?"

John nodded. That was another strange part of it all; robbery could no longer be thought of as a motive and yet all the connections he'd thought of so far had some money woven through them.

"Money's in there somewhere, though," he said, half to himself.

"How?"

"You know you said Glover had paid off Willie Johnston?"

"Aye."

"Well, Willie's been passing it on to Jessie. Says he owed it to Jimmie."

"What?"

"And there was a full purse in Jimmie's ditty box. I found it in the bow of his new boat and took it along to Jessie."

For a change, Tom was silent. When John went on to tell him about the invoice he'd found and the interest that Glover had in the box, it was too much for him to take in.

"Hang on, hang on," he said. "Now you're sayin' the money's mixed up with Anderson?"

"Look," replied John, organizing his thoughts with care, "Anderson paid the editor, right?"

Tom nodded.

"And there was nothing in the paper. So, if he wasn't paying to put something in, maybe he was paying to keep something out."

"Somethin' Anderson doesna want people to know about."

"Right. So he's paying to keep it quiet. And if somebody else finds out about it, he has to pay them, too."

"And if it's in Jimmie's box, it's Jimmie who's found out about it."

"So he's paying Jimmie and that's where all this extra money's coming from."

Tom gave a sudden yell of pleasure as if they'd solved everything.

"Christ, you're clever, John," he said, a grin splitting his face. "Here's to you."

He raised his mug, emptied then refilled it and they began trying to tie Anderson's blackmail into the other threads they'd found.

"I canna understand women," said Tom, after a long pause in which each of them had sat looking out to sea, swigging from their mugs and following their diverging thoughts.

John didn't reply.

"I mean, how can Winnie Simpson let Donald shag her?"

The question was so far from what John was thinking that he laughed out loud.

"Aye," said Tom, assuming the laugh signified agreement. "I went to see him this mornin'. She was there with their two lassies. Bonny wee things. And he's standin' there over his barrel of tar, dippin' a skein of seamin' twine in it, hangin' it up and rubbin' it down with his bare hands. There's grease everywhere, 'specially on his head, and he's sweatin' and... Christ, I could barely stand bein' in the same sail loft, never mind jumpin' into bed beside him."

The image was not an exaggeration. John could picture the sailmaker in the canvas blouse and trousers he'd made for himself. The idea was that there should be no loose areas or buttons which might catch up the threads he was using to sew the sails, but the material soaked up all the tars and greases that Donald used in his work and on his person. The effect was to make him look like a bundle of oily rags.

"Anyway, I was askin' him about the man he saw with Jimmie and Joe last Saturday. He said it could easy have been Glover."

"We'll need to ask Joe."

"Aye."

"In fact, there's lots we need to ask Joe," said John.

"How?" asked Tom.

The drink had loosened John's reticence about handing secrets over to Tom and he told him about the row he'd had with Joe in the bar. When Tom heard about the black pebble, he whistled.

"That looks bad," he said. "Jimmie would never have given that away, no' his lucky stone. Joe must've took it."

"They had a fight about a lassie. Maybe it got pulled off then," said John, not really believing it himself.

"We'll have to ask him, though."

John just nodded.

The darkness was beginning to crawl in from the horizon. The jug was empty and John, his defenses already lowered by what he'd drunk so far, went back to his house to fetch a bottle of whisky. It was one of three he'd bought for last Hogmanay. Only a quarter of it had been drunk and the other two were still full. When he got back, he tipped the bottle over Tom's mug. Its size encouraged him to pour big measures and, as they downed them, the clarity of their analysis of the murder began to fade very quickly and their minds began to wander over other things. Tom's musings hopped everywhere and his changes of subject in the end held no surprises and became the norm.

"Wonder what happened to Bobbie," he said at one point.

"Bobbie who?"

"You know. Bobbie. The Eskimo. Lived with William Penny on Riverside Drive."

"Oh aye, what was his real name again?"

The conversation then deteriorated into stupid noises and laughter as they tried to pronounce the word Eenoolooapik. He'd been brought back from a whaling trip by Captain Penny and feted by the people of Aberdeen, who, unlike Tom and John, had given up trying to pronounce his name and christened him Bobbie instead. They watched him fish from his canoe in the Dee and there was a special dinner party given to see how he would behave. Eenoolooapik was more than a match for them; he realized the value of aping the things he saw people doing around him and the evening was a huge success. He'd been a feature of the Aberdeen scene through the past winter, eventually leaving in April, just a few weeks before. He sailed with Captain Penny on the Bon Accord to go home to Baffin Island because he found Aberdeen was too cold and there was, in his words, "too much cough" there.

Another silence wallowed between them. They sat, eyelids blinking slowly, warmed by the air outside and the whisky inside. Again, it was Tom who restarted the conversation.

"Of course, with Eskimos, borrowin' a married woman's normal," he said.

"Is it?"

"Yes."

"Would you lend your Mary then?"

"I'm no' talkin' about that," replied Tom. "It's no' about lendin' your own wife, it's about borrowin' somebody else's."

John couldn't help laughing at the contradiction.

"Aye, you can laugh, but it's just natural," said Tom.

"And you think that's all right?"

"Course it is."

"Whoever's doing it?"

"Aye. Everybody."

"Even if somebody's borrowing your Mary?"

"No. I already said that."

"How about Wee Tam, then?"

Tom was about to continue his insisting but the question stopped him completely. What did Wee Tam have to do with it? Internally, John was screaming at himself for what he'd said. Once again, a combination of tiredness and alcohol had cut through the restraints that normally kept him away from disputes.

"What d'you mean?" asked Tom, sounding more sober than he had before.

John shook his head and gave a deep sigh. The words were out and he would have to justify them. It would be easy to pretend that they had no real import and find a way to laugh them off but it was something that had been on his mind for a while and it needed to be brought into the open to complete their picture of the things surrounding Jimmie's death. His only regret was that he'd introduced it in such a way. His anger with himself shifted toward Tom.

"Come on, what?" Tom insisted.

"Leave it."

"No. You musta' meant somethin'. What was it?"

John swore. There was no road away from it. "Right," he said. "You told Rose you haven't seen Jessie since last Sunday."

"Aye, well?"

"Haven't had any contact with her at all."

"That's right."

"And you haven't sent anythin' round to her?"

"No. Why?"

"Well, I was there earlier in the week. So was Wee Tam. He said he was bringing her stuff from you. Said you'd be calling round yourself. That was for my benefit. And last night, when I took her the ditty box. I smelled tobacco. It was the one he smokes."

"Aye, him and hundreds more."

"I know. It's maybe nothing."

"Christ, John."

"Aye. Sorry. It's this bloody whisky. I should never touch the stuff."

Tom said nothing.

"Just forget it, eh?" said John. "It was the drink talking."

Tom stood up and looked out into the darkness that now covered the sea and beach. "He was late home last night," he said, quietly. "Smellin' of women and fish."

CHAPTER TWENTY

Rose held up both arms to protect her head. She'd rather have the bruises on them than on her face. It didn't lessen the pain but, if she kept her sleeves rolled down, she could hide the shame.

Joe hadn't been fishing for a few days and his money had run out again. He'd been looking for the jar in which Rose kept the coins with which she bought their food and other things for the house. She knew that, if she let him have it, it would mean a week or more of bread and little else for her. She curled herself into a ball in the corner, her arms still clutched around her head, her legs pulled up, her body turned in to the wall so that his punches and kicks all fell on her left side and her back. She was crying quietly, holding back the screams she wanted to let out, depriving the neighbors of the ascendancy that pitying her would give them.

Joe reached down, grabbed her arm and pulled her to her feet. He slapped at her face but, again, she turned away, catching the blows on her shoulder. He dragged her across the kitchen to the dresser, opened the middle drawer and scrabbled among the cutlery. His hand found the bread knife. He took it out and held it against her throat.

"I'll cut you, you whore. Where is it?" he spat at her, his mouth inches from her eyes.

She shook her head, the muscles of her neck tensing as his fist pushed harder into her throat. He angled the blade upwards, lying its edge across her cheek. She closed her eyes, not wanting him to see the fear there, and at once felt the pain as he pulled the knife across her cheek bone.

The blood that flowed took Joe by surprise. He hadn't intended to cut her. Her head had moved forward. He stepped back, his arms at his sides, and watched the line of blood run down her cheek and along her jaw before it dripped onto her dress. He swore and threw the knife onto the table.

"I didn't..." he said, but he couldn't bring himself to say sorry. "It was... You moved... You should've..."

Rose was looking at her hand, which she'd put to her cheek to press against the stickiness oozing from the split flesh over the bone. She stumbled across to the bowl on the stand in the corner, splashed water into it from the jug and lowered her face into it. The cold made the cut sting and she pulled back, leaving a thick pink swirling against the white china.

Joe swore again, grabbed his coat and went out, slamming the door behind him. Automatically, he felt in his pocket for the money he needed to buy a drink. There was nothing there, not even a halfpenny. Only the hard little nugget of Jimmie's black stone. He shouldn't have taken it. You couldn't borrow somebody's luck. Since that Saturday night, he'd had nothing but troubles. And, anyway, if it was such a lucky stone, why had it not saved Jimmie? He took it out and, without looking at it, threw it into the deep grass at the side of the road. He had to change things, make some different luck for himself. He wasn't finding the shoals any more. Living with Rose was a constant fight. And now, he'd cut her. He was never proud of the beatings he gave her; it made him feel bad, and that, too, was her fault. It was time to go away, sign up for a longer trip. There were plenty of skippers who could sail the boat in his place.

And, of course, the moment he signed on, they'd give him an advance on his wages. He quickened his step and headed for the shipping offices on Waterloo Quay.

****

John was up before six. His constitution and general fitness were good and, despite the fact that he drank only rarely, he had no hangover. What he did feel, though, was just as bad. It was a deep anger with himself for his lapse. His curiosity about Wee Tam and his connection with Jessie was real enough, but it should have been handled better. He should have found out for himself and not upset Tom with it. His mood made his work harder. It came between him and Helen, blunting his perceptions of the delicacies of her face. He shifted his efforts from the head, preferring the almost mechanical job of cutting away excess material around the place where he would eventually shape her waist and the folds of her dress. And all the time, the thought at the front of his mind was one of self-disgust.

Jamie had sensed the oppression coming from him and worked steadily on his own task, never wishing to step into the heavy silence in which John was buried. He was glad when, half way through the morning, John announced that he had some errands to do and walked out onto the quay.

The weather had broken. There was no rain but the clouds had climbed up out of the sea and bunched themselves over the coast and away inland to the Cairngorms and beyond. They were thick and unbroken. There would be no sun for a while. John pulled his coat around him and kept his eyes on the cobbles, acknowledging only those passers-by who actually called to him.

As he'd worked, his thoughts had reverted to the brutishness of Jimmie's death and the questions that he and Tom had been asking one another. His mood was better suited to raking about in those than to creating a thing of quality. There were people he needed to see and he might as well talk to them while the anger was still in him because he would never want to when the fogs had lifted from his mind.

Willie Johnston's sawpit was ringing with activity. He'd already finished the spars and masts for Anderson's boat and was into his next commission. John found him supervising the harnessing of one of the horses which drove the saw.

"I need to talk," he said.

Willie shook his head.

"Busy, John."

"Won't take long. Just a couple of questions."

"Questions?"

"Do you just want to waste time repeating what I'm saying?"

Willie caught the difference from John's usual tone.

"What is it?" he asked.

John flicked his head to indicate that Willie should come with him, away from the boy who was buckling the leather around the horse's girth. He walked off, not turning to see whether Willie was following. When he got to the passageway that led to the main shop, he stopped. Willie appeared almost right away.

"This had better be..."

John ignored him.

"I hear Jimmie's debts have been paid."

There was a quick turn of Willie's head. Guilty.

"It's none o' your business."

"Glover paid them. Very thoughtful of him."

Willie shook his head. He wasn't sure what this was about and didn't want to know.

"Then somebody tells me it wasn't Jimmie who owed you, it was you who owed Jimmie."

The anger was building in John's voice. Willie couldn't know that its source was elsewhere.

"What's this, John?" he said. "Why're you tryin'..."

Again, John spoke through his words.

"So either you're playing at charity, handing out money to Jessie, or you really owed it. And if you did, why did you take the money Glover gave you? See, Willie, it doesn't make much sense to me."

His tone sparked a resentment in Willie.

"I don't care whether it does or no. Like I said, it's none o' your business."

"Oh aye, it is," said John, his anger flashing in his eyes, his finger jabbing into Willie's chest. "It's my business because Jimmie had two holes in him and a rope round his neck and because you said you looked through his pockets on the beach and didn't find anything. But I know he had money. Lots of money. So something's not right, Willie. I need you to help me. I need to hear the truth from somebody."

His words came faster. Once he'd released some of the rage in him, more began building up, pushing to get through. He dropped his hand and, without realizing it, held his clenched fists slightly raised at his waist as if ready to use them.

"Look, John, there's nothin'. The money for Jessie... I just wanted to see she was all right, help her out."

"Seven pounds worth of help? That's a lot of charity, even for a big man like you."

John seemed to know a lot of details. Willie fell silent.

"I'll tell you what, I'll help you, Willie, shall I? I'll tell you all about it. Bessie finds Jimmie. She has a quick look, lifts his watch, but puts back the wee purse she finds... well, not so wee. Too big for her to risk it, anyway. And then there's folk everywhere. But when the police take Jimmie away and go through his clothes, the cupboard's bare. No purse. No money."

Willie opened his mouth to speak but John put up a warning hand, its fingers still bunched, ready.

"Now, you told me that you looked through his pockets, too. And there was nothing there. When did you do that?"

"I told you, just before they took him away."

"Aye. Anybody see you?"

"Of course not. I wouldna want folk seein' me in his pockets."

"That's what I thought."

John stopped. He stared hard into Willie's face.

"What?" said Willie, completely confused by the whole exchange and feeling the pressure of the accusation.

"Whoever took it did it without anybody seeing them. I was thinking how that could've been you. Nobody's watching. There's the purse. He owes you money. You help yourself."

"No," shouted Willie, but John saw at once that it was a lie.

"Yes," he said, just as loudly.

He waited. Willie was shaking his head but saying nothing.

"Tell me, Willie. Better me than the police."

Willie shook his head harder, then suddenly stopped and slammed the flat of his hand against the wall beside him.

"He owed me. He bloody owed me," he said, now matching John's anger. "Aye, that's what I took, the money I was due."

John felt surprise and relief. He hadn't expected anything much of the visit, only a release of some of his own frustration. He had to work to conceal his reaction.

"So why give it back to Jessie?"

"It was somethin' I did without thinkin'," he said. "I mean, Christ, robbin' a dead man, robbin' Jimmie when he's dead, it's no' normal. It's no' somethin' to be proud of."

His anger had gone as quickly as it had appeared.

"I felt bad, bad. Then Glover comes and pays me off. Says he's settlin' everythin', wants a clean slate. So there's me a thief. A real thief, no' just somebody takin' what he's owed. The money I gave Jessie, that was what I took out of his pocket. I couldna keep it."

John looked at him and noticed that Willie couldn't meet his eyes.

"Have you told anybody else?" he asked.

Willie just shook his head.

"Did you kill him?"

Willie's head snapped up and his eyes blazed.

"No."

John held his stare. At the edge of his vision, he noticed a white curl of wood caught on Willie's collar. He reached out, brushed it off, then turned and walked away.

****

Glover was adding columns of figures in the hut office. His efforts so far with his various suppliers had been very productive. Paying off some of Jimmie's debts had earned him extra credit and favorable treatment and almost all the materials he needed to finish the job had been delivered and were lying at the quayside or up on the deck of the Elizabeth Anderson. His calculations were not so reassuring, however, since, until he received the final payment from Anderson on completion, he would be running into debt. It was not yet serious and he was banking on the fact that he had earned enough good will to see him through but he would have to be careful.

John's arrival coincided with him drawing a final line under the right hand column and turning to a new page. John saw that he was wearing a clean shirt under his overalls and that he seemed to have taken more care of his appearance than before. His beard had been trimmed and his thick hair was plastered back over his head. Altogether, he seemed to belong more with the books on the table in front of him than with the usual nails, tools and timbers of his trade.

"Good morning, John. Trouble?" he said with a smile.

John shook his head, irritated again by Glover's familiarity.

"Just need to get one or two things straight," he said.

"What, measurements? Design? Times?"

"None of that. The job's in hand."

"What then? You only have to say."

John looked out of the window at the men crawling and climbing around the hull of the new boat, wanting his world to get back to the familiarity of building ships and sailing them, away from the darkness which Jimmie's death had thrown across it. There was no point in trying to be subtle. His anger had had time to recede on the way over from Willie's but, on Waterloo Quay, the sight of a carter lashing away at his horse, which had slipped on the granite cobblestones and fallen, still harnessed between its shafts, had stoked it again and his mistrust of Glover kept it bubbling.

"It's Jimmie Crombie I want to know about," he said. "And Mr. Anderson. And Willie Johnston."

The list of names put Glover on his guard. The smile slid away. He said nothing, waiting for more information.

"Been settling Jimmie's bills, I hear," said John. "Generous."

"No. It's good business. Why? Do you have an account outstanding?"

"It's not about money. Not money of mine anyway."

"Well, what then? The names you mention hardly seem to be part of..."

As he had with Willie, John cut into his words, looking to unsettle him. "When did you come up from Dundee?"

"Why?"

"I'm curious. I mean, you've slipped so easily into this contract. It's as if you already knew about it."

Glover shrugged. "Contracts are mostly the same."

"But knowing who's owed what, settling with them so quickly."

"I'm a professional."

"And you knew about me. Knew I wasn't from Aberdeen."

Glover frowned. "There's no mystery about that. Your reputation's spread further than you maybe know. And you don't make the sounds of the north east."

"But..."

It was Glover's turn to interrupt. "I've got a ship to build. What's this about?"

"Jimmie dying," said John, trying to grab the initiative back from him.

Glover seemed unmoved by the words. "His misfortune is my advantage, is that what you mean?"

"No. It's more than that. Aye, you got his job, but that's not enough, is it? What do you gain from paying his debts?"

"They're part of the job."

"Is his ditty box part of the job, too?"

At last, John got the sort of reaction he was seeking. The revelation obviously surprised Glover. His face closed. Once again, he waited.

"Why? Why ask Jessie for the box? What was in it for you?"

Glover continued to think before answering slowly, "More papers. More bills. I didn't know for sure."

"How did you know there was a box?"

"He told me."

"When? Saturday night? When you were drinking with him in Pensioners' Court?"

"I don't drink."

"Folk saw you."

"I still don't drink. Am I accused of something?"

John ignored the question. "Is that when he told you?"

"Yes," said Glover. "I don't know if he was a friend of yours but if he was, none of your secrets is safe. He was babbling to all and sundry about Mr. Anderson, the extra money he was making from him, the crimes Anderson was guilty of. If anyone else there had been sober, they would have been able to make a living out of what they learned."

"But there was only you."

"It seemed so. His brother-in-law... Joe, was even more drunk."

"Did he hear all this about Anderson?"

Glover laughed. It was a sharp, unpleasant sound.

"I'm not sure Joe heard anything at all. If he did, he wasn't interested. His mind was on fornication."

He pronounced the word in the manner of a hellfire preacher and followed it with the same, grating laugh, before adding, "Did your informant tell you that there was a whore with them, too?"

"There are whores everywhere in Pensioners' Court."

"But this one was hardly more than a child. And they put her to particularly disgusting use. They even fought over her. On the steps of one of the houses, they conducted an anatomy lesson, baring the girl's organs and comparing them with those of the two sisters they'd married. It was little more than a contest in depravity."

"Why were you there, if it disgusts you so?" asked John.

"I'd come to see Mr. Crombie, to find out whether he had work for me. After a while I saw that there was no sense to be had from him."

"So you left?"

"Yes. Joe went away with the girl, Crombie said he was going home to get the box."

"You're lying. I was told he went to his boat."

Glover's eyes flashed.

"I lie when it suits me but I'm not lying now," he said. "He was going to get the box. That is the truth and I remember it so clearly because I preferred it to the alternative that he'd suggested."

"What alternative?"

Glover shook his head as he recalled the incidents.

"I told you, they were comparing the girl's organs to those of their wives."

"And?"

"Crombie had the revolting idea of the two of them trying out one another's wives. Out of interest."

"He actually said that?" said John, his anger momentarily stilled by the words.

"Yes. To see whether sisters were different."

"What about Joe? What did he say?"

"'Help yourself.'"

John shook his head. For all his curiosity about people, there were still things he didn't understand. Glover sensed the effect that he'd had and continued, "He said that Jimmie would be doing him a favor because, with all the drinking he'd been doing, he wouldn't manage to do anything himself."

"But he still went off with the girl."

"Yes. He was calling her his princess."

"Where did they go?"

"I don't know."

"Well, which direction? Union Street? The Links?"

"No. Towards the quays. It was disgusting."

"And what did you do?"

"Went to my lodgings. I hoped to speak to Crombie again when he was sober, but... well, I didn't get the chance, of course."

"Who saw you at your lodgings?"

Glover looked at him and once again, to John's irritation, barked his laugh.

"No one. I am both abstinent and celibate. I have a profession to pursue."

He was in control of himself and John began to wonder whether he had misread Glover and was making a mistake.

"This girl," he said. "Do you think you might recognize her again?"

"Why should I?"

"Because Jimmie died," said John. "And because the watch will need to investigate everything about that night."

Immediately, from the expression that flashed into Glover's face, he realized that he should have used the threat of the watch earlier.

"Why should they?" said Glover. "The man was drunk. He fell and drowned."

"And you've profited from it."

The fear had disappeared as quickly as it had arrived. Glover's face was serious as he spoke again.

"John, I told you I intend to make my way here. Crombie's misfortune was for me a happy accident. I make no pretense at being sorry about that. Now, I must make sure that I take proper advantage of it. Paying debts is one way of making a start. Crombie owed me money, too. When I came up, it was to try to get some of it. That's why I was with him on Saturday. And the drink made him talk and, from everything he said, I knew I could do a better job than he was, make the right contacts. I needed to establish myself here."

"Then you'll have nothing to fear when the watch calls," said John.

Glover was silent for a moment.

"I think I would perhaps recognize the girl if I were to see her again," he said at last.

"Good," said John. "Then you and I will pay a visit to Pensioners' Court this evening."

Glover was about to protest but he stopped himself and gave a short laugh. "I didn't know you had such hungers," he said.

"There's much you don't know, for all your researches," said John.

"No doubt," said Glover. "You know, I even offered to work for Crombie, unpaid, just to get a foothold in the city."

John nodded his head slowly. "Well, you've got that now, haven't you? You could hardly have chosen better than Mr. Anderson."

Glover inclined his head, acknowledging that he was indeed fortunate.

"Do you plan to do more for him?"

"If he needs more, of course."

"And are you as close to him as Jimmie was?"

Glover looked at him, judging him, trying to read the thoughts behind his words.

"Close?"

"Closer than a shipwright usually gets to the man he's building for."

"What do you mean?"

"Close enough to be doing different sorts of business."

Glover just smiled. It was a smile that told John that he'd lost. It showed that none of the surprises or accusations had really disturbed him and that, if there was anything else between him and Anderson, John would certainly not find out about it.

"John," he said. "You're as new to the ship as I am. In fact, I'm the one who recommended you to Mr. Anderson."

It was information that John would rather not have had. Instead of defusing his anger, the meeting had turned it more sour, made him aware that he was wasting nervous energy on issues that he normally avoided. On the other hand, it had opened up the events of Saturday evening and given him new questions to ask. He shook his head and turned to go. Glover followed him out. They stopped at the door.

"Pensioners' Court, nine o'clock," said John.

Glover nodded.

The two of them looked across at the Elizabeth Anderson. Even under heavy cloud cover, her timbers seemed to glow.

"Ships shouldn't be mixed up in all this," said John, for himself rather than for Glover.

Glover nodded.

"I know that some people are asking questions," he said. "But it'll get done now, and people will be paid, and Mr. Anderson will have the ship he deserves, won't he?"

It was true. Whatever nastiness was being stirred by the people responsible for her, she was a good-looking vessel. John started to walk toward her.

"After all," Glover called after him, "he's paying enough for it."

CHAPTER TWENTY-ONE

Anderson was in his office, studying two sets of figures on the desk in front of him. Each was a balance sheet of one year's trading with a particular agency in Boston and he was looking for the evidence that their fees had been raised without the required notice being given. It was an absorbing task and, when a knock came at the door, he hardly heard it. After a pause, the door opened and he was astonished to see Helen standing there. He stood up immediately, the figures forgotten, and went to welcome her. He'd sensed at breakfast that all was not well with her; she'd been unusually silent and withdrawn. It was an impression that was confirmed by the solemn expression that she now wore.

"What a pleasant surprise," he said, kissing her on the cheek.

"Perhaps not so much as you think," she said.

He led her to an armchair in the window and sat opposite her.

"Another of your mysteries?"

She was silent for a moment. She hadn't returned his smile. It was clear that there was indeed something which was troubling her.

"I... I rather think that... that... the mystery is yours," she said at last.

"Tell me," said Anderson, feeling a little anxious at her obvious discomfort.

She clasped her hands tightly together in her lap, her fingers squeezing and releasing, squeezing and releasing. He reached across and placed his own hand gently on top of them. She looked up at him quickly and let her eyes fall back to look at their hands again.

"You were right," she said. "The world you work in is not pretty."

"No."

Anderson waited, knowing that she needed to say whatever it was in her own time.

"I looked at your papers," she went on. "In your study. As you said I could."

"Yes."

She looked at him again, encouraged by the softness of his tone, and this time held his gaze.

"I saw the letter," she said.

"Which letter?"

"The testimonial. The one you wrote praising Captain Thorsen."

"Ah."

"It was false, wasn't it?"

"False?"

"Yes. You were pretending to be a passenger. Bearing false witness."

"I see," said Anderson.

He tapped her hand, then stood and turned to look out of the window.

"Do you not think, then, that Captain Thorsen's passengers are treated well?" he said.

"I don't know."

"And are the estates which are being settled in America vile places, unfit for habitation?"

Helen shook her head. He reached down, took her hand and raised her to stand beside him at the window.

"You're right," he said, looking out again at the bustle in the street. "It's not a pretty pursuit. But I did warn you of that. Indeed, you've come to the conclusion I hoped for far more quickly than I expected."

She shook her head and turned to face him.

"I expected the flaws to be in others, not in you," she said. "Why do you have to deceive people? You're powerful enough to succeed without such... tricks."

Anderson smiled at her.

"My dear, you've spent a very short time looking at some papers in a study and already you're making judgments about how my world works. Deceit is at the heart of commerce. Merchants borrow and buy on the strength of cargoes that may already be at the bottom of the sea. It's a vile, vile way to behave, but it's a necessity."

Helen had expected him to be ashamed, even angry perhaps, but he spoke wearily and with tenderness. It increased the confusion that the letter had sparked in her. She'd been confident that, with her education and the sharpness of her mind, she could become part of his business, add to his successes, but she was lost already. She would have to set aside the rules by which she'd been taught to live and learn a new morality.

"I knew that some men did wicked things," she said, "but I thought that others might deal honorably. I thought that you would be..."

She stopped, unwilling to brand her father as unworthy. Anderson smiled and shook his head.

"It would be wonderful if we could all tell the truth, but those who try are quickly swallowed by the others. Truth equates to weakness. It destroys."

"You're right," she said. "I'm young, naïve. I know nothing of any of this."

"Do you still want to?" he asked.

"I don't know," she said. "Are you not angry with me?"

"For what?"

"Reading your private letters."

He smiled again.

"I knew they were there. They're part of my whole enterprise. If I'd hidden them from you, that would have been truly deceitful. It would mean that I was treating you as I treat my competitors. I would never do such a thing."

Helen felt a lump in her throat. Her father was so much more complicated than she'd ever realized.

"Will you help me to understand?" she asked, her voice breaking slightly.

He held out his arms and pulled her to him, kissing her hair.

"I fear that it will only bring you more distress," he said, "but I know that there's little that I can say to stop you."

She looked up and kissed him on the cheek.

"I only hope your mother will forgive me," he said. "Now, come and look at these figures. There's a little man in an office in Boston. He wears cravats of an outrageous color and boots with the highest heels, and I think he's trying to deceive me."

****

John was back in his workshop and, gradually, the rhythm of his mallet, the demands of the grain and the slow emergence of folds and shapes from the wood, had begun to catch at his mind and turn it away from the questions that his day's visits had multiplied. He hadn't yet done enough to see the whole figure in the wood but he was beginning to know that it was there and he eased his gouges through the surface in search of it. It was as if the tree had grown around the woman; his task was simply to release her. By late afternoon, he was ready to start working on the curves of the head and the planes of the face. As they began to appear, he chose a smaller mallet, tapping at the surface with even greater care, fearing that if he bit too deeply, the wood might bleed.

Jamie had left and John was still gratefully absorbed in his work when the big door of his shop swung open and Tom came in. As he saw him, John's spirits fell again as details of the previous evening and the day's encounters came rushing back into his head to dispel the calm of the work and remind him of his weaknesses.

Tom looked at the carving, saying nothing, showing no sign of how he judged it. John gave a few more taps with his mallet, but with no intention of making any significant cuts. He was annoyed that Tom had interrupted him but he also felt guilty about him and knew that the sooner it was dealt with, the better. He stopped and, like Tom, just looked at the wood in perfect stillness.

At last, without shifting his gaze, he said, "Sorry, Tom."

"No need."

The stillness returned. This time, it was Tom who broke it.

"I wish it was all like this," he said, pointing to the carving. "We'd know where we were, ken what to do."

"Aye, maybe."

"Anyway," said Tom, heaving a deep sigh and seeming to shake himself out of a dream, "we need to go to Jessie's."

"What for?"

"We need to."

His voice was quiet and although the words were insistent, the tone wasn't. If anything, he seemed resigned, even reluctant. John knew that, by the time he worked his concentration back to the carving, it would be too dark to continue, so he put his tools in their racks, took off his apron, pulled on his coat and followed Tom out into the gray evening.

The clouds were allowing none of the sparkling light of the past few days through and their leaden cover brought gloom to the quays and made the water look heavy and dull. As they walked toward York Place, John forced himself to recount his meetings with Willie and Glover. Tom listened but asked few questions. It was as if the information was of no interest to him and there was certainly no sign of his previous enthusiasm. John was surprised. Blurting out that his son had maybe paid Jessie a visit or two had been insensitive but did it really deserve such a strong reaction?

At Jessie's door, Tom gave a tap and pushed it open without waiting for an invitation to come in. John followed him and, in the light of the single lamp, was surprised to see not only Jessie but Wee Tam. She was in her usual chair and Wee Tam was sitting on the floor at her feet, leaning back against the side of it. His knees were drawn up in front of him and she had her arm on his shoulder, with the backs of her fingers moving slowly up and down the side of his neck. They looked up at him and he was grateful when Jessie's face broke into a smile.

"You're a terrible man, Big John," she said.

John looked from her to Wee Tam. There was nothing he could say. The look on Wee Tam's face told him that he was not as forgiving as Jessie. Tom had sat down on a bench under the window and started to fill his pipe. Jessie's smile got wider. It was as if she were enjoying the tension between them.

"You should join Davie Donne in the watch," she said. "They never seem to find out nothin'. But you... Just a sniff of 'baccy and you're huntin' down the criminals."

"Not criminals, Jessie. I was just..."

She nodded and raised a hand to stop him.

"I was jokin'."

"I'm sorry, Jessie. You, too, Wee Tam. It was no joke. None of my business. It was just, you know, the things we were finding out about Jimmie." He stopped, then added lamely, "And the whisky."

"Pokin' your nose in where it doesna belong," said Wee Tam, unimpressed by the apology.

John nodded. Jessie gave Wee Tam a tap on the neck.

"Leave him be," she said. "Can you no' see he's sufferin'? Anyway, it's your fault, no' his, with your 'baccy and your half-baked excuses."

As Wee Tam turned to argue with her, she switched her smile to him and he was left shaking his head, his protest blown away.

"So, what do you think?" she said.

"What about?" said John.

"Us. This."

John shrugged.

"Nothing, Jessie. Really. Like I said, it was because Tom and I were asking questions about Jimmie, making up all sorts of daft stories. I suppose I started taking it too seriously."

As he spoke, he wondered himself how he'd let the game of explaining Jimmie's death creep into the reality of their lives. If Wee Tam and Jessie were seeing each other, they should be left to get on with it. It was, as Wee Tam said, none of his business.

"Wee Tam's been comin' to see me for months," said Jessie, her hand stroking the big man's neck again. "I'm surprised it's still a secret. You know what folk are like when others is carryin' on."

"It doesn't matter, Jessie," said John. "You've no need to say anything."

"Aye, I do. I wanted to tell you. That's why I asked Tom to bring you along. You've a right."

The look Wee Tam flashed at him contradicted her words but he said nothing.

And Jessie told him their love story. The way she told it, it was love, too. It had started as a friendship, Wee Tam taking delight in the company of a woman who made him laugh and feel comfortable, Jessie appreciating a man who was much bigger than her husband but treated her with gentleness and respect. It had been weeks before either of them had begun to feel the pressure of the inevitable sexual excitement that was at the center of their attraction and yet more weeks before they had given in to it. Even then, they'd somehow managed to restrict themselves to kisses and embraces and tolerate the frustrations their abstinence ignited.

When they'd eventually made love, one Saturday night when Jimmie was away at his drinking, it had been glorious, but the aftermath of guilt had almost spoiled things for them. That, too, was gradually dealt with and, although sex was still exciting, their relationship had now gone beyond mere appetites and they wanted to be married.

Jessie told the story simply, embellishing nothing and acknowledging that, as a married woman, she'd been doing wrong. Wee Tam listened, nodding now and then, reaching to touch her still-caressing hand, and sometimes flicking a look at John to make sure that he was not judging them or amused by the details of a relationship that sometimes seemed more suited to a couple ten years younger than himself and Jessie. There was no need for his concern. John recognized the hungers that had driven them, appreciated the restraint they'd managed to maintain for so long and silently applauded them for the honesty of their dealings with one another. For his part, Tom sat sucking on his pipe, his face showing no sign of what he felt or indeed, if he felt anything at all.

"See, that's why I was askin' you not to ask about Jimmie," Jessie was saying, "why I said I maybe didna want you to find out who killed him."

John's frown showed that he didn't understand.

Jessie smiled again.

"Ach, for all your brains, you don't understand much, do you?"

"Probably not," said John.

Her smile lingered, then fell away as her lips set tighter.

"I... Well, when you said somebody'd..."

She stopped, shook her head and gave up trying to explain. Wee Tam reached up, took her hand and kissed it.

"She thought it was me that killed him," he said.

"Why?"

"I would have if I'd got to him first." Wee Tam's voice was hard, fierce. He glared at John. "So would you if you'd seen what he did to her."

Jessie tried to hush him but he was angry.

"No, Jessie," he insisted. "It's no' right. Folk ought to know." He turned to John again. "I was here Saturday. I usually am, with him out on the drink. You should have seen her. She didna say nothin', but I knew. I knew she wasna right." His anger gave way to tenderness. "Quiet, no' sayin' much. Sort of... holdin' herself in. I asked her what it was but she wouldna say. Then I put my arm round her and she jumps and I can see she's hurtin'."

Jessie was shaking her head.

"It was nothin' new, Tam," she said. "You know that. If he took it into his head to hit me, there wasna much I could do. I didna want you worryin about it."

Her smile came back. Wee Tam kissed her hand again.

"I went lookin' for him," he said, turning back to John. "I wanted to give him a beatin'. Aye, if I'd caught him, I'd maybe have killed him myself. The bastard deserved it."

As she heard the anger coming back, Jessie hushed Wee Tam again.

"I thought it was him," she said. "When I heard that Jimmie hadna drowned, when they started saying somebody'd killed him, I was terrified it was Wee Tam. If you'd seen him stampin' away, his great feet kickin' at poor wee stones..."

Wee Tam looked at her. There was no smile on his face.

"If Big John had seen the marks he left on you, he'd have wanted to murder him, too."

"Oh aye, I show everybody my marks," said Jessie. "There's usually queues of men here to squint at my firm wee body."

Wee Tam shook his head. The memory of her hurt couldn't be dismissed so easily. But, once again, John marveled at Jessie's strength, the delicate way she shuffled off seriousness, refused to stoop under the weight of her experiences. It was true; she'd been far ,too good for Jimmie. It was easy to see why Wee Tam was so determined to protect her; not that she showed many signs that she actually needed looking after.

Her joking had the effect she'd wanted. They were able to move away from revelations and seriousness and talk about the plans that Jessie and Wee Tam wanted to make. They both thought that they would only be able to live properly and naturally if they left Aberdeen and Wee Tam had already started talking to people with connections in the Clyde yards. Tom's stillness deepened further when he heard this. He clearly didn't find it easy to accept the normality of his son's arrangements. John sensed his disappointment and, once more, felt the guilt of having been the cause of it. The low opinion of himself he'd been carrying since the previous evening rose in him again and he felt shame at the way he'd started prying into people's motives and movements as if they were playing cards. Nothing in the way people behaved was simple, there was no easy cause and effect. The threads which held them together were tangled into impossible ropes and led in unimaginable directions. He wanted to be away from others and away from himself, back with his carving.

CHAPTER TWENTY-TWO

Dinner at the Andersons was more somber than usual. Helen was quiet, her father seemed preoccupied and Elizabeth sensed that some change had taken place. Her attempts to discover what it was simply led to denials and changes of subject that confirmed that she was right. It was only at the end of the meal that the reason for it all became clear. Her husband pushed back his chair and said that he was going to his study.

"Can I come with you?" said Helen.

Anderson gave a quick nod.

"Later. I have one or two commissions to complete first."

"Ah, I see," said Elizabeth. "My daughter has become an Anderson and I must prepare myself for a lonely old age."

"Yes, that would be advisable," said Helen, before allowing herself a small giggle and giving her mother a hug.

Anderson left them together and, as Molly came to clear the table, they went to sit in the drawing room and Elizabeth immediately wanted to hear about the new pact that seemed to have been formed between Helen and her father. Helen told her how she'd looked through his papers, read share certificates, followed manifests of cargoes and, despite the fact that they were all dull documents listing amounts, figures and things devoid of apparent immediate interest, it was obvious to Elizabeth that they excited her. Helen said nothing of the testimonial letter and the conversation she'd had with her father about deceit. She was half aware that, by suppressing it, she was perhaps already playing the commercial game and, although she'd never kept secrets from her mother before, she felt a shiver of excitement at the thought.

"Well, I'm pleased that your father is being so liberal with you," said Elizabeth, "but I hope that he shows you the sorrows as well as the joys of the world in which he moves."

"You need have no fear of that," said Helen. "Joy seems to have no place in the transactions he's spoken of so far."

"I'm glad to hear it."

"Indeed, I suspect that he intends to paint the blackest possible picture in order to persuade me to look elsewhere for my occupations."

Elizabeth nodded slowly and was silent for a moment, lost in her thoughts.

"Yes," she said at last, "I think his work has been very lonely for him."

"Lonely?" said Helen.

"Yes. He seems to trust no one. Everyone is his enemy."

"Is that true?"

"It's the way he chooses to see it. Ever since his father died. I used to think he was somehow trying to avenge his death."

"Avenge?"

Elizabeth shook her head.

"It's too strong a word, I know," she said. "But his energies came from something other than profits." She made a gesture to indicate the room and its contents. "He wants comforts for us, all these lovely things, but I always feel that, when he's devising his schemes, he has a deeper motive, one that he's never spoken of."

"How mysterious," said Helen, with a smile.

Elizabeth didn't return it.

"It's caused him much pain," she said.

"And you think it came from his father's death? Did he suffer, too?"

"Yes, he did," said Elizabeth, "and I'm fearful that, if you become entangled with it all, it will take the joy from your life as well. That's why I hope the time you spend in the study with him will be laden with gloom."

"You are a witch," said Helen.

"Yes," said Elizabeth. "And I'd rather speak of other things."

****

Glover arrived at the entrance to Pensioners' Court a little after nine o'clock. The fears the place held made him want to be sure that John was already there. There was no guarantee that John's size would protect them but, alone, Glover might be an easy prey. Neither of them said much in the way of a greeting and they turned into the dank passageway, their eyes already flicking from side to side, catching dark movements in doorways and closes. Girls and women stepped out to ease themselves against them and trail their hands around their waists, pushing their fingers into the tops of their trousers. But, even if the two men had had such hungers, the smell of the creatures would quickly have stilled them.

They found the one they were looking for sitting on a step beside an older woman. Glover tugged at John's sleeve and pointed to her.

"You're certain?" said John.

Glover just nodded. John stepped up to the pair. The woman pushed the girl to her feet and out of the shadows to meet him. John held up his hand to stop her and she stood looking at him. There was no attempt to attract him, no smile, no words. She really was only a child, with breasts just barely beginning to form, a thin, straight shape and dirty tangles of hair hanging down past her shoulders. Her face was empty.

"She's never been had," said the woman. "She's a Madonna."

John beckoned the girl forward. Obediently, she came and he bent to put himself at her level.

"Don't be afraid," he said. "I don't want to do anything. I just want to ask you something."

She looked at him, her expression unchanged. A woman screamed twice in a nearby alleyway. Still the girl didn't move.

"Will you come with me?" said John. "We'll just walk a little way away from here, somewhere a little quieter."

The girl looked round at the woman, who flapped a hand to tell her to go. She turned back to look at John again.

"Come on, then," he said.

The three of them walked away, bringing shouts and whistles and cackles of laughter from various doorways. Glover walked quickly and was soon ahead of them.

"You go," John called to him.

Glover turned his head, nodded and quickened his pace even more, soon disappearing into the darkness. John and the girl turned toward The Links.

"How much money do men give you?" he asked.

She shrugged her shoulders.

"A shillin'," she said.

She wasn't a good liar. John knew that three or four pence was nearer the mark.

"Well, that's what I'll give you then," he said. "If you tell me about last Saturday night."

"What shall I tell you?" she said.

"Do you remember the man who just left us?"

181

She shook her head, then dug her fingers into her hair and began to scratch.

"He saw you last Saturday. He was with two other men. They were drunk. They both... wanted you. You went this way with one of them. To The Links."

She shook her head again.

"Are you sure?" said John.

"Will I still get the shillin'?" she asked.

"You'll get the shilling whether you say anything or not."

"Well, it's true. Honest to God. I didna come this way with nobody."

John wondered if Glover had made a mistake. Pensioners' Court was full of girls like this one, all dirty, all underfed. Perhaps his fear had made him eager to identify her quickly so that he could leave. Perhaps he had other reasons for misidentifying her.

"And you don't remember two men fighting over you, touching you."

She nodded.

"Aye. In the doorway."

"That's right. And you went with one of them..." John didn't know how to say the rest of it. She was so young. "For sex," he added.

She nodded again.

"Aye, but we didna come this way," she said.

"You did go to The Links, though."

"No. He wanted to go to a boat."

"A boat. Which one?"

The girl shrugged again. Her fingers were still digging into her scalp and the back of her neck.

"Don't know. New one. Being built. He was laughin'. He said it'd be bad luck."

"What would?"

"Me goin' on board. He wanted the boat to have bad luck."

"Did he say why?"

She shook her head.

"Could you show me which boat it was?"

"In the boatyard. I didna go on it. I'm afraid o' boats."

"Which yard was it?"

"No' the Duthies'. The one beside it."

John wasn't surprised to hear that it was where the Elizabeth Anderson was sitting.

"And that's where you... did it," he said.

Again the nod.

"The other man came, too," she said.

"What other man?"

"The one who was fightin'."

"He came with you?"

"No. I was with the big man, but I saw the other one in the yard."

"Did he see you?"

"No."

"Did the big man see him?"

"Don't know. Don't think so. He was lyin' on his back. I was suckin' him. I'll suck you if you want."

John shook his head quickly.

"No," he said. "Just tell me about the boatyard."

"There's nothin' else. We stopped. He told me to go away. Wouldna give me any money. Didn't matter. I took some from his pocket while I was suckin' him. Only two pennies."

"And you didn't see them again? They didn't say anything?"

Her scratching fingers had moved to her chest.

"No," she said.

"Come on," said John. "I'll take you back."

They turned back toward the way they'd come and John asked more questions, trying hard to think of what else she could add to the picture. But she'd already given him all she knew. For her, Saturday's transaction had been a single, typical event, not memorable, not distinct from the others. At the entrance to Pensioners' Court, he took out a shilling and held it out for her. She looked at it, then up at him.

"Have you got pennies instead?" she asked.

"Why?"

She gestured toward the alleyway.

"She'll want what you gave me. If you had pennies, I could keep some."

So the innocence was already compromised. John looked in his pocket and found a sixpence and some coppers. He counted them out and gave them to her. She grabbed them and turned without a word to slip away into the darkness and back to the old woman. She didn't look at him, smile, thank him. It had been the most profitable night she'd had for a long time, and certainly the easiest and least painful.

John walked slowly, trying to organize the tumbling, contradictory thoughts she'd provoked. Joe had said that they'd gone to The Links but he'd taken her to the boatyard. And Jimmie had been there, too. When Joe got back from his fishing again, there were lots of questions for him to answer.

CHAPTER TWENTY-THREE

Egil Thorsen would have preferred to be in his cabin on board ship. It was the main saloon cabin aft and had a small stateroom leading off it, but the two of them together were still smaller and had about half the headroom of Anderson's office. In spite of the room's size, as he stood across the desk from his employer, he felt the claustrophobia of the processes that went on here and itched for the seclusion and liberty of his own domain. His report had been delivered but, once again, Anderson had other propositions to explore.

"It takes... what, a month?... to unload a timber cargo," he said. "And all the time, I'm paying crew wages, insurance, port dues, the costs of loading and discharging. And an extra month's worth of provisions and supplies. And the level of commission the Canadian agents and brokers are asking is close to criminal."

As usual, Thorsen said nothing.

"I take it you've heard of Chile saltpeter?"

Thorsen thought, then nodded.

"And guano?"

This time he shook his head.

"Fertilizers, very good ones, too. Now, I know you pay little heed to what's going on onshore, but there are more and more mouths to be fed and the people feeding them are the farmers. They need these fertilizers, and they'll pay a premium to have them. We can get them from anchorage ports in northern Chile and Peru. They're lightered out to the ships by boatmen willing to be paid for quantity rather than time, and at excellent rates."

Thorsen listened, giving nothing away.

"What are your thoughts on passages to and from Chile and Peru?" asked Anderson.

"The saltpeter, I've heard it's dangerous," said Thorsen.

Anderson was quick to agree.

"We would have to take care with it, certainly. But, with properly equipped holds and good seals around the hatches, there's nothing to alarm us."

Thorsen resisted the temptation to say that one part of the "us" would be sailing with the substance while the other sat thousands of miles away in this office.

"You'll line the holds then?"

"Yes."

"And fit the seals?"

"Yes."

Thorsen shrugged. Anderson took it to mean that he was prepared to make the trip. Lining the holds and sealing the hatches would cost money but the new trade was generating real profits and he was hoping that, with some judicious publicity, he might begin to propose that the western coast of South America held special attractions for emigrants. Communications with the area took some two months so it would be a long time before anyone disputed the suggestion; it seemed an ideal opportunity.

It was true that these particular cargoes could cause some concern. The saltpeter gave off a dangerous gas if it got wet and, while news of guano had only started to be heard the previous year, those involved in handling it knew already that, sealed in a damp, dark hold, it produced ammonia fumes which could have lethal effects. Anderson, though, was confident that he could equip his ships and brief his masters in such a way that these dangers were avoided. In any case, the plan was simply to make three or perhaps four runs before returning to the idea of opening trade with New Zealand.

Thorsen left the office just before half past nine, fully briefed on what he needed to prepare in order to satisfy the needs of the new project, grateful that it would not be starting until the winter and glad that soon he would be out in the Atlantic with time and space to think about it all properly. As he turned onto the quay, he passed Glover going in the opposite direction. He answered the shipwright's loud greeting with a nod and made for the peace of his ship and his cabin.

As Glover was shown into his office, Anderson noticed, as had John, how much smarter he was. There were no overalls or other outward signs of his trade. He wore a black woolen jacket over well-fitting trousers. His leather boots shone and the dark blue cravat at his neck was held by a silver pin. The effect was to make Anderson trust him even less. The man was a shipwright and yet he clearly had pretensions.

"Once again, I'm surprised you have time to leave the ship," he said. "Have you special news?"

"No, sir. Everything is proceeding well and we are already ahead of the timetable I made out for you."

Anderson spread his hands as if to ask why, therefore, the man had come. Glover smiled, explained exactly what tasks were being performed at the yard and why they didn't need him to be there to oversee them. Anderson nodded, not allowing his satisfaction at the news to show.

"I'm sure that you know part of the reason why we've been able to advance so much more quickly," said Glover.

Anderson said nothing, giving no ground.

"It's a matter of which I've spoken before. Mr. Crombie and his lying. I cannot believe that a person with your appreciation of commerce could remain ignorant of the fact that he was conducting himself in some... inappropriate ways."

They were back on ground that made Anderson even more wary but Glover had prepared his arguments with care. He took two sheets of paper from his pocket and handed them across.

"In short, you were being robbed. The lists you have there cover costs of timber that was either never supplied or not needed, wages for workers who did not exist, transportation of materials that were already in the yard. While I would be pleased to take the credit for the progress we're now making, the truth is that the job could have been finished weeks ago."

Anderson had kept his eyes on Glover but now looked down at the figures on the pieces of paper. When he looked up again, Glover could read nothing in his expression or in his tone as he spoke.

"I know all this," he said.

"I suspected that you would."

"Why, then, are you telling me of it?"

So far, the two men had stood facing one another as if in some sort of confrontation. In the short silence that followed Anderson's question, Glover half turned away then asked if they could sit down to continue their talk.

"I don't think that's necessary. It's unlikely to be prolonged," replied Anderson.

Glover pursed his lips, nodded, and then took some time to brush the front of his waistcoat, seeming to relish the tension.

"I think it would be better for both of us if we were totally honest with one another," he said at last.

"You're building me a boat, not joining my club," said Anderson.

Glover smiled.

"I would never aspire that high. But I do wish to improve my lot. I told you before what I thought of success and of how an association with you could bring me closer to it."

"An 'association'?" Anderson managed to fill the word with both scorn and disbelief. It had little impact on Glover.

"Your protection, if you prefer," he went on. "That's still my goal and, unlike Mr. Crombie, I know that I'd be foolish to try to exploit you to achieve it. You've been successful too long to be undermined by men like him. Or me."

Anderson snorted with impatience. He had little time for flattery and no desire to protect this man. At one point he'd promised to be a worthy enough opponent, but no longer. Anderson's intention was still to pack him off back to Dundee the moment the Elizabeth Anderson was afloat. His protests, however, were stilled by Glover's next words.

"You allowed him to extort money from you because he knew that some of your business practices would find little favor if they were revealed."

Glover spoke fast. It was not an accusation but it was a challenge.

"He told me things, spoke loudly when drink had loosened his tongue. The notes of his I found were on the same subject. But you have no reason to fear..."

"I fear no one," said Anderson.

"No. Be reassured, Mr. Anderson, there's no need in my case. I can keep my counsel. I have no wish to take advantage of the information. He told me of your dealings with the Journal, your need to keep news of the additional expenses faced by your emigrants out of its pages."

To give himself time to prepare a response, Anderson walked round behind his desk and sat down. His features still betrayed nothing and there was ice in his voice when he spoke.

"If that's indeed the case, why have you come here now? Why are you saying all this?"

"Because the world is changing, sir. Because you know that and so do I."

"I have no time for riddles or philosophy. Say what you want."

Glover smiled again.

"Success," he said. "I wish to be free of the debts and disputes of little contracts. I wish to make my way."

"Ah, and I suppose I am to pay for it."

"No, sir. All I want is that you should see that I am capable of greater things, that my aims are higher, and help me to move into circles where I may realize them."

"It is extortion in another form, that's all."

"Is it? And what if I tell you that I know of a merchant in Dundee whose intention is to move into whaling and who would pay a handsome price for the machinery in the boil houses of the Union Whale Fishing Company?"

Anderson held his gaze for a moment. There was obviously much more to Glover than he'd realized.

"Why should that interest me?"

Glover gave a knowing smile.

"Mr. Anderson, you've made an offer to buy the boil houses and I don't really think you'll be using them for whaling."

Anderson had been expecting a variation on the pressure that Crombie had tried to exert and which he'd been able to divert so easily with sums which, to him, were trivial. But this man was operating in a different area. He'd thought carefully about his plans, done some investigating. It was also astute of him to make his first move one which had no apparent benefits for himself but strengthened Anderson's position with regard to the boil houses.

"You speak of protection," said Anderson. "From what?"

"The unexpected. For me to advance, I may have to break rules, negotiate short cuts. As an incomer, any... misdemeanors might be dealt with more harshly."

"Do you mean crimes?"

Glover smiled briefly, without humor.

"We're all guilty, aren't we?" he said.

Again, Anderson realized that he must take great care with him.

"How exactly do you imagine that I can further these ambitions of yours?" he asked.

Glover paused, took a deep breath and leaned forward.

"By letting me build you an iron ship."

"You're a shipwright," he said.

"Yes," said Glover, not understanding what he meant.

"So you must have some idea of how much such vessels cost."

"Yes."

"I see. So I am to finance one simply to make your name."

"On the contrary, it will spread your own influence even wider."

Anderson waited for him to explain.

"The Elizabeth Anderson is a beautiful ship but listen to her when she's eventually floated off. She'll groan and creak like they all do, changing her shape as the water presses against her."

"And?" said Anderson, unsure of the point being made.

"All the buoyancy's in the middle, as it should be, but it'll make her hog, dip her ends lower and stress the keelson."

Despite the fact that he was describing a vessel for which he was responsible, he sounded almost enthusiastic about the problems she would face.

"They flex too much. When she's deep-laden with heavy cargo, it'll pull in her topsides and slacken her rigging."

"Mr. Glover," said Anderson, tiring of the flow, "you make it sound as if you are building me a wreck."

"No, no. She's a fine ship. She'll serve you for many, many years. But the future is in iron. It's stronger, there are no dangers of fire. An iron ship is made of bigger pieces, not just planks fitted together. And they last forever."

Anderson had heard all the arguments before and was not convinced that the extra costs could be as easily recouped as Glover was suggesting. He shook his head.

"The fleet I have suits my purposes. I do not speculate."

Glover lifted a hand.

"May I suggest just one thing?"

Anderson listened.

"Next month, we'll be visited by the Archimedes. She's on a national tour and creating enthusiasm wherever she goes."

"I've heard of her and her... screw propeller."

"Yes, which drives her forward whether the wind blows or no. She spins on a penny piece and is as easy to maneuver as a rowing skiff. Before you say no to iron, go to see her."

Anderson remained seated, looking at him, assessing him. Although the talk had turned to shipbuilding, the initial threat of extortion still lay behind it. He wondered exactly how much Glover knew.

"I have little taste for the way you began this discussion," he said.

"Mr. Anderson, I've told you exactly what I believe you can do for me. I see an association with you, however remote, as the key to my progress here. How can I reassure you?"

"Oh you can't. You never will be able to. Who knows who else might benefit from more drunken ramblings. This time from you."

"I do not drink and I promise you I will say nothing."

"Promises," said Anderson, dismissing them with a wave that showed how little he thought of them.

He thought for a moment, studying his hands and rubbing a finger across one of his nails.

"These notes, these papers Crombie has written..." he began.

Glover held up a hand, palm outward.

"Ah, that was clumsy. I was lying. The truth is that he spoke of an item he had found in the papers relating to the boat. It was an account paid by you to the Journal. He'd hidden it in a box but I've not yet found it. When I do, I shall return it to you at once."

He stopped. They continued to look at one another.

"As a token of my good faith," he added.

CHAPTER TWENTY-FOUR

At last, John had found time to make his way over to Joe's house. Rose was leaving just as he got there. John frowned as he saw the red welt which angled down from the corner of her left eye toward her mouth. It was still open and weeping in one or two places and Rose held her head so that it was turned away from him. She'd have preferred to stay at home until it had healed more but, with Joe away, she had to work as much as she could.

"Nasty cut," said John.

"Aye. Cupboard door swung open. I wasna even drunk," she said.

Dutifully, John smiled. He guessed that the true explanation was more sinister. He walked along beside her.

"I was looking to have a wee word with Joe," he said.

"What for?"

"Just some things."

Rose stopped.

"Is it Jimmie again?" she asked. "'cause if it is, I'm no' havin' it. I've told you, you're upsettin' Jessie. Why d'you do it, John? It's no' like you."

She turned and continued down the street.

"I know, Rose," said John, falling in beside her again. "I'm nosy, maybe, but there's things I've been told, I can't just say nothing about them. I'll not do anything to make Jessie miserable. She told me that Davie Donne's been bothering her already. I want to help her."

"Aye, maybe. Well, you'll no' be speakin' with Joe for a while. He's signed on with the Glenns. He never told me but that's what I heard."

"Has he sailed?"

"Aye. Deep sea trawlin'. Greenland or Iceland, one of them. What did you want with him?"

John raised a hand, a throwaway gesture.

"Just things about Saturday night. I was wondering about them, that's all."

"I can tell you where he was. He was drinkin'."

"I know. With Jimmie."

"Aye. All night. I dinna ken where he slept. Probably with his wee whore in the Court."

"Has he said anything to you?" said John. "About what they were doing that night?"

"He never tells me nothin'. We dinna speak no more."

"He didn't say who else was with them, then?"

"You mean the new man? The shipwright?"

"Yes."

"Aye, and if you're wantin' to look for somebody, he's the one," said Rose.

"Why?" said John, surprised at the seeming change.

"Some box he was after, Joe said. Jimmie's. Somethin' to do with Anderson."

She stopped again and reached for his sleeve to turn him toward her.

"But leave it, John. Don't make things worse for Jessie. If you go on scratchin' at it and upsettin' her, you're no' the man I thought you were."

John lifted her hand and held it in both his own. She was frowning, anxious.

"Rose, love. I promise you I'll do nothing to hurt Jessie," he said, shaking away the thought that he'd already done enough damage by uncovering her affair with Wee Tam. "The things she said about Davie... he's out to cause trouble as usual. If I can get there before him, we'll shut him up."

She shook her head and there were tears in her eyes.

"No good'll come of it, John," she said.

It was hopeless. John noticed that, as well as the cut, there were other hurts. She was limping and her hand rubbed occasionally at her back. Joe had given her something to remember him by while he was away and her bitterness, added to the fierce protection she felt for Jessie, made her close in upon herself. John could understand why she didn't want yet another man stirring up troubles. They walked on in silence for a while then began to talk of trivial everyday things. It brought Rose out more, pushed her abrasiveness back a little, but John didn't risk reviving it with more questions. When they parted at the quayside, he bent to give her a peck on the cheek and managed to get a smile out of her.

****

A short while later, the therapy of carving was beginning to work again. While Jamie chipped away at the scrolls of the trailboards, John felt his way gently into the area in which her arm was buried. As it appeared, it was held gracefully in front of her, a long bend in the wrist, the back of the hand facing forward, the fingers held lightly curled, forming with the palm a cup that tilted slightly upwards toward the top of her breast. None of it yet had any finesse or detail but its rhythms were unmistakable.

Outside, on the quay, Helen heard the double tapping of the two mallets and finally gave in to her curiosity. When Sarah and Bella had called for her, she'd persuaded them to take a turn along the water's edge. Normally, it was an area into which they would not venture and it was only the opportunity to show one another how daring they were that had made them all agree. Now, the other two had gone ahead to look at the ships moored in the deeper water (and hope that they might glimpse some of the crewmen on board). She'd told them she had a commission from her father for John and promised to join them soon. If being on the quay was dangerous, being there alone was unforgivable but, especially in her present mood, Helen cared nothing for convention.

She knocked, but immediately realized that they would not hear her above their own hammerings so stepped through the half open door. John was bending over his work, his right side toward her with his arm rocking up and down as he tapped against the gouge. His hair hung forward, flicking to and fro with his movements. It was only when she moved toward him and her shadow fell across the floor beside him that he looked up and immediately straightened. He was unable to hide the surprise in his face.

She smiled and quickly apologized for disturbing him, explaining that she was so curious about how the work was progressing that she couldn't resist coming to see for herself, even though it was against all the rules. He could only mumble answers that meant little. Swinging so quickly from the intimacy of her cupped wooden hand to her very full, very real presence was a shock. Her face, which had lost its smile when she saw how confused she had made him, was framed by the large brim of a striped silk taffeta bonnet with a high domed crown. Over her shoulders was a deep burgundy colored pelerine made of the same material as her long full-sleeved dress.

He suddenly realized that he was staring at her, taking pleasure in the sight but saying nothing. Helen was holding his stare, returning it. Jamie had stopped working, too, and was looking at the fascinating tableau. To break the spell, Helen moved across to look at the trailboards.

"My brooch," she said, a little lift of delight in her voice. "You copied it."

Jamie pointed at John, who just nodded.

"That's very clever. I do envy you," Helen said to Jamie.

"I just do what he tells me," he replied.

She gave him a smile which made him blush, then went back to John's carving. Although not yet a whole person, there were enough shapes and features to make it live.

"It looks wonderful," she said, meaning it.

"It will when it's been finished and mounted," he said, recovering slowly from his surprise. "Onshore like this..." He stopped, shrugged and added, very simply, "... the ship's missing."

"I thought the figurehead was supposed to be the ship, capture its nature."

"It is. It does. But only when they're together. The ship... knows who she is. She doesn't need my trimmings for that. She's got her own... self."

He spoke hesitantly, feeling a little adrift in this totally unexpected conversation.

"And this one's my mother. And me," said Helen, trying to lighten the mood, free him from his apparent embarrassment and herself from the little ache that lay within her brightness.

It was his turn to smile. She saw little lines curling up at the corners of his eyes and lips.

"It is for now," he said.

"What do you mean?"

"I've had too many owners change their mind about the name of their ship. One day, I'm carving a goddess, the next it has to be a beast of some sort."

"Is that true?"

"You'll see two barques in Leith, the Leopard and the Eagle. They started as the Diana and the Betty Lee. The work isn't mine, but look carefully at their figureheads; the beasts are remarkably human."

Helen laughed.

"Do you mind if I ask you some questions while I'm here?" she said.

"What could I possibly tell you?"

She stepped closer to the carving to run her hand over its shapes.

"Everything," she said, raising her hand and gesturing at the wood. "This... alchemy you're doing here. This blending of Mama and myself into... well, into a third woman, but one who'll see the oceans and the Americas and the Orient."

There was no playfulness in her tone; John could hear that she truly was fascinated by what she was imagining.

"I don't know what to tell you," he said. "I'm commissioned to produce a piece and my hands work the timber."

He ended with a small shrug, as if that was all there was to it. She gave him another of her easy smiles, tilted her head to the side and wagged a finger at him. Her hand was china white, fragile, exquisite. John's eyes flicked to the carved hand. It looked heavy, too dense.

"Modesty does not become you, Mr. Grant," she said. "I know of your reputation as I'm sure you do yourself. This is more than carpentry."

Her smile allowed no protest. Instead, he was drawn into her eagerness to treat ship's carving as a mystery rather than a trade. He told her of how the early builders thought that ships needed eyes to find their way across the waters and how the figureheads were offerings to Neptune and began in blood. She listened, setting aside the decorum that she'd been taught, as he described how, on the Coromandel Coast, sheep were slaughtered and their heads were stuck on the prow, and how, in Melanesia, the sacrifices were human and the heads on their canoes were all too real. Her curiosity insisted on more and, when he described the fashion for horns which were part of the boats' structure and whose purpose was not nautical but simply to provide a convenient pike on which to fix the hearts of enemies, she gave a slight shiver and he saw, for the briefest of moments, that her eyes flashed with the thrill of it. She put both her hands on the carving again, running them up its sides and over its shoulders. As she got to the neck, she drew her palms away from the surface so that it was just the tips of her fingers that caressed it. Their movement continued as she looked directly at him.

"If only Papa knew what he was buying from you," she said.

"I think he does. Your father isn't known for wasting his money."

She seemed to pick up the slight coldness of his tone.

"He chose you because he said you're the best. He could have spent less elsewhere."

"And he would have got what he paid for."

Again, John was surprising himself with his words. Why was he suddenly attacking her father? Or was he defending himself because of his association with him? Whatever it was, it was prompted by a strange need to distance himself from Anderson's world.

"Well, well," she said, the smile gone, her eyes now seeming to measure him. "Then you, too, know the values of the market place."

"Forgive me," said John, his tone formal. "I have rather foolish ideas about commerce and finance. They'll serve me ill in the end."

She surprised him by laughing.

"Ah, Mr. Grant," she said. "If you had to live every day with it, it would drive you mad. It makes victims of us all."

"I hardly see you as a victim," he said.

"Perhaps that is because you hardly see at all," she replied, a sudden spark of anger in her face.

John let the insult lie. He didn't know its origin or its target. Suddenly, they seemed to be a long way from their musings on the wonder of figureheads. Helen shook her head, gave a quick sigh and turned from the carving.

"Oh, I'm sorry, Mr. Grant. That was extremely rude and it meant nothing at all. It's just that I'm always being reminded that I am my father's daughter."

"Then I, too, am sorry. It was not my intention to..."

"And he has been more troubled with this ship than I care to remember."

"In what way?"

"Oh, I don't know really. Mr. Crombie... I don't think he was being very... helpful. There were things happening which seemed to be hampering the work."

She walked round to the other side of the carving, her hand still tracing along its surface.

"I've tried to ask about it. Papa thinks I don't need to know. But I'm his heir, Mr. Grant. One day, I shall need to know everything about his work to continue it."

"A difficult task," said John.

"What do you think of him?" she asked. "An honest opinion. Please."

They were both surprised by the sound of Jamie's mallet. He had been taking tools to and from a cabinet at the far end of the workshop during their conversation and trying not to listen to it. In the end, though, he'd run out of excuses and could either stand there like some idiotic spectator or get on with his work. John called to him and flicked his head toward the door to indicate that Jamie should go outside somewhere. Jamie was glad of the excuse, said goodbye to Helen and, gratefully, escaped from a situation that had become incomprehensible to him.

"Was that wrong?" asked John. "To send Jamie away, I mean? Does it trouble you that there are just the two of us here?"

"Oh, was Jamie a chaperone?"

John smiled. The incident had allowed a little thaw into their exchanges.

"I would still like you to answer my question," said Helen.

"It isn't a fair one," said John. "I have no wish at all to hide anything from you or be anything other than totally honest, but you're asking me about your father. Can you not see that, even if I think he's the lord Jesus, I can say nothing of him?"

"Why not?"

"He's your father."

"Yes, and I know he isn't the lord Jesus and that he's probably closer in the mind of everyone in Aberdeen to Judas Iscariot or Herod or Pontius Pilate, but I'm asking you what you, John Grant, think of him."

The flashes were back in her eyes. This was no lady in love with the small talk of salons. She spoke only of things that mattered to her and seemed to make no attempt to hide her passions. John tried to push back the suspicions concerning Anderson's dealings with Jimmie and be as honest as possible with what was left.

"He's successful. He bargains hard but I think that his business gives work to many others. The distance between our stations makes it unlikely that we'd ever be acquaintances but, even if that were not the case, I find it difficult to believe that he could ever be my friend. I respect him but I don't understand what lies behind his dealings."

She nodded her head as she thought about his words.

"Thank you. And why could he not be your friend?"

John didn't want this to continue. It would only lead back to anger.

"He has different... interests, different preferences in life. I'm a very simple man."

"Please," said Helen, "don't say foolish things."

John began to protest.

"I've heard the way you speak about your work," she said. "You're not a simple man."

"Very well, but real things, society, enterprises—they're beyond me."

"Because you wish it that way."

"Perhaps."

She nodded as if they'd agreed on some fundamental point. When she spoke again, her tone was different, more casual.

"Do you think Mr. Crombie was a good shipwright?" she asked.

John shrugged.

"As good as most."

"But why was he delaying the building so much?"

"I don't know that he was."

"Papa says he was. It's a terrible thing to say, but it does seem that his dying has made things easier. I must confess to wondering at its convenience. For a man so used to the harbor to simply fall in and drown... it seems hard to believe."

"There are others saying the same thing," said John.

She turned and looked quickly at him.

"Do they suspect... other things?"

"People always suspect things."

"Then it must be investigated," she said.

"I... I think that's happening."

"Oh? The watch?"

"Yes. But I wouldn't expect too much of them. Their successes with real crimes are few."

"Then whom should I ask?"

John shrugged. He wanted to change the subject and yet he would love to have taken her into his confidence, talk of the hanging and the theft. It was as he remembered the money which had vanished from Jimmie's pocket that he saw an opportunity of involving her without having to give anything away.

"It has had one unfortunate consequence," he said.

"What?"

"A woman is in jail. Bessie Rennie. She's to appear at the next courts. She tried to steal a purse."

"But how is that connected with Mr. Crombie?"

"It isn't. But I think she may know something about his death."

"What?"

He shook his head.

"I don't know. I may be completely wrong. I'd like to talk to her, ask her some things. She's a harmless enough person. She doesn't deserve to be treated harshly."

Helen was looking at him, seeming to judge him.

"Are you investigating the death?" she asked.

The directness took John by surprise.

"I am interested in it, certainly," he said.

"I see. And why are you telling me of this woman?"

John took a deep breath.

"You mentioned earlier the burden you carried for being your father's daughter."

A little frown creased her brow.

"It has advantages, too," he added.

"I know that."

"I just wondered how much influence you or he might have with the judges or the court officers. The simplest representation on her behalf would make them treat her much more kindly."

Helen considered his words, then nodded.

"Of course. What did you say her name was?"

"Bessie Rennie."

"I shall do what I can."

"Thank you."

They fell silent. Helen was looking at the carving again. The light in the workshop was gray but it still managed to silver her shoulders and the folds of the back of her dress.

"There is a price," she said.

He looked a question at her.

"In return, I shall expect you to tell me what you learn from her and from your investigations."

She was serious but, in her eyes, he could see the pleasure she was taking from the arrangement she was suggesting.

"You are your father's daughter in more ways than one," he said.

"Is that a compliment?"

John couldn't help being drawn into the intimacy of her tone.

"Yes, and there are many more I could think of," he said.

She gave a little bow and laughed.

"Then we have a business agreement?" she said. "Miss Rennie's rescue in exchange for information."

"Very well."

She stepped toward him and held out her hand.

"Then we must seal it," she said.

She was almost a foot shorter than he was and, for all the fullness of her skirts, seemed slim and delicate. John felt a quick desire to put his arms around her. In spite of himself, he reached out, took her hand, then bent to kiss it. As he straightened, she kept on holding his hand. A slight flush had come into her face but her eyes were still wide, bold and direct.

"A handshake would have sufficed," she said with a smile.

Gently, he pulled his hand away from hers. After a moment, he reached toward her face and trailed the backs of his fingers slowly down her cheek, barely touching the surface.

"No, it would not," he said.

CHAPTER TWENTY-FIVE

John whistled as he walked up Union Street on his way to the Bridewell. It was crowded and noisy with shoppers and strollers. He looked over the parapet of the bridge to the Den Burn flowing down from Gilcomston and saw the specks of more figures walking along its banks. The weather was still gray but this was Saturday afternoon and work was nearly over for the week and folk were taking the air.

Bessie and her helpless, wheezing neighbors would be lucky ever to have the freedom to roam around Aberdeen again. The air they were most likely to breathe was that which blew in from the Tasman Sea or out from the hot desert in the heart of Australia. Last time he'd come, John had stepped from sunshine into gloom; this time, even though the contrast was less strident, he still felt the chill of the corridors leach into him as he walked along beside Charlie Dodds.

Charlie was a remarkable man. Thin as a stair rod, with skin made pale gray by the hours he spent in the Bridewell's darkness, he had almost no interest in his prisoners. John had brought him a big flask of whisky and his thoughts didn't go beyond the anticipation of the pleasure it would give him to drink it. John supposed that his objectivity was necessary to do the job properly. The slightest sensitivity to the plight of the people he was guarding would drive him screaming mad or leaping from the Union Bridge in despair. Far better to think of the prisoners as numbers or bundles filling particular spaces in his honeycomb.

Once again, he stayed just inside Bessie's gray cell door as John moved slowly across to her. She was hunched in the same corner as if she hadn't moved since his last visit. The smell was worse and Bessie had huddled closer into herself. There was none of the hope she'd shown the last time. She looked up at John, barely moving her head and giving no sign of recognition or any sort of greeting. There was a tin cup beside her. John picked it up and turned to ask Charlie to tip a shot of whisky into it from the flask he'd brought. Charlie frowned but, since there was plenty of it, sloshed a couple of mouthfuls into the cup. John went back, sat down beside Bessie and handed it over. For a while, she looked at it. After a quick glance at John as if to ask what his game was, she took it, sipped and immediately coughed and spat on the floor beside her.

"Slainte," said John.

Without looking at him, she raised the cup a few millimeters in reply.

"How're they treating you, Bessie?"

"Like an animal," she said, after a pause and another sip, which had less drastic consequences.

"Aye," said John.

He let a little silence fall between them, wanting her to feel that he was there for a while, ready to chat about whatever she wanted. At last, she spoke again, elaborating on what she meant, describing the thin liquids and pastes that were served up as foods, speaking of her fears that some of the others with whom she worked were capable of slitting her throat and other unspeakable practices. It was clear that she still saw herself as a relative innocent amongst these thieves and murderers. John thought that that was probably true, although he suspected that the same could be said for many of the others crouched in the darkness. The confession he eventually drew from Bessie, though, made him wonder just how much he really did know about people. It was something he'd already suspected, the reason for his visit, in fact, but having it confirmed made him heave a deep sigh of recognition that, most of the time, he was looking at surfaces and knowing nothing of the depths beneath them.

He told her of the promise he'd got from Helen to get her father to intervene on her behalf. It had the effect he hoped for. The prospect of having at least one voice speaking for her, and one as powerful as Anderson's, renewed the hopes that had been dying with each hour in the cell. She was grateful and her gratitude took the form of a willingness to be completely open about the Sunday morning find on the beach.

"Did you see it was Jimmie right away?" he asked.

"Aye, more or less."

"But you didn't come up to the street."

She was silent. He heard a rustle as she changed her position and took another sip.

"He was dead, John. Honest he was."

"I know. I saw him."

"But I still... I couldna believe it. And there was his watch and chain."

"Temptation, was it?"

"You dinna see watches like that along the shore. Bits an' pieces of rubbish, that's all I ever see. An there's him with a watch he winna need no more."

"So what did you do?"

Again the silence. It was John who broke it.

"I think I know, Bessie."

"Aye. I told you. I took it. But I put the money back."

"No. I mean before you took the watch. I know what you did to Jimmie."

"I didna do nothin'."

"Bessie, I'm helping you. I'm trying to get you out of this. Trust me."

"I dinna trust nobody."

Another silence. Then.

"He didn't bleed much, did he?" said John, too quietly for Charlie to hear.

"What? When?"

"When you used your fid."

Bessie didn't speak, which meant that she wasn't denying it.

"People don't bleed when they've been dead for a while. No blood flowing round in their body."

He could hear that her breathing had changed. She was catching at her breaths, holding them.

"You see, when I saw him with the two holes in him, I wondered why there wasn't more blood around. He should've been covered in it. It should've been all over the sand."

Still nothing from Bessie.

"You stuck it into him, didn't you?" said John. "In his neck and chest."

"I didna."

Bessie's voice was even quieter than John's. Her tone was unconvincing.

"What did you do it for?"

This time, the silence stretched on. Bessie finished the whisky and put the cup on the floor. Still she said nothing. John waited.

"I was glad he was dead," she said at last.

"Why?"

"Things he's done. To some of the girls in Pensioners' Court, Mason's Court. To me. He was more wicked than half the folk that's in here."

"What sort of things did he do?" asked John.

"He was an evil man to the women. Old ones, young ones, even wee girls. Didna matter to him. Hit them, cut them. Just used them for hisself. I was glad he was dead."

A certain defiance had come to her now.

"I knew he was gone but I just wanted to make sure." She stopped, then repeated, "I wanted to make sure."

"And nobody would think you'd done it, would they? Nobody would think you were a murderer."

"I'm no' a murderer."

Bessie's protest was loud enough for Charlie to hear. He stirred by the door then leaned back again in his habitual boredom.

"I know, but if he hadn't already been dead, you would've killed him. That's murder, Bessie."

"He deserved it. Anyway, he was dead. You canna kill a drowned man."

John was surprised by these words. She'd inspected Jimmie's body pretty closely and yet she still believed he'd drowned.

"Didn't you see the mark on his neck?" he asked.

"What mark? I didna see nothin'. I saw the watch and chain there... I was... all mixed up. Didna ken what to do. I dinna ken why I did it."

She'd cried when she'd first been brought here but then had no tears left. Suddenly, they came back again: tears of pain for what she'd lived through and tears of fear for what was still to come.

"It's all right, Bessie. He was dead. You didn't kill him."

As he spoke, John patted her arm, feeling the stickiness of her dress under his fingers. He'd confirmed his suspicions and yet he felt guilty at his desire to be away from her. The extremes of his day were oppressive. From an hour spent in the radiance of Helen, he'd fallen into this pit with a tired, diseased old woman who'd pushed a sharp fid into a corpse to settle old scores and steal a watch. While Charlie Dodds leaned patiently and unconcerned against the door, John forced himself to stay and talk some more with Bessie, trying to build in her the hope that he'd brought with him and all the time dimly aware that, by sharing her degradation, he was in a way opening a clearer perspective on his own good fortune.

****

Later, John sat quietly beside the lamp in his workshop, eating his supper and looking at his carving. The light wasn't good for working. Each time he contemplated starting on any details, he realized that the potential for error was too great. In the end, he was saved, just before eight o'clock, when the door opened and Tom came in.

"What are you doin' here?" said Tom. "I've been waitin' at your place for ages."

"I just had a few things I wanted to finish."

"I thought you was hidin' away."

The residue of guilt from Thursday evening still clung in John's mind and he wondered whether this was Tom's way of rekindling it.

"How's Wee Tam?" he asked.

"Like a kid at Christmas. Best thing you coulda done for him, tellin' me about him and Jessie. No' for me, though. I'm sick of hearin' her name. Talks of nothin' else. Work, home, it's all the same."

John was reassured. Despite his apparent complaining, Tom was obviously happy at the pleasure Wee Tam was taking in being free to talk of Jessie.

"So you're here to get away from it?"

"Aye. Thought we might go and have a wee drink."

John held up his hands to protest.

"Oh no. Never again. I did enough damage the other night."

"Just a wee sup. A jug or two."

It was more than an invitation to drink; it was an attempt to clear the air, get back to normal.

"Who's paying?" asked John.

"You are."

"I thought so."

He put the plates and knife away, wrapped the food and stuck it in a box in the cupboard. The box was a necessary extra; the paper was strong enough but if he left it overnight, the rats would make short work of it.

The London Tavern wasn't the nearest place but it was bigger than the Pilots Tavern and they knew they'd be able to find a seat there. Inside it was warm and so full of smoke that John felt it catch at his throat. Most of the drinkers were standing around near the long bar, barking out laughter, stories and indisputable truths. The light barely reached into the corners at the back, where squat stools were pushed close to round tables with wrought iron legs. Tom went to sit at one while John bought the ale. Near the bar, the sawdust on the floor was sticky and lumpy and the smells of beer and bodies were strong. The memory of Bessie's cell flashed into John's head. Sawdust, even as clotted as this, would represent a luxurious upgrading of her lodgings.

At the table, he told Tom of his visit and of Bessie's confession to having used the fid on Jimmie. The smile with which Tom greeted the news was huge.

"So... we're just lookin' for a hangin'?"

John laughed.

"Aye, that's all."

"Makes it much easier, John."

"Go on, then. Who did it?"

Tom's expression suggested that he was considering whether to reveal the information or not.

"I've no idea," he said at last.

It was good that they were joking again. John's mind had been churning away all day. The confusions provoked by Helen's visit still lingered, and he hadn't yet been able to suppress completely the memory of how he'd hurt Tom and of how silent his friend had been when they were at Jessie's. On top of that, he still needed to sort out the turmoil of Joe's comings and goings with the girl.

"Have Wee Tam and Jessie decided what to do yet?" he asked.

Tom shook his head.

"No. They're glad it's out in the open, though. Me, too, really."

"They'll have to be careful for a while. Folk'll start getting all sorts of ideas otherwise."

"Aye, I ken. Wee Tam and me's been speakin' about it."

There were sudden shouts from the bar. Some crewmen from a Dutch coaster had misunderstood a comment made by a fisherman and decided he was insulting Dutch women. A big, bearded sailor had the fisherman by the front of his jacket and was shoving him hard against the bar. Others tried to drag them apart and started their own wrestlings and pushings. It took the landlord and three others to herd them all out into the street, where they could settle their differences without damaging his interior. They were forgotten as soon as the door shut on them.

"He was tellin' me about Jimmie, too," said Tom, as if nothing had happened to interrupt him. "What a monster he was, John. I mean, I'd heard some tales but I never knew he was as bad as that."

"Aye, he treated Jessie bad."

"Worse than you ken. Tied her to her bed one time and left her all night while he was out whoring."

"Bessie said he was hard to his women."

"Hard? He was evil. He treated them all like they was whores. Neighbors, the girls workin' round the quays, everybody. Nobody was safe with him. Know young Ailsa Drew?"

John nodded. She was the daughter of a carter who lived in York Place.

"Nine year old. She came in to see Jessie one day. Jessie was tellin' Wee Tam. Jimmie was there. Had his hands all over her. A nine year old, for Christ's sake."

John shared Tom's disgust, but he also wondered how many of the men around this tavern and walking the streets outside were carrying secrets with just as much darkness in them. He'd never liked Jimmie, never spent any time with him, either at work or outside it, but he hadn't suspected just how corrosive an influence he'd been and how miserable he'd made Jessie's life. It made her liveliness and good humor even more remarkable. It also, incidentally, added many more names to the list of people who would want him dead. It seemed that, in every way, the killer was an agent of God and not the devil.

"D'you think we should tell her about Bessie and the fid?" asked John.

Tom pushed his glass to and fro on the table, spreading the ring of ale it had made. He looked at it as he did so, thinking about John's question.

"I'm no' sure. She's wantin' to forget it."

"Aye. Seems Davie Donne's been upsetting her again. Rose was telling me."

"Aye. Wee Tam was sayin' it looks like he's thinkin' she did it herself."

John shook his head and was quiet in his turn.

"You had any more ideas about it?" he asked.

"No," said Tom.

"Me neither. That's why I'd still like to talk to her. Ask her about Saturday. I mean, now she knows it wasn't Wee Tam, she could maybe help us."

Bessie's revelations had added a venom to the circumstances of Jimmie's death that had given fresh impetus to his curiosity about it. It now had the personal edge that was his real motivation. Right from the start, the urge to act had been triggered by memories of Marie, the bitterness at the fact that no one had ever identified her killer. Even though Jimmie had deserved what he got, a passive acceptance of the death as accidental would be a second betrayal of Marie.

Tom's involvement had grown from similar impulses. For him, the discovery of his son's liaison with Jessie had at first pushed everything else into the dark, making him want to go back to the safe monotony of his regular days. Wee Tam's stories of the man's depravity, though, set his curiosity burning even more than before. Now, he wanted to find out who had killed him and maybe buy him a drink.

"Wee Tam's there with her now," he said simply.

It amounted to a suggestion that they should visit. They both knew it and, with a look at one another, they swallowed their drinks and left, keeping well clear of the flailing arms and legs of the various Dutchmen and fishermen who were still battling in the street outside.

CHAPTER TWENTY-SIX

The York Place interior was already showing signs that Wee Tam was spending more time there. His boots were set neatly together by the skirting board just inside the door, two of his big, black coats were hanging on hooks in an alcove and Wee Tam himself was sitting in a sagging armchair by the range. Jessie, in the chair opposite him, was sewing the seam of a shirt and the two of them looked as if they'd been sitting together for years.

They greeted Tom and John warmly enough, although John sensed that Wee Tam hadn't yet forgiven his meddling in their affairs. There was no real outward sign but his eyes held a coldness that used not to be there. Jessie was as lively as ever, putting aside the sewing, giving both of them a peck on the cheek and filling the kettle to put on the range. She pulled two chairs out from the table for them.

"What now?" she asked as she reached for the tea caddy on the mantelpiece.

"What d'you mean?" said Tom.

She looked at him and put her head to one side.

"Tom," she said, "it's Saturday night and you're drinkin' tea."

"I've maybe seen the light."

"Aye, and I'm the queen."

She spooned the tea leaves into the pot and set it on the range near the kettle.

"You havena come just to blether, so what's been happenin'?" she said.

"Why d'you want to know?" asked Wee Tam. "It'll just upset you again."

She put her arms round his neck and kissed his cheek.

211

"Because these two rogues'll just keep comin' back till they're satisfied. I'm wantin' to be rid o' them for good."

Tom looked at John and nodded, encouraging him to do the talking. In a way, he and Jessie were now family so it was proper that the latest news should come from someone with a bit more objectivity. An outsider.

John had decided to say nothing yet to Jessie of what Jimmie and Joe had been doing in Pensioners' Court. Choosing his words and the way he approached the news very carefully, he told them instead about his visit to Bessie. When he came to the stabbing with the fid, he saw that Wee Tam's brow wrinkled into a frown as he gave a little shake of the head. Jessie, on the other hand, paused in her tea-making and said, "well, well, well" with something like admiration. When he spoke of Bessie's decision to put the money back into Jimmie's pocket, Jessie actually laughed.

"My God, she musta' hated him," she said.

"Aye, her and plenty of others," said Wee Tam.

"Stickin' a fid in him. And him already dead." She shook her head at the thought. The focus was on Bessie, not Jimmie. John's revelation that it was Willie Johnston who'd taken the money had the same effect. For all the things that Jimmie had done, all the damage he'd caused, he was nothing now. His only importance lay in the patterns of behavior his death had generated in others.

Jessie's apparent amusement had quickly died. Fascinating as the latest discoveries were, their effect was to keep the death open. Until Jimmie was allowed to vanish completely, she and Wee Tam would be unable to take full possession of their affection for one another and start to live it.

"It doesna get you any further, though," she said to John.

"In what way?"

"Why are you askin' the questions? What are you lookin' for?"

John shrugged.

"He was killed," he said.

It seemed an inadequate answer. Somehow irrelevant.

"Just curious, are you?" said Wee Tam, his tone revealing what he thought of John's motive.

"Aw, come on," said Tom, feeling that he, too, was being accused of something. "You canna blame us. Money, stabbin's, hangin'—it's no' the sort of thing that happens to you every day."

"No, but why dig about in it, Pa? What for? Specially when it upsets Jessie. She had enough to put up with from him when he was alive. And now there's that fat bastard Davie Donne, too."

"I don't want to upset Jessie," said John, his voice quiet, grave. The tone caught their attention. "It was just... Marie. The way they found her.

The way she died, all on her own. The pain she..." He stopped, thought for a moment. "And nobody paid for it. Whoever it was took a knife to her neck and face and just walked away. If I let the same thing happen with Jimmie... it'd be wrong."

His voice fell as his explanation petered out to a weak, unsatisfactory conclusion. Fundamentally, it was true; Marie had provided the initial impulse, but it had grown, taken other shapes and directions, and she'd occupied little enough time in his thoughts of late.

"If you want us to go," he said, "just say so and we will. I don't want to cause any more trouble than I already have. But..." he added, as Wee Tam started to speak, "just let me ask one more thing."

"What?" said Wee Tam.

"Tom and I were saying," said John, "that it would help if we knew what happened last Saturday. Maybe there's something that..."

"No," said Wee Tam, his voice loud, angry. "Good Christ, John. I'm sorry about Marie. I understand what you say about it, but one minute you're no' wantin to cause trouble, the next, you're draggin' Jessie back to Jimmie's dyin'. That's enough, man. Leave it alone."

There was no option but to accept what he said. If all that was driving them was curiosity, its satisfaction was too high a price to pay if it involved more misery for Jessie. John looked at Tom, who nodded. There was no point in pursuing it.

"He went out straight after supper and came home about eight, drunk as a pig."

It was Jessie's voice, quiet but firm. Wee Tam flashed a glance at her. She smiled at him and poured tea into cups. She'd taken out her best china.

"He wanted his ditty box. Fell about lookin' for it. Mutterin' all the time about wantin' to put it somewhere where the new man wouldna find it."

"The new man?" said Tom.

"Aye. Glover. He'd been drinkin' with him and told him things he shouldn't have."

"What things?"

"Dinna ken. It was all stuff he was sayin' as he was lookin' for the box. Didna make no sense to me."

She handed them their cups one by one, still speaking as she did so.

"I tried to help him find it. Just to get rid of him. I knew Wee Tam was comin', see?"

Wee Tam was looking at her, his concern for her obvious in his eyes and the tight set of his mouth.

"Got in his way. That's when he hit me."

She shrugged, almost apologetic.

213

"Knocked me over. Kicked me. Ach, the usual. He found it in the end. Where he'd left it. Took some money out and put it in his pocket. Just as well for Willie Johnston, eh?"

She managed a laugh. It was tainted with the bitterness of the night she was describing.

"That was that. He took the box and went out again. Never saw him after that. Not till they found him Sunday mornin'."

"That better?" asked Wee Tam, his eyes fierce as he stared at John. "Learned somethin', have you?"

"You said he was here about eight," said John, ignoring the anger in his tone. "How long did he stay?"

"Long as it takes to punch and kick a woman around," said Wee Tam.

Jessie smiled and hushed him.

"Wee Tam came just after he left. Musta' been gettin' on for nine. That right, love?"

Wee Tam was looking at them, the fury still in his eyes. He gave a sharp nod.

"Aye, and as soon as I saw what he'd done, I was away out again after him. And I still wish it had been me that caught the evil bastard."

Strangely, of the two it was Wee Tam who was nearer tears. Jessie's telling of the story had calmed her, helped her to push it outside herself, into the distance at which she needed to maintain it.

"Anything else?" John insisted, avoiding Wee Tam's stare.

Jessie shook her head.

"I was hurtin'. I was just sittin' here for a while. Then I boiled up some water, washed myself. Tried to ease the soreness."

She stopped suddenly.

"I think somebody saw me," she said, a frown on her face. "I had the bowl in here. I was washin' in front of the range there, and I coulda sworn somebody looked through the window." The frown deepened as she tried to recall the event. "It was just a quick flash outside. White, like. I caught it out of the corner of my eye. I pulled my blouse down and went to look but I couldna see nobody."

"You never told me that," said Wee Tam.

"Maybe it was nobody. Maybe I was dreamin'. I was that tired. I just went back inside and straight to bed. Folk had to wake me in the mornin' to tell me Jimmie was dead."

"And you could start livin' your own life," said Tom.

The words were spoken with affection. He wanted to help her get away from the nastiness she'd been talking about. Jessie smiled at him, a quick, reflexive smile which broadened as the truth of what he was saying became more obvious.

"Aye. You'll maybe have me as a daughter-in-law one of these days," she said.

"You'll be welcome, lass."

They drank their tea and, gratefully, moved onto the plans that she and Wee Tam had been making. The Clyde was still their favored location but Jessie surprised them all when they started talking about where the couple might live. After airing their imperfect knowledge of what Glasgow had to offer, they tried making comparisons with the types of property they might aspire to in Aberdeen.

"Bon-Accord Terrace. That's bonny," said Jessie, and everyone nodded agreement.

"But know where I'd like to live most of all?" she went on.

"The Castlegate," said Wee Tam, sure of his ground.

To his surprise, she shook her head.

"Guestrow. Or maybe Broadgait," said Tom.

Another shake of the head.

"The Ferry Hill," said John.

"Wrong, wrong, wrong," she said, pointing at them one by one.

"Where then?" asked Wee Tam.

Jessie folded her arms in her lap, looked round at them all again and, with a smile full of mischief, said, "Montreal."

****

Despite the persistent grayness of the weather, the following morning John went to sit at the top of the beach, not far from the spot where Jimmie had been found just a week before. He'd brought an apple with him, which he was polishing on the lapel of his jacket. The sounds of a hymn being sung in St Clement's church drifted across on the wind coming from the west, broken only by the regular wash of the waves up and down the sand. There were plenty of men in the church but the women's voices still predominated. Faint though it was, the music sounded miserable. It was a phenomenon that John could never understand. Here were these people, lifted out of their heavy, work-filled little lives to a level where they were being promised all sorts of delights, eternal painlessness and a love beyond time and space, and yet all they could produce by way of celebration was a dreary complaint. It made salvation sound thoroughly depressing.

Two barques and a brig were anchored near the harbor mouth, waiting for the Sabbath to pass so that they could be winched into their berths. Most of their crews had come ashore in longboats the previous evening and were spread through the streets and houses, sleeping off their excesses. As John bit into his apple and watched the sway of the distant masts in the

215

light easterly swell, he was humming his own tune, far brighter than the hymn, an outward indication of his feeling that all was right with the world. He'd thought a little about Jessie's version of Jimmie's last evening. It gave him a sequence, a timetable which he didn't have before but, apart from the shape at the window that might or might not have been a face, there was little else of interest. What he next had to do was set Jessie's story alongside that of the girl from Pensioners' Court.

CHAPTER TWENTY-SEVEN

On the Plainstones, the fact that it was Sunday seemed to make little difference. The men were, for the most part, more smartly dressed than at other times, but the choreography of their walking was unchanged and the smoke from their pipes drifted over them and curled in the little eddies and breezes. Anderson had been talking with two of his bankers but, seeing Glover strolling alone and obviously waiting to approach him, he excused himself and beckoned the shipwright over.

Glover was wearing the same jacket and trousers but his cravat was a dark plum red. It was held by the same silver pin, which Anderson noticed was in the form of the letter G.

"More threats?" he said, pre-empting any approach which Glover might have planned.

The shipwright was unperturbed.

"There never were any. And I hope we have left all such matters behind us."

"Do you?" said Anderson, setting out across the Plainstones once more. "Then you'll never achieve the success you're pursuing with such diligence. Why are you here?"

Glover walked easily beside him, looking around and taking obvious pleasure in the fact that he'd slid himself into one of Aberdeen's best known commercial rituals.

"Your iron ship..."

"I have no iron ship."

Glover smiled and inclined his head.

"The iron ship we were discussing," he corrected himself. "I've spoken with an acquaintance from Dundee who was here on business. He specializes in the manufacture of iron wire rigging."

Anderson stopped. Glover turned to face him.

"We were not 'discussing' an iron ship," said Anderson. "You were trying to sell me one. If no such ship exists, I see little point in talking of its rigging."

Glover raised a hand in a gesture that was both apology and protest.

"I was simply putting the advantages before you."

"Why? What's to be gained from it?"

"Mr. Anderson, when I speak to you of success, I don't just mean as a shipwright. My aim is much higher. I knew, many weeks ago, that Aberdeen would be looking for a resident superintendent and director of works and operations at the harbor. The word is that the man appointed will receive not less than two hundred and fifty pounds a year. Building ships of iron is only the first step of the journey I am hoping to make."

Anderson knew better than Glover just how dramatic the increase in activity around the harbor would be in the coming months. He'd already bought pieces of land and entered into agreements with constructors which would keep him even closer to the heart of things than Glover could imagine. The shipwright's ambition was a shadow of his own but Anderson was beginning to appreciate the man for it. He'd come to Aberdeen with bold thoughts of acquisition but the foundations beneath them had been carefully layered. Unless he had some motive, which he'd so far managed to conceal, he might prove to be a useful ally in some of the projects which lay ahead.

"Mr. Glover," he said. "I think, after all, that we may be able to work together."

****

Later, dinner at the Andersons was as sumptuous as ever: venison roasted with diced pork, served with braised celery and garnished with a sauce of port wine and rowanberry jelly. The smells were delicious, the meat was cooked to perfection and the flavors were strong and insistent.'

Helen found it all irritating. Her mind was too preoccupied for her to be able to give any attention to such basics. She ate quickly, sparingly and contributed so little to the conversation that neither Anderson nor Elizabeth was surprised when she asked if she might be excused to go back to the study and continue her commercial education.

"She seems eager to learn," said Anderson, when she'd left.

Elizabeth simply shook her head, a little frown on her brow.

"I wonder if my talk of marriage has unsettled her?" Anderson went on.

"No. She would have said something to me if it were that, I'm sure," said Elizabeth.

Anderson shook his head.

"Why is she such a complicated young woman?"

Elizabeth smiled.

"Because she has such complicated parents. Don't fret, she'll tell me whatever it is when she's ready."

In the study, Helen's thoughts were far from marriage and not even particularly focused on the papers through which she was leafing. Her meeting with John had excited her and she could still feel the whisper of his fingers on her cheek. The thought that those fingers were also coaxing her from the wood on his workshop floor was dizzying and she tried to force her attention onto the papers before her. By now, cargoes, manifests, tonnages, costs, and ships' specifications were becoming familiar and she moved quickly to other cabinets, looking for letters, scribbled notes, or anything that appeared to be different from the other things around them. Her interest in her father's business was still keen, but the world beyond the papers was bringing her new excitements. She wanted to know more about the mystery of the shipwright's murder and, most of all, she wanted to feel those fingers on her cheek again.

She looked out of the window but it was too dark to see any of the ships or masts. Ahead of her lay a Sunday evening turning on the same treadmill as always. The thought was too much. She got up, went quickly to her room and started looking through her wardrobe. Folded at the bottom of a heap on a shelf in the darkest corner, almost out of reach, she found a fine cotton chemise with a silk drawstring and delicate embroidery at the front and along the edges of its short sleeves. It was a present from an aunt who lived in Edinburgh and had brought it back from Paris for her. Helen had never worn it, finding it ridiculous to decorate a garment that was for wearing under a dress and would therefore never be seen. She folded it carefully in white paper and tied it with a length of cream silk. She pulled on a dark blue hooded woolen cape, tucked the white package under it and went quietly down the stairs again. Her parents were still talking in the dining room and she let herself out, knowing that the door would click when she shut it but that, even if they did hear it, by the time they came to see what it was, she would be far enough away to avoid them.

As she hurried along, she knew that she might be walking into danger. There were figures everywhere and, from the shouts and songs that came from some of them, they had already spent some time in one or more of the taverns. She stayed to the right, over near the edge of the quay, watching for bollards and mooring ropes. On the other side, nearer the houses, there was more light, but there were also more people. She saw sailors with their arms round girls, some of them astonishingly young. Now and then, a normal, seemingly respectable couple would walk by, their pace rather faster than usual. But mostly, the people in the streets were men. Some stood in doorways, scanning the passers-by, looking as if they were waiting for something, others scouted quickly along, their heads turning from side to side, watchful or searching. Only the drunks looked content, swaying and singing in their self-contained worlds. To Helen, it was a hostile place, very different from the quay she walked in daylight. Stationary or stalking, the men were menacing. The sight or smell of a young woman, especially one whose dress betrayed her as being someone of means, would draw them beyond reason, offering a fast and brutal satisfaction of the appetites they were carrying through the darkness.

Twice, she was greeted by seamen who'd just climbed down from their moored ship to start a night ashore. Each time, she quickened her pace, her dark cape and hood helping her to disappear into the gloom which hung beneath the hulls along the quay's edge. The night was not silent. The lapping water beside her and the tapping, singing rigging above were overlaid with the murmurings of the passing people. Occasionally she heard shouts and cries, sometimes from the streets off the quay, sometimes on board one of the ships. Halfway down Waterloo Quay, where there were fewer people but where even more menace lurked in the empty stone yards and workshops, she suddenly heard the breaking of glass and a man's voice screaming. Other shouting voices joined in and, still staying as close as possible to the water's edge, she hurried even more urgently away from the screams as they grew more shrill from the terror of whatever was tormenting the man.

She was already beginning to feel how unwise it was for her to be there, but she felt such a strong urge to talk of John that she'd determined to visit Jessie. Jessie was already far more interesting than Bella or Sarah and she knew that she would understand her. They would talk, laugh, and Helen knew that her excitement would be approved of. As she turned gratefully into York Place, she was eager to be inside the little house and speaking of things which would decide how she would live the next few weeks of her life.

But her senses had been sharpened by the fears which had grown in her since she'd left Regent Quay. York Place was completely dark, with only four or five windows showing any light behind them and none of them bright enough to illuminate the street outside. Ahead of her, though, she thought she saw movement. Maybe a dark shape. She stopped and immediately heard footsteps. It was the long and heavy stride of a man, the steel tips of his boots striking hard against the cobblestones. Helen couldn't quite see how far away he was but it was obvious that he was coming toward her. Jessie's house was only three more doors away but could she risk hurrying to it and knocking? What if Jessie were not there? Or if she decided not to answer, or was busy with something and couldn't come to the door? Helen pressed herself back against the wall, knowing that she had no time to debate things. The doorway of the house beside which she'd stopped was just a few yards further along. As the boots came nearer, she ran forward as lightly as she could and stepped into its recess. It was not nearly deep enough. She pulled at her skirts to hold them back against her legs but still they jutted out and, even if the man didn't see her, he'd be certain to brush against the material and turn to investigate whatever was in the doorway.

Then, just as she decided to run back to Waterloo Quay, the footsteps stopped and she heard a knocking. She heaved a silent sigh. The man was going into one of the houses. Her imagination was once again creating troubles where none existed. She heard a door open and leaned her head forward to look along the street. She saw no one. The man had obviously stepped inside, but the door was still open and a flickering light fell across the pavement. To Helen's alarm, she saw that it came from Jessie's house. She would have no option but to go back through the streets to her home again. But then, as she waited for the door to close, the man stepped back out onto the pavement. He was big and Helen thought that she had seen him before. Jessie stepped out into the street beside him. She reached up, locked her arms around his neck and lifted her head for him to kiss her. It was not the kiss of strangers or of a neighbor. This, without doubt, was Jessie's lover.

Helen drew herself back quickly. She heard murmurs from the couple, then laughter from Jessie. At last, the man said goodnight and, after another short silence, during which they were no doubt kissing again, Helen heard his footsteps start to clatter away up the street. There was a final call of goodnight from Jessie and the door was closed.

It meant that Helen would have to wait for a little longer in the doorway. Having come all this way through the darkness, she was disinclined to go straight back home, but she felt instinctively that it would be wise to leave a decent interval before taking her turn at knocking on Jessie's door. The image of the kiss she'd just witnessed was clear and troubling in her mind and, to shake herself free of it, she tried counting, then rehearsing the things she might say, then thinking of Jessie's dead husband. The darkness seemed to press against her in the doorway and, quite quickly, she decided that enough time had passed. She stepped out, walked the few paces to Jessie's house and knocked.

Jessie's surprise when she opened the door was obvious.

"Helen," she said. "What are you doin' out at this time o' night? Come away in."

Helen stepped inside and was immediately confused to see another woman sitting beside the table.

"Oh, dear," she said. "I'm sorry, I didn't know you..."

"Hush," said Jessie. "This is my sister, Rose."

Rose was equally embarrassed. She half stood, then, uncertain as to how to greet Helen, sat down again, contenting herself with a nod of the head.

"How do you do, Mrs.—er?" said Helen.

"Och," said Jessie, "we canna have you callin' me Jessie and her Mrs. Drummond. It's just Rose. Right Rose?"

Rose smiled and nodded.

"And I'm Helen."

"I ken," said Rose.

Helen tried once more to apologize for disturbing them but the two sisters both brushed her words aside. They seemed content to see her.

"I've brought you a present," she said, putting the paper package on the table.

Jessie looked from the parcel to Helen and back again.

"You must stop doin' this," she said.

"Why?"

"Because I've nothin' I can give you."

It hadn't occurred to Helen that her generosity might prove embarrassing.

"You give me your friendship," she said and, as Jessie began shaking her head, added, "And cups of really most awful tea."

Jessie laughed with her, then stood up, loosened the silk ribbon, unfolded the paper, picked up the chemise and looked with obvious delight at the material and the fine embroidery. Again, though, she shook her head.

"This is too good for me," she said. "You canna give it to me."

"But I have. It's yours."

"In that case," said Jessie, putting on a special voice, "we must have a cup of 'most awful tea.'"

The three of them laughed and, once again, Helen was charmed with the way that they pushed ceremony and correctness aside. She felt totally at ease.

"I have a confession to make," she said.

"Oh?" said Jessie.

"Yes. When I arrived in your street, I... I saw a man visiting you."

Jessie was silent for a moment.

"His name's Tam. They call him Wee Tam," she said.

"It isn't any of my business."

The smile was still on Jessie's lips.

"It doesna matter," she said. "It seems my business is everybody's business these days."

"What do you mean?"

"Oh, it's just Jimmie's dyin'. Folk canna just let it be."

Although that was one of the things Helen wanted to talk about, she decided to take the words as a warning not to. Nonetheless, as they chatted on, and Rose's understandable reticence began to thaw, references to the death kept recurring and, at last, Helen was provoked into saying, "Well, I'm sure people will invent the silliest ideas about it. I did."

"Oh?" said Jessie.

"Yes. In my stupidity, I started thinking that... oh, it's so silly when I remember it... I started thinking that, if a wife is happy about losing her husband, and if she has a man, then perhaps... perhaps it would not be too far-fetched to imagine that they had conspired to..."

She stopped, not able to make the full accusation. Jessie looked at her.

"You thought I could do that, did you?"

"Of course not. My mind was wild, my thinking was giddy..."

Jessie didn't move.

"I'm sorry, Jessie," said Helen, "but do you not see that if I could imagine such a thing, then others might easily do the same? And if enough gossip started spreading, it might cause you difficulties."

Jessie picked up the chemise, held it in her lap, and began stroking the cotton as she thought about Helen's words. Helen was surprised to see that there were tears in her eyes.

"Why do folk no' leave you to get on with your life?" said Rose. "The number of them I've told to leave her alone."

"I'm sorry," said Helen, feeling the rebuke.

"Ah, it's no' just you I'm speakin' about. It's... everybody. Questions all the time. They winna let it rest."

"Well, in a way, that's what I mean," said Helen. "If somebody doesn't find out what happened, it'll always be like that. People will go on wondering, guessing, saying hurtful things."

"No," said Rose. Her voice was sharp and there was real anger in her face. "Look, I know you've been kind to Jessie but you dinna ken nothin'."

Jessie tried to hush her but she ignored her.

"Jimmie was buildin' your father's ship, and he was maybe no' doin' it as quick as he might, but you dinna ken all the other things he was up to, all the folk he was harmin' with his... habits, and his filth. But others do know, other men, other women, even their bairns. They'll just be glad he's away. And they'll forget. There's other things to keep them amused."

"I'm sorry," said Helen, suddenly aware of how trivial and even insulting her curiosity was alongside the deeper hurts and more violent passions Jimmie stirred in those who knew him as a man.

"Behave yourself, Rose," said Jessie, putting the chemise back on its paper wrapping and standing to go and get more tea. "And you too, Miss Helen Anderson. I'm the widow. It's up to me, and I don't want to know who killed him."

She brought her cup back to the table.

"Anyway," she said, "I'm afraid to find out who did it."

"Afraid?" said Helen.

Jessie nodded.

"It'll be somebody I know, somebody he worked with or somethin'. God forgive me, for a while I even thought myself that it might be Wee Tam who'd done it."

"Wee Tam?"

Jessie shook her head, waving away the notion as foolish. The distress had gone from her face and been replaced by a fierceness, a defiance.

"I don't want to know," she said. "And I'll tell you somethin' else."

"What?"

"Even if they do find out who it was, they shouldna be punished, they should be thanked."

CHAPTER TWENTY-EIGHT

Jamie had finished the trailboards long before John had progressed to the finer details of the figure itself. With no other immediate orders to meet, John preferred to give him the time off to finish all the arrangements for his emigration, which was now only days away.

Toward the end of the week, he had a visitor. He'd just finished shaving tiny splinters of wood away from the eyes to form the upper lids. It was a critical process. Losing the balance between them would destroy the likeness and create an unnatural, even freakish effect. In this particular case, the task was made more difficult by the fact that they were composite eyes. As well as marking the little differences he'd noted between the right and the left in both mother and daughter, he had to blend youth and age. To complicate things further, he'd also made a conscious decision to give them a suggestion of the feline slant that had made Marie's gaze so distinctive. It was a tiny homage to Marie, an apology for allowing Helen to supplant her in his thinking.

As he stood back to check his progress, the door opened and, with a short tap on it to announce his presence, Anderson came in. John put down his mallet and gouge. Anderson nodded a greeting and looked immediately at the carving.

"I felt the need to spend some time away from my office," he said. "It occurred to me to come and see how far you'd got. Do you mind?"

John shook his head and waited, saying nothing as Anderson walked round the work, which was lying on its back on two wooden horses. At last, he nodded and looked at John again.

"Excellent," he said. "Congratulations."

John gave a quick nod of acknowledgement.

"Difficult to appreciate it properly as it lies, of course," said Anderson. "The head stretching back in such a way."

It was very perceptive of him. As it lay, the head did seem to be held artificially, at a false angle back from the trunk, but that was the way the work had to be done. John knew that, once it was raised to the vertical, then tilted forward so that the face was looking straight ahead, its character would change utterly. The whole thrust and arch of the body would be carried through the shoulders and neck into the head.

"I could lift it for you, balance it, show you how it'll sit against the prow," he said.

"No, no. I'll wait for that pleasure."

He bent and looked closely at the eyes.

"Remarkable," he said. "Already, they have Elizabeth's look about them. Although there is a certain... Oriental aspect to them, too."

He looked up at John, expecting a response to his observation.

"It's for when we begin trading with China again," said John, improvising quickly. "I think that, perhaps without knowing that I'm doing so, I try to make my figures more acceptable to those with different ideas of beauty from our own."

"Interesting," said Anderson, looking back at the carved face. "You think these opium wars will soon be over, then?"

John shrugged. He had no idea. He was just pleased to have been so quick with a convincing answer and, more importantly, relieved that the person that Anderson had identified in the figure was Elizabeth and not Helen.

Anderson held himself very still as he continued to look at the figure, but his admiration of it was clear. As he watched him, John realized that it was natural that, for him, the woman in the timber was Elizabeth rather than Helen. He'd commissioned a likeness of his wife and he was therefore seeing only what he expected to see. Perhaps, too, this younger version of her was closer to his image of the woman he'd married. Whatever the forces at work, John felt vindicated in the choices he'd made.

His sense of ease was banished as quickly as it had formed.

"I believe you know something of a woman called Bessie Rennie," said Anderson, his stillness unchanging and his attention still on the carving.

"Yes," said John, instantly alert.

Anderson looked across at him, appraising him. "Who is she? What is she?" he asked.

"A fairly wretched creature," said John. "She makes her way by finding things along the beach, begging a little."

"Stealing a little," Anderson added.

John gestured an acknowledgement that that, too, was possible.

"Which is why she's in the Bridewell," said Anderson.

"How do you know of her?" asked John, looking for some way to get his bearings.

"My daughter has a will stronger than that of most men," said Anderson. "For some reason, she's taken it into her head that this woman deserves to be helped."

"I believe she's right," said John.

"Yes. She said that you were one of the people whose support the woman had mustered. I don't know where she gets her information but she seems to have heard much about Miss Rennie and is determined to be of service."

It was clear from his words that Helen had said nothing of her visit to the workshop and their private conversation.

"It would be a Christian act," said John.

The look Anderson gave him showed exactly what he thought of Christian charity.

"But if she's in prison, there must be a reason."

"Perhaps, but it's also possible that those who detained her were mistaken. She's a harmless old woman, with little hope of anything in her life. Condemning her would be a waste of time and money."

Anderson lifted his hand and held it just clear of the surface of the carving, moving it slowly and following the curve of the face and neck. He seemed in no hurry to be away. John wondered why they were having this conversation and what other issues he wanted to raise.

"I've always found that it's politic to stay well away from things which aren't my concern," said Anderson. "We think we know about the affairs of others but we're usually guessing."

He was referring to Bessie and yet the words seemed more general.

"Yes, that's the... reasonable attitude," replied John. "But reason's not everything."

Anderson looked at him, a question in his face. John shrugged.

"It's destructive," he said. "It's taking the place of compassion."

"You don't hold with reason, then?"

"I have to. But sometimes I don't much like what it does."

"Such as?"

"It colonizes everything," John said slowly. "Makes things like instincts worthless. Science, what we know, is everything. There's little room for passion."

Anderson laid his hand on the carving. "There's passion here," he said. "Of a sort. But what purpose does it serve? Nowadays, things are judged by one thing, their usefulness. What use is this? Does it help the master to control his vessel? Get the yards round or the sails set more quickly? No. And yet I'm paying you to make it."

"Your crews believe she'll help them through the storms," said John.

Anderson gave one of his little laughs. "The same crews think it's unlucky to allow a woman on board." He lifted his hand and turned away from the oak figure. "Why should I help this woman in her cell?" he asked suddenly.

"She has no one else," said John.

"None of us does."

John felt a little rush of annoyance that Anderson could imply that he shared or even understood Bessie's condition.

"That's not true," he said. "Some have everything."

Anderson heard the change in his tone and looked at him. Once again, he seemed to be judging John. Without looking at the carving, he pointed toward it.

"Do you think, because you can make likenesses, that you know or understand the people you see? Do you think your opinion of this Rennie woman is worth more than mine?"

"I've seen her. I know her."

"You've seen me. D'you think you know me, too? Are you so gifted that you can judge me on the basis of your... imaginings?"

"I can guess."

Anderson shook his head. "No, I don't think so. At least, not with any certainty. You see surfaces. You're drawn into everyone else's ideas. Let me tell you how you see me. I'm greedy. I search for profits and discard those who stand in my way. I love money more than people. Is that the picture? More or less?"

This was dangerous territory.

"I would imagine you to be less simple than that," said John.

"Well, you're right. Ask yourself, I'm a rich man; why do I want more money? Well, maybe I don't. Maybe there's something else."

"Yes, I see that there could be."

"If I stand back, if I renounce all these enterprises, what happens to the structures they're part of? What happens to the people I employ?"

"So your actions are all based in altruism?" said John, his annoyance stirring again.

"No. Reality," Anderson snapped back. "Our world needs to be dynamic, to move forward, develop, change, get better. I'm comfortable enough to step aside from it but I choose not to. I want things to be governed by people who've made their own way, not by those who've inherited wealth and don't even know why they're in power. What I do makes me rich, but it also makes society work."

"And crushes those who get in the way."

"Yes. Sometimes."

"Like Jimmie Crombie," said John, surprising himself.

It didn't quite amount to an accusation but it brought a frown to Anderson's face. "What do you mean?" he said.

Already, John was shaking his head. "Forgive me," he said. "I've been rather preoccupied with Jimmie's death. It... Forgive me."

"And you think I may be connected with it?"

John said nothing.

"Responsible for it?" said Anderson. His voice, like John's, had been loud before, echoing around the workshop. Now, it had dropped to a murmur. "I would prefer you to be honest with me," he said.

John flapped a hand, trying to wave away the accusation. "I meant nothing. My anger speaks when I should be still," he said.

"Then the connection was there. You do think I know something of the death."

John sighed. "I'm an interfering man," he said. "Ask anyone around the harbor. I poke around in puzzles. I speculate about things. Jimmie was working for you and so you were part of my thinking."

"Fascinating," said Anderson, who seemed undisturbed by the information. "Well, it serves to confirm what I've been saying. We know so little of one another. For all that you imagine my life to be governed by profits, you must not think that I value them more highly than people's lives. Mr. Crombie was indeed costing me more than I need have paid, but I could have found many ways to rectify that, and murder was not one of them."

"I know," said John. "I'm sorry that I was so rude."

To compose himself, Anderson turned once more to the carving. The eerie sensation that it was his wife lying there behind them, witnessing their anger and John's accusation, defused some of the tension in him. He looked at her eyes, staring blindly up into the joists, and sensed the directness of her look, the warning that it would have sent him had Elizabeth herself been there. He gave a small shake of the head.

"It's I who should be asking your pardon," he said. "The morning has been rather trying. I've lost a cargo in Canada. And I've spent too much time with customs officers and other people who also assume they know what I'm thinking."

John's eyes flashed again.

"Not you," said Anderson, waving a hand to indicate the problems were elsewhere. "Others. Silly people."

John nodded. Anderson's apology surprised him and served to ease some of his own strain. "We're both to blame," he said. "I know you no

229

better than you know me." He gave a small shrug. "We have different views."

"Anger is a dangerous master, even if it's justified," said Anderson. "We should listen to the old wisdoms, 'Always conduct yourself toward your enemy as if he were one day to be your friend'."

"I hope I'm not your enemy," said John.

It brought a smile from Anderson.

"Everyone is my enemy," he said, before adding, "No, that's too dramatic. Or, if it is true, it's my own fault. I look for confrontations. I expect to find enemies and so... people oblige me."

"Why?"

"Why what?"

"Why look for enemies? Life's hard enough already."

Anderson nodded. "True," he said, "but it's something which... Oh, it's too far back, buried too deep to explain. And of no interest to anyone but me."

The words had a different resonance. They were spoken as much for himself as for John. John was surprised to glimpse a different man, someone who refused to conform to his image. Anderson trailed his fingers across the carving.

"My hope was that this commission would be different from the others. Mr. Crombie made that difficult. I'm sorry for that. This ship means a great deal to me." He paused, stroked the side of the figurehead. "That's why I'm naming her for my wife."

"He treated you badly, didn't he?" said John.

Anderson shrugged.

"Mr. Crombie? He tried to, yes. Oh, I know that he charged me more than I owed, delayed things. Even so, I wouldn't wish him dead."

John looked at him and knew that he meant it. Jimmie had abused his trust, been dishonest in his business dealings with him, and even tried to dig deeper using the enigmatic invoice from the Journal. Little wonder that the man was so skeptical about relationships. And yet he could still respond charitably to Jimmie's death. John remembered his own suspicions about him and felt a slight blush of shame. He made a quick decision and went to a chest of drawers in the corner.

"I have something for you," he said.

Anderson looked up, a frown on his face.

John took out some papers, sorted through them, chose the invoice and put the rest on the top of the chest. He carried it across to Anderson and handed it over. Anderson glanced at it, then quickly up at John.

"Where did you get it?" he asked.

"Jimmie Crombie's ditty box. He'd hidden it there."

230

"And why are you giving it to me now?"

"Because I think he was using it to extort money from you and that others might have the same idea."

Anderson nodded very slowly.

"Yes," he said. "But you're not one of them."

John looked at him, the flash of his anger rekindling briefly deep in his eyes.

"You still don't know me. It's not my way. Oh, it did occur to me, of course, that I might put it to some use. Not for cheap extortion but... well, there's still the matter of his death to be resolved. This may well be an important piece of paper."

Anderson was looking at him all the time, his face betraying nothing.

"In that case, perhaps returning it to me is... irresponsible."

"It's a charitable act."

The two of them held each other's gaze. John was right; giving the invoice to him had disorientated Anderson. It was an act of faith and there was nothing in the rules of his game that allowed for such a thing.

"You're a surprising man, Mr. Grant," he said. "Thank you."

John shook his head, dismissing the matter.

"I have no time for the evils that Jimmie Crombie perpetrated. He was even worse to others than he was to you. I suspect he had other things planned for you."

"Oh?"

John went back to the chest of drawers, sifted through the papers again and picked out another. Once again, he handed it to Anderson. It was the item about his father's death. To John's surprise, as Anderson read it, the color drained from his face.

"My God," he said, his voice low, almost a gasp.

John waited. Anderson took a long time to compose himself. In the end, he held the paper toward John.

"I have no need of it," said John.

Anderson lowered his hand again.

"What do you know of this?" he asked.

John shook his head.

"Nothing. I read it, that's all."

"Well... well," said Anderson, visibly working to regain control. "I had no idea how far he was prepared to go. And I revise my previous opinion."

"About what?"

"Had I known about this, I would not only have wished him dead, I'd have taken steps to cause his death myself."

"Murder?" said John.

"Yes."

"But you told me that..."

"I told you that I would never murder for profit."

He held out the cutting.

"This has nothing to do with money. This is... personal. There are some things for which I would kill."

His tone was cold, measured again. It was the William Anderson that John was used to.

"Are you sure you want nothing in exchange for these kindnesses?" asked Anderson.

It brought John back to the present. He thought of mentioning Bessie Rennie again. The paper might be useful leverage in persuading Anderson to intervene, but it would be just another piece of barter. He'd surrendered the invoice to show that not everyone could be bought and that, sometimes, trust was a valid currency; asking a favor would make the gesture pointless. If Helen was pleading for Bessie, that should suffice to sway Anderson eventually. John shook his head.

"Nothing," he said.

Anderson held his gaze for a while before folding the invoice and the cutting and putting them in his pocket. He looked again at the carving.

"This truly is a wonderful piece of work," he said.

"Thank you," said John.

"And you've unsettled me, Mr. Grant."

He nodded and went to the door. Before leaving, he stopped and, without looking back, said, "I'll do what I can for Miss Rennie."

CHAPTER TWENTY-NINE

The following day, to fix his eyes on wider horizons and stretch his cramped muscles, John strolled over to the Elizabeth Anderson to check some of the measurements he'd made of the prow. The heavy clouds had given way to a lighter scrim of bright, pale swirls. There was still no sky to be seen but the oppression of the early part of the week had lifted.

As he was noting angles and dimensions, he was joined by Glover.

"I saw you were here. Wanted to ask how the work's going."

"Well," said John. He tapped the deck. "It'll be ready before she is."

"Good."

He stood there, nodding slowly. It was obvious that there was more to come. John went on with his measuring then, as the silence stretched, stopped and looked at him.

"What is it?" he said.

"What?"

"You're not here to pass the time of day. What is it?"

Glover smiled, clapped him on the shoulder and stood up.

"Straight to the matter as usual, John, eh?"

John said nothing. Waited.

"What did the girl tell you?" asked Glover. "From Pensioners' Court."

John shook his head.

"Nothing of any import," he said, adding, "I'm not even sure she was the right one."

"They do all look the same," said Glover. "I thought it was her, though."

John bent to the timbers again.

"Why did you give that bill to Anderson?" asked Glover.

It came out of the blue. John kept his head lowered.

233

"Because it was his," he said.
"Did you know what it was?"
John felt annoyance at the questions.
"Why?" he said.
"He told me you'd given it to him."
"What are you, his confessor?"
"His colleague."
John laughed and stood up, dwarfing the other man.
"You have some very big, very wild dreams, Mr. Glover. Take care that your 'colleague' doesn't push them back into your throat and up into your brain."
Glover echoed his laugh, untroubled by the fierceness of the words.
"If I'd found the invoice, I'd have done exactly as you did."
"Is that why you wanted the ditty box?"
Glover paused only briefly but quickly covered his surprise.
"No. I'm a professional. It might have contained papers relevant to this commission. I leave nothing to chance."
He smiled and walked away. John promised himself that he would never trust the man.

****

May twenty-fourth was the Queen's birthday and work of all sorts was interrupted by the need to prepare for the festivities. The flag was hoisted on the Tollbooth, ships broke out their colors, which fluttered from masthead to masthead, along all the yards and down to the decks. All the mail and stage coaches were decorated and everywhere, colors and cloths flashed and waved against the buildings, lighting up the city's granite. Most of the men around the harbor and on the ships took the opportunity to drink even more and two ship's carpenters were so overwhelmed by her majesty's special day that they tore a spike off the Tollgate of the Wellington Suspension Bridge and broke the Toll House windows. Their celebrations would earn them each a ten shilling fine and the cost of the repairs.

John worked on his carving as usual, happy to hear constant laughter and greetings all around him. The day became brighter at three-thirty in the afternoon with the arrival of Helen. This time, she hadn't bothered to use Sarah and Bella to furnish an excuse. She'd already spoken to them of John far too often, and proposing more walks around the harbor with them, only for her to disappear in the vicinity of his workshop, would free their tongues and minds to invent the wildest of romances. In fact, neither her friends nor her family knew where she was and there would be no need to tell them.

She knocked, walked in, said nothing by way of greeting, and went straight to the carving. Her fingers ran over its surfaces, explored its now finely-detailed features and cupped over its cheeks, chin and head. With a single outstretched index finger she traced the line of each eyebrow, the nose and the upper lip. John said nothing, watching her, seeing his vision and its expression in that close relationship.

At last, she turned away from the figure, her hand still resting on its neck.

"She's even finer than she promised to be when I first saw her," she said. "Really, Mr. Grant, you're a magician."

He simply shrugged.

"One learns tricks," he said.

She smiled again and patted the figure.

"This is no trick," she said. "It's alive."

He shook his head.

"I confess that I'm not displeased with it, but one learns how to achieve the effects."

"Oh?"

"When Lord Sandwich was at the Admiralty, he had a liking for classical antiquities on the ships. His carvers simply whittled away to produce a male figure, gave it a trident and called it Neptune. Or, if it was a female figure, they added dogs, a crescent Moon, a bow and called it Diana. This is the same. I follow my sketches as closely as I can, but by using the pattern of your brooch, I... persuade you that I'm creating a likeness."

"I don't believe a word you're saying. And I don't think you do either," she said, with a final pat on the figure's head. "Now, I've come because we had a bargain and I've fulfilled my part of it."

He was becoming accustomed to her directness and no longer wondered whether it was a deliberate attempt at disorientation.

"I know," he said. "Your father came to see me. He said that he would help."

"He will. You need have no fears of that."

"I have no fears. Reservations, perhaps, but no fears."

"Reservations?"

"Yes. I have little faith in commercial activities."

"And that is how you judge my father?" asked Helen.

"In part," said John, a pulse of anger rising in response to the sarcasm in her tone.

"I find your dislike of commerce surprising," she said, her quick temper matching his. "Papa is bringing vast quantities of materials to Scotland which make it a richer place. He's opening people's eyes to other possibilities. Is commerce really such a terrible pursuit? What of the sailors who catch albatrosses and sell their skins in London for twenty shillings, or make pipe stems from their wing bones and tobacco pouches from their webbed feet? Do you dislike them also? Do you object to furriers paying young boys three shillings for a hundred rat skins? Or is it only the larger enterprises which pain you?"

"I am pained not by commerce but by what it does to people."

"Well, well," said Helen. "A very fine sentiment."

Both had raised their voices and, as they were speaking, each of them felt the absurd self-destruction they were practicing. How and why had they so quickly slid from the pleasure of another meeting into a sort of jousting contest? The silence bulged around them. John's anger turned back onto himself.

"I'm sorry," he said. "Your father is an admirable man. I don't know why I said the things I did. You... confuse me."

She shook her head.

"No, no. It was my fault," she said. "The devil gets into me. I... taunt people, provoke them, try to shock them, I suppose. And I've no idea why. I'm truly a dreadful person."

He nodded, she smiled, and the silence rose around them again.

"We're very stupid people," she said.

John laughed. "Yes."

She held out her hand. He took it and began to bend to kiss it.

"A handshake will suffice," she said, her smile wider.

He bowed and, holding her hand in the tips of his fingers, he shook it with a very slow, very formal gesture.

"Good," she said. "Now, what did you learn from Miss Rennie?"

****

As John gave her the details of Bessie's confession about using the fid on the dead body, he tried to soften its brutality. Helen, though, was greedy for information. She listened as he described the horror of the early morning beach, with the ragged old woman hunched over the corpse, a spike in her hand and evil in her heart. She noted his words calmly and urged him to be more precise and repeat some of the details of what he'd seen. John responded by dwelling on the lacerations on the body and the welt burned into the throat by the hemp. Her cool, thoughtful reactions drew them into a bizarre complicity.

"Then you think he was hanged?" she said.

"Yes."

"But his hands were not tied?"

"No. Why?"

"I was wondering why he would submit to being hoisted like a pennant without fighting. Surely the person who hanged him would need to subdue him in some way?"

"Perhaps he was unconscious. Or just unable to resist. He'd taken lots of drink."

Helen nodded and fell silent, considering his suggestion.

"Were there any marks on his head? Any signs of blows?" she asked.

John shook his head, recalling the sight of Jimmie's body.

"Nothing really serious. There were some scratches, but all the damage was on his body. His head was... intact."

"Then why was he unconscious?"

"I don't know, but that does seem the likely explanation."

Helen tutted.

"Mr. Grant, it's as well that you're not a member of the watch."

"Why?"

"If you were charged with solving all their mysteries, you'd be far too reasonable. Crimes are dark things, conceived and committed in the night of people's souls. The reasons for them defy analysis. They belong to the devil."

John thought that her words betrayed the sort of reading she did.

"They may belong to the devil," he replied, "but they're committed by men. And men leave the marks of their passage. I believe that a study of the marks will reveal the man."

"Or the woman," said Helen.

"I think that's unlikely."

"Why?"

"It shames me to say so but it's men who are responsible for most of the infernal things that happen. Crime is their country. When women are found there, it's invariably because they've been hauled there by a man."

He spoke softly, with a gentle conviction that needed no emphasis. Slowly, she lifted her hand and reached for his face, trailing the backs of her fingers over his cheek to repeat exactly his own gesture at their last meeting.

"There are more things in heaven and earth..." she said, adding "Do you like Shakespeare?"

He almost laughed at the incongruity of the question and welcomed the chance to break the spell which had gripped him.

"I read the great speeches but have difficulty grasping the rest."

"You prefer books of reason, logic, philosophy?"

"Certainly not. They would make my head hurt."

The trivia helped them to slip away from their intensity.

"Ah, so you've not yet heard of Charles Lyell's 'Principles of Geology'?" she asked.

He shook his head.

"He writes that the earth is much older than anyone ever thought," she said. "We shall have to change the way we think about it."

"You mean God didn't create it all in seven days? Well, well."

She laughed. "Tut, tut, Mr. Grant. Making fun of religion. Do you not fear the wrath of the Almighty?"

"I've no time for gods shaped to suit the priests who preach them."

"I'm not sure that that's an answer."

They both laughed and Helen began to walk around the workshop, looking at the timbers stacked against its walls and the tools hanging from various hooks. John remained by the carving, watching her slow movements. She came up to the chest of drawers in the corner, where she stopped and looked at the sketches laid on top of it. John went to join her, opened a drawer and pushed papers around until he found what he was looking for. It was a small scrap of paper. He handed it to her.

"People need something," he said. "Not all have the ease of living you and I enjoy. This is written on a stone in St Clement's churchyard. I copied it one evening last summer."

Helen unfolded the paper and read the inscription, which had been written with great care.

"WILLIAM CHRISTIE Labourer in Aberdeen, in memory of his children JANE, died March 1821, aged 1 year and 3 months. WILLIAM, died Septr 1830, aged 3 years and 8 Months. DIANA, died May 1834, aged 2 years and 4 Months. WILLIAM ROSE, died 8th Aug. 1837, aged 3 years and 6 months."

She looked up at him and he saw the understanding in her eyes.

"There was more space at the bottom of the stone," he said. "It may even have been filled since then. But you see, whatever I feel myself, I would hate to take away William Christie's dreams."

She was touched by his compassion and sincerity and resisted the impulse to say that the dreams were precisely what pinned William Christie in his misery. It made her angry that people comforting themselves with the promises of the hereafter were always more willing to acquiesce to the inequity of the now.

The chime of a church clock pulled them back to the moment and Helen realized that, if she did not soon appear at home, she would be questioned in too much detail about how she'd spent her afternoon.

"I must go," she said.

"Yes."

"May I come again?"

"Of course."

She looked at the figurehead then back at him and walked quickly back out onto the quay.

CHAPTER THIRTY

The following Friday, the usual crowds of porters, seamen, dockers and tradesmen on Waterloo Quay were swelled by others who rarely visited the harbor and had nothing to do with it. Some of them had come from as far away as Inverurie and Elgin, some were lost and afraid amongst the unfamiliar sights, sounds and smells. It was a special day because the strangers were there either to board the Clarissa or to say goodbye to friends and family who were doing so to go to their new lives in America. In the streets and on the quay near the ship, bewildered individuals wandered along, looking for familiar faces or lost pieces of luggage. Men and women, fathers, mothers, sons and daughters hugged one another, spoke in strained voices, forced out bursts of laughter, and were unable to hide their tears.

Jamie and his fiancée, Jenny, looked young, vulnerable and uncomfortable in their Sunday best clothes. Their trunks and bundles had been taken on board and stowed away for them by friends of Jamie's who worked as shore porters and they were standing on the quayside with nothing more to do, having no option but to accept the repeated embraces and advice of their parents.

The Clarissa was a three-masted barque, fully rigged on the fore and mainmasts and with a spanker, gaff topsail and two staysails on the mizzen. She had already made a dozen or more Atlantic crossings and was a solid, dependable ship, whose master had a reputation for seamanship and, just as important, honesty. With all the cargo on board, the crew was making fast the final lashings on the detachable wooden hut on deck which would serve as the galley. The master's custom was to get the cook to serve them a coffee royal to keep them sweet as they prepared the ship for sea. It was a grand title for what was simply the normal mug of coffee with a tot of rum in it, but it broke the routine and set the men singing as they heaved at the ropes to sweat them down tight around their cleats. The master had stowed three quarter casks of Demerara rum in his own stateroom to fortify them during the journey and try to keep them loyal.

As soon as Jamie saw John amongst the crowds, he excused himself from the clutch of his folks, leaving them to focus all their anxieties on Jenny, and pushed his way through the crush. The two men shook hands and John, with a nod of his head, beckoned Jamie to follow him to a far corner of the quay where there was less bustle.

"Well, big man. No turning back now," said Jamie, when they got there and stopped to look back at the people boiling around in the shadow of Clarissa's hull.

"D'you want to?"

Jamie shook his head. "No. But I'm no' a sailor, John. Neither's Jenny. Yon ship looks awful small when you think o' her in the middle o' the ocean."

"She's been back and forth often enough to find her own way there. And the skipper knows what he's doing."

"Aye, I ken. It's no' that, though, it's all sorts o' other things." Jamie waved a hand to encompass everything around them. "All this. I ken where I am, what's goin' on. I had a good job with the best carver in the North East. And I'm givin' it all up. What for?"

"Well, what?"

Jamie shrugged his shoulders. The expression on his face was one of genuine concern. "I've no idea really. I'm takin' Jenny over there and God knows what's waitin' for us."

John put a hand on his shoulder. "Well, for a start, there's diseases," he said.

Jamie looked quickly at him, saw his grin and let out a big laugh, which took away some of his tension.

"Aye, you're right. Might even catch somethin' on the way across, with so many folks on board."

"Inevitable," said John.

"No point worryin' about America, then," said Jamie. "We won't even get there. You're a great one for cheerin' folk up, John."

They stood side by side, watching the continuing swirl of people.

"When's Anderson's boat bein' launched?" asked Jamie.

"Next Wednesday."

"Pity. I'd like to have seen it with the figurehead and boards fitted."

"She'll look good," said John. "Your boards are perfect."

Jamie nodded. "How about Glover?" he asked. "Is he any good?"

John shrugged.

"He couldna be worse than Jimmie, though," said Jamie.

John gave a small laugh. "Maybe not."

There was a pause before Jamie spoke again. "You found out who killed him yet?"

John shook his head.

"Good."

"Why?"

"I hope you don't find out nothin'. He deserved it."

John looked at him to see where the sudden little edge of bitterness had come from and, briefly, the thought came to him that any of the people leaving on the Clarissa, including Jamie himself, could be responsible for Jimmie's death.

"You should see the stuff Jenny's Ma's made us take," said Jamie, changing his tone of voice and the subject. "Rice, candles, dried ham, sugar, tea. And enough biscuits to feed everybody on board."

John reached inside his jacket and produced a bottle, which he handed to Jamie.

"Did she not think of this?" he said.

Jamie looked at it. It was a pint of brandy. He didn't understand; John knew that neither he nor Jenny drank very much.

"Out there," said John, pointing seawards, "there's nowhere to spend money so it's not much use. But if the trip's longer than expected, rations can get a bit low." He tapped the bottle. "This'll be just the thing to offer the cook to make sure he keeps you fed and happy."

Jamie gave him a big smile. "How did you get to be so wise, John?"

"Easy. Worked with idiots so that I always looked clever." He reached into his coat again and took out a small wooden figure. It was about ten inches high, a perfect miniature of a female figurehead with its right arm across its chest, a bunch of flowers in the hand and a dress with long, sweeping folds.

"Recognize her?" he said, giving it to Jamie.

Jamie lifted it and looked closely at it, turning it in his hands to study it from every side. The tight curls along the forehead, the wide set eyes, the tilt of the nose and the slight downturn at the sides of the mouth made it instantly recognizable. It was Jenny. John had whittled it from a small piece of lime, a wood as easy to carve as butter, and he'd been able to scratch tiny creases into the face and textures into the hair and dress which gave the creamy figure a startling individuality.

Jamie looked from it to John and there were tears in his eyes. He shook his head and suddenly opened his arms and clasped John hard. John returned the hug, patting Jamie on the back and gulping back a lump which had come into his own throat.

"You're a great wee carver," he said. "If you get the chance to do it over there, take it. You'll get lots of work." With a final hug, Jamie drew back. "I owe you much more than seven pounds," he said, wiping the tears away.

"Well, just make sure I get that back before you start worrying about the rest," said John. "Come on, Jenny'll be fretting."

They went back to where the families were still fussing and laughing and crying and hugging. When Jamie showed Jenny the figure, she gave John a big kiss and he picked her up and made as if to carry her away into the crowds.

The Clarissa was due to be launched on the flood. Apart from the advantages this gave in terms of letting go the mooring ropes and swinging the ship round on the tide to head out of the harbor, it was a lucky time, a time of promise. Traditionally, ebb tides were felt to be depressing, bringing low not only the water but also people's spirits.

The crew began hurrying the passengers on board, which signaled more tears and frantic clutchings and embraces. With final hugs for his family and John, Jamie, the tears running freely down his face, put his arm round Jenny and helped her to climb the gangway up to the deck. They pushed their way to the rail on the starboard quarter and, along with all the other passengers, waved and waved to the pale sea of faces on the quay.

With the bow line still secured, the company's onshore crew let go the stern lines and the springs and threw them into the water. On deck, the crew hauled them inboard, coiling them near the capstans. Slowly, the incoming tide began to push the stern away from the dock and the Clarissa's quarters swung out into the flood. Held now by her bow ropes, she turned slowly through one hundred and eighty degrees and the passengers moved across to the larboard side to keep contact with the shore for the longest possible time. With a final call from the bo's'n of "Stand clear the checks there," and "Let go, for'ard," the ship began to move out from the dock into the flood and Jamie, Jenny and all the others were bound for America.

****

In the past few days, Jamie had spent very little time in the workshop, and yet, later that afternoon, when John sat there looking around it, it felt very empty, despite the presence of the two young lads he'd taken on who were hacking away at newly delivered pieces of elm at the back of the shed. The commissions were still coming in but it would be many weeks before they were ready to start any of the finer work. All the real carving had to be done by John and he knew that he would have little time to spare until the winter came.

He'd intended to put the finishing touches to the Anderson carving but instead, had wandered around, finding little memories of Jamie everywhere, tools stowed in places he wouldn't himself have chosen, little sketches, rags and an old apron. He ran his eyes and hands over the trailboards, feeling the cuts and shavings that were the last Jamie would ever do for him. Jamie's face and laughter came to him and he shivered to think that, for the days to come, he'd be bucketing about on an ocean that could be as savage as any in the world.

John was still steeped in memories and regrets when, toward four o'clock, after the new lads had left, the door opened and Helen walked in.. She felt the somberness of his mood and, at first, was afraid that she was its cause. His smile was less ready, his eyes held a sadness and his low, slow voice carried more shadows. She was careful to confine her questions to details of the carving and the preparations for fitting it to the ship. It was when John was describing how the trailboards would extend the figure on either side of the bow that he spoke of Jamie's departure and she realized why he was so changed. She asked him about Jamie and, gradually, as they spoke, the specter of loss was replaced by memories of all the good things that had happened during his time as John's apprentice.

"I was surprised when he said he wanted to emigrate," said John. "Didn't realize that was part of him at all."

"But you must have known him well."

"I thought I did. How can you know what people are thinking, though?"

"We do it all the time," she said.

"What?"

"Assume we know what people are thinking. We label them whether they like it or not, whether it fits or not. They become designated and the designation is their truth."

John smiled at her. She wasn't sure what the smile meant and felt a quick annoyance with herself for speaking before thinking.

"However," she said, "it's not philosophy which brings me here."

"No?"

"No, your investigations into Mr. Crombie's death intrigue me."

"To speak the truth, I've almost forgotten them," said John. He pointed at the carving. "With this to finish and Jamie's departure, my mind has been somewhat distracted."

"Then we must reopen the enquiry," she said. "You owe it to Mr. Crombie. And, anyway, your descriptions of it all have quickened my own curiosity further. Indeed, I've thought a great deal about what you told me on my last visit and I find your arguments somewhat flawed."

John grinned. For all the seriousness of her tone, she'd become an eager young girl again, playing some society game.

"Do you?"

"Yes. For example, I find your explanation of how he allowed himself to be hauled aloft without protest very limited."

"Really?"

"Yes. Frankly, it lacks imagination."

"Then perhaps you'll enlighten me."

Helen's face suddenly became grave. She'd been pacing about as she spoke, her long dress swishing through the shavings on the floor, but now she stopped before him and looked straight into his face, her eyes looking into his. She raised a hand and put her forefinger on his chin.

"Indeed I will," she said.

She lowered her hand and looked around the workshop. A large block and tackle, which they used to hoist the bigger pieces of timber and carvings on and off the horses, hung from a rafter. She went across and held the rope, looking closely at it.

"The rope which was used to hang him; was it like this?"

John shook his head and went across to her.

"No. This has been made up. Jimmie was strangled with raw hemp."

"Have you any?"

He looked around.

"Perhaps."

"Could you show it to me?"

John smiled, bowed and began to look among the scraps and shavings on the floor and shelves. He found two lengths at the bottom of the cupboard which Jamie had used for storing his efforts at more complicated patterns.

"There, you see," he said, putting them on the bench before her. "Just strands. No plaiting."

She looked down at them.

"But they'd need to be in a loop, wouldn't they?"

John picked up the longer piece and quickly tied a slip knot in it, holding it for her to see. She looked, took the loop from him and nodded.

"Did you know that Jessie Crombie thinks that a woman might be responsible?"

"No. How do you know that?"

"She told me. I've paid her one or two visits. We've talked about it."

"Did she say why she thought such a thing?"

"No. There were things she knew, things her husband had done, which were beyond mention. From her words, I would guess that his victims on those occasions were women. Jessie seemed to think that their reasons for killing him were greater than those of his business acquaintances."

"And did she say who they might be, these women?"

Helen lowered her eyes, remembering Jessie's tears.

"She didn't want to talk about it. She didn't want to find out. She was afraid it would be someone she knew."

"Aye, I know," said John. "But we can't just let folk be killed. It doesn't matter whether they deserve it or not. We may not have to do anything about it, but we have to find him."

"Her."

"No, him. Jimmie had a rope looped around his neck and somebody hoisted him up over a spar. No woman could have done that."

"Not a single woman, perhaps, but if there were many of them. If he'd offended so many that..."

She stopped when she saw the smile on John's face.

"You think I'm too fanciful," she said.

"I think that you may be asking too much of reality," he replied.

"Oh, so that is what you think."

Her tone made him look at her. She turned away, apparently in deep thought. When she turned back, there was a new look in her eyes, one John hadn't seen before. She was directly in front of him. She reached up with her hands, put them on his shoulders and gently pushed him down so that he was sitting on the bench, her hands still resting on him.

"You asked me why I came here. Let me ask you, too, why do you tolerate my visits?"

He looked up at her, unsure whether this was still a game. There was a different intensity in her expression now.

"I don't tolerate them, I welcome them. I look forward to them. They... entertain me."

She put a finger to his lips.

"Hush," she said.

He raised his hand but she stepped away from his touch. Only when he lowered it again did she move back.

"We're neither of us fools, Mr. Grant. We both know that there's some of Dr. Mesmer's animal magnetism flowing between us when we're together, isn't that so?"

"I know nothing of Dr. Mesmer."

She leaned forward, keeping her eyes locked on his. Her lips parted, her hands slid down his arms.

"And it is only decorum, correctness, fashion that inhibits its expression."

John had never felt such power in a woman. He was held, willingly, inside the spell she was creating. He sensed that it was part of another of her games but it was one he enjoyed. He felt her right hand brush over his left. She lifted her fingers and, again, trailed their backs down his cheek, then upwards across his eyes, which he closed to feel her fingertips like gossamer on his lids. Their faces were very close and he felt her warmth and breathed a smell of sweetness.

Suddenly, without warning, she straightened up and, simultaneously, John felt a scratching below his left ear. A reflex brought his hands up and he felt the loop of hemp around his neck. She stepped back and, immediately after the surprise, John felt a rush of anger. There were some games which were too close to reality to be played without cruelty.

Helen saw the flash in his eyes and raised a hand.

"Forgive me. I'm sorry. I did not wish to make either of us feel foolish or cheated. It was my way of..."

"No apologies are needed," said John, interrupting her with a voice suddenly very cold. "It was I who was foolish. I should know my place."

"Oh nonsense," said Helen. "I just wanted to show you that Mr. Crombie might easily have been vulnerable to a woman. There are forces other than brute strength which..."

John grabbed at the loose end of the hemp, which was still around his neck, and held it toward her.

"Perhaps you know, too, how the whore who slipped on the halter then hoisted him with it. Perhaps you could show me that force, too."

The emphasis he put on the word "whore" brought a flush to Helen's cheeks. She pressed her lips together, biting back the sharp reply which came to her.

"I meant no harm," she said.

John dragged the hemp from his neck and threw it into a corner.

"You should leave," he said. "The game has finished."

She glared at him, angry at her own stupidity and his extreme reaction to it.

"I wasn't playing a game," she said, her own anger now as hot as his.

"Leave," he repeated. "I've had dealings enough with the Andersons."

She clenched her fists and made a sound that was just less than a scream before walking quickly to the door. As she got there, she stopped and, in a voice too loud and angry for the words she was saying, shouted, "It was not a game. I do not toy with people or affections in such ways. You are a boorish, bad-tempered, vile man."

"Thank you," said John. "You are perfect."

CHAPTER THIRTY-ONE

Gossip stales very quickly, and Joe Drummond hoped that other things of interest would be occupying the people living and working around the harbor by the time he returned. He'd been away for several days and the work had been cold and hard. He was ready for a drink and a woman. As his ship swung into her berth, he was getting the baskets on deck ready for slinging up onto the quay but, as he looked up for the slingers, he knew that some things had stayed the same. John Grant was standing there again.

Unloading took the best part of two hours and when Joe finally came ashore hauling his kit bag onto his shoulder, John stepped up beside him.

"Give us a chance to get home," said Joe, already angry. "I've a wife to see."

"You'll see her soon enough," said John. "Probably too soon for her liking."

Suddenly, Joe swung his arm at John's head. John swayed back and the punch just caught the point of his chin. Joe dropped his bag and stood ready, fists clenched.

"You'll talk with me," said John. "I'm sick of you lying."

Joe lunged forward, his arms around John's chest, and the two of them fell onto the flagstones. John managed to roll sideways as they fell but he still came down heavily on his left shoulder. The people nearby stood back in order not to get tangled up with it all. Very quickly, a circle had formed around them.

John rolled so that he was on top. Joe had freed one arm and brought a punch up into John's stomach, knocking the breath out of him. John grabbed the arm and dragged his knee up to press down on it and hold it against the ground. His left hand grabbed at Joe's hair, lifted his head and slammed it down again. Joe arched his back and bucked John off him so that he pitched forward, his face grazing across the stones. Quickly, they were both on their feet. Blood was flowing from Joe's nose and a cut at the back of his head. John's cheek was weeping blood from beneath his eye down to his jaw. Simultaneously, the two of them flung themselves forward again, each scrabbling for a hold, digging with nails, trying to bring a knee up into the other's groin. Joe's head snapped forward, aiming at John's nose, but John twisted his neck and caught the blow on his already damaged cheek. He dropped suddenly, caught Joe's leg and upended him again. Quickly, he was astride his chest, his knees once more pinning his arms. His right fist slammed into Joe's face and neck again and again. Joe's left eye was nearly closed and the blood from his nose was now a thick stream running down into his beard.

John was unloading many frustrations: his own treatment of Helen, the memory of what Joe had done to Rose, and Joe's refusal to talk about the night out with Jimmie. As he pummeled at Joe's head, there was an exhilaration in him, a satisfaction that he was imposing himself. Winning. After a very short time, with Joe now obviously too weakened and damaged to resist, two men stepped into the circle, grabbed John by the shoulders and pulled him off. At first, he tried to shrug them away but, as soon as he was clear of Joe and he saw that there was no fight left in him, he stopped struggling and the two men bent to help Joe. Joe pushed them away and, after looking at the two fighters, the men decided that it was all over and, along with the rest of the crowd, went back to their work. Fights were common enough happenings on the quays and, soon, John and Joe were left to themselves again.

"You know about Jimmie and you'll tell me," said John. "I didn't want any fighting, but I've a taste for it now, so what's your choice?"

Joe was sore. John's anger had surprised him and he needed to wash his cuts and stop his head from throbbing. One day, he'd get his revenge, but not now.

"I need to clean myself," he said.

"We'll go to my workshop," said John.

"And I want a drink."

"After," said John.

Joe stood up, picked up his kit bag and started to walk down the quay. John followed him, just a pace away, ready to renew his assault if needed. Everyone they passed looked at the blood on their faces and clothes, many wishing they'd been there to see it happening. As they walked, John had time to gather himself once more and start regretting that he'd let his temper take control again. He also felt disgusted at himself for having enjoyed landing all those punches and for taking pleasure, however briefly, from the pain he was giving.

At the workshop, they washed the worst of it all away in cold water and sat on the bench beside the table. Joe's nose continued to drip blood, his head still throbbed and both men were aching from their bruises. John wanted to get it over as quickly as possible.

"Now," he said. "I've heard all sorts of things about that night, and if you don't start telling me some truths, I'm taking you straight to the watch and telling them you know who killed Jimmie."

"I don't," said Joe.

"You've been lying all the time."

Joe started to protest but John raised his voice and continued.

"No, listen. You said you took the girl to The Links. You didn't. One minute you're saying Jimmie went to his boat, the next you say he went to see a woman. You said you went home after you'd finished with the lassie. You didn't. You didn't get home till late on the Sunday."

Joe stood up. John leaned forward and slapped him hard across the face, spraying blood across the table. He pushed Joe back down again.

"Stay there," he said, the anger back in his voice. "I want the truth. Let's start with the girl. Where did you go with her?"

"I told you. The Links."

It was John's turn to jump to his feet. He grabbed Joe by the hair and wrenched his head back. The blood started running from the cut on his head again.

"Liar," he shouted. "Look, I don't have time for this. You tell me, or you tell the watch, and I'll take you there myself, now."

Joe pulled at his wrist to loosen his grip. John's fingers stayed tangled in his hair.

"Now," he repeated.

"All right, all right," said Joe.

John released him and sat down again. He held a finger to his face, pointing a threat.

"So where did you take her?" he said.

Joe rubbed his head and looked around the workshop before answering. He kept his eyes lowered as he spoke.

"Jimmie's yard," he said.

"Why?"

"To take her on board the new boat."

"What for?"

Joe was slow to answer. John prodded his finger into his chest to prompt him.

"It'd be bad luck. For Anderson."

"How?"

"Everybody knows. A woman on board ship. Worst thing you can have."

"Why Anderson?"

"He deserves it, the bastard."

"And you were on your own there with her?"

"Yes."

"Where was Jimmie? You said he went to the boat."

"He didna. He... he went home."

The hesitation was obvious. This still wasn't the truth. Or, at least, not all of it.

"Home?" said John. "I thought he went to look for a woman."

Joe shook his head.

"No. I was... That wasna right. He went home."

John tried a different tack.

"Did he give you his pebble before he left?" he asked.

The quick look Joe gave him and the wildness in his eyes told John that his tactic had worked.

"I know you had it, and Jimmie would never give it away. It was his lucky stone. Everybody knew that. And I know you saw him at the yard. That's why you said he went there. Because you saw him."

Joe's eyes looked down at the floor, his fingers scratched at the material of his trousers.

"You didn't kill him for his lucky stone, did you?"

"I didna kill him," said Joe, looking straight at John.

"How did you get it then?"

Joe's breathing was short, coming in little gasps.

"You saw him at the yard, didn't you? When you were there with the girl."

"I didna kill him," said Joe again. "He was asleep. That's what I thought."

"Where?"

"In the yard. I sent the girl home."

John waited. Now that he'd started, Joe would want to tell it all.

"I went for a drink. I didna have much money left, though. I started to go home, then I got the idea that... I was stupid, no' thinkin'. I thought I'd go on board the boat anyway."

"What for?"

Joe shrugged.

"Do some damage. I don't know. But I never went on board."

"Why not?"

"I saw him. Round the stern of the boat. Just lyin' there. I thought he was asleep."

"With all the marks on him?"

Joe shook his head.

"He didna have no marks on him. Nothin'. Honest, John, he was just lyin' there like he was asleep."

"What did you do?"

"I shook him. But he didna make no noise or nothin'."

"What about the pebble?"

"It came out on his collar when I shook him. I saw it. Took it. It was lucky."

He grunted a bitter little laugh.

"And you didn't see the marks on his neck?"

"I told you, there wasna any marks. Nowhere."

"And you didn't think to take any money? His pockets were full."

Joe's head was already shaking.

"There was a shillin' lyin' beside him. It must've fell out of his pocket. I took that. But I wasna thinkin' right. I was drunk. The stone was just a thing, an idea. I didna... I didna think I was stealin' it."

"And you told nobody about seeing him? Didn't try to get help."

"No."

"What did you do?"

Joe was silent for a moment, then, "I went for a drink."

"And left him there?"

"What could I do? We was fightin' earlier in Pensioners' Court. If I'd stayed, they'd have said I killed him."

John still wasn't convinced that he hadn't killed him. He'd said himself that he was acting stupidly, that he was drunk and didn't really know what he was doing. Or perhaps this was all true, and Jimmie had simply hidden the box on board, come ashore, and dropped dead. But then, why the lacerations? Why strangle him? Why take him to the beach? Joe's story had filled some gaps but opened others.

"I'm no' saying nothin' to the watch," said Joe. "I'll tell nobody nothin'. He's dead. Leave it be. Think about Jessie."

John remembered Rose's cut face.

"Aye, like you think about Rose," he said.

He wanted Joe to be away. He needed to make sense of the new information. There was already too much to explain.

"Listen," he said. "Go away now. Go and fill yourself with more ale. But remember you've told me all this. And remember I'll be straight to the watch if I think I need to tell them."

Slowly, Joe stood up. His head ached more and the pain of his cuts stabbed at him. He really needed to drink. He limped to the door.

"And don't think of signing on for any more long trips. Not until this is all over," said John.

Joe showed no sign of having heard him. He went out and closed the door.

****

That evening, John found it impossible to stay at home. He ate chunks of bread and cheese, washed them down with strong coffee and found himself incapable of sitting still by his lamp. His argument with Helen had been overwhelmed by Joe's confessions and his mind whirled, feeding on its own confusions. To ease away the pain of his bruises and try to tire himself, he walked along the beach, striding through the sand, kicking at pieces of flotsam, picking up pieces of wood and flinging them out into the waves.

He walked all the way to the mouth of the river Don and back again and, tiring at last as he came near to Footdee, he forced himself to recall everything that others had said about Jimmie. If Joe was telling the truth, he'd seen his body in a normal condition, so where had all the marks come from? And why? Helen's demonstration with the hemp, stripped of the angers and misunderstandings it had generated, had been telling. There were many other ways that Jimmie could have been strangled, many other explanations for his actions that evening and the marks that had been left on him.

He stopped at last near the brae leading back up into Footdee and looked at the sand, picturing Jimmie's body, hearing Bessie's moaning and the murmuring of all the others as they'd arrived to look at the dead man. He heard a woman calling for a child in one of the nearby streets and the perpetual wash of the sea up the sand. He thought of Jamie in the Clarissa somewhere out over the horizon. More distant calls suggested that another ship was being prepared for undocking the following morning and a single horse clopped along the other side of the harbor wall on its way to the lower basin.

It was as he was trying to bring together the stories of Joe, the girl, Jessie and Glover that he suddenly saw how, after all, Helen's suggestions could be right. His thinking had been very narrow. He'd concentrated on Jimmie the trader and not Jimmie the man, who was even more culpable in his personal habits than in his commercial ones. If John allowed Helen's view to prevail, the possible Saturday night encounters took on a different character, with different individuals inhabiting them. The forces driving the killer changed their direction and John saw how strength might not be a factor.

The more he thought about it, the further he moved from his previous thinking. Trade might still be a motive but, if it was, then there were accomplices involved. Slowly, an explanation began to form in him that had never been part of his deductions, a different way of seeing Jimmie's final trip to the place where he was found. He tested it against all the pieces of evidence he'd gathered one by one and none of them worked against it. Attaching names to the guilty parties was a little more difficult but there were obvious candidates. It wasn't something he wanted to do but, being now so far in, he couldn't draw back. It would be a hard, painful process that would make him few friends.

But it might help to lay the ghost of Marie.

CHAPTER THIRTY-TWO

While Joe's revelations had helped take John's mind away from the unpleasantness of the dispute with Helen, she had had no such diversion and his hard words had stayed with her. Her way of dealing with them was to try to bury herself in studying more of her father's papers. Once again, she excused herself after dinner and went to sit in his study. She pushed aside all those documents whose contents she could guess, glancing occasionally at a bill of lading to admire the range of materials in which he traded and the sums he'd managed to accumulate, but looking again for the more personal items.

When her father joined her later, he found her reading a copy of the Journal dated Wednesday, 12 March 1817.

"Interesting?" he asked.

Helen gave a little frown. "Yes, but I'm puzzled at why you should keep such a thing."

He smiled. "Are you really?" he said. "Let me show you."

He took the paper from her, opened it at the third page and pointed to a small item in the fourth column.

"BIRTH. At Aberdeen, on the 22nd ult., Mrs. Elizabeth Anderson, wife of William Anderson, of a daughter."

Helen smiled and put the paper on the desk. "Not one of your more profitable announcements," she said.

"On the contrary, it was perhaps the best."

"Perhaps?" she said, with mock surprise.

"Definitely," he replied. "Why? Are you forming an impression that profit is all that concerns me?"

"Certainly not. Although it's clear, even to my mere woman's perceptions, that you have a talent for making inspired choices."

Anderson pulled a chair across to sit beside her. "And your ability to make such assessments," he said, "Suggests that you may well have inherited that talent. Even though, as you say, you're only a woman."

"I wish so much that were true," she said. "I would then be better fitted to control my impulses."

"Then you would not be you."

"Perhaps. But it's so frustrating. An idea comes to me and I leap at it, giving no thought to its consequences. I create bedlam, not for others but for myself."

Anderson could not, of course, guess that her thoughts were provoked by recalling the harsh words she and John had spoken earlier. He wondered what, in his papers, could have started her thinking in such a way. Her next question did nothing to clarify things.

"When you were my age," said Helen, "what were you like?"

Anderson frowned. "I've no idea. Probably much as you are. Inquisitive, independent, usually ready to disagree with my elders."

"Were you a passionate man?"

Anderson laughed. "What an extraordinary question," he said.

"But were you?"

He thought about it. "About some things, yes."

"What?"

"My work. Your mother."

"That's an excellent answer," said Helen.

"Yes. I succeeded in deceiving her sufficiently for her to marry me."

"Deceiving her?"

"Yes. She believed that I'd protect her against that little Frenchman, Bonaparte."

Helen giggled.

"He was occupying almost everywhere in Europe at the time," said Anderson. "Everyone was terrified of him. I told your mother that I was ready to join the army to fight him. She thought that was heroic."

"It was, if it was true."

"Actually, if she'd encouraged me to do it, I would have, so I suppose I must have meant it. But, fortunately, she just believed me and she didn't require such a sacrifice. I could concentrate on making life comfortable for us instead."

"Oh, how disappointing. You preferred comfort to passion."

"Oh no, there were moments. Our parents had matched us. Your mother was obliged to accept me but, fortunately, we did love one another, too. I'm sure there were fires and pains... But too long ago for me to rekindle them now. Anyway, passion is too destructive."

The argument with John was too recent for Helen to disagree with such a conclusion, but these glimpses of her father's vulnerability were tantalizing. She reached across the desk to some other old copies of the Journal which she'd found at the bottom of a chest.

"Are these more examples of the passions of William Anderson, or simply records of his commercial successes?" she asked.

Anderson picked them up and flicked through them, shaking his head. "I don't recall why I kept them," he said. "If I read them thoroughly, I would probably remember. But I thought it was commerce, not passion, that brought you here. Have you tired of it already?"

Helen took the papers from him and began to look for one which she'd noted earlier.

"No," she answered, "but what intrigues me is when the two coincide."

"It's a dangerous combination. Your judgments must remain clear. Passion clouds them."

Helen found the item she was looking for. It was the announcement of the death of Anderson's father and the loss of the vessel, its crew and cargo which had preceded it, the same item that John had found in Jimmie's ditty box. She handed it to her father and saw at once the effect it had on him.

"Tell me about my grandfather," she said.

Before she'd uttered the words, his head was already shaking. He sighed deeply. "You do have my talents," he said.

She didn't understand what he meant and waited for him to go on.

"Showing me this as we speak of passion and judgment, it's a clever strategy."

"Not strategy, Papa. Curiosity. Mama said that she thought that you changed a lot when your father died."

Anderson nodded. "I did. It was..." He stopped and appeared to be considering the words he was about to utter. The silence in the study was deep and velvet. "What else did your mother say?"

"Nothing. Except that he was a clever, successful merchant."

Anderson nodded. Once again, the silence pressed around them. Anderson's fingers began tapping on the desk. At last, he seemed to make up his mind.

"He was. And it destroyed him," he said. "It destroyed him and made me what I am and gave us all the comforts we enjoy." He pushed the newspapers aside and leaned toward Helen. "Are you sure you want me to speak of this?" he said. "It concerns more than commerce."

Helen felt his solemnity. Thoughts of John had long gone and there was a thrill in this quiet intimacy with her father.

"Yes," she said.

Anderson nodded again. "He was a ruthless man, hard in his dealings. Hard with my mother and me, too. But he provided for us. Handsomely. And it cost him his life. If he hadn't died, our family might have had nothing."

"Why?"

"It's an unpleasant story. He'd overstretched his resources. He had cargoes in several ports, but not enough ships to carry them. Others saw their opportunity and forced him into... special arrangements. It was simple. They saw the chance to undermine his power and his wealth; that was what they wanted most. But he was always a match for them. He made sure that those arrangements involved activities outside the law. Everything was hypothecated on his word but he'd tied the agreements up in such a way that, if he died, none of them could make any claims against his estate without revealing their own transgressions."

"I'm sure that..." Helen began, but her father held up a hand to stop her.

"This is about business," he said, "but it's beyond the things we've been speaking of. Don't judge or comment until you've heard. Yes, the transactions strayed outside the law, but their outcome was devastating."

He reached forward and took her hands in his.

"I'm telling you something which I haven't even told you mother. Because I think you need to understand everything before you let your curiosity drag you further into my world. Your grandfather was a clever man indeed, but he paid dearly for it. You see..."

He stopped. It was clearly difficult for him to continue. Helen waited, then said, "Tell me, Papa."

Anderson looked into her eyes and gave her a small smile in which she saw a deep sadness. "Well then," he continued, "he made all these arrangements, secured his contracts. Then, the moment he'd put the last safeguard in place, he came home, had a meal with us, then went down to the cellar and hanged himself from a beam."

Helen gasped. This was beyond anything she could have imagined. As he went on, her father's voice was quiet but steady.

"I'm very sorry to say such a thing to you. I've given you a terrible burden. But it's part of who we are, my dear."

Helen's head was buzzing with questions and confusion. She could find no words.

"Perhaps that tells you why I trust no one," her father said. "It's why I drive such hard bargains. I owe everything to my father and none of the people who drove him down into that cellar will ever get the better of me."

Helen felt enormous depths opening up in her mind. This was no longer a game. She stood up, put her arms around her father's shoulders and leaned into him, kissing his cheek. The two of them were silent for a long time. At last, she whispered, "I'm so sorry, Papa."

Anderson gave a little shake of his head. "There you have it," he said. "Trade in Aberdeen."

****

On the Tuesday night before the Elizabeth Anderson was due to be launched, as Glover and Anderson were supervising the final preparations, John and Tom were sitting on the Footdee wall, looking out over the beach at the usual sails, near and distant, beating toward the harbor mouth or squaring off to run downwind toward Dundee, Leith, London and Holland. There was enough light left to give the sand a warm orange shine as it curved up and around to Peterhead.

At first, their talk was of the launch and of the reputation Glover had already earned for himself around the docks and in the town.

"He's no' the only one who's bein' noticed," said Tom.

"Oh?"

"Aye. I saw your lassie on the bow. I've never seen you do a better one. You're flatterin' the woman but it's a grand piece o' work. They'll all be askin' for you now."

"They already do," said John, wanting to shift the emphasis away from the carving.

"It's probably because you're so modest."

"Aye. Must be."

Tom sucked at his pipe and spat onto the sand.

"Well, we wouldna have been this far ahead if Jimmie'd still been in charge."

John reached over and picked up a long splinter of wood that had been washed ashore. It looked as if it had been split from a spar. He poked it into the sand and scratched patterns at his feet.

"Have you been thinking any more about how he died?" he asked.

Tom spat again and inspected the stem of his pipe to see where the bitter taste was coming from.

"No. It's funny," he said. "Findin' out about Wee Tam and Jessie has put everythin' else out of my mind. It's like... it's more personal, now."

"How?"

"Well, my boy, he's with Jimmie's wife. It's no' a game. It's too close. I... och, I dinna ken. I..."

He gave up with a shrug and began to poke at his pipe with his knife. The silence stretched as John kept on scratching at the sand and Tom cleaned out the obstruction he'd found.

"I'm getting an idea about it," said John at last.

"What?"

"Och, I just tried thinking about it a bit more... clearly. I mean, where it was done and who could've been there. I talked to Joe again."

Tom pointed to the grazes on John's cheek.

"Aye, I heard," he said.

John smiled.

"You know, Tom, we were supposing all sorts of things before," he said.

"What d'you mean, 'Supposin''?"

"Look, take it bit by bit. Who could have done it?"

"Anybody."

"No. You were with your pals in the Union and the Royal. It couldn't have been you. It must've been somebody who was on their own that night. So?"

Tom cast his mind back over the things they'd talked about in connection with that Saturday night.

"There's nobody," he said. "They were all with somebody else."

"Not Jessie or Wee Tam, or Glover or Joe."

"Not you either," said Tom, uneasy at the mention of his son.

"Aye, me as well," agreed John. "I was walking along the beach, but I can't prove it."

"Ach, there's hundreds o' others, too. Who says it was anybody we know?"

John nodded.

"I think it is, Tom."

"What? Who?"

"I'll tell you in a while. You see, I'm still not really sure."

"You're worse than a woman for teasin'."

John smiled.

"Just think of what we know about it. Try to see it a different way. I mean, he was drunk. Where did he go after he'd been with Glover and Joe in Pensioners' Court? Where did Glover go? Or Joe? And when Wee Tam went looking for him, how do we know he didn't find him? And what did Jessie do?"

The constant inclusion of Wee Tam in the equation was annoying Tom. He turned away in exasperation.

"And the hanging," John went on. "How was he strung up? You wouldn't find raw, unlaid hemp rove through a block, so did somebody just heave a length over a spar and hoist up Jimmie's dead weight? If he did, he'd need to be a big man."

"Like Wee Tam, you mean. And him with all the hemp he needed at the rope walk."

Tom's anger was obvious.

"No, no," said John. "But we've got to look at everybody."

"Aye, well, just look around the quays. There's big men everywhere. And I bet none of them has a good word to say about Jimmie."

"But it's maybe not a man we're looking for."

"What?"

"That's what we've been saying all along, isn't it?"

"Of course it is. How's Jimmie goin' to let a woman hang him up? And what woman's goin' to..."

John put a hand on his arm and stopped him.

"I know, I know. That's what I've been saying myself all along. But we've thought and thought about men and we never got any further ahead. That's why I started thinking about other things."

"Like women with muscles?"

John smiled and shook his head.

"Another thing," he said. "All those scratches and cuts on him. We thought somebody had made them to hide the marks of the fids. But if it was Bessie who stabbed him, there was no need to. The marks were all there before the fids went in. So why? Where did they come from?"

"Listen, big man, you're the one with the brains," said Tom, forcing himself to calm down. "You're the one who says he knows who did it, so why are you askin' me all these questions?"

John smiled and shrugged.

"Because we asked them all before and didn't think about the answers properly. We... assumed things, talked about how Jimmie had so many enemies because of the money he owed. We didn't look far enough. Didn't think about people who might have stronger reasons to get rid of him. Maybe it wasn't his greed for money that got him killed. It was maybe his greed for other things."

Tom held up a hand. John noticed the inward curve of the two middle fingers, the dislocated ones which he'd reset. They'd never been completely straight since the accident.

"John," he said, with a long sigh and an inflexion that conveyed that he was now being very patient. "Try to remember who you're talkin' to. This is me, Tom. Thinkin' doesna come easy to me."

John laughed and drew some more patterns at his feet. Tom returned to his pipe and, at last satisfied that he'd cleared it, relit it and enveloped them in swirls of pale blue smoke. Then, slowly and in detail, John explained to him what he thought might have happened to Jimmie. Tom listened, intrigued by his reasoning and, at intervals, nodding his appreciation and agreement, even whistling in surprise and admiration. But when John mentioned two names and said that his guess was that, although he couldn't really believe they'd done it, they were the guilty ones, Tom immediately shook his head and said, "No."

John spread his hands and said nothing more. Tom continued to think about his words, his head still shaking.

"You're as bad as Davie Donne," he said. Then "no" again.

CHAPTER THIRTY-THREE

The next morning, there was an extra brightness to the bustle around the quays and a feeling of excitement that infiltrated everyone and everything. The launch of a new ship was always a time of hope and an excuse for all sorts of excesses and indulgence. All the houses and streets in Footdee were strung with bunting, and tiny flags and pennants fluttered along the rails and down the sides of the shining hull of the Elizabeth Anderson.

Onshore in the yard, the small army of shipwrights, laborers, carpenters and their apprentices were busy around the ropes and cables, rechecking everything, greasing the slips and making sure that their own part of the operation would go quickly and smoothly. The crowds up in Castle Street were thicker than usual with citizens who always came to see the ceremonies, and the thieves who trained young boys to pick pockets in the east end of town were making their usual, quiet profits.

Still and massive at the center of all the activity was the ship herself, one hundred and eighteen feet long, twenty-five across, with a hold seventeen feet deep. Lying along the nearby quayside were the thick lower masts, which would be stepped the following day when she was towed alongside. The big sheerlegs that would hoist them were already set and the ship's own capstans and winches would heave them on board for lowering into the keelson. Above the fo'c's'le hatch gleamed a brand new horseshoe, nailed there earlier in the morning by the ship's carpenter.

John's role in the process had ended the moment he'd been satisfied that the figurehead was secure but, like everyone else, he loved a launching and he was keen to see how his work complemented the vessel once she was in the water. He walked among the crowds in the yard, nodding greetings at some, moving aside as apprentices ran by, trailing ropes behind them or carrying huge wooden wedges. He saw Willie Johnston deep in conversation with Donald Simpson as Donald's wife and daughters stood dutifully beside him, patient as ever and far too pretty to be tied to such a charmless man. Further on, near the bow, he was surprised to see Joe Drummond with Wee Tam and Jessie arm in arm beside him. Even though he and Tom had known about their affair for weeks, Tom had said that they hadn't yet spoken of it to others. This must be their first appearance together in public and the way Jessie clung close to Wee Tam left no doubt as to the nature of their relationship. As he approached them, John saw the looks some were giving them and knew, as did Wee Tam and Jessie themselves, that many tongues would be wagging in the days ahead. He came up beside them and was surprised at the greeting he got. Jessie and Wee Tam just gave a little nod, Wee Tam continuing to stare at him and Jessie dropping her eyes away and hanging on to Wee Tam's arm. Joe's face still bore the marks of their fight but he said "Good morning" and pointed up at the figurehead which arched high above them, its colors gleaming against the dark grain of the bowsprit, adding, "Best you've ever done".

"Aye," said Wee Tam. "Pa said she looked good. She does."

Jessie said nothing, gave no sign of agreement or disagreement. She seemed to have none of her usual vivacity. It was perhaps the nervousness of being in public with Wee Tam.

"Where is Tom?" asked John.

Wee Tam shook his head.

"He's at the rope walk. Got some idea in his head about somethin'. Dinna ken what it is, but I don't think he'll be comin'."

The four of them set off to stroll along toward the stern, looking up at the hull from time to time and saying very little. As they came to the starboard quarter, John looked across and, through the crowd fifteen or so yards away, saw Anderson and Glover facing one another. Both wore top hats and Glover had a wide smile on his face and was talking eagerly. Anderson seemed to be paying careful attention to what he was saying. All the time, the two men were shaking hands.

"That's the future," said John.

"God help us," said Wee Tam.

They all turned to look again at the tight sweep of the hull's planking as the babble of voices licked up the sides and echoed back over their heads. Then, as they began to stroll forward, John heard his name called and felt a hand on his shoulder. He turned and was surprised to see that it was Anderson. He gave a slight bow to Jessie and the others and said, "Mr. Grant, would you mind walking with me a moment? I'd appreciate a word with you."

John looked at the others. Their expressions revealed nothing. John nodded to them and turned to walk away from the ship.

"I'm glad you're here," Anderson began. "You should be at the center of the celebrations. That figurehead is a masterpiece. I thought so in your workshop, but now that I see it sitting in its rightful place... Well..."

John bowed a small acknowledgement.

"You'll be wondering why I should take you away from your friends, " said Anderson.

"Well, yes."

"I have a proposition. I wanted to ask you... I have plans for two more ships, ships to carry people and cargoes to New Zealand. I'd be honored if you'd take charge of all their carvings. There's something else, too."

John waited. Suddenly, Anderson seemed strangely shy. He was considering his words before uttering them. At last, he gave a quick nod and said, "I'd also like you to consider aligning yourself more closely with me in a wider business arrangement. I have plans to extend my trade into the southern oceans. It will certainly mean we encounter new cultures, new types of communication."

John said nothing, content to watch as Anderson searched for the right expressions.

"The truth is," said Anderson at last, "I would value the opinion of someone who seems prepared to question values which others see as immutable. We shall need to send different signals of our intent to the southern islands, adopt different methods of trade, perhaps even carve different messages into the bows of our vessels. But it is your way of thinking that would be useful to me as well as your skills with timber."

He threw up a hand in exasperation.

"You see? I speak in riddles. I need to settle my thoughts and present them to you more clearly. I ask only that you keep yourself open and agree to speak further of this."

John simply nodded. The proposal took him by surprise. He had no idea what such an arrangement might be. Despite his present workload and the inexperience of his new apprentices, he could easily undertake the two new commissions, and they'd take his reputation even higher. But the Elizabeth Anderson had been a special task and he was uncertain whether he could move easily to a straightforward commercial contract, especially with the memory of his recent argument between himself and Helen still bitter and his suspicions about Jimmie's death gnawing at him.

"I realize that you may need to see whether your schedules allow for it but there's lots of time," said Anderson. "The business arrangement will need some discussion but as for the ships, the plans are not yet drawn up... And I shall pay whatever fee you think appropriate."

John shook his head.

"It's neither the time nor the fee that makes me hesitate," he said. "I'm flattered by your words, but the work I've just done for you was... special. If you'll forgive me for saying so, your wife is a beautiful, charming woman. It was a pleasure to look for her likeness."

"And, unless I mistake myself, that of my daughter."

John felt a blush come to his neck and looked quickly at him. Anderson's eyes were on his face, but there was a smile in them.

"I don't think you're a flatterer, Mr. Grant, and you certainly know what you're doing, so giving my wife back her youth in your work suggests that you perhaps had other inspirations."

"It was a challenge," said John, knowing the words to be inadequate.

"And a very natural one," said Anderson. "She's a beautiful young woman."

It was a reference not to his wife but to Helen. John could think of nothing to say. Revealing the deception he'd been asked to perpetrate was out of the question.

"Your silence is quite eloquent, I think," said Anderson.

"Am I so easy to read then?" said John, angry at his own confusion.

"I think you're honest, that you don't dissemble."

"If only you knew."

"Oh, you might well now and then. Perhaps to preserve your pride."

John stopped walking.

"When you visited my workshop, you warned me against judging by appearances. Aren't you guilty of the same thing?"

"Completely," said Anderson. "But my proposal is based on a deeper instinct."

"I thought you preferred reason."

Anderson smiled.

"I do. But I've thought a lot about your giving me that invoice. It was a rare occasion. I can think of none of my acquaintances, even the close ones, who would have done so without asking something in return."

John waved his hand to dismiss the observation.

"Perhaps you should change your acquaintances," he said.

"Oh no. I prefer them that way. Trust no one; that's the key to success."

"A sad philosophy."

There was a pause, then Anderson shook his head, turned and resumed walking, almost stumbling over two small boys who galloped past them, screaming like banshees. John walked with him again.

"Anyway," he said, "My action earned its reward."

"Oh?" said Anderson, the surprise evident in his voice.

"Yes. I saw Bessie Rennie among the crowds back there. They'd only have let her out if someone had spoken for her."

Anderson smiled and waved a hand in a dismissive gesture.

"The jails are too full already. Most of the wretches inside them are harmless. The real crime is that all it needs is a word from someone such as myself to gain them their liberty."

"Nevertheless, it was an honorable gesture. Even though her hand is probably in someone's pocket as we speak."

Anderson smiled.

"Well then, since we're both honorable men, what do you say?" he said.

"To what?"

"Will you undertake these commissions?"

"Yes."

"And the other proposition?"

"I'd like time to consider it once these celebrations are over."

Anderson took his arm, turned him back toward the ship and started walking with him.

"Good, then come and talk to Mr. Glover. He's as enchanted by your work as I."

Glover was still standing outside the office and, to John's confusion, he was in conversation with Elizabeth and Helen. When he saw them coming, he came toward them, his hat raised and his hand outstretched.

"John," he said. "How can I congratulate you? I've never seen a better marriage between a ship and its figurehead. I hope you'll honor me with more of your artistry."

John said nothing. The compliments should have soothed him but, instead, his mind was galloping with the implications of Anderson's recent offer and from the impact of Helen's presence. He contented himself with a little bow.

"You'll find that my wife and daughter are equally content with your handiwork. Isn't that so, my dear?" said Anderson.

Helen's eyes were fixed on a point somewhere on his waistcoat. The flush in her cheeks was obvious and she hung back a little, letting her mother talk for her. Elizabeth held out her hand, which John duly took and kissed.

"It's more flattering than I could possibly have hoped," she said. "I fear that those of my husband's trading acquaintances who have never met me will be sorely deceived if they judge my appearance by your work."

John still found nothing to say but, again, he saw an intensity in her eyes which went further than her words.

"Well, Helen? Have you nothing to add?" said Anderson, with a quick look from her to John.

Helen looked up and was forced to meet John's eyes. In turn, she forced herself to stretch out her hand. Its trembling was stilled by John as he reached to take her fingers. His lips barely touched the lace of her glove and she immediately drew her hand away and clasped it in the other.

"It's a very competent piece of work," she said.

"Competent?" echoed her father. "My dear, your standards are excessively demanding."

She flashed another quick look at John's face.

"Yes, they are," she said.

"I'd be honored if you would join our party for the launch," said Anderson.

"The honor would be mine entirely," said John, his voice slower, more careful than normal. "But I regret that I must decline."

"Oh?" said Anderson.

"Yes," said John, searching frantically in his imagination for an excuse. "I... I must confess to being somewhat superstitious."

"Indeed?"

"Yes. I... er... I prefer always to be at the very edge of the water whenever a ship with one of my carvings on it is launched."

"Of course," said Anderson, with a little shake of his head. "Then that is what you must do."

"But come and have tea with us. I should like to thank you properly."

The invitation came from Elizabeth. Helen looked quickly at her but she was looking straight at John, a neutral expression on her face. There was no way in which he could refuse her without being grossly impolite.

"I would be honored," he said, resisting the urge to look at Helen as he spoke.

"Good, then I shall send a servant round tomorrow to arrange a convenient time."

John gave a little bow and, saying a general farewell and allowing his eyes the briefest of glances at Helen, he moved away into the crowds, his mind boiling with confusion and frustration.

Glover shook his head.

"Such talent, and yet he'll never make his way in the world," he said.

"Why do you say that?" asked Anderson.

Glover shook his head and raised his hand to scratch at his beard.

"Somehow he lacks... grace."

John pushed through the crowds, looking for Wee Tam and the others and was surprised when Jessie suddenly appeared beside him, pushing her way past two women and the three screeching children they were trying to control, and grabbed his arm.

"John. I need to ask you somethin'," she said, looking around as if she was afraid that someone was looking at or for her.

"Of course, Jessie," he said.

"No' here. What are you doin' after the launch?"

"Nothing."

"Come and see me. At home. Yes?"

"Aye, all right." He was suddenly aware of the fear in her eyes and suspected that he knew what had caused it. "Is something wrong, Jessie?" he asked.

She shuddered, her grip on his arm very tight. "Aye. But just come and see me. I'll tell you then."

"Right," he said.

She gave him a final look, her eyes haunted, afraid, and moved quickly away to get back to Wee Tam.

CHAPTER THIRTY-FOUR

Launching ships in Aberdeen harbor called for particular precautions. There was only just room for the ship to glide into the water and it was important to stop her momentum before she struck the opposite bank. Glover's men had set big anchors in gravel runs and shackled their straining cables to various points on the ship. As she ran down the slips and into the water, they would drag through the gravel and bring her slowly to a halt. The cables could not stretch and, if their anchors had been set in anything other than gravel and not free to move, the sudden strain on them would cause them to snap. As an extra safety measure, shipwrights stood by the anchors with large timbers ready to throw into them to stop their progress if the vessel threatened to go too far.

Toward eleven o'clock, with the tide almost at the flood, Glover gave the final orders to make ready. His only concern was the efficiency of the launch; others preoccupied themselves with the various rituals needed to make sure that the Elizabeth Anderson would be a lucky ship. There was no minister of the church present; these rituals derived from pagan rites and practices.

Cheers and excited babblings ran through the crowd as the sequence of orders was called out and the shipwrights and their apprentices wielded sledgehammers and levers along either side of the hull. The hollow bangs and knockings echoed over the water and around the yard. Some timbers gave way easily, others needed more persistent attention and more brutal treatment. At last, all the restraining supports had been knocked away, leaving only the dog shores, which held the huge cradle on which the ship rested. Glover called to those in charge at various points along the sides of the hull and around the bow, checking that all was well with their part of the process. Then, he gave a final shout of "Stand clear", the last

273

preventers were knocked away and the Elizabeth Anderson's four hundred and twenty-eight tons began to slip, stern first, down toward the water.

In order to give his excuse some respectability, John had moved down to the water's edge. Near him were two ships' carpenters who had brought two apprentices with them, young lads who knew nothing of launches and what their duties were. Their masters just told them that they were needed for a special maneuver as the ship dipped clear.

The hull loomed over them, gliding down the launching ways, picking up more and more speed, its timbers creaking and the cradle's beams squealing at the friction against the slips. As it hit the water, it threw up a huge wave that washed away from it and climbed up the beach. To their surprise, the two apprentices were grabbed by the carpenters and plunged head over heels into the cold wave. They came up spluttering and yelling and were immediately ducked once more. Luckily for them, the ducking was a mere parody of a ritual that had originally involved a real human sacrifice. As they shook themselves and shouted obscenities at their masters, the Elizabeth Anderson pushed on out into the river, the wave created by her surge growing all the time. The cables screamed and rattled along the granite quay, straightening and dragging the squealing anchors through the resisting gravel. The shipwrights watched anxiously, their timbers ready to be rammed home. And the crowd's cheers grew louder and louder.

At last, with something like a curtsey back toward the throng on the shore, the hull dipped against the cables and was held floating on her true element. With her keel submerged and only her topsides showing, she looked beautiful, perfectly balanced, ready for the ocean.

She had not yet been named since another superstition decreed that it was unlucky to name a ship before she was afloat. The custom was to break a bottle of whisky over whichever part of the ship had first entered the water but, in a variation that was becoming quite common, Anderson had given the office boy a shilling to go to the grocer at the corner of Garvock Wynd and buy a bottle of christening wine. As the bottle swung and shattered against the stern, the ship's master said, almost to himself, "From rocks and sands, and barren lands, and ill men's hands, keep us free," and the apprentices who'd managed to hide themselves on board grabbed at the pieces of silk ribbon which had held the bottle. These were the prizes they would give their girl-friends that evening in the hope of making them sweeter and more compliant.

The cheers were subsiding now and the shipwrights began the tidying up and squaring away of all the cables and ropes they'd used. The soaked apprentices went home to change and everyone connected with the launch started getting ready for the bread, cheese and whisky that would be waiting for them in the hall that Anderson had reserved for the feast. They would also be served with pieces of large fresh skate, boiled, covered in butter and mustard and served with copious amounts of jacket potatoes. There would be no knives or forks, but plenty of singing, dancing and drinking. Launches were popular not just for the hope they represented or the mysticism of the old traditions but for the license they gave to be gluttonous, licentious and unreservedly intemperate.

****

John walked away from the hubbub, content that the ship had looked so good in the water and still needing to find some quiet in order to resolve the confusions that the meeting with Helen, her mother's invitation and, most of all, Anderson's propositions and revelations had bred in him. The thrill and color of the launch had held his attention but the usual aftermath, with its sense of anti-climax, had dulled his spirits. For the moment, the thoughts of Helen had been pushed into the background as he remembered Jessie and her anxiety. As she'd left him, he'd guessed the reason for her nervousness, but there were too many possibilities and he had no real idea of the secret she was reserving for him.

He'd allowed her plenty of time to get home and, as he turned into York Place, he wondered whether Wee Tam was part of whatever they were about to discuss. When he knocked at Jessie's door and she opened it, he realized that he wasn't. The only other person there was Rose and he saw at once why she hadn't been at the launch. The weal he'd seen on her face before had reopened, her left cheek and temple were one big bruise and the flesh around her eye was swollen so much that it was almost shut.

No one spoke as he came in and sat down. Far, far away, they heard a sudden burst of whoopings and callings. The celebrations were well under way. Their distant echoes made the silence of Jessie's house seem thicker. It was warm and dark, and the smell of fish that was always there was mixed with that of Wee Tam's tobacco. John looked at the black coat in the alcove.

"Where's Wee Tam?" he asked.

"Back at work. Gone to see his Pa," said Jessie.

"He said you're still askin' about Jimmie," said Rose.

John nodded, his eyes unable to avoid dwelling on the marks on her face. There was another silence before she added, "He says you told his Pa who did it."

John was embarrassed.

"No. I don't know for sure. I just... had some ideas. I was just..."

Jessie had been standing by the range. Suddenly she turned and said, quickly and angrily, "Why did you no' leave it, John? Why stir it all up, cause more trouble? You shoulda' let it be."

"Aye, maybe," he said.

"Never mind maybe. You shoulda'."

He'd never seen her angry before. It was surprising, disturbing. When Rose spoke, her voice was quiet, controlled and contrasted very strongly with that of her sister.

"I told you to leave Jessie alone. I told you no' to make her worse. You've hurt her, John. Made her sad."

"I'm sorry," said John, knowing how empty the words sounded.

"Aye, well, if you go on with all this, it'll make her worse."

"I'm not going on with anything, Rose," he said. "It was Jessie who asked me to come along."

"Aye, I did," said Jessie, struggling to control her anger. "Why did you do it?"

"What?"

Jessie flung a hand to gesture at nothing in particular.

"This. Diggin' around. Playin' games with Jimmie's dyin'."

John shrugged. "I wasn't playing games, Jessie. I wanted to help."

Jessie snorted a laugh. The sound was empty. John could only nod in agreement with such a response to the inappropriateness of his words.

"I was curious at first," he went on. "It was all mixed up with Marie and... well, it just kept going. It was a puzzle. Then, when you said Davie Donne was asking questions, I... well, I wanted to help."

"Help?"

There was scorn in Rose's voice as she repeated the word.

"Yes. Jessie said he was asking her questions. You know what he's like. He'd have her in the Bridewell just for saying nothing. I wanted to stop him. Wanted to find out who did it so he couldn't blame her."

The silence came back, letting in the same faraway sounds of revelry.

"What did you want to tell me?" he asked at last.

"I thought you knew," said Jessie.

He looked at her, then at Rose, who was staring straight at him, tears seeping out of her swollen eye.

"I think I do," he said. "But I'm only guessing."

"Well?"

Jessie's voice was defiant, challenging. It left him no choice.

"I think Jimmie died in his yard," he said. "After he'd gone to hide the ditty box on the boat. I don't know how, but it couldn't have been natural."

"Why not?" asked Jessie.

"Because he was dragged to the beach, had water thrown over him. It was to hide something. If he'd just died of apoplexy, we'd have just found him where he fell."

"Who did it then?" she asked, the challenge still there.

John looked at her but found it difficult to hold her gaze. His eyes dropped away.

"You know, Jessie," he said. "That mark round his neck, from the rope. It wasn't a hanging, was it? It was where a horse dragged him along the road to the beach. That's where all the cuts came from, too. And we know that it was Bessie who stuck the fids in him. But he was long dead by then."

"So how did he die, then?"

"I don't know. Bang on the head maybe. Poison?"

Jessie laughed.

"Did you see any bangs on his head? And what sort o' poison? Were there any marks? Were his lips blue? Was there foam in his mouth? You dinna ken nothin', John."

"No," said John. "And I don't care about it. I've satisfied my curiosity, scratched the itching I had. You'll hear no more from me about it."

He stopped. He wanted Jessie to understand that he knew that she was guilty, but that she had nothing to fear. But she was just looking at him, an expression of surprise on her face and her head shaking slightly. It was Rose who spoke.

"You think Jessie killed him?" she said, making it only just a question.

"Hush," said Jessie. "He dinna ken nothin'."

"He should, then," said Rose.

"No," said Jessie.

But Rose simply reached across and trailed her hand over her sister's hair and down across her shoulders.

"Aye, he should."

John looked from one to the other. Rose gave Jessie a final pat and turned to him.

"Jimmie came round to my house," she said. "Late, it was. After he'd left here with his box. He was drunk as a pig and he told me he'd been with Joe in Pensioners' Court."

"Aye, I knew he was there," said John.

Rose nodded.

"Aye," she said, her voice calm and eerily unaffected by the tears which were in her eyes. "He was even boastin' about it, tellin' me what they'd been doin' with some poor wee lassie they'd had there. He said that's why he came round. Said that Joe wouldna be home 'cause he was out of his head with the drink. And away somewhere with the lassie."

She stopped, her head shaking.

"My God, John," said Jessie. "You men..."

She was blinking back her own tears.

"It was Joe's fault," said Rose. "He shouldna have said it. He shouldna..."

Then the tears took over.

CHAPTER THIRTY-FIVE

Jessie and Rose were comforting one another, each trying to hold back tears with great heaving sighs, each angry with herself that she was being so weak.

"I'm sorry," said John. "I promise I'll leave it. I won't say another word about it. It's..."

"Och, John, it's too late for that," said Jessie. "It's done."

"Aye, but..."

"Aye, but nothin'," said Rose. "You wanted to find out, well, just listen."

After a few sighs and gulps to drag her back from the crying, Rose began to tell him her story. She needed to let everything out, was glad to unburden herself at last after the weeks of silence and guilt. She told John the things Jimmie had said when he'd visited her that night, evil things from an evil man. He'd described what he and Joe had been doing to the young whore on the steps, the way they'd prodded their fingers into her and talked of the differences between her and Rose and Jessie. She spoke simply and with no acknowledgement of the fact that these were subjects that women didn't raise in conversations with men.

"He said he was wantin' to try two sisters," she said. "Wantin' to see who'd got the best one, him or Joe. The biggest, he said. The widest. The wettest. He said Joe told him to help hisself. That's what I mean. If Joe hadna said that, Jimmie would maybe no' have come round. He'd've..."

"You treat us like whores," said Jessie, her tears driven completely away by a cold anger at Joe and Jimmie's antics.

"Aye. He was pawin' at me all the time like I was just one o' his whores," said Rose. She leaned her head sideways and kissed Jessie's hand, which was on her shoulder. "But it was when he started on about

279

Jessie... I couldna listen to that. The things he said. Awful things. Called her such names. I just kicked him out."

"And he went?" asked John.

"Aye. Just laughed and staggered away. He had his wee box. He was takin' it to his work."

John nodded. There was no need to ask questions. Rose was well into her story and it seemed to be helping her to tell someone else about it.

"I went round to see Jessie. Had to. I wanted to tell her, try to... I dinna ken, do somethin'. He was such a pig."

As her attention turned to the hurts which had been done to her sister, she was still managing to control the tears but he could hear them behind her words. Jessie's hand was gently stroking Rose's shoulder.

"I was just ready to go in when I saw her through the window," said Rose. "She was washin' herself in that big white bowl, splashin' the water up over her face and shoulders." She turned her head to look up at Jessie. "And you turned round and I saw the marks on you. Round the side and back. Red. Purple. I knew it was Jimmie who'd done it."

"Aye," said Jessie, with a sigh.

Rose patted her hand.

"Why did you no' come in?" asked Jessie.

Rose shook her head and wiped at her eyes.

"You don't need to ask me that. You never liked me seein' you like that. You liked to pretend it wasna happenin'. Same as me." She turned back to John. "See, it's both o' us. We're ashamed o' ourselves for lettin' it happen, for no' tellin' folk... We always keep quiet."

"Folk don't want to know," said Jessie, simply.

"So what did you do?" asked John.

Rose gave a laugh.

"Oh, I was that blazin' by then. That was just the last straw. I went to his yard. Went to find him to tell him what I thought of him. But he couldna even understand what I was sayin'. He was even drunker than before and he starts maulin' at me again, grabbin' at my chest, my dress, pullin' at my hair. His hands was all over me."

She gave an anxious glance at Jessie, who squeezed her shoulder gently to reassure her. She looked back at John then her eyes dropped and she was staring at the dark floorboards. Jessie looked at John and gave a small shake of her head, warning him to say nothing, just to wait. Then Rose lifted her right hand and pushed it out in front of her, a tired, helpless little gesture.

"I just... pushed him away. Just a wee push. But he fell over. And he just lies there. And he's laughin'."

She was reliving the moment, seeing Jimmie on the ground before her.

"And then his laughin' makes him sick," she went on. "It dribbles out of his mouth and he starts coughin' and chokin'. And then he goes quiet."

In the silence, she turned her eyes to Jessie again. "Honest, Jessie. I thought he'd fell asleep."

"Aye, he did, love," said Jessie. "He was always fallin' down and just sleepin' where he fell."

"I just left him there," said Rose. "I wanted to kick him and spit on him but... I was just disgusted with him, and I left him. I went home to wait for Joe. But he didna come. And I kept thinkin' o' Jimmie and how still he'd been lyin' and... well, I went back to see. It was the middle o' the night. There was nobody about. He was still there. In the same place. But he didna look asleep that time. Didna seem to be breathin'. Maybe he was. I dinna ken."

The tone of her voice betrayed how vivid the memory was for her. She was speaking as much for herself as for John and Jessie.

"But he was goin' blue. Like you see them when they've drowned. Blue. I s'pose it was his sick that done it. Drowned him, I mean. That can happen, you know. That's how I got the idea. Make it look like he'd drowned and Jessie would be rid of him and the wee girls round about wouldna be bothered by him no more..."

She stopped as she realized the effect her words might have on Jessie but Jessie just nodded.

"I ken, I ken. He was an evil man," she said.

John hated himself for opening up the pain the two women had been going through and now forcing them to speak of it and relive its horrors.

"Now you see why I wanted to speak to you?" said Jessie.

John nodded and held his hands out in a gesture of apology.

"It was you that made her tell me," said Jessie.

"It's all right, Jessie, I'm glad I did," said Rose. "I could never have gone on without tellin' somebody."

The two women seemed more composed and, for Rose, the worst part of it all seemed to be over.

"I went to get big Duke," she said.

Duke was one of the horses she looked after and used for taking the bigger loads of fish to market and into town. Their stables were just across the way from Jimmie's yard and it would take very little time to throw on a harness and lead him across.

"There was plenty of bits of rope lyin' about the place. I just got the longest one I could find and kinda looped it round Jimmie. I wanted to get it round his shoulders, hitch it under his arms, but he was too heavy."

"You shoulda' seen him without his clothes," said Jessie, trying to help Rose to shake off the misery of it all. Rose gave a quick smile.

"I tried and tried, but I couldna lift him. I just had to put it round his neck. I didna ken whether that'd be strong enough to take all that weight so I was careful to go slow and steady when we went down the street. Duke's a grand wee horse. Does everythin' I tell him. Just as well. I didna want to pull Jimmie's head off."

She stopped and, almost immediately, Jessie giggled. It betrayed not amusement, but nervousness. It was enough to set the two of them laughing.

John smiled with them but felt very uneasy. Into the horror of what was being described, laughter came as a sinister intrusion.

"There was nobody about," Rose went on. "No' at that time of night. I dragged him all the way to the beach and left him hitched up to Duke while I went down to the sea. I'd brought a bucket with me, so I gave him a good soakin'. Three bucketfuls. Then I just took off the noose, brought Duke up the brae, took a stick and brushed away the marks we'd made. And that was that. I took Duke back to the stables and went home."

She paused for a moment, then nodded her head.

"And you know this," she said. "I felt good."

It was only the details that surprised John. He'd already worked out the mechanics of how it had happened. The way in which Helen had shown him that women were capable of strategies unavailable to men had released him from the restrictions of his previous imaginings. As soon as he began to consider the possibility of a woman being responsible, the whole problem, about which he'd been thinking constantly, shifted its perspectives, renewed its fascination. A man would have been strong enough to carry Jimmie or put him on a cart and both of those options would have been safer and easier. There were lots of women around the harbor who worked with horses, and any of them could have been involved. But Rose and Jessie were directly linked with Jimmie. John hadn't been aware before just how much justification they had for getting rid of him but, in the excitement of his new approach to the whole puzzle, he'd thought only of the fact that they both had access to horses and knew their ways. On top of all that, he knew that they'd both been alone on Saturday night. When he'd spoken to Tom about it, he'd been supposing that, since Jessie had the motive, she'd been the one who'd done it. Now that he'd heard Rose's story, though, he understood very well why there had been almost an inevitability about it all. Jimmie's contempt for others, his insistence that the women of the family were at his disposal, however grotesque his appetites, deserved to be punished. That the punishment had been so comprehensive had a sort of justice to it. With the degree of provocation to which Rose had been subjected, John even thought that she'd done the right thing.

"How d'you feel about it now?" he asked.

"I'm glad I've said it," she replied. "I needed to. It was too much on my own."

She thought for a moment and added, her voice strong, determined, "I'm glad he's dead. I don't feel bad about it. Jessie's got her new man."

The two sisters smiled at each other. Rose looked back at John, a fierceness and defiance in her face. As he nodded, she held his gaze then dropped her eyes away again.

"But I feel guilty, too," she said. "I havena been to church since. I'm afraid to go."

"Don't be," said John. "Whatever your minister tells you, he's wrong. God's been on your side all the time."

"D'you think so?" said Rose, with hope in her voice and a desperate need for him to be right pleading in her eyes.

"I'm sure of it," he said. "Go and tell Him about it."

Rose smiled again.

"What now then?" asked Jessie.

John got up.

"What?" he said.

"What happens? Now you know."

He shook his head.

"Nothing," he said. "I won't be saying anything to anybody."

"But Tom knows..."

John shook his head again.

"No, he doesn't. He knows I've had some stupid ideas. And he cares more about you and Wee Tam being happy than about what happened to a waster like Jimmie."

"I'll tell him," said Rose.

Jessie made to protest but Rose shushed her.

"He should know. He'll understand."

Jessie looked anxiously at her, then nodded.

John felt the distances between them and sensed that the usual goodbyes might be awkward. He went to the door, knowing there was nothing else to say, wanting to get out into the night, still the tumult in his head and come to terms with the guilt he was feeling. He opened the door and turned, his big, black silhouette almost filling the doorway.

"I'm sorry," he said.

Almost immediately, Rose stood up and came across to him. She reached up, put her arms round his neck and kissed him on the cheek.

"It's no' your fault, big John," she said.

He bent and kissed her in turn, making sure to choose the right hand side of her face. As Rose released him, Jessie came across and she, too, hugged him. As he smiled, nodded and went out into the street, he was aware that, for all their fragility, they were the strong ones.

CHAPTER THIRTY-SIX

At eight o'clock that evening, John was sitting on one of the Elizabeth Anderson's masts on the quayside. The tide was rising again and lifting the ship, which was moored alongside. Her figurehead had just been raised clear of the quay's edge and was level with John's eye line.

The reveling was still going on, but it had drifted away to the taverns nearer the bottom of Commerce Street, James Street and Marischal Street. The last shipwrights and carpenters had left the ship as soon as they were satisfied that she was secure and, while the celebrations of her launch continued far away, she was left alone to settle in the water and begin to feel the sway and movement for which she'd been created.

The day had started in a thin mist which had partly cleared for the launch and had now vanished completely. John couldn't see the sun from where he sat, but its light still filled the sky and spilled across the headland on the south bank of the river. The water lapped between the sides of the boat and the quay wall and John breathed deeply, drawing in the peace of the evening to try to still the conflicting thoughts of Jessie, Rose and Jimmie which continued to spin within him.

He saw Helen long before she was close enough to speak and, although he turned his head to look in the opposite direction, he still felt her gradual approach and, eventually, heard the swish of her dress on the cobbles as she came near.

"I knew you'd be here," said Helen.

He stood up.

"I love new ships," he said. "Beginnings."

Helen looked at the Elizabeth Anderson.

"She's very beautiful."

"Yes. But I'm not sure how many more there'll be."

"Why?"

"We're to be visited by the Archimedes on the twenty-fourth. An iron ship, with a device under the water to drive her. There may be no place for sail next year."

"Not even the Scottish Maid?"

John raised his shoulders.

"Perhaps."

Their words were controlled. Neither looked at the other as they spoke.

"What will become of your carvings if builders prefer iron?"

He shrugged again.

"They'll still want a figure to guide them, protect them."

"And there are none finer than yours," said Helen.

John looked across at it.

"It's competent," he said.

She laughed.

"Forgive me. I don't know the words to use. It's more than beautiful."

John shook his head.

"No. The beautiful one is gone. It's underneath the paint. It was the one lying in my workshop before I started to coat the timber with colors."

"But it's the same figure."

"No. It has different details. Paint blunts the sharpness of the features, covers the grain. All the curls and rhythms I found in the oak are hidden now. They were there before. That was the true figure. I saw it only for a brief while. Alone in my workshop. It's hidden now under all the paint. Gone."

"To me, it looks very alive."

"I'm glad."

"And it looks like my mother, and me. And itself."

"Well, it won't grow old. Ever. It's bound you and your mother together even more closely than life has."

Helen nodded and said nothing. John was anxious to keep talking.

"You were right about Jimmie Crombie, by the way," he said.

She looked quickly across at him.

"In what way?"

"He was killed by a woman."

"Who?"

John didn't like lying to her but his desire to protect Rose was too strong.

"A woman who works on the quay. He'd treated her very badly. She lost patience with him."

It was not enough to satisfy Helen's curiosity and he had to tell her more. She listened, fascinated and appalled at the torments to which Crombie had subjected the woman, and asked no more about her identity. Like John, she believed that, in the wider context of things, whoever she was, the woman was blameless.

Once again, they fell silent as, having talked of the enormity of the murder, they were left with thoughts of their own disagreement and the need to separate again. In each of them, avalanches of words were ready to pour out but each felt the fragility of this contact and was afraid of doing anything that might destroy it as they had destroyed it before. John risked turning to look at her. For a moment, she kept her eyes on the ship, then slowly turned to meet his gaze. In her face was an unaccustomed timidity. She looked much younger even than her years. And on his brow she saw not the strength and silence that had first attracted her but a little frown of anxiety.

"We have no more reasons to meet," he said.

"We have. Mama has invited you to tea. Will you come?"

"Of course."

"Good. I shall see you then."

She held out her hand. He took it and bent to kiss it, this time letting his lips press against her knuckles and dwell there. He straightened and said, "Before you leave, will you walk to the figurehead with me?"

Slowly, correctly, she put her arm through his and they moved across the quay to stand by the ship's bow. The figurehead leaned proudly forward, pushing out from the stem post, her lovely head lifted to look out over the waters but turned slightly to the right to protect her from their worst furies.

"Do you see the hem of her dress?" asked John.

"Of course."

"Look more closely."

Helen leaned forward, following the folds. John had picked out the edges of the material in gold leaf.

"What am I supposed to see?" she asked.

He pointed to a fold almost hidden on the side nearer to them. In the shadow, she saw that he'd painted three letters, E, A and P.

"Oh yes," she said. "What do they signify?"

"One day, I'll tell you."

Helen turned quickly to him.

"Mr. Grant, you're worse than Bella. That's not fair."

"It may bring you back," he said.

They looked at one another for several seconds. At last, Helen said, "I must go. Mama and Papa are waiting for me."

"Of course."

She turned but immediately spun back to face him. Quickly, she raised her hands to his face and pulled him down toward her. As he leaned forward, he saw her lips part and then, suddenly, felt them warm and soft against his own. It was a lover's kiss.

When she eventually drew away, she gave him a final long look, then turned and left him without another word. He watched her go, his heart still jumping from the kiss. When she at last disappeared, he turned back to the ship and looked again at her image on the bow.

The three letters he had carved were initials. Since the beginning of his acquaintance with her, he'd been re-reading some of the poets that he'd enjoyed when he was younger. There was a fragment of verse which he half remembered and which he searched for until he found it in a volume by the American, Edgar Allan Poe. The letters "EAP" etched in the gilt of the hem were there to honor the poet and to carry out to sea the secret of the words John had spoken so often as he shaped the oak alone in his workshop.

He moved as close as he could to the figure and, his eyes on its face, he recited, in a whisper,

"Helen, thy beauty is to me
Like those Nicean barks of yore,
That gently, o'er a perfum'd sea,
The weary, way-worn wanderer bore
To his own native shore."

As he finished, he smiled, then, suddenly aware of himself as a lone figure on a quayside whispering words of love to a piece of oak, he began to laugh loudly and the sound echoed along the ship's sides and out over the water.

THE END

Unsafe Acts:

"…a polished and extremely enjoyable thriller. A real page turner."
—Fleur Smithwick

"Everything you look for in a police procedural is here - tight prose, a tight plot and a set of characters you take "home" with you when life intrudes on your reading of the book. When you buy yourself a Bill Kirton book, quality is assured."
—Michael J. Malone, author of Blood Tears.

SATIRE

The Sparrow Conundrum:

1st Place Winner, Humor, 2011 Forward National Literature Awards

"…*The Sparrow Conundrum* is the demon love child of Spike Milligan and John Le Carre. I absolutely adore this one—hysterically funny, with this weirdly tender wickedness."
—Maria Bustillos, author of *Dorkismo: the Macho of the Dork* and *Act Like a Gentleman, Think Like a Woman*

"…You have combined the elements of *The Tall Blond Man with the One Black Shoe* with *The Biederbecke Affair* and thrown in Happer from *Local Hero* for good measure. It is killingly funny, and for those who love farce—from *Scapin* to *Noises Off*—this is utterly brilliant, divine, and classic, and couldn't be bettered."
—M.M. Bennetts, author of *May 1812* and *Of Honest Fame*

Alternative Dimension: (written as Jack Lefebre):

"… for all its dystopian menace, the story is carried along by Lefebre's sparkling humour and we find ourselves enjoying the fate of those seduced by the promise of virtual bliss."
—Edgar.

"I liked the humor … and the sometimes absurdly comical events that take place in AD's world"
—Heikki Hietala

"... there is humour aplenty. Like a picaresque novel, or a weird modern version of *Pilgrim's Progress*, or maybe even a *Canterbury Tales* for our times"
—Cally Philips

CHILDREN'S BOOKS (written as Jack Rosse)

The Loch Ewe Mystery

HOW-TO BOOKS

Brilliant Study Skills

"This will be a book I refer back to again and again."
—M. Nikodem

"...an excellent guide for the fresher, but also a learning resource throughout the undergraduate years."
—Max Roach

"...any parent wishing to give their son or daughter a helping hand would be wise to make sure they are equipped with 'Brilliant Study Skills'."
—Prof. J.M.King

Brilliant Essay

Brilliant Dissertation

Brilliant Workplace Skills

Brilliant Academic Writing

ABOUT THE AUTHOR

Bill Kirton was born in Plymouth, England but has lived in Aberdeen, Scotland for most of his life. He's been a university lecturer, presented TV programmes, written and performed songs and sketches at the Edinburgh Festival, and had many radio plays broadcast by the BBC and the Australian BC. He's written five books on study and writing skills in Pearson's 'Brilliant' series and his crime novels, *Material Evidence, Rough Justice, The Darkness, Shadow Selves, Unsafe Acts* and the historical novel *The Figurehead*, set in Aberdeen in 1840, have been published in the UK and USA. He's also written a hilarious satire of the spy and crime genres, *The Sparrow Conundrum*, and another, *Alternative Dimension*, on online role-playing games. His short stories have appeared in several anthologies and *Love Hurts* was chosen for the *Mammoth Book of Best British Crime 2010*.

Two of his books have won awards. *The Sparrow Conundrum* was the winner of the 'Humor' category in the 2011 Forward National Literature Awards and *The Darkness* was second in the 'Mystery' category. *The Figurehead* was also long-listed for the International Rubery Award, 2012.

His blog and website are at http://www.bill-kirton.co.uk